SHADOWOLF VOLUME 1
THE CELENIC EARTH CHRONICLES

BOOK 3

SADGI

An epic fantasy novel
by Shaun M Jooste

NOVELS BY AUTHOR

THE CELENIC EARTH CHRONICLES
1. Windfarer
2. DragonRider
3. Sadgi

Silent Hill: Betrayal

CONTENTS

PART THREE: HORN OF MASARA

PART FOUR: BOW OF CELENE

CONTENTS

PART THREE: HORN OF MASARA

PART FOUR: BOW OF CELENE

PART FIVE: SOUL OF THE SADGI

ANNEXURES

This novel is dedicated to my loving wife and wonderful children, who as always have shown great love, patience, support and encouragement while writing my novels

To see the full quality map, please visit
https://celenicearth.wordpress.com/visual-glossary and click on the map

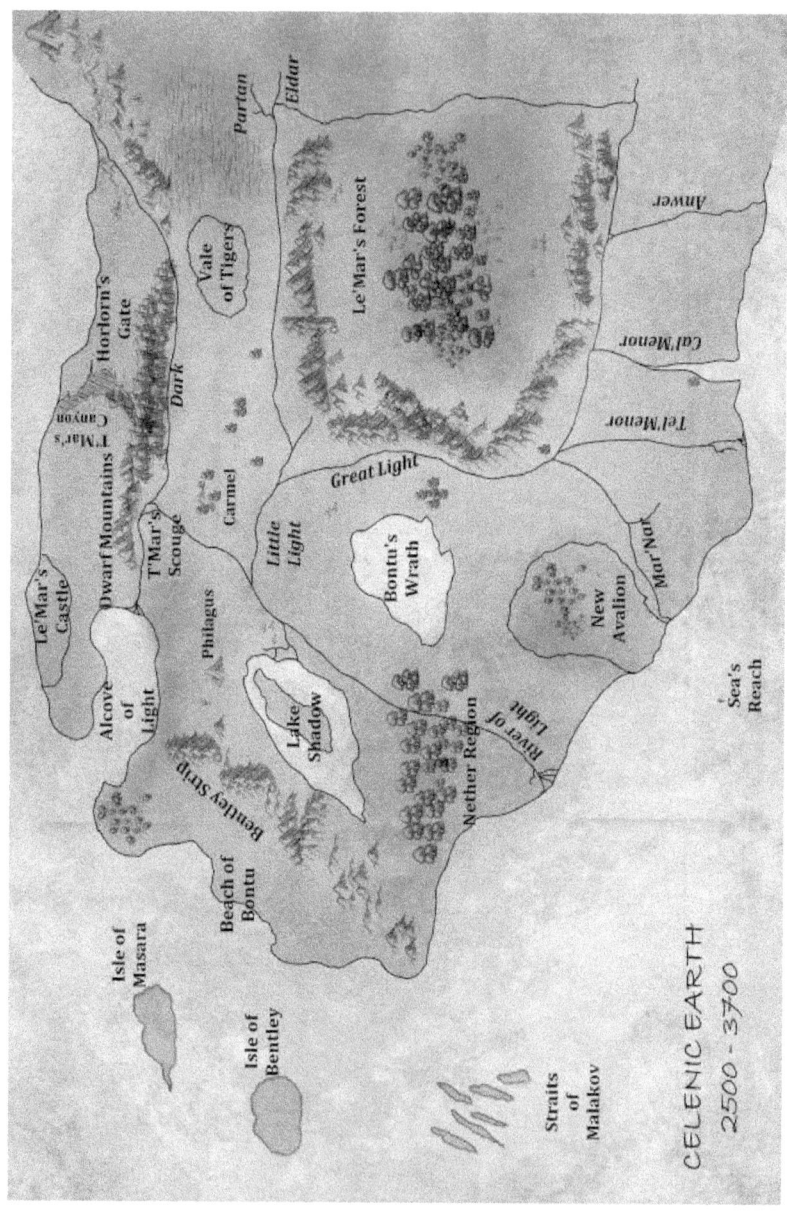

FULFILMENT OF THE WINDFARER PROPHECY
PROLOGUE A

Eldor walked up the steps to the dais. The Elders were seated upon white chairs atop the stage, and he nodded to them as he turned to face the Druids of the Isle of Masara seated within the Hall.

"My fellow elves," he said, his age written upon his dark, green face and the timber of time ringing in his ancient voice. "It has been a year since I sought solitude for the elves of Eldor's Forest upon your island, and until now I chose not to speak of the occurrences that forced me to do so."

The eloquence of his words slipped off his tongue as he savoured their attention, but the sadness of Le'Mar's rule crept over his heart again and he bowed his head in a moment's contemplation.

"Eldor," one of the Elders behind him spoke, "we know it weighs heavy on you. But we need you to start from the time of the Windfarer."

"You wish me to go that far back?" Eldor turned to face the ancient elf.

"Indeed it is necessary," the elf replied, "if we are to understand the true context of your woes."

"We only really understand some of the rumours and tales," a Druid elf from the hall interrupted. "It is time we understand the full scope of things."

Eldor nodded in agreement and reached into his green robe and extracted a few, stained pages.

"I requested of Nighthale two years ago to write on the occurrences of the age of the Windfarer," Eldor said, opening the pages. "I will read to you what he wrote."

"Very well," the Elder said and waited in anticipation for him to begin.

"It has been a year since the fulfilment of the Windfarer Prophecy. I pen this down in the hopes that there will be a generation to read it. It may be that my knowledge of what had transpired last year will be essential in the event of my death.

"Much has passed since the power node had been released, and none of them favourable. Eldor has lost the area that once contained the *Pernonil* forest. The mountains and forest adjoining the area has been taken by Le'Mar, the dark lord. He keeps creatures on watch, waiting for the moment that he obtains the Heart of Tigers.

"Asbec Island and the land south of it has been taken and named "The Dark Boundary". Le'Mar's camps that were once housed in the east of Eldor's Forest have been divided in order to fortify the Boundary.

"Ah, I see I forget myself. I have gotten ahead of the story. I need to explain the tale that led up to these dark times. I need to explain how the Windfarer Prophecy started...

"Although my son Shadowolf played the essential role in the prophecy, and it indeed began with his birth, I feel I must go back a few years more. It was a time of hardship and the orcs had first showed signs of their existence. They attacked villages, killing humans in order to resurrect them for their army. We did not know where they had come from, or if anyone ruled them, but a man named Mercius led one of these orc armies.

"Mercius had hoped to catch my Degron tribe off-guard. Although the walls of Avalion were quite secure, the volume of his army would have destroyed us. But our Lord Bontu watched over us, and my friend Malkius Saphin in Costen saw the army creeping along the river on his border. Malkius gathered his troops and journeyed to Avalion, arriving just in time to save us. We had victory that night, and captured Mercius. He was imprisoned in Eldor's Dungeons north of Avalion. Unfortunately, Mercius's four elemental leaders, known as the Sandrihelin, escaped.

"According to Masara (who brought news of my son's disappearance last year), Mercius had split his soul as they dragged him to the prisons. While his dark half lay enclosed by the magical cell, his better half roamed the world. This better half named himself Farnerd Malerus.

"I was blessed with two sons a few years later. One was dropped by my doorstep a few months before Shadowolf's birth. His origin is unknown, but we named him Darcwulf. When we had to travel to Carmel for the Masaran Phenomenon we left Darcwulf in the care of my sister Listren in Costen.

"It was during our travel to Carmel that we were attacked by a band of orcs. During the attack, Shadowolf was born. The men of the ship fought valiantly and in the end five of us defended the new-born babe and his mother with wind, fire, water, earth and spirit. Masara commented that he feels this power created the power node beneath Shadowolf's body. We did not realise it was there at that moment, however, having just expelled all of our energy.

"But the power node was felt by other elementals. Mercius must have stirred in his cell when it raced through his veins, and I am sure his counterpart Farnerd cringed with excitement too. One other felt it, although he was unknown to me at the time. His name is Le'Mar, and he is the true conductor of the war.

"Farnerd was the first to react. He started construction of a College above the node, and when Shadowolf was two, it was completed. The node gave the school elemental properties, and because he was an elemental too he decided it best to teach Elementalism as tertiary education to young adults.

"The four Sandrihelin heard of the school, and decided it was time to use their elemental abilities as an occupation. I am not sure at what point Farnerd revealed his duel nature to them, but he employed them nevertheless.

"The power node distressed many people, as no one knew what its purpose was. Many greedy elementals hungered to obtain the power with the assumption that they would become Sagdis. Everyone wanted to know how to release the power, and turned to the high elf king, Eldor. Eldor was as bewildered as we were and sent some of his elder elves to investigate. Farnerd permitted them entry, but also commissioned three Orion sages in fear that the elves would keep the secret to themselves.

"Many writings were jotted by the sages, but the most

prominent of note was by the Orion sage, Philgarn Asmuth. Philgarn warned that the power should not be left open, and upon instruction by the Orion, went to the College to conceal the node by lore and passages within the foundation of the College.

"The writings of Philgarn became widely accepted, and one prophecy, divided into three sub-prophecies, became infamous: The Windfarer, The DragonRider and The *Sadgi* prophecy. In "A Compendium to the Trichotomic Prophecy", Philgarn mentions the rise of a dark lord to lead the orcs, and that only the Windfarer could claim the power node as his own. But he also said that once the power was claimed it did not mean the end of the war, but only the beginning, leading to the fulfilment of the other two prophecies.

"We feared for the worst. Mercius had been called a Windfarer (or *Enodhim* as the elves name it) many times as his skill with the wind was remarkable. Le'Mar probably knew this, but for some reason did not react immediately.

"When my son was twenty and in his final year at the college, Le'Mar must have realised that the only way to know the truth was to release Mercius from the prison. The prophecy states that "The Masaran Phenomenon will awaken his power", and he had already missed five in the twenty years of the node's existence to do so.

"We have puzzled and debated at length the dark lord's decision not to release the node himself. Masara claims that Le'Mar is an accomplished *Enodhim*, and did not need Mercius at all. We feel that he is up to something that we have not yet deciphered. Either that or he had tried without our knowledge and failed.

"It was during this time that my son became involved with the prophecy. Masara says that he had always been a part of it from the conception of the node, but my son was, as all of us were, unaware of it.

"The mer-Kingdom from *Marsandil* tried to warn him, but they were attacked by aVampyere and Lellian became the new mer-king. The city Shenama was then destroyed by Mercius and McCaniban to the north of the College at the same time that Le'Mar attempted to steal the Heart of Tigers from Jin-Tai Sanctuary.

"This produced two respective results: The College was closed by Farnerd, as he needed to keep the node secure in preparation for the Phenomenon. And Chenesia from the Vale of Tigers decided to journey to Eldor's Forest to seek protection for the Sanctuary.

"My son returned home to the War Council with a gift from the mer-Kingdom. Shedaaij the Merlani took to his heart and I could see that he cared for her deeply. But the war stopped any love developing between them as he took it upon himself to visit Mercius's old prison.

"There he found Dren, Fornoren and Masnen, the gargoyles. They agreed to join him, if he would help them find the Lapis Pins, magical gems that would stop them from turning into stone in the sun.

"Shadowolf accepted, but Masara placed another task on us. Abutja Blue of Iceland was being manipulated into believing that there was no war by Le'Mar through an Amethyst pendant. Iceland's defences remained low. We needed to remove the pendant.

"My son succeeded in obtaining the Lapis Pins, but Mercius killed Fornoren and Masnen. Thereafter, Shadowolf failed to meet with Abutja Blue, and so I went to meet with him. I was denied my request, but it was decided that Shedaaij use her mermaid powers to seduce him into taking the Amethyst off.

"We did not anticipate that the Amethyst would allow Abutja to withstand her powers. She was taken as prisoner, but Shadowolf intercepted through stealth, freeing her and removing the pendant. An attendee of the castle saw Abutja's generals enter his chamber. There was a cry of death, and the generals, now in their true purorc forms, left.

"We lost Iceland. Although Shadowolf and I tried our best, we could not save it. I took as many refugees to Hasner as I could, while Shadowolf continued fighting.

"The next morning Shadowolf returned to Iceland alone to search for refugees. In his absence, the War Council decided to move Hasner to Costen, and then both Hasner and Costen to Avalion. It was also in his absence that the Shadow Clan was formed by those loyal to my son.

"My son rode into Hasner with one of the enemy's horses and a refugee. There the Hand of the Orion, a special group of warriors, met him and journeyed with him to Costen. The Hand joined the

Clan.

"But Lellian had sent a message to Shedaaij and Shadowolf about the war occurring in the oceans between the mermaids and the sirens. Shedaaij left Avalion to assist the mer-King, and Shadowolf returned to the War Council to ask if the mer-Kingdom could be offered warrens beneath Avalion.

"We had two months of peace. Shadowolf grew restless as the Masaran Phenomenon was close, and I am sure Le'Mar and Mercius felt the same. I do not know if Farnerd and Mercius became one again, but Masara assures me it would have been necessary if he wanted the strength to release the node.

"Masara also informed me that he had realised that Mercius could not possibly be the correct Windfarer and that he had sent this message to Shadowolf in the Mists of Celene. But, knowing my son, he obviously ignored this information in the event that Masara was wrong.

"What happened in the College no one knows. We all felt the power being released. We all feared for the worst. Masara found the remains of two of the Sandrihelin, with no knowledge of where the third and fourth were.

"Mercius's body was also gone, and we assume Farnerd's with it too. But Mercius did not join Le'Mar in attacking Eldor's Forest when *Pernonil* fell. He was not there when the dark lord was enraged and captured Chenesia and fled. Something had gone terribly wrong for Le'Mar, and we can only hope that Shadowolf had destroyed Mercius and claimed the node as his own.

"But my son is gone. Masara informs me Asgorna the Dragon King had taken him into the mountains. This is the only hope I have, yet I have still heard no further news. Masara resides with Eldor in the forest, but when I ask he simply says that Shadowolf will return when the time is right.

"We have seen signs of dragons traversing the skies. It seems that Le'Mar has already chosen his champion for the DragonRider Prophecy. And still, I do not know when my son will return to us…

Nighthale Degron
Degron Core
New Avalion"

FULFILMENT OF THE DRAGONRIDER PROPHECY PROLOGUE B

Eldor closed Nighthale's expose of the prophecy, and faced the Druid hall again. He heard the Elders murmur behind him and he awaited the outcome.

"So the Windfarer prophecy was fulfilled?" an Elder asked. Eldor shifted his stance and looked at him. "You disagree?"

"I think we need to look at the precise words again," Eldor replied slowly. "There is a chance we misunderstood what was prophesied. Maybe we trusted Philgarn's words too much."

The Druids spoke louder, and the Elders stared in disbelief at Eldor.

"Maybe the prophecy was nothing but deception from Farnerd when the sages were studying the power node."

"This is preposterous!" an Elder hit the arms of his chair and stood up. "How do you come to that conclusion?!"

Eldor calmly retrieved another set of pages from his robe, less stained and smaller than the first, and the Elder sat down.

"I, too, have written on the Prophecy, more specifically of last year's events," Eldor said, facing the Druids again. "It gave me the time I needed to gather my thoughts and address you properly. If you will listen and consider the words of the prophecy, you will see that there is little connection with what has happened, and what was prophesied to happen."

The Elders and Druids spoke among themselves again, until the eldest arose and stood beside Eldor.

"We will listen and hear your words," he said. "But in no way will we abide by your condemnation of the prophecy until we have studied the facts."

"Very well," Eldor said, lifting the page as the Elder sat down.

"Let me begin…

"We have sustained many losses and the dark lord's hand wreaks havoc on the land. We have lost the forest I have kept for so many centuries, and the Shadow Clan is no more. I fear that Le'Mar's rule will be unchallenged, and that the Prophecy was nothing more than a ruse.

"What happened three years ago was no secret. Nighthale documented the adventures of his son, and then they all thought that he had mysteriously disappeared, although Masara had informed me of the truth.

"The Dragon King, Asgorna, was called by Ursula the unicorn to assist us. He was hesitant, as a dragon in his world named Maneto had started an uprising against him, and they feared a dragon war was imminent

"Yet, he listened to her words, and agreed he would assist as much as he could. He asked her to bring Shadowolf to him in Bentley Strip so that they may discuss the matter.

"But Shadowolf did not listen to Ursula's counsel, and went to stop Mercius from retrieving the power node. Shadowolf released the power, destroyed Mercius and Farnerd, and was almost killed by the two Sandrihelin. Asgorna managed to make it in time and kill the two, taking Shado's unconscious body to his world.

"War broke out there, and Shado stayed to assist in the Dragon War for two years. In that time, Maneto and a select few dragons came to Celenic Earth and pledged allegiance to Le'Mar. The dark lord realised, with the Windfarer Prophecy supposedly fulfilled, that the DragonRider Prophecy would follow.

"Le'Mar chose an *Enodhim* by the name of Sonersaat to follow as champion in Mercius's absence. We lived in two years fear and tyranny as the dragons took over land in the name of the dark lord. The Heart of Tigers that protected my elvin kingdom still resided with Maren-Ti, the Baron of the Vale of Tigers, but that protection was very slim indeed.

"Le'Mar had kidnapped Chenesia, his daughter, in a moment of desperation when Shado had released the power node, and she still remained locked in his dungeons. Le'Mar waited for the moment of weakness when Maren-Ti would relinquish the Heart. I argued many days with the Baron, and his heart cramped many nights as he feared for her life. Yet, he kept the Heart safe.

"It was two years after his disappearance that Shado finally returned. Asgorna sent an invitation by eagle to four of his closest comrades, thereby alerting the Shadow Clan and his father. The Shadow Clan journeyed to Bentley Strip, and watched Shado undergo a trial to leave the Temple of Asgorna.

"Once reunited, a former Saneth of Le'Mar by the name of Trimistus left the Temple of Mynisna, one of Asgorna's dragons. Trimistus joined the Clan and indicated the true location of Le'Mar's castle by the Alcove of Light. He also stated that he had been absent from Celenic Earth for two years, after narrowly escaping Nolraldun, the assassin.

"Shado's plan of action was to journey across the land and view the devastation caused by Le'Mar. Ursula used this plan to convince him to search for her horn lost in the Battle of T'Mar's Scourge. The Clan agreed to the quest and left.

"Le'Mar at this time sent Sonersaat to attack the Harhonsa Village in Bontu's Wrath. Lucian, former Sandrihelin and Wind tutor at the Asbec College of Elements, resided there with his wife and son. The dragons of Sonersaat destroyed the village and the Orion left the sands, travelling south to New Avalion, home of the southern wolf tribes.

"Chenesia escaped with a pegasus named Genewiu from the dungeons of Le'Mar. We don't know at what point he realised their absence, but Le'Mar attempted one last time to take the Heart of Tigers from Maren-Ti, but I intercepted. I finally made the decision to change the Keeper of the Heart, and Nighthale accepted the position.

"Shadowolf journeyed south to the Dark Border, and then north to T'Mar's Scourge to retrieve the lost horn of Ursula. Along the way, he battled three witches and was rescued from demons by two centaurs, Millon and Kentaur. The two centaurs and one of the witches named Heula joined the Clan.

"The centaurs informed Shado that their ruler, Kraakis the Butcher of Philagis, wished an audience with the *Enodhim*. Shado then conceded to visit him, and met an old man named Malanite in Meëntis.

"The other half of Malanite's soul resided in my throne room in the forest. Masara had split his soul much the same way that Mercius had in order to journey with Ursula and assist the Clan.

"After defeating the Butcher, trapping the other centaurs in the cave (with the exception of Millon and Kentaur), and undergoing the Trial of the *Enodhim*, Shado and the Clan rode north, destroyed McCaniban's army in Shenama and reached the Scourge.

"Lellian the mer-King joined Shado and his brother Darcwulf in swimming down into the depths of the waterfall. There they solved the riddle of the horn and retrieved the ancient object. But they returned to a deserted camp, and saw the assassin Nolraldun enter Dwarf Mountains.

"Le'Mar had an army waiting in Dwarf Mountains to attack Horlorn's Gate from the west, while Sonersaat waited with Maneto and another army in the east. During Shadowolf's quest to save the Clan, they destroyed the mountain army and Shado went through the Trial of the *KariemsaPh*.

"Chenesia reached Carmel with Genewiu and an old peddlar Nucial, and met Lucian and Simnab the Crethan. Nucial strangely disappeared, but Lucian informed Chenesia that the Heart of Tigers no longer resided with her father. Lucian and Simnab joined her on her journey to the Vale.

"Horlorn's Gate welcomed the Clan heroes with open arms. Shado met his old college friends Lanel, Harmony, Mourna and Theroy at the Gate, and passed the *Goudlem* Trial. Sonersaat attacked on Le'Mar's orders, and although the Clan had at first decided to remain out of the battle, Shado and Trimistus summoned Asgorna and Mynisna and flew to battle the dragons.

"Le'Mar must have stopped the battle, for Sonersaat's army retreated. We realised that he was saving the Dragon War and the prophecy for the battle he longed for the most; the battle where he planned to finally conquer the forest of the elves. Shadowolf and Asgorna's presence must have been a frustrating surprise to the dark lord.

"Shadowolf and the Clan journeyed back to the Scourge at the same time that Chenesia, Lucian and Simnab reached the Vale, where I met with them. Lucian informed us of his plan to find uPendus, the mythical valley of the Pegasi. I took Chenesia and

Simnab with me to the elvin forest.

"Shado journeyed to Carmel, with a plan to meet me. In a tavern called the Blue Periwinkle, they heard of a portal that would take anyone to my forest. Ursula and Masara were distressed, as the only entrance they knew of was the Fairiwell, the underground home of the Fairies and Fairdievells.

"They found the mystical portal in Lasglow, and were taken to Trimistus's home planet. It was destroyed by a fog Le'Mar had sent upon them. There, the Clan met the elements *Enodhim*, *Merlandsi*, *Goudlem* and *KariemsaPh*. Le'Mar paid them a visit, but could not find Shado. Upon his departure, the elements sent the Clan back to Celenic Earth.

"Shado now hastened to the elvin forest, going through the Fairiwell, saving the fairies from Le'Mar's fletchlings and entering my forest through the hidden passage. They made it to Tholoi-Temh, one of the elvin villages.

"I gave the Clan and the elves a presentation that evening, and brought Nighthale to the forest. I had decided that Le'Mar was going to find a way to break the defence of the forest anyway, so I was no longer willing to sacrifice any human life for the sake of the Heart. Once Nighthale entered my forest, the magical defence of my forest disappeared.

"Shado passed *Merlandsi*'s trial, but I had other problems. I went to visit the Heart of Tigers in my chambers while the armies moved south to Lard's Den. Horlorn's warriors had joined us and entered the forest. I walked to the gem and touched it, and it passed a horrible vision to me.

"Le'Mar had entered the Heart shortly before Nighthale had been brought to the forest. He had attempted to break its secret, but had failed. After the defence of the forest had fallen, and the gem placed in my throne, Le'Mar had left the Heart and found himself in my kingdom. Not only had I left the way open for him, but had brought him to the forest myself!

"I sat in deep contemplation of this terrible truth as Masara (now reunited with his other half, Malanite) and Shado came to inform me of the armies moving south. We left the throne and made for Lard's Den.

"To prepare the armies for Le'Mar's war, I showed them the

history of the Battle of T'Mar's Scourge, revealing to them that T'Mar had been Masara's step-father, thereby making Le'Mar Masara's half-brother. When the show ended, Le'Mar attacked.

"Looking back at the battle, I can say that there were three stages to it. The first phase has been labelled by many as 'The darkest hour'. Most of our men were killed, the Shadow Clan destroyed and Nelnar, Shado's faithful pet wolf, murdered by Sonersaat. Despite these victories, Le'Mar realised that he was losing, and started the Dragon War.

"Trimistus and Mynisna faced Sonersaat and Maneto. Somehow Trimistus was as much part of the prophecy as Shado was. Shado tried to get through to Asgorna and the dragons, but found that he was being blocked from reaching them. As Masara and Ursula met Le'Mar and his black pegasus in battle, Trimistus was nearly killed. Shado fought Sonersaat, receiving a killing blow in his chest, but he finally became the DragonRider, or *Wisoum* as we elves call it, and destroyed Sonersaat and Maneto.

"The Dragon War had ended, the second phase of the battle complete, and Asgorna was taking his dragons back to his world. Shado had vowed to return with him once the war was over, but Shado could not leave until Le'Mar was dead. Trimistus took his place as the DragonWourd, thereby making Mynisna the new Dragon King.

"In the ocean, the mer-Kingdom faced the demon-queens and their sirens under the rule of Blosom, Mercius's former lover. Lellian faced Blosom as the warrens under New Avalion crumbled, and was killed. James grabbed the trident and killed as many as he could, including Blosom. He became the new mer-King, falling under the ruins of *Avalendil*.

"New Avalion was also under attack by the Dark Border's army under the leadership of the two Saneths, Lister and Ru-maak. Mercius's last Sandrihelin, Sona Nelma, finally emerged from within the city and destroyed the Avalion defence walls with her earth powers.

"But in a strange twist, Darcwulf's former fiancé Angelicus was found in the midst of the dark lord's Crethans. Somehow she found the power to overcome her Creth-master, and she led the wolf-humans away from the forest to New Avalion and assisted

Nighthale.

"In the last phase, Le'Mar raised demons, but Shado ignored them and went for Le'Mar. As he got there, the dark lord killed Masara and trapped his soul in his staff. Le'Mar used Masara's spirit to increase his power, and showed us the power of the Sagdi. He claimed that he had fulfilled the final prophecy. Shado fought him as we left the forest.

"I watched as Le'Mar almost killed Shado. Shado used his last strength to teleport Shedaaij, who was pregnant with their child, to New Avalion. Elgoth, the son of Masara and Ursula, became a unicorn and caught the falling Shado on his back. Chenesia and Genewiu opened a portal for them, and they disappeared.

"I do not know where they went. Le'Mar summoned his black fog and proclaimed himself ruler of the land. His armies disappeared and he left New Avalion to Nighthale. The elvin forest is now called Le'Mar's Forest and his castle is still north of the Alcove of Light.

"Le'Mar has been silent this last year, but his rule has been passed to Shado's brother, Darcwulf, who was turned by Le'Mar in the last moments of the battle. All seems lost and the remnants of the Shadow Clan are gone. We can only accept that Le'Mar is now ruler of Celenic Earth, and leave the inhabitants of the land to live in his fog.

Eldor, Lord of the Eastern Elves
Land of Illusiam
Isle of Masara"

Eldor looked at the silent room and then turned to the Elders.

"Bontu will find a way," the eldest said.

"What if this is the way?" Eldor asked respectfully.

"We must have hope!" the Elder shouted and stood to address the Druids. "The Masaran Phenomenon is upon us next year and....."

"The Prophecy was false!" Eldor intercepted and grabbed his papers, walking out the hall. "There is nothing more that can be done!"

****

PRELUDE

a year later….

He rode over the hot plains, the dust rising into the air behind him. The three companions beside him rode silently.

His aura was still, his power silent. Within the core of his soul, it thrummed against the walls of his spirit for release. He hardly cast a thought to keep it at bay as the power swirled, for his spirit was stronger.

The green, hooded cloak stretched out behind him as the strong, black mare beneath him raced to the edge of the cliff. The sand coiled around her thick legs, and the wind teased the muscles that bulged beneath his body. Her eyes flared red in the sunken pits of her skull, and her ghostly mane flew up against his chest.

His staff clinked in the saddle-strap by his left knee. Its mottled, white surface glistened in the sharp sunlight. Strapped behind him in a bag on the saddle were the only other possessions he owned.

The group of four came to an abrupt halt on the edge of the cliff. The sand swayed around them, and the Dark River lay still in the valley of the mountain.

He looked to his left and spoke in a deep voice.

"Chenesia," he said. She looked at him from Genewiu's unsaddled back. The pegasus unfurled her wings in preparation. "Good luck and I hope you find her."

She nodded, and Genewiu sprang off the cliffs and soared down into the fog of Celenic Earth.

"Lucian," he address the man to his right mounted on Lancenat. "He should be in Bentley Strip."

"I'll find him," Lucian replied and teleported with his horse onto the land below.

"Anuxis," he said, turning to the last one. He wore a dark, black robe with the hood covering his wolf-head. His golden sceptre was strapped to the three-headed hound beneath his legs that was the same height as Mandy. "I hope you find your servants."

"Cerexus and I will hunt them down," Anuxis's voice echoed across the northern plains, "once I have located the Gate."

Anuxis hollered deeply and Cerexus charged down the mountain side, rocks falling behind them and dust rising in the air.

Shadowolf patted Mandy's neck and looked over the land hidden by fog. He knew he would no longer see the fog once he was in it. Trimistus had taught him that much.

He looked at the mottled staff and smiled.

"Well, Nelnar," he said. "Time to take back to the land."

****

PART ONE

DAGGER OF BENTLEY

MISTS OF THE PAST
CHAPTER ONE

New Avalion loomed before him. The warm sun soothed the skin on his arms and the breeze softly caressed his cheeks.

Shadowolf sat lazily on Mandy's back as she walked slowly across the grassland to his father's land. He remembered a time when Avalion had defensive walls around it, with the three concentric circles surrounding the Degron Core.

Now the city was open to the land, the Core visible to all eyes on the raised hill in the centre. The houses and villages were located on the sides of the hill, and the people were milling around, tending to gardens and visiting the taverns.

Degron Castle was not the only castle of note. On different locations, which the circular walls once protected, were three other castles. One belonged to Malkius Saphin, lord of the Saphin Tribe of Costen. Another was Sjedwolf Watre, lord of the Watre Tribe of Hasner. And lastly, there was Jasnon Lowle, lord of the Lowle Tribe of Iceland.

The Orion Tribe had also been situated amongst the villages, but due to their late entry had not received land of their own. Also, their leader Amon Harhonsa had been killed by Sonersaat, Le'Mar's DragonRider, and no new leader had been chosen when Shadowolf had last stepped foot in Avalion.

As Mandy idly walked into Lowle Village, entering through a gate set in a wooden fence, the people stopped raking their gardens and gossiping on the lawns to look his way. They didn't seem to feel threatened or elated by his presence, merely observing him pass through their land.

A few children stopped running and pointed at the black mare he rode on. Her sunken eyes amazed them, and they seemed not to fear such a dark creature. Shadowolf wondered what they had seen recently to overcome such fear.

But the men and women of the land were not looking at the mare but at his face. His light brown hair had streaks of blond from the sunlight, and reached down to his shoulders. A goatee was around his mouth, with a thin line of hair stretching from his bottom lip to his chin. He had three rings on his fingers and a white, mottled staff attached to his saddle.

Even from a distance they could see the deep blue of his eyes that penetrated them with his glare. He offered them a smile, at which they frowned, and then faced his father's castle again.

He received the same response in Watre Hills, but Mandy stopped calmly in her tracks as kids ran before them. Their parents were anxious to pick them up and carry them away.

Shadowolf rode forward again and saw a woman running down the hill towards him. She wore a simple white and red skirt with a blue, sleeveless top, her black hair bouncing behind her head.

He dismounted and let Mandy graze on the yellow grass as Heula embraced him. As they walked up the path looking at each other and smiling stupidly, Mandy followed in their wake.

"So….you're back?" Heula said, laughing at herself.

"Yes, it would seem so," Shadowolf replied. "How have you been?"

"Coping," she shrugged and nodded her head simultaneously. Her lips pouted as she tried to find the right words. "I am….no longer a witch, so to speak."

"Really?" he said in amazement, his eyebrows rising.

"I decided to forsake that which the dark…well, anything to do with him," she said, shifting her eyes around the village. Shadowolf looked at her in confusion, but left her in peace.

"Who made it through the war?" he asked, his throat struggling to remain calm.

"Skywolf and Angelia are here, if that's what you mean," she said, looking away from his eyes. She studied the townsfolk for a while as they entered Saphin Vale. "Lastgorn was last seen in Lowle Village, as Costen only reminds him of Sny-Ten and Gwyn."

Her sweet voice trailed away as he swallowed the dry spit down his throat. He sighed as he tried to enjoy the strange serenity he felt in Avalion.

"And Shedaaij?" he finally asked. Heula shook her head, and it seemed as if she was not going to reply.

"I don't know," she said.

Mandy neighed behind him, more to herself than to anyone else. His steps to his father's castle became heavier when suddenly he stopped and turned around in circles.

"What's the matter?" Heula asked, watching him.

"Where's *Avalendil*?" he asked. "Where's the moat that used to surround Degron Core?"

"The mer-Kingdom's warren was destroyed by the sirens during our battle with Le'Mar two years ago," she replied. "The earth and water elementals closed the moat."

Shadowolf wouldn't allow this to get to him right now. He closed off his emotions and walked on. Heula stood still and studied his face before following.

"Darcwulf?" he attempted, almost afraid of the answer.

"Le'Mar has been quiet since his rule on the land," she said, and Shadowolf turned to stare at her.

"Rule?" he asked.

"Believe it or not, we have only had peace since he defeated us in what was once called Eldor's Forest," she said defensively. "We don't complain. We get to live."

Shadowolf ground his teeth together, but calmed his rising temper as he walked on.

"Darcwulf has been seen," she continued. "He still serves Le'Mar and doesn't speak to any of us anymore."

He held his hands behind his back, his mind in contemplation. The archway of his father's court was before them, and he only turned his attention from his thoughts when he realised there were no guards by the archway. He pushed the low, steel fence open and walked in.

He went through to the courtyard that led to his parents chambers. Above him on the second floor he could see his mother walking to the kitchens speaking earnestly with a cook. She was carrying plates and cutlery in her hand, opening her mouth to answer the cook and then dropping the items when she looked down into the courtyard.

Shadowolf tried to smile in comfort, but he somehow felt it insufficient to describe his feelings. She began running down to him, her arms outstretched in greeting, but he saved her the trouble and teleported to the second floor.

The wind rushed into her as he appeared and she ran right into his arms. He held her tight, her soft tears falling on his chest. She pulled away and looked into his face.

"You've grown so much," she whispered, touching his cheeks.

"I wondered if you'd remember me?" he jibed, realising how much huskier his voice sounded.

"Come," she said, and looked passed Shadowolf's shoulder to see Heula approaching them from the stairs. "We were just getting ready for lunch."

They walked passed his old room towards the stairwell that led to the tower where his father held the War Council meetings. They climbed it steadily, Shadowolf taking his time and counting his breaths until they reached the tower top.

When his mother eased the door open, his heart sank when he saw the room was empty except for a solitary, circular table which had never been there before.

"Where's dad?" he asked.

"He's with Franklin and Nowles by Malkius's place, honey," she replied and offered him a seat. He took it, and she blew a kiss from her hands through an open window. Little dots of light sprang from her palm and drifted down to Saphin Castle.

"I see the tower is no longer used," he said.

"It is," she replied, sitting between him and Heula, "but no longer for meetings of war. The people eat in their own homes now, and the dining hall is used less than it used to be. Your father and I eat here, with any few friends who wish to join us."

His mother suddenly looked at Heula. He looked from one to the other as Heula opened her eyes in shock and gaped.

"I'll do it," Heula said and ran from the tower, forgetting to close the door again in her haste.

"Oh, my dear, you must have been so worried," his mother grabbed his hand in hers on the table and looked into his eyes.

He frowned and tried to speak, but he assumed she was referring to Shedaaij. He remembered that he had teleported Shedaaij to Avalion at the height of the battle in the forest and her current absence dismayed him.

There was a rush of wind from the passage leading up the tower and his father laughed at something Malkius said as they, Franklin and Nowles entered the room.

"I got the message, Karla," he said, as he turned his head from Malkius's direction. "Is it...."

The four men stopped. Nighthale gripped the chair before him and continued to stare at his son.

"No matter how many times you vanish and reappear," Nighthale murmured as Shadowolf stood to embrace him, "I can never get used to it."

They held each other tight as the other men sat down. Men with snacks and drinks entered the room, laid it on the table and left.

"If I could spank you for every time you run away..." Nighthale began.

"My bum would be purple," Shadowolf smiled as he finished. Wet tears strolled down his cheeks.

"I think we played too much hide and seek with you as a child," Karla joked, and they both sat down laughing and crying at the same time.

"So much has changed," Shadowolf said.

"Wait until you see the Mists of Celene," Nighthale warned him. Shadowolf stared at him in disbelief.

"I could almost swear you've given in to Le'Mar," he said more seriously, looking into his father's eyes.

"We have," Nighthale said, averting his gaze. "There is nothing to fight against. Le'Mar poses no opposition."

Shadowolf looked at his father, his lips pursed. He nodded in acknowledgement, but only because he did not want to upset them on the first day of his return.

"We know you don't understand," Karla tugged on his elbow and he faced her. "But why should we fight when there is peace? Our land is thriving."

Footsteps echoed from the passage and Shadowolf looked towards it. His power was surging in his soul, rising with his temper. Heula appeared in the doorway with a little girl cradled in her arms holding her fingers. Shadowolf sprang up in shock, the chair falling backwards.

"She's yours," Karla said and watched Shadowolf's expression.

"Shedaaij left her in our custody when she disappeared a few months ago."

Shadowolf walked passed his father and the others, oblivious to their presence. The girl smiled up at him as he bent over her, and he stroked her cheeks.

"She has my eyes," he said in awe, "but her mother's face. What's her name?"

"Shedaaij was waiting for you to return before she named her," Nighthale said as Shadowolf held out his hands to hold her. His daughter pulled back shyly, unsure of his intensions.

"She'll have to get to know you first," Karla laughed softly. "She seems to have gained your mistrust for strangers.

Shadowolf beamed down at his daughter, taking in every part of her face.

"How old is she?"

"Give or take 14 months," Karla replied. "Anyway, will you be joining us for dinner?"

"Of course!" Shadowolf exclaimed joyfully.

His mother nodded and, with a last wave from Shadowolf, left the hall with the baby.

Shadowolf's stomach grumbled in pleasure that evening as he stared out the window of his room. Mandy was sleeping in the stable yard and his staff leaned against the white wardrobe along the wall.

Behind him was his bed that still held the faint scent of Shedaaij. He had found a strand or two of her hair on the pillow and some of the clothes his mother had loaned her in his wardrobe.

He looked down on the western land and remembered the first time he had met the Merlani. She had walked out from *Marsandil*, the original home of the mer-people of Shadow Lake, and she had introduced herself as the only one of mer- and human conception.

Since then it had been attempt after attempt on Shedaaij's part to ensnare him in her heart, until she had succeeded and he had fallen inlove with her. His soul stirred and he smiled softly, missing her love and wondering where she was.

"Why is it that I always find you contemplating?" Nighthale stepped into the room. He joined Shadowolf looking out the window onto the moonlit landscape.

"Because there always seems to be something to contemplate," he replied, Shedaaij's scent disappearing in the smell of the bath salts from his father's skin.

"Are they ghosts of the past, or plans for the future?"

"Past, present and future," Shadowolf replied. "My mind is exercising its free will."

Shadowolf looked down at the trees that once bordered the western wall of Avalion. He used to walk among those trees, when the blue mist caressed the grass and imbued the atmosphere with soul-refreshing vigour. It had been the Mists of Celene where he had first met the unicorn Ursula on one of his quests.

"Do you know what happened to Ursula?" he asked.

"She led the refugees from Le'Mar's Forest back to Horlorn's Gate at the time of the war," Nighthale replied. "The elves have returned to the Far Isles and I assume she went with them, especially after Masara...."

Nighthale's voice trailed off, but he knew what his father had wanted to say. The old saint Masara had fought valiantly against Le'Mar, but in the end had failed against him and died. Yet, his death had seemed pale in contrast to when the dark lord had imprisoned his soul in his staff. It had been this turn of events that had marked victory for the dark lord. Once again, Le'Mar had disregarded Shadowolf as if he were a mere ant.

Shadowolf bowed his head, closed his eyes and pushed the pride away. He would not allow Le'Mar's belittling attitude to affect him. He focused on the presence of Bontu when he heard his father bid him goodnight and shuffle out the room.

LORD DANAKA
CHAPTER TWO

Lancenat's hooves pounded onto the cliff. Lucian Par'Mal shifted his eyes in the dimming light, making sure no one had seen him teleport. The wind blew listlessly in the air, unable to clear the dense fog that was now visible to the *Enodhim* from his view on the cliff.

Lucian turned Lancenat to the mouth of the cave. They rode in gingerly, not knowing if the dragons still resided in Bentley Strip or if Le'Mar had extended his kingdom there too.

It was a minute later when Lucian entered the hall he assumed Shadowolf had referred to. There were no bon fires to warm the skin, nor tables laden with meat and drink to sate the body, but he had followed the waterfall to the cliff just above it and hoped he had taken the right entrance.

Lucian smiled forlornly as he realised it did not really matter which entrance he took. The problem would be to find the correct entrance to Mynisna's temple. Within the bowels of the mountains of Bentley Strip was a DragonWourd that rode Mynisna, the Dragon King. It was this *Wisoum* that Lucian had to find in order to complete his part of the quest, and he hoped that Lord Danaka still remembered old alliances.

The tunnel narrowed the further he rode in. There were no torches to light the way and no heralds to announce the path. Lancenat scuffled on the soil of the tunnel, apparently being able to pierce the dark veil with his sight better than the rider could.

They passed a door on the left and Lucian pulled the reins softly. As Lancenat slowed to a halt, Lucian removed from under his shirt the Amulet of Larna Thorn that Shadowolf had handed him.

The amulet consisted of two silver dragons entwining their

bodies. Their heads reared at the top where they faced each other. Holding them in place to the silver chain was a large ring to which they were fused.

Lucian had hesitated in accepting the amulet, wondering if Shadowolf would not need it more. But the young man had insisted that he take it, impressing upon him that he would not require its service immediately and that he would need Asgorna's help in locating Mynisna and his DragonRider.

But Lucian knew Asgorna, the former Dragon King, would not present a warm reception, for he had lost the title because of Shadowolf. This was not, however, the reason that Shadowolf had sent Lucian on the quest. Rather it had been for the sake of the prophecy that they had agreed it better that Shadowolf not go.

The amulet lay silent in his hand, only emitting a soft, grey sheen from the summoning power it held within. Lucian moved on, passing a few more doors to his left and right until the amulet began to vibrate.

He looked to the left wall and dismounted. He felt on the surface for a hole in the centre and then pushed the amulet into it. The amulet winked brighter for a moment and the door creaked open.

Everything was as Shadowolf had explained it. He first passed through a triangular room, where Shadowolf had battled four gigantic elementëls to escape the room. Then there was the narrow, dark passage stretching endlessly from left to right.

Next, he stepped out of the bark of a tree into a forest and made his way to the field where Shadowolf had fought the minor elementëls to open the way to the dark passage. He entered a second forest, making sure to avoid the lit glades where the nymphs and dryads were located.

Finally, he stepped into a clearing where the Temple of Asgorna stood majestically in the light of the mountain. On the right side was a shimmering lake that held the sirens that posed as mermaids. At the bed of the lake was the trident that would light the way out.

Lucian led Lancenat by the reins and walked before the temple. The walls and columns that supported the roof were white stone, while the roof, window and door frames were green. The central steps leading up to the main doors were silver.

Lucian held the amulet that was thrumming with power and closed his eyes. The lids glared a soft white and then returned to normal.

Lancenat walked along the grass and started grazing. The Windfarer sat cross-legged on the ground and waited.

***

Shadowolf could not help laughing at his daughter the next morning. She crawled around the courtyard, took a moment to stand on her legs and then walked over to him with a bright smile.

"Come here, you!" he grabbed her as she reached his arms. He lay flat on his back and held her above him. Slowly he threw her up in the air and caught her. He watched as her face turned from anxiety to delight. He threw her again; her face went into a mixture of tension and joy. She giggled as he caught her again, clearly wanting more.

He bent his legs up and put her on them. He straightened his legs up and then dropped it down. She laughed out loud as she descended, ending with their faces close together. He moved her in the air again and dropped her down, this time with her laughter ringing on the walls of the courtyard.

"Where's daddy, where's daddy, where's daddy?" he said as he raised her up again, and then dropping his legs. "There's daddy!!!"

She laughed; her faced was screwed up in happiness and her eyes narrow slits. Her milk teeth glittered above him and he laughed with her.

"I see you two are having fun," Karla said as she strode across the grass. His daughter was hopping up and down his knee in unmasked impatience as he watched his mother approach.

"I vaguely remember dad doing this to me when I was a lad," he replied, moving his legs up and down slowly to please his baby.

"He was doing that and all the other sorts of things with her in your absence," she smiled fondly at the memories. "I dare say she's taken a liking to her grandpa."

"Paaa...paaa," his daughter said, and Shadowolf looked up in amazement.

"She's been saying things like that for a while now," his mother informed him. "It's her name for your father."

"And Shedaaij?" he asked.

"She was saying 'mamamamama' before Shedaaij disappeared," Karla replied, and then fell silent.

"You understand that I have to search for her?"

"Of course, my son," she said. "I wouldn't expect anything less."

"If I know her, she went in search of the mer-Kingdom," he said. "She should have been back by now. Are there still sirens in the ocean?"

"We don't know, sweetie," she said. "Will you come in for breakfast?"

"In a moment, I want to check up on Mandy first."

"Ok, but this little monster must eat," his mother said, removing the girl from his knees.

"Byss.....bysss," his daughter said, clutching the crude quartz hanging from Karla's chain.

"She loves crystals," she said, "just trying to get her to say the word properly. Say tata to daddy."

"Dadadada," the baby mumbled, flapping her hand up and down in an effort to wave.

Shadowolf watched them leave the courtyard and then made his way to the stableyard. From a distance he could see that a stableboy was trying to groom Mandy, but it was through no rebellion on her part that the boy failed.

Her mane still flowed from her neck in ghostly proportions and the tail refused to look elegant. The only effect that the brush had on her coat was that it looked darker than ever, which he knew pleased Mandy more than it did the boy.

"I think her nose is bleeding," the boy said as Shadowolf nuzzled his face into her mane in greeting.

"Why do you say that, Eldricht?" he asked, trying not to laugh.

"Every time she exhales there's a stench of blood in it," Eldricht replied.

Mandy snorted and glared at the boy and Shadowolf no longer contained his mirth. Eldricht recoiled from the smell of brimstone in the air.

"Thank you for attending to her," Shadowolf said, his face

becoming politely serious. Eldricht nodded at the silent instruction and left them alone.

Shadowolf peered into the black pits of Mandy's left eye. Her red pupil burnt warmly in its depths, pulsing to the beat of her heart, but he could not detect any messages from Lucian, Chenesia or Anuxis.

He patted her neck and mounted her bare back, riding into villages to search for Angelia and Skywolf.

***

Lucian woke up from the grass as he heard something stir in the air. Lancenat had waded into the forest while he had slept the night, but he knew the difference between its hooves and the new sound.

He stood up; flexing his muscles and body, he waited for the dragon to appear from the temple. He had feared that Asgorna had decided not to respond to the amulet anymore. But his hopes were alight as he heard movement within the temple, quickly to be confused when the doors opened. Didn't Shadowolf warn that Asgorna would rise through the roof?

It was not a dragon that emerged from the oak doors. A strong, bulky man walked down the silvery steps to the grass. On his hip dangled a wide sword with a dragon emblem embossed on each side. It had no sheath, but was tied with a red sash to his waist.

The main constituent of his skin was hardened scales that looked like small pebbles clustered close together to the casual observer. The scales were green, the only exception being the yellow on his chest and abdomen.

Yet, one would only notice the scales if the attention was drawn away from the man's face. Like Mandy, his eyes were sockets that sank into his head with red pupils burning in the abyss. In place of a nose he had two small slits above pinched lips.

"Lord Danaka," Lucian bowed down on one knee as he approached.

"I was expecting someone else," the reptilian man said.

"The expected one sent me to search for you," he replied. "I summoned Asgorna in the hope of finding you."

"And Asgorna informed me of the summons to Celenic Earth, but I decided to attend to the matter personally," the man replied. "By whose name did he send you?"

"Shadowolf," Lucian replied. "It is he who gave me the Amulet of Larna Thorn."

It sounded as if the man sighed and in a friendlier tone asked that Lucian rise.

"I come with a request, Lord Danaka," Lucian continued.

"Please," he said, "call me Trimistus."

"Very well, Trimistus," Lucian said. "Shadowolf has asked if you can assist me in finding an ancient artefact."

"And what may that be?" Trimistus asked.

"Bentley's Dagger."

TALES OF BENTLEY
CHAPTER THREE

It was the third time in her life that Chenesia found herself standing by the disc. Genewiu pattered the arid sand beside the Fairiwell portal as the girl stared down at it anxiously.

"Do you think the fairdievells are still down there?" the pegasus asked.

"I do not know," Chenesia answered honestly, quelling her hopes. "But if the rumours are true, she will be with them. Like Shadowolf said, we need to find her if we are to locate the relic."

Genewiu spread her wings out and rose into the air. They had returned from a long flight over and around Le'Mar's Forest, inspecting Le'Mar's new camps and surveying the *KariemsaPh* Throne in the centre. Before Chenesia started her quest however, she had a personal errand to run.

They soared through the air towards the Vale of Tigers. For a few moments they enjoyed respite from the fog before flying back into it and landing at the entrance to the city.

Genewiu landed on the sand, looking for the gate but finding none. Chenesia gaped as she saw that the Vale was unprotected. There were no walls to bar entry, no gates to swing open in welcome and no guards to stall intruders.

"What happened?" Genewiu wondered.

"It can only be the work of the dark lord," Chenesia assumed. "Let's go."

The people of the Vale were walking around, either doing their work or visiting friends. The houses were still standing as they once had and seemed to have escaped the dark lord's tyranny. They rode on to her father's castle, passing the Jin-Tai Sanctuary to the south.

Chenesia dismounted and walked into the castle. Genewiu tucked her wings to the sides of her white body and looked around at Baron Maren-Ti's home.

Chenesia found one of the dwarf wardens walking away down a side corridor to an open courtyard. She ran lightly on her feet and touched his shoulder to stop him.

"Excuse me, master dwarf," she said formally, "but do you perhaps know where lady Larnesia is?"

"I do not hold court for the holders of the city," he said simply and turned to continue down the passage.

"Perhaps you know the where-abouts of master dwarf Hargon?" she persisted.

"The adviser to King Gallon is in the mountains," he said, trailing away from her, "as are most of the dwarf wardens."

"Dwarf Mountains?" she asked.

"Yes," he sighed impatiently, disappearing from sight.

"I see hospitality and courtesy have left the city too," Genewiu commented.

Chenesia moved at a faster pace and Genewiu trotted to keep up. They eventually made it to the sleeping quarters of her parents and she opened the doors in a rush.

"Mother?" she called walking into the carpeted room. "Father?"

There was no one present. A soft, musty smell permeated the room and as she walked dust rose from the floor and fell onto her sandaled toes.

She walked to a window that revealed the Jin-Tai Sanctuary to the south. The sun caressed her serene face, trying hard to warm her open shoulders and arms but only to be swayed by a slight breeze.

The wind flowed over the small, pretty freckles on her cheeks, over her ears and down her shoulder-length black hair. She let her arms rest on the window ledge, her firm round breasts lying upon them as she stared down at the Vale in search of her parents.

A short breath escaped her lips as she spotted her mother. She was walking among several men and women, smiling softly to them in the sunlight and making gentle gestures with her hands when she spoke. Chenesia frowned; those were the people her father usually held court with.

"She's in the city," she informed the pegasus.

"Get on," Genewiu instructed.

Chenesia mounted her and watched as the wall before them shimmered.

"It's amazing that I managed to get used to that," Chenesia smiled and held onto Genewiu's mane as the pegasus ran for the wall. Her hooves dug into the floor and she jumped through.

The two passed through the solid structure to the sky outside and glided down to Larnesia. The wall they had passed through stopped shimmering and became solid again, untainted by their passing. Larnesia covered her brow with her hand, looking up at the shadow that glided down beneath the sun towards her.

The hooves dropped on the pebbled road and Larnesia's hand fell as she saw her daughter. Chenesia didn't dismount immediately, waiting for her mother's reaction. Larnesia walked calmly to the pegasus's side and looked up at her.

"I've missed you," she said, and Chenesia jumped down and embraced her mother. The two stood with the courtiers around them. Genewiu flapped her wings before tucking them neatly to her sides.

"Where is father?" Chenesia asked as they broke the embrace.

"That is why I have missed you the most," Larnesia replied, bowing her head and fiddling with her hands. Chenesia's eyes widened slowly, horror teasing the tension in her mind.

"What has happened?" she barely stammered, retreating a few steps.

"I have needed you so much," Larnesia said, coughing into her hand and tears rolling down her cheeks. More out of respect for her mother's need than her own, Chenesia held her again, Larnesia's head falling on her breasts as she cried. The men and women left them in peace.

"Genewiu," Chenesia whispered. The pegasus nodded and walked around them twice. The sand between the pebbles on the road rose in the air and they vanished.

They appeared in Larnesia's bedroom from where Chenesia had spotted her only moments before. The two sat on the edge of the bed as Genewiu left the room, the doors closing of their own accord behind her.

"He couldn't bear losing you a second time," Larnesia began. "But he didn't lose me...."

"Eldor told us you were safe in uPendus?" her mother looked at her and she nodded her head. "Even so, it had a devastating effect on your father. His old heart cramps returned..."

"Oh no," Chenesia said, remembering how he had complained of his heart many times during her youth. Her cheeks were wet from her own tears now as she clutched her mother's hands.

"It became more severe," Larnesia continued, "until one day he claimed it was gone. Many times that day he told me he loved me, and I knew what was coming. He told me.....to tell you he loves you."

"Was it peaceful?" Chenesia managed to say, barely keeping the sobs at bay.

"Yes; he passed away in his sleep that night." Larnesia cried out loud, her head falling on Chenesia's lap drenching the skirt she wore. Chenesia looked down and stroked her mother's hair, her lips quivering from the pain and her face contorted in sadness.

Finally she succumbed to the anguish and released the flood of tears upon her mother's hair....

***

Lucian sat at the desk in the musty study. Torches flared on brackets along the walls, but the table was well-lit with candles and orbs of blue light. He stared at the books lining the walls, all covered in the dust of time. Pages ruffled behind him as Trimistus searched through documents.

"Ahhh," the reptilian DragonWourd said. Lucian shifted in his seat. They were in one of the rooms of the Temple of Asgorna, well hidden from the source of light outside. He stirred the air with his mind, allowing the wind blow the dust off the table's surface just before Trimistus dumped a scroll on it.

He picked up the scroll and unrolled it, letting the loose end run down to the floor and across it by his feet. It was entitled "Treatise on Falgan Earth".

"This document is indeed old," Lucian murmured.

"As I am not originally from this world," Trimistus said, wiping the seat of a chair with a rag and sitting opposite him, "maybe you could indulge me as to how you now that, besides the obvious age of the document."

"Before the Masaran Age," Lucian replied, scanning the elvin words briefly, "we referred to the first twelve hundred years as the Falgan Earth, or "First Earth". But we discovered that we had made an error. Falgar was the first man to leave the Nether Region, but was not the first man to be created. It was Bentley that first roamed the world, and it was the elves that informed us through Masara."

"What does this mean in terms of the document?" Trimistus asked.

"We renamed the first six hundred years the Bentlic Age," Lucian replied, looking up at him. "This document must be a couple of centuries old; although, it does make reference to Bentley...."

"Well, I am in no rush to return to the kingdoms," Trimistus smiled, planting his feet on the table. "Maybe you could interpret the document for me."

"Certainly," Lucian said, screwing his eyes in concentration as he deciphered the words.

Treatise on Falgan Earth
1 – 1200yrs
Bentley

The passage of time cannot erase the name of Bentley. He is the forefather of time, the one who was the sole disciple of Bontu the Almighty. When he awoke on the River of Light, it is said he opened his eyes to the beginning of creation; when the paths of space and time were first constructed. The Jehnisan, or Angels as we refer to them today, were said to have blessed Bentley with the gift of life. Bentley, on the other hand, knew no such thing....

The River of Light

When Bentley first awoke on the southern shores of what was referred to as the "First Earth" by Falgar, he felt numbed by the spray of the ocean upon his legs. After a few hours of collecting his energy he finally arose and witnessed a river spreading to the north-east. The cold of the river made his head pound and he turned to see a large orb arise on the eastern horizon. He felt how the orb radiated heat and emitted light upon the earth, and watched as it travelled across the sky.

The light dazzled upon the newly-formed river, which was no longer a gentle stream but rather becoming a deep torrent. No longer permitting his curiosity to delay him, he followed the river north.

Life on Falgan Earth

Earth was not lacking life. A day or two's travel found Bentley witnessing deer cross the River of Light. There were teems of fish in the stream and rabbits burrowing holes in what appeared to be low hills of moss. Bentley was amused by the colours upon the earth. The grass followed the river towards the north-west. Deciding to leave the river, he followed a path trodden by deer.

Three days after his appearance on the southern shores, a mysterious incident occurred. Bentley realised that Creotos the sun was finally by the western horizon. A new orb appeared in the eastern sky. It was smaller in size and softer in heat and radiance. The earth was dark after Creotos set and was barely lit by the new orb he called Sothos, the moon. Feeling the pangs of exhaustion, he settled down upon the flowers to rest. Yet, the excitement of the world kept his mind awake and an hour after Sothos's rising, another orb broke the north-eastern horizon. It had rings upon its surface and was twice the size of Creotos, albeit it bestowed upon the land a little less illumination. The land was lit again with light, Sothos and the new orb Ringos travelling the sky; Sothos went west, while Ringos went south-west.

Bentley was mesmerised by their journey. He saw that Ringos travelled at a much faster rate than Sothos. Within three hours of the ringed-planet's rising, it set again in the south-west, leaving Sothos as close to the eastern horizon as it had been before. The earth was plunged into darkness again, Sothos inching its way to the western sky. It would take another three hours before Ringos rose in the north-east again, with no sign of Creotos anywhere. Sothos continued its slow journey west.

Bentley could no longer hold the exhaustion at bay. He stared up at the apex of the sky, and fell asleep…

The Forest of Purity

Bentley slept through the moon's forty-two day journey across the sky. When he awoke, the last vestige of light set in the west. Ringos was as small as a star now in the sky, no longer orbiting earth. Bentley would soon learn that the sun only lit the sky at day and the moon at night. The rare occasion of the appearance of Ringos would occur every four years.

These matters were the last thing on his mind, however, when he opened his eyes to a forest. He raised his upper body to see that the forest was filled with life. Around each tree there was a hue of light sacred to perceive and there were creatures, similar to Bentley, but with narrow eyes, pointed ears and bright auras. One being stood out among the faces staring at him in awe, human as he was but with obvious differences. He was immediately attracted to her and he named her Marhelen, for she was the first woman of the earth.

The love he felt for Marhelen was not lost upon her. By the time Creotos returned to start its natural orbit across the sky, Marhelen, Bentley and the elves had formed a basis of communication and order within the Forest of Purity, and Bentley and Marhelen were the rulers of all.

Mikinos and Elhorin

Mikinos and Shardenel were born to the rulers within two years. Mikinos resembled his father in stature and strength and

Shardenel's eyes gleamed as the stars up high.

It was the fourth year of his age, two years after the reappearance of Ringos, that Mikinos first showed promise of true power. His touch with the trees of purity was unmatched and his love for all the animals of fur, feather, fin and scale was remarkable.

But, at the age of sixteen, Mikinos had a deep desire for one of the elf daughters. Against the wishes of his father, he walked into one of the elvish encampments in the region. His father willed that he love his sister in order to bring more children to the earth. But all men have greedy desires and Mikinos, with growing pride and power, began to feel lust in his loins and desire for that which he was denied.

So it was that he met Elhorin, great-granddaughter of Saldheron the wise. She was fairer in complexion than most elves and, like her mother, had skin more akin to a human's than the green hue of the elves. And his heart bled for her and her smile captured his mind. But Elhorin was humble and obedient and would not betray her father, Malherin, albeit her love for Mikinos was true and pure.

Mikinos had no care for such foolish obedience in the presence of 'love', and believed his power above all. Thus it was that, on a cool clear night, he broke into Elhorin's chalhela through the open window. When she refused to court with him and run away, he hit her across the cheek. Such a force of power against the will of another did not go unnoticed by the nodes of power throughout the forest. Malherin appeared before Mikinos as if he had been there all along. Tension grew between the two as power surged within them.

"Let us go to the plains and the decision make in battle," Mikinos suggested. Although the plains were days' travel to the north, they were there in an instant.

The Battle of Powers

Malherin was a wise elf and well loved by his followers. Not a day was lost when he meditated and concentrated his power on Bontu. But wisdom is best found in serene moments. The tension and anger he felt at this abuse against his daughter made him lose his calm.

Malherin stared with blue eyes towards Mikinos, who was gathering energy from the earth. Closing his eyes, Malherin focussed on the wind. The night became colder as static built around the two and the battle began. They alternated between vicious physical and power-filled torturous blows. The earth began to quake, the wind uncontrollable as the battle raged on.

In the end, Malherin had the upper hand. Mikinos had depleted his power and lay panting on the grass for breath. Malherin prepared in his had a ball of power, small in size but devastating once released. He was about to deliver his final blow when he found himself in a distant plain. No forest was near him and he pulled the power back into his soul. He looked up into the serene face of Bentley. The man had just saved the elf from committing the first act of murder, but to all appearances it seemed that Malherin was ignorant of this fact.

"Your son has betrayed us, Bentley," Malherin said.

"He is young, Malherin, and has yet to learn. We have only encountered such an act for the first time and we should wisen ourselves against it."

"Don't lecture me on wisdom! What think you to your daughter with an elf?"

"Do not deign to threaten me," Bentley said calmly, "or you will find a most unwelcomed greeting in my heart when next we meet."

As Bentley turned to leave, Malherin roared with the fury of the wind and struck towards the back of his head with an evil blow. The earth rose to block the blow and, as Malherin chased Bentley across the plains, the earth quaked again and spewed forth hot flames to protect Bentley's pure honour.

Maddened, Malherin formed his greatest power within the palm of his right hand and aimed it at Bentley. The man moved with the wind to the elf and, as the power was released, pushed against it with his arms. The two stood locked around the power orb, pushing against each other. Malherin's mind ached to release the power while Bentley strained to keep it contained.

"Do not let the evil consume you!" Bentley shouted, but Malherin ignored him. They rose in the air, the power lifting them up. The landscape changed and lightning broke out from their bodies. Mountains rose from the earth beneath them as their arms bulged against the orb.

Before Malherin could retort or shout, Bentley drew the complete power-orb of Malherin into his hand and transformed it into a dagger of wind. He thrust it into the elf's abdomen.

Malherin's own power killed him, surging through his soul and veins as his eyes turned black and melted from the inside. The earth cried at the murder, the skies ran with the wails of lightning…and then all was quiet.

Malherin slipped off the dagger and fell down to the newly-formed mountain peaks of Bentley's Strip. Bentley let the dagger fall from his hand.

Before the first tear caressed his cheek, Bentley turned and saw a light shining from the western oceans. He followed it.

The Forest Lost

At the forest of purity, a strange wind blew to awaken Mikinos. He arose with a pain within his chest, not only form the battle, but also from the guilt of his actions. Saldheron the wise appeared before him.

"You have destroyed the sanctity and haven of the children of Bontu with your evil desire and now the forest and the earth repel us. We must leave. Know that your actions will be the downfall of many. Yours is a power we cannot qualm."

As Saldheron turned to leave, he spoke a last verse to Mikinos.

"One will come with the power to save,
Pure in nature to undue this pain.
United we will stand again in this forest,
With fire, earth, wind and water, elements unbested.
The one with the store of power unclaimed."

Saldheron and the elves vanished, leaving Mikinos and Shardenel with the fate of the world. He named the forest the Nether Region, for all purity had left the trees and he did not know what would become of them.

The Beach of Bontu

"I have sinned against you Lord," Bentley said, kneeling on the beach and bowing his head to light in the west.

IT IS UNFORTUNATE THAT EVIL HAS ENTERED THE HEART OF THE WORLD, BUT YOU HAVE SAVED THE WORLD FROM THE DESTRUCTION MALHERIN WOULD HAVE CAUSED.

I WILL NO LONGER PERMIT YOU TO LIVE IN THIS WORLD WHERE EVIL HAS ENTERED, BUT WILL LEAVE IT TO YOUR CHILDREN TO CARE FOR. YOU WILL RETIRE TO AN ISLAND OFF THE CONTINENT.

It sounded like his own voice ringing in his head, but knew it was Bontu. He wanted to ask the fate of Marhelen, but decided to trust the Lord's will. He nodded and was taken to the Isle of Bentley. There he met with Saldheron and the elves, and his trust was rewarded when his wife rushed into his arms.

"The rest of the parchment has been torn off," Lucian said, looking at the end of the scroll.

"Do you think there was more?" Trimistus asked, his thoughts lingering on the tale Lucian had just read.

"Yes," Lucian replied. "I think the rest concerned Falgar leaving the Nether Region and his acquisition of the staff that Le'Mar now has."

Trimistus thought back two years to when Eldor had revealed the relationship between Masara and Le'Mar to everyone in the forest.

"Was that the staff that Firewolf mysteriously found?" Trimistus asked. "The one that bothered the elves and Masara so much and that T'Mar took when he killed him?"

"I think so," Lucian nodded. "Le'Mar inherited it when Masara killed T'Mar."

"Darcwulf has been seen with the staff."

Lucian sat quietly for a moment and absorbed the news.

"At the moment my first concern is the dagger," he finally said. "And I still have no idea where it is."

DEAD SERVANTS
CHAPTER 4

The fire burned softly in the dark of the mountain's cave. The beast with the body of a man sat chewing beside the warmth. The remaining meat sizzled over the dying flames, the fat and juice dripping down on the coals.

His three-headed dog sat beside him chewing the bony remains of the antelope they had caught before entering Dwarf Mountains. The hair on the three heads fell onto the snouts and hidden beneath the curls were maroon eyes, each with silver, diamond-shaped pupils.

The fur on Cerexus's back fell down on each side from the centre, forming a red path along the spine from neck to tail. The fur curled around the legs, ending in tufts on top of the paws. Three bushy tails descended from the back, twirled around each other and tranquil as the hound chewed.

Anuxis was different to behold entirely. His hood was now lowered, but still clung to the robe upon his body. Human hands held the meat which he ate, and a human chest was clothed by the dark robe. Similarly, his human legs were crossed before the fire, supporting his tall, broad frame.

But where the top of his chest ended, his mane began. Fur streaked down from the wolf head, his yellow pupils burning from his black eyes. His canine teeth dug into the meat, and upon his snout his whiskers tingled from the swirling smoke of the carbon coals that were being teased by the falling fat.

His head ended above with spiky ears that rose like towers towards the roof in perfect proportions to the size of his head. They were attuned to the sounds of the world, able to detect even the most distant noises. He had grown accustomed to the idiosyncratic noises made by nature, those of allies and of foes. Even the ethereal approach of a demon or spirit could not escape them.

It was this gift that made his ears twitch in the direction of the disturbance. First it had been the soft, heavy steps coming from the tunnel entrance on the opposite side of the cavern. Then it had been a slow, determined unsheathing from a belt around the waist. Finally, it was the silent whistling of the axe flying across the air towards him.

In a fluid movement, Anuxis grabbed his golden scepter and hit the axe aside with its stem. Cerexus jumped from the floor and growled to the darkness.

Several dwarves emerged into the cavern, holding their hefty axes in hand and watching him carefully. Almost self-consciously, Anuxis pulled the hood over his head and held his scepter in defence. Shadowolf had informed him of the allies on Celenic Earth; he would have to convince them he was on their side.

Another throwing-axe crossed the air, but this time it headed for Cerexus. The hound's central head caught the double-edged weapon in its mouth. Its jaws bit down into the immaculately hardened steel and the remainder of the axe fell to the floor. Cerexus chewed on the steel it had bitten off, watching as the dwarves approached.

Anuxis walked to meet them, strapping his scepter to his back and raising his hands at chest-height in a show of surrender. He noticed that one of the larger dwarves, reaching just above Anuxis's chest, wore a white-gold crown encrusted with rose quartz studs. Closer observation revealed that there were circles of banded agate surrounding the studs.

"Lord Gallon," Anuxis greeted, and the dwarves murmured behind their king. Gallon looked up into the hood of the stranger and narrowed his eyes in suspicion.

"How is it that a Creth-Demon knows my name?" Gallon asked. A low moan seemed to escape the depths of Anuxis's robe, and Gallon wondered if he had angered him.

"My name is Anuxis, and I am not a *Haniegke*, or Creth-Demon as you Celenics refer to it," Anuxis replied, lowering his arms. The dwarves raised their axes tentatively.

"Celenics?" Gallon echoed, but chose to ignore the phrase. "You haven't answered the question concerning my name."

"Shadowolf and Chenesia have told me all about you," he

replied. Gallon raised his brows in surprise. "The princess said to ask for Hargon were you to doubt my word."

Another dwarf, almost as tall as Gallon, stepped forward. He looked up at the cloaked figure, his eyes wide between the bushy hairs of his beard and head.

"Chenesia is alright?" he asked. Gallon shifted his gaze to Hargon.

"That she is, and has returned," Anuxis replied. The dwarves lowered their weapons and walked forward to inspect the stranger and his mount.

"Where is she now?" Gallon asked, the last remnants of suspicion dwindling from his eyes.

"Her purpose and destination remain a riddle for the present," Anuxis said, and then added, "for her safety."

Gallon and Hargon nodded together.

"I am heading to Horlorn's Gate," he informed them, "after my business in the mountain is done. If you wish to see the princess again, you may wait for her there."

"What business do you have in the mountain?" the dwarf king asked.

"I am here looking for my servants," Anuxis replied. "You refer to them as Crethans."

"I see Shadowolf is aligning with dark warriors once more," Gallon said. Anuxis could feel the dwarf king's wall of defence rise again. "The Crethans he had in his Clan almost killed us in the Battle for Eldor's Forest."

"I know you do not understand right now," Anuxis replied, "but it will be explained in due course. Do you know where I may find them?"

"No," Gallon shook his head, "but there is one in our warrens who was once a journeyman with Chenesia."

"Simnab," Anuxis said, filling Gallon's silence.

"Ok, he isn't lying," Hargon told Gallon. "Only Chenesia could have told him that."

"Or Darcwulf," Gallon cautioned. "Be that as it may, we will lead you to Simnab."

Anuxis nodded and the dwarves returned to the tunnel entrance. He called for Cerexus to follow, but the hound collected one of the antelope's bones before obeying.

They had been travelling at a steady pace through the mountain for an hour or two when they entered another, larger cavern. The roof was not visible, even by the light of the torches. The cave was filled with huts and abodes written across the walls, an almost equal amount inhabiting the cave floor. Dwarves walked among the huts, only the guards having weapons strapped to their backs or hips.

"It is not here that Simnab resides," Gallon replied, "but you may rest for a moment before continuing."

"I do not need rest...." Anuxis started to say as Cerexus barked behind him, the echo of the three barks resounding on the walls. The hound pounded its way to the left, far wall where no huts littered the floor. Its large paws raised dust to the air when it slid to a halt by what seemed to be a grey, frozen river.

"Why are there no huts there?" Anuxis said as he walked to Cerexus, followed only by Gallon and Hargon.

"It was once a flowing river of magma and fire," Hargon replied. "It has gone cold over the years, but we believe it's still flowing beneath the crust of the surface."

Cerexus sniffed at the river and the central head looked up at its master. Anuxis pulled his robe off and the dwarves in the village stopped and watched the wolf-man remove his golden staff from its strap.

"I will return," Anuxis said, but Gallon forestalled him with a warning.

"We threw the remains of a few Crethans in the river when we returned to the mountain."

"I know," Anuxis said, his canine eyes glistening as he stepped onto the upper crust.

Smoke rose from the touch and the crust began to give way. The colour of his feet turned brilliant red up to his ankles as the crust melted below him. He sank into the frozen lava river the further he walked until he entered the dormant fire that waited beneath. Soon he was consumed by the lava and could not be seen by anyone on the cave's floor.

Anuxis was surrounded by a slow current of fire, his scepter glistening in the wan light and heat. His feet drifted down to the bed of the river and he walked around until he found what Cerexus had discovered with its nose.

The brimstone ashes drifted on the floor like flower petals in a gentle breeze, resembling loesse blown from land to settle upon the bed of the river. Yet, time could not erase the beings that had once been the wolves that the ashes resembled.

Anuxis raised his free hand, his fingers tense as he summoned the Crethans. The ashes shifted and became four skeletons in the forms of deformed wolves. They changed and developed until they stood upright like humans, their skulls grinning in the fire.

"Lord!" they cried in shrill voices as they sank to their knees.

"Where is your *Haniegke*?" Anuxis asked.

"We do not know," the Crethans replied. "We assume the humans killed him."

"How long have you served the dark lord Le'Mar?" Anuxis asked, spitting the name out in disgust.

"For two years before our demise," they replied. "We were informed by our *Haniegke* that it was upon your instruction that we reside upon Celenic Earth."

"You have been fooled and I betrayed," Anuxis said. With a wave of his hand the skeletons returned to ashes, and faint lights flickered from the dust to his abdomen. He absorbed them into his soul before returning to the land.

The fire dripped like warm magma off his skin and he took the robe from Hargon and donned it, the robe sizzling in places where it touched his skin.

"Lead me to Simnab."

A FATHER'S PLEDGE
CHAPTER FIVE

Shadowolf walked down the grassy hillock until he reached the house. It stood upright, despite the leaning land. The sun was bright in the beautiful sky and he felt a trickle of sweat swim down his face.

He took a long breath in the shade of the house's roof, willing himself to knock on the wooden door. He reached out, his knuckles barely touching the door, when it swung open.

"I was wondering when you would pay me a visit," the lady of the house said.

Shadowolf smiled and entered upon her welcome. The house was cooler within. He found a large round cushion to sit on and waited as she poured a refreshingly cold drink from a storage bar. He looked passed her thin frame to see that someone had used the water element to create frames of ice in the bar to keep the contents cool.

Kailan handed him the drink and he thanked her.

"I thought it was prohibited to use the elements in the fog?" Shadowolf asked after his first sip.

"We use it in small measurements and see if it incurs the dark lord's wrath," she smiled, sitting down on a white, wooden chair. "Besides, I think he is more worried about us using the elements in preparation for war than keeping our food and drinks cool."

"Yeah, I guess he can't deny you that," Shadowolf thought out loud, taking another sip.

"So what news do you bring of my husband?" Kailan asked in a non-chalant tone.

"Lucian….."

A boy of four years ran into the room. He stopped mid-way to his mom, eyes wide as he stared at Shadowolf, and ran back to the room he had come from.

"I don't think I have ever properly met Philanus," Shadowolf said, smiling as the boy's room closed.

"At least you know his name," Kailan said, and he picked up on a trace of bitterness in the words.

"Lucian spoke a lot of you two while we were in uPendus."

Now it was Kailan's eyes that stretched wide. She had almost dropped the drink from her hand and the bitterness had disappeared.

"He found uPendus?" she asked in awe.

"Yes," he replied. "When he travelled with Chenesia to the Vale of Tigers, before....well, anyway, Genewiu informed him how to find uPendus and he had decided to search for it instead of entering Eldor's Forest."

"Was this after he arrived at the Blue Periwinkle?" she asked. He detected a hint of insecurity.

"Yes," he said, offering her no more in way of an answer. She nodded in reply.

"Where is he now?"

"He's in Bentley Strip, trying to find...." Shadowolf went silent.

"Yes?" she asked, sitting forward.

"Trying to find an old friend of mine," he answered, deciding not to tell her of the relic as yet.

"You don't need to keep secrets from me, Shado," she said sweetly, falling back in her seat. "He's my husband."

"I know," he replied, looking away from her piercing gaze before returning it. "But I would prefer if he spoke in confidence with you concerning it, and not me."

"Of course," she smiled, "ever the gentleman. Well, how long will I have to wait for his return?"

"Hopefully he will be home soon if everything works out as planned."

"Another mission?" she snidely asked.

Shadowolf sighed. The inactivity of the people against Le'Mar was frustrating him again.

"I have to get going," he said, standing and throwing the empty bottle in the pine rubbish bin. "As soon as I hear from Lucian I will let you know."

"Thank you, Shado," she said apologetically. "I just wish he would come home."

"He will," Shadowolf replied and bid her farewell.

***

Anuxis followed the dwarves, lost in his own thoughts. Cerexus walked behind him. Hargon and Gallon walked at the fore of the group as was customary in the dwarves' military tradition.

Although the dwarves seem equipped for battle, there was very little upon the face of the earth that Anuxis could have warranted worthy of fighting against. He knew of no one that would challenge the dwarves or their warm home in the mountains, although Shadowolf had enlightened him of the battle that took place within it two years before.

The illusionary wall that the human had spoken of was also on his mind. By the sound of the dwarf king's conversation and the direction they were heading, it seemed as though the dwarf throne room was built in the same cavern as the wall. If his fears were realised and the wall had been closed from gaining the outside, he would have to request another path to Horlorn's Gate...or make one with Cerexus. His hound had a passion for digging.

When they reached the dwarven throne, Anuxis realised the illusionary wall was indeed no longer there. However, he breathed a sigh of relief when he saw that there was another way out in its stead. Large, ornate silver-wrought doors hung closed against the mountain's rocky wall. It reached high up into the mountain and covered a large width across the gap that had once served as Le'Mar's deceptive wall.

Here were dwarf dwellings too, but instead of huts there were marble and concrete homes. The throne itself consisted of stairs that ran over the lava river to a large, domed abode. The domed building rested on a ledge that protruded from the wall to hang over the river.

The river was different in the throne hall. There was no cold, magma crust on the surface. The fire burnt freely, although not as warm as it had been years before. Dwarf mechanisms and rigs were planted in the bed of the river. These were used to extract lava for blacksmiths in the tents along the beach of the river. Anuxis assumed the tents were used to preserve heat in the tent workshops, for there was no sun to shade against.

Gallon whispered to a guard, who ran off in the direction of the tents. Anuxis approached the dwarf king. Hargon and Gallon waited silently for the guard to return.

"How long since you've tested your new axes?" Anuxis asked.

"We haven't had the chance," Gallon said, almost forlornly as if he hungered for battle, "since the Battle for Eldor's Forest. There have been no enemies to battle, unless you count the occasional skirmishes with a few stranded orcs."

"You will get your chance," Anuxis warned, and the two dwarves looked up questioningly. Gallon was about to speak, when the dwarf guard returned.

"There is a report that Simnab has left," the guard said.

"What!?" Gallon and Hargon shouted simultaneously.

"They say that he left to visit his wife in Carmel," the guard said, lowering his head, "in a place called the Blue Periwinkle."

"Oh," Gallon said, and then turned to Anuxis. "He will be back in short time. A week or two."

Anuxis did not really care for much more detail, as he was only interested in the essence of the Crethan. Simnab could keep his human soul, but it was the servant within that Anuxis required.

"I must leave for Horlorn's Gate immediately," he informed the dwarves. "I shall concern myself with Simnab another day. May I pass through your gates to the land outside?"

"Of course," Gallon said, and sent a hand signal to men in towers on each side of the gates. "Hargon, I want you to go with Anuxis."

"That will not be necessary," Anuxis said, rising onto Cerexus's back and grabbing the rein that was tied to straps from all three heads.

"I wish Hargon to accompany you so that he can report to me in due course," Gallon said, his eyes attempting to stare the demand to the robed warrior.

Anuxis contemplated debating the matter further, but could see that Hargon enjoyed the thought as little as he did. If he was to gain the dwarves' trust and allegiance, he would have to comply with even a simple request as this one.

"Very well," Anuxis said, his face grinning maliciously beneath the hood as he added, "hop on."

Hargon swallowed hard, his beard quivering as he approached the hound. As he neared the right head, it growled deeply and bore its teeth at him to taunt him. Anuxis pulled his proffered arm and lifted him before him onto Cerexus's back.

"Bring back a good report!" Gallon shouted, laughing beneath his beard as Cerexus bounded away; Hargon was shouting out loud as he bounced up and down on its back.

Gallon narrowed his eyes and his face took on a solemn complexion.

"If there is to be a battle again for the earth," he murmured softly, "then the dwarves will be part of it from the start this time."

***

"You sent for me?"

"Yes, lord Shadowolf," Eldricht said. Shadowolf smiled uncomfortably at the formality. "You asked me to call you if Mandy should act strange in any way."

"So I have," he asked, curiousity creasing his brow into a frown.

"Well, a light caught my attention and then Mandy became fretful and would not remain still until I sent for you."

"Very well," Shadowolf said, grabbing Mandy's reins. "I'll speak with her."

Eldricht frowned.

"Figuratively, of course," Shadowolf added.

Shadowolf led Mandy away from the stables until he was relatively alone with her.

"Do you bear a message for me?" he asked. Mandy neighed and nodded her head.

Shadowolf patted her ghostly mane and looked into the pit of her left eye. The red pupils deep within the void slowly dissipated until he saw Lucian's face within. Mandy's lips moved and, when she spoke, it carried upon it the voice of Lucian.

"Trimistus has shown me a scroll which should be of some interest to you," the image of Lucian said. "The last part of the document is missing and we assume it concerns Falgar. It may be that the second scroll lies with the staff of Falgar.

"As for the mission, there is still no sign of discovering the dagger. We are meeting with Mynisna and Asgorna shortly to determine which dragons were the first to enter Bentley's Strip. It may be that one of them holds the dagger as a treasure."

The image disappeared. Shadowolf patted Mandy as she became herself again and led her back to Eldricht.

"Thank you, my friend," he said. Eldricht looked up at him in delight. Within Shadowolf's eyes he could tell that Shadowolf trusted him with Mandy's life.

Shadowolf walked away, his thoughts spinning as he considered Lucian's words. The scrolls seemed insignificant at the moment, but they could assist in finding the dagger. A nerve within him twitched. He was starting to feel that he was wasting time, even though he had enough of it. He needed to leave immediately.

He stopped in his walk and closed his eyes. He breathed slowly, and opened them again. He took in the land around him, the oxen on the distant plains, the sheep bleating in the villages and the grass beneath his shoes. He relaxed the tension inside.

Yes, he had to leave but it would be in a serene state. There was no need to stress over time. Even were he to jump into the ocean at that very moment, it would not stop the fog from lying over the land and it would not stop Le'Mar.

Now that he was composed and his power quiet once again within his soul, he continued towards Degron Castle.

Shadowolf heard the footsteps behind him in the room as he grabbed his staff. His father waited until he was done donning his green cloak.

"How long do you think you will have to search?" Nighthale asked him as they both looked out of the window. The ocean was a brilliant blue, even in the hue of the fog. The sun sparkled on its soft surface, inviting them to its depths.

"I'm not sure," he replied, "as long as it takes, I guess."

"Well, I hope you have a good journey," Nighthale said, and they both turned to the patter of baby steps.

"Come here, girl," he said to his daughter and then dropped to a knee as she waddled into his arms. He picked her up and pointed to the ocean through the window. "That's where daddy is going to find mommy. And then we will come back and give you a name."

His daughter stared out at the water, her wide eyes intensely focused on the ocean.

"I'll come back to you with her," he said, and then looked into his father's eyes. "I promise."

"What if...." Nighthale started to say, but ended it in a sigh.

"I will find her," Shadowolf repeated, "even if it's with one last breath."

ABANDONED WARRENS
CHAPTER 6

As per his father's wishes, Shadowolf rode on Mandy's back to the southern beach that opened up to the ocean. He had wanted to teleport to save time, but his father's words held good advice. The dark lord might allow small powers for the purpose of preservation, but he may be alerted if he felt constant use of power within the fog.

His hood was drawn over his head in the light of the sun. It was not merely for shade, but also as a guard. He was worried that he might meet old "friends" in Le'Mar's army or that the orcs might recognise him, as frail as their minds were.

His temporary plan ran through his mind as he rode down to the beach at a steady pace, his staff clinking in the saddle-strap. His best bet would be to head for Sea's Reach first, the warrens where the mer-King once ruled his kingdom before *Avalendil*. Sea's Reach was also where Shedaaij's family had once lived.

Something stirred in the heat wave of the beach in the distance. He slowed Mandy's run when he saw that they were orcs, four or five of them, strolling east along the sands. He veered right, hoping to avoid them if at all possible.

One of them pointed at him and he realised it was too late. He continued straight when he saw that they walked in his direction. He pulled on the reins and Mandy stopped when they stood before him.

"I have no business with you," he said. The orcs stared up into his hood, trying to make out his face. Mandy remained still, not betraying the lust for battle that stirred within her. Their greedy eyes took her in, mentally calculating her worth and the staff that regally rested against her side.

"The dark lord requires payment for travel upon his lands," one of the orcs hissed. Shadowolf assumed it was a purorc, for there was no vestige of human upon any of their faces.

"The fog is enough payment, I would think," he replied. He knew they were bluffing. Le'Mar didn't need any form of payment; he took what he wanted.

Nonetheless, the orcs drew their crude, damaged swords and laughed at him. Shadowolf simply stared at them as one of the orcs slashed down on his leg.

He swung his leg under the swinging arm and curled it over the other side until his foot had twisted onto the inner joint of the elbow. He pushed his foot into it, forcing the elbow to bend. The forearm swung forward and the back edge of the sword broke into its skull. The orc blinked for a second and then fell backward, staring blankly at its comrades.

Shadowolf had already descended onto the grass, staff in hand, when the other orcs recovered. His cloak and hood swayed in a wind that seemed to warn him against using his power. An orc shouted and lunged forward with its sword, but Mandy kicked into its head and the neck snapped before reaching the ground.

Shadowolf swung his staff around his body, the wood whistling in the air as the last two orcs approached. Mandy stayed out of the staff's way. He lifted the staff horizontally, blocking both swords simultaneously. He slid under the staff and, supporting his body with his left hand, kicked the left orc's legs out so that it collapsed on its back.

The other orc was striking again. Shadowolf let the blade slip beside his chest and grabbed the arm. He kicked into the orc's knee, his elbow crashing into its face, before twisting around and bringing his staff level into its cheek.

The first orc rose again, sword glistening in the sun. Shadowolf twisted his body to avoid the blade, which narrowly missed his neck. The orc drew the blade across and Shadowolf danced his neck under the sword. With quick efficiency, he used one end of the staff to hit a leg up into air, then the other end to smack the spine of the beast hard and finally straight up into the chin of the orc.

The orc rose into the air. Shadowolf jumped and turned, his leg lashing out like a snake into the orc's chest. The orc flew backwards, its scream silenced when its spine met Mandy's rear hooves.

Shadowolf once again spun the staff around his body and caught it in both hands, standing in a stance to intimidate the final orc. The orc looked at him with wide eyes and then ran down the beach in an attempt to save its pathetic life.

Mandy snorted and then stared at Shadowolf. Burnt smoke rose from her nostrils and her eyes flared with desire.

"Hunt him down and kill him," Shadowolf said, tying his staff to the saddle-strap, "then return to Avalion."

She broke into a run in the orc's wake and the beast's voice rose in fear.

Shadowolf walked to the beach, ignoring the three dead orc's around him. He pulled off the cloak, his top and shoes, leaving only his swimming joggens on his legs, and dived into the waves of the ocean.

***

Chenesia was lying on the grass, her fingers gently playing with the blades. The sun reached the courtyard of the Jin-Tai Sanctuary through the square opening above her. Corridors held the courtyard between them, and off to one side was her room.

Soft footsteps reached her ears, gentle footsteps that walked over to the bench behind her. Chenesia turned her face on her arm until she looked at the aged toes of her mother.

"I see you are enjoying the weather," Larnesia said.

"It was cold in uPendus," Chenesia commented, standing up and sitting beside her mother, "thanks to the snow."

"This mission or quest that you spoke of," her mother said for the hundredth time, "is it really neces..."

"Yes, mother," she replied sweetly. "I need to find Sorceress. She has the butterfly pendant."

Larnesia nodded, but Chenesia could see she was still calculating persuasions in her mind.

"Have you figured out how you will find her?" Larnesia said. Chenesia sighed in relief; she was finally accepting that her daughter would have to leave again.

"I will be heading to the Fairiwell," Chenesia said. "I have heard rumours of her presence there. It corresponds with what Elgoth told me about the pendant."

"And what is that?"

"The fairdievells are attracted to it," she replied. "Apparently it's a power that Ursula left with the pendant so that, if ever they were to search for it, they only need follow the trail of the fairies."

Chenesia looked at her mother's hands. She was twisting them, her taut nerves straining against the conflict in her heart. Chenesia leaned over and held her mother in her arms.

"I will see you shortly again," Chenesia said.

"You promise?"

"I promise," she said. "As you told me, Le'Mar hasn't attacked in two years, and Sorceress is on our side. So no harm will come to me. Just remember, you need to convince the others to leave the Vale."

Larnesia nodded. She seemed reassured, but Chenesia knew it wouldn't be long before the doubts returned. She had to leave....soon.

***

The sun began to set and cast the upper lands into shadow. Anuxis slowed Cerexus's run until they were barely wading through the grass of the forest. His wolf-head swiveled to the side as the sound caught him again.

He dismounted and pointed into the heights of one of the trees. Hargon held fast to the beast's neck as Cerexus obliged by clawing its way up to the branches and rested upon one, watching.

It didn't take long before the cause of the noise became visible. Anuxis drifted upon the wind and melted into the shadows behind a tree. Three silhouettes walked cautiously passed him, their eyes alight with fear and their steps precise over the roots protruding from the earth.

"I know what I felt," one of the shades whispered. "And it wasn't one of the Haniegkes."

"But what does it mean?" another asked.

"I don't know," the first replied again. "Could it be that judgement is upon us?"

The three shades looked at each other, growling deeply, before proceeding on their path.

"Let us return to the kennels," the third said, "before the night swallows us whole."

They moved north. Anuxis materialised from the shadows and nodded to Cerexus to descend. He mounted the dark beast and followed them in silence.

It took twenty minutes before they reached the kennels. The grassland was open and flat, save for the rolling hillocks. Anuxis had spied several buffalo and antelope along the way, but his hunger was not for meat.

Cerexus padded softly through the grass maintaining his distance, its three heads down low between the blades. Anuxis kept his head low on the mount's back, ready to dematerialise into the shadows should it be necessary.

The three shapes topped the apex of a hill, but Anuxis led Cerexus around the side so that they would not be visible to anyone peering from below. Three hillocks seemed to form a bowl from which several small lights flickered, and between two hills Cerexus crept to view the kennels.

Holes had been dug into the earth of the hills. Fires flared in various areas in the bowl around which beasts that looked very much human sat. But Anuxis knew that they were not human, for their souls cried out to him in silence. He knew his flock.

They were not the Crethans that Shadowolf had told him of. Crethans were humans of Celenic Earth that had either been bitten by a *Hieragke* or been struck dead by a *Haniegke*. The *Haniegke* were what the Celenics referred to as Creth-Demons.

But Shadowolf had not encountered a *Hieragke* in its true form. Its essence was held in the form of a rabid wolf, enraged by the darkness it held within. They could take on the form of any creature around them, but their true appearance was that of the dark wolf.

It was the essence within a Crethan that transformed the human against his will into a deformed wolf in the presence of a Creth-Demon. The *Hieragke* within the Crethan overpowered the will of the human when summoned by the *Haniegke*, a curse that could only be lifted by Anuxis.

Anuxis watched as the three shapes entered the light of the bowl. Their wolf bodies walked placidly towards a group of men, transforming as they edged closer. Their fur sank into skin, and their snouts vanished to reveal a human face. The only physical attribute that betrayed their human nature was the feint pulsing of their purple pupils.

"Any luck, Basgon?" one of the *Hieragke* asked.

"No, Taliga," Basgon replied dryly. "There is no sign of the Crethans. The one they call 'Creth-Angel' is hiding them quite well."

The bowl fell back into silence as they contemplated this. Anuxis asked Hargon to dismount and stay behind the hills. He then urged Cerexus into the kennel glade. The hound deliberately stomped on the ground to mark its entry. The *Hieragke*s jumped from their fires as they entered the light.

"It's him!" one of the original three men shouted. "I knew I felt his presence earlier!"

The *Hieragke*s fell to their knees as Anuxis dismounted. Cerexus watched them carefully, all three heads growling at the servants.

"We are graced by your presence, my lord," Taliga said as Anuxis stepped before him with staff in hand. Anuxis detected a hint of insincerity in Taliga's voice.

"How long is it that you have been absent from Hadides?" Anuxis queried, referring to the world of brimstone and fire that they belonged to.

"We are only here upon your orders," he replied. Anuxis listened closer than any man could. He felt the lie beneath the veiled truth. He drew in breath between his teeth, sounding almost like a hiss, as he realised he had found the one that he had been searching for.

"So it is you that has turned traitor?" Anuxis said, and to his surprise Taliga rose. The other *Hieragke*s murmured at the audacity.

"How long did you think I would serve you?" Taliga laughed. "I am tired of servitude! I will have my own way!"

"Is the command of Le'Mar not servitude as well?" Anuxis questioned.

"No," Taliga replied. "He has given us free reign."

"Perhaps because it is not he who had summoned you from the darkest depths of Hadides."

Taliga growled in anger.

"I should have left you in the pits of Crenopus to die in your own filth," Anuxis continued to push.

Taliga charged forward, his face turning into a wolf but, when he reached the robed lord, Anuxis grabbed the *Hieragke* around his furry throat and glared into his eyes. Taliga moaned in pain as Anuxis tightened is grip.

Without any words, although it had been his intent to speak many, he hurled Taliga into the air. The wolf howled in pain as the golden scepter glowed. His fur began to burn and smoke rose around it. Before the dying corpse hit the ground, it smouldered in a chaos of fire and its ashes drifted to the earth.

"Who else defies me!?" Anuxis roared to the bowed faces before him.

"My lord," Basgon whimpered, "we truly did believe we were under your service all along."

At last, Anuxis could detect the truth. From the ranks before him, not one disagreed with Basgon's statement. They had all been fooled by Taliga.

Anuxis stretched forth his free hand. The beasts' skins glowed a green hue and they slowly vapourised into the air. The green mist drifted into his tense fingers and floated into his soul.

When they were all stored within him, he called for a very cautious Hargon to join him. The dwarf inched closer to them, looking up with fear into Anuxis's hood. They mounted Cerexus and continued to Horlorn's Gate.

***

The ocean was eerily quiet. The pressure of the ocean squeezed against his liquid head, but it was not that which disturbed him.

Sothos the moon could not send the reflected light of the sun's rays deep enough in the water to reach him. He could feel small fish swim through him, maybe a shark or two behind him, as he made way down to Sea's Reach.

The only light that shone in the water was an ethereal one. His body was no longer skin, but part of the water. Where he drifted through the ocean, the liquid was denser and more concentrated.

In sufficient light, one would have seen a body of water floating down to the warrens, but in the darkness all that could be seen was a soft light emanating from his soul that was the power keeping him from drowning in the ocean. Water and fish passed through him as if he were a ghost.

He reached out with his liquid hand and slid down the coral surface of the undersea mountain. It took moments before he found an opening into Sea's Reach and floated in.

The fact that he could not see anything within the warren confirmed his fears. He remembered a time when Lellian ruled Sea's Reach with his power and trident. The caverns were filled with abodes for the mer-people and at the top, suspended from the roof of the warren, had been a large dome that was the throne of the mer-King.

Shadowolf moved there now, and by the light of his power he saw that the dome had broken and crumbled in several places. The corals were dim along the walls, no longer projecting those spectral rainbows of colour into the warren. He did not need much intelligence to know that Sea's Reach had been abandoned.

What Shadowolf found strange was that he had encountered no sirens so far. Surely they would have sensed the power he had used to become water? He knew the Demon-queen sirens were as sensitive to power in the water as Le'Mar was to elements in the fog.

Putting all other questions aside, Shadowolf focused on only one now. If the mer-Kingdom still existed, where would Shedaaij search for them? Where would she go when she had found the warren of her family deserted?

There was only one answer. She would go back to the place she had met Shadowolf, back to the place where Lellian the mer-King had sent her to assist Shadowolf in the war against Le'Mar.

Shadowolf left Sea's Reach and headed for *Marsandil*.

GUARDIAN OF THE DAGGER
CHAPTER SEVEN

Lucian stood by the temple's grounds and waited for the dragons to appear. Trimistus had summoned Mynisna and Asgorna, but their prolonged absence had caused him to return to their world. Meanwhile Lucian paced, slept and ate. The anxiety crept through his nerves, tingling the wind essence within him and stirring the trees behind him.

He thought on the scroll concerning Bentley. It had bothered him a few times in the course of his patience. His thoughts mostly centered on Mikinos. The son of Bentley had been so close to committing murder for the sake of his desire, so close to crossing the path from good to evil.

Malherin had acted out of paternal protection and righteous anger. Had Bentley watched the battle from the start, would he have stopped Malherin from protecting his daughter's honour? Surely Bentley would not have allowed the desires haunting his son to control him?

Yet, what started out as a lesson for Mikinos had turned for the worse. Malherin had been ready to strike Mikinos down forever. Malherin became the one who was prepared to take a life. Had the motive been pure: was it to destroy the evil lurking within Mikinos he wanted to be rid of, or could he not contain the dark anger within himself?

Whichever was the case, Bentley had intervened to stop his friend from making the greatest spiritual mistake of his elvin life. He had not merely wanted to protect his son, but to prevent Malherin from releasing his own dark desires of revenge. In the end, Bentley had sacrificed his own purity and been the first to commit murder.

But the Lord had seen fit to grant him sanctuary from the world. Lucian could almost feel the remorse within Bentley as the dagger that had dealt the death blow fell from his numb fingers. Remorse that, Lucian was almost certain, Malherin would not have felt upon avenging his daughter's honour.

Lucian shook his head at his own misguided speculations. For some odd reason, one not associated with his quest, he wished that he could have seen that battle. Only Bontu knew what had been in all three hearts, and that it was only Bentley that deserved sanctuary from the new evil in the world.

Lucian also knew that he was just as susceptible to the attraction of evil desires, to the wrong choice made in the heat of revenge or anger. He looked at Lancenat, spying the "Treatise on Falgan Earth" scroll protruding from a bag. He hoped that further study of the scroll at a later stage would reveal some hidden secrets.

A welcome distraction removed him from his thoughts in the direction of the temple. Between him and the building, the air grew denser and rippled. Two dragons and a rider appeared from the haze.

"Couldn't get both of you in the temple?" Lucian joked, forgetting that humour was lost on the dragons like sand thrown on a wall.

Trimistus slid down Mynisna's back to the grass, Asgorna eyeing the Amulet of Larna Thorn around Lucian's neck.

"He unfortunately had family matters to attend to," Lucian said to the dragon. It was not the real reason Shadowolf could not personally be available, but it was as close to the truth as Lucian could manage in the line of Asgorna's angry glare.

"I believe you search for the Dagger of Bentley," Asgorna said dryly. "It will not be an easy feat to accomplish; obtaining it that is."

"For what purpose will the dagger be served?" Mynisna asked. Trimistus turned to look at Lucian expectantly.

"It is a relic of ancient power," Lucian said, revealing only as much as Elgoth, the son of Masara, had revealed to them in uPendus. "We believe it will assist us against Le'Mar and the prison of fog he has contained the world in. Do you know where it resides?"

"There is an ancient dragon," Asgorna replied, spreading his wings in the air and settling it down again, "who is said to have arrived on Celenic Earth a few years before Bentley Strip was created."

"Apparently she was only three years of age when she saw Bentley and Malherin battle in the sky above him," Mynisna continued. "When the mountains were raised, she was caught in its embrace."

"She fought to get out of the earth's grip," Asgorna said, "struggling with her young wings to rise above the rapidly rising peaks. It was a tortuous flight, one that left many permanent marks on her scales."

"And just when she thought she had made it out and the land fell silent, a dead corpse struck her and they tumbled back onto the peaks."

"Malherin," Lucian said, and Asgorna nodded.

"She landed on her back, sorely injured," Mynisna continued. "Her heart pulsed with the power to rejuvenate her health, the corpse lying on her belly. She stirred, unable to rise from her back, when a dagger of immense power fell through the corpse's abdomen and into her heart."

"She collapsed into a gaping hole in the mountain," Asgorna said, "falling deep into the mountain. It is said she slumbers there for eternity with the dagger still within her heart, too afraid to move should the dagger cut the essential organ."

Lucian gaped for a few moments then looked at the grass as he contemplated this news.

"Is she still in the mountain?" he finally asked.

"We don't know," Asgorna replied. "It is only a myth, after all."

"Ok," Lucian said. "Thank you."

The dragons nodded and turned to leave. The haze appeared and the dragons departed. Lucian waited for Trimistus to join them, but the haze vanished without him.

"Aren't you returning?" he asked.

"No," the reptilian man replied. "I want to help you find the dagger."

"And the real reason?" he asked humourously.

"Maybe my DragonWourd influence might help," Trimistus replied.

Lucian mounted Lancenat. He turned to ask Trimistus if he

wanted to hop on the back when he saw it wasn't necessary. A creature was descending the temple's stairs upon Trimistus's whistling command.

The *Enodhim* had never laid eyes on such a creature before. It had the same reptilian features as Trimistus, but strode on two trunk-like legs.

It had two forearms hunched close to its chest with talons nearly as big as his head. Its enormous head held two large roaming eyes and its mouth had fangs as long as his forearm. Even with Lucian mounted, the creature could have easily rested its lower jaw on the top of his head.

When its rider mounted the back and slapped two reins attached to the straps on its neck, the beast rode beside him. Trimistus's knee reached Lucian's nose, and he looked up to ask him what on earth the reptile was.

"It is called a saurex in the Kingdoms," Trimistus replied to his frowning face. "This one is still a dinopup by two years."

"Deadly," Lucian said, and then coughed as the saurex puffed acrid smoke into his face.

"Let's go find that relic," Trimistus said, the beast lurching at a fast speed away from them.

THE REFUSED ALLIANCE
CHAPTER EIGHT

Shadowolf eased into Shadow River that broke off like a branch from the River of Light. He knew the Dark Boundary would be ahead which protected dark camps of Le'Mar. Uncertainty rang inside his mind again: would the mer-Kingdom really rebuild a warren in the dark lord's territory?

His fears were both realised and assuaged when the river stopped abruptly shorter than it should have. Shadowolf became human and walked out the water in his dripping wet joggens and stared at the open land.

The Dark Boundary was no longer contained as before. The large walls had been removed just like Avalion's. Across the lands Shadowolf could see encampments he assumed still contained orcs and other creatures of Le'Mar.

Before him, the lake that held Asbec Island shimmered in the sunlight. The island still stood in the deep waters, but Shadow River no longer reached it. The rubble that once had been the Asbec College of Elements still littered the grass of the land; the gaping hole that Shadowolf had created four years before when he had released the power node still lay open to the sky.

His doubts returned again. Would the mer-people have crossed the land to gain the lake? Shadowolf walked to the lake's edge anyway, knowing that, if they were not in *Marsandil*, then he would not know where to look. He jumped into the water and swam around the foundation of the island.

By the light of his soul he followed the water down to the bed of the water. He barely recalled where the warrens once were but he was determined to find them. He had been hoping that he would be drawn to the power of the trident, but he could not sense any power within the water; perhaps the trident no longer existed…

Something familiar about the lake's bed caught his memory and he swam upright for a moment to look at his surroundings. He saw the foundation of Asbec Island to his right and vaguely remembered swimming there with Hurticule and Lellian to discuss the power node.

They had been so ignorant then. Mercius had escaped from his magical imprisonment and they had all thought him to be the greater threat. Had they known at that stage that Mercius was merely a puppet for Le'Mar, would things have been different?

Shadowolf had been so engaged with Mercius that year that he had barely spared a thought on the dark lord. True, stopping the evil Windfarer from obtaining the node had set Le'Mar back. But even during the attempt to stop Sonersaat from winning the Dragon War, it was only in the elvin forest that Shadowolf had truly seen Le'Mar properly for the first time.

The power from Le'Mar had been so great. Masara's words rang in mind again as it had so many times that year.

Do not face him until you are ready…

In the end, when Sonersaat had been defeated and the Dragon War won, he had watched as Masara was killed and his soul consumed by Le'Mar's elemental staff. While the others fled the forest from the rising demons, he had chosen to face Le'Mar. Only he had remained to confront him while Elgoth mourned his father's death and Eldor and Ursula ensured the safety of people within the forest.

But, as was always the case, Masara's words rang true. Le'Mar didn't even sweat as he cast Shadowolf aside like a toy. Even with the wind, Le'Mar had been far more powerful than he could have imagined.

Shadowolf awoke from his daydream. His thoughts on the dark lord and the war had caused his anger to rise. The water was boiling around his liquid form and his aura was pulsing from the adrenaline pumping through his veins. He calmed his spirit and let the power subside again. The water remained warm around him, but stopped boiling.

He moved away from the island base. It took him several minutes before he reached the place where he had followed Blosom to *Marsandil*, and then another few minutes before he had the warren in sight.

As he had feared, the warren looked uncomfortably silent. It was still situated in the bottom of the bowl and shaped like a coral ball with random holes on its domed circumference. But he could detect no mer-presence. There were no scaly tails or naked torsos swimming anywhere near the warren. Yet, against his misgivings, he swam down to the old city, hoping against hope.

He landed with his watery foot on the landing he had used when he had first arrived at *Marsandil*. He stopped. His heart pulsed as he realised there had to be someone within the city, for a rocky door barred him from entering the warren. When he had last been there, the entrances had been freely accessible. He ran his hand over the coarse surface. Yes; there had to be someone inside.

He became air and let his essence flow into rocky cracks by the side of the door. He seeped through, moving between the rock and coral until he was on the other side. When he realised that he had passed into dry air, he became human.

The interior was completely devoid of water and was humid. There was a wan light from the torches that burnt softly on the walls. The coral that had once lit the warren still clung on the surfaces, but had died some time ago.

Shadowolf frowned. It was obvious that there were no mer-people within the warren, but who had barred the entrances? Had Lellian returned and closed off the city from the sirens for some future purpose?

He looked up at the torches and realised he was wrong. Someone was replenishing the torches, which meant that there was someone within the city. Shadowolf became cautious and walked silently around *Marsandil*.

The statue of a forgotten mer-King still stood among the abandoned coral buildings at the bottom of the warren. The hand reached up to hold an absent trident that was now with the current mer-King. The once-white floor and walls were covered by moss and fungi.

Then something which had never been in the city before caught Shadowolf's attention. A pair of coffins hung from the walls, the wood deep red in colour. The surfaces were smooth and reflected the torch light ominously.

He reached the two hanging coffins and touched the lid of the right one. Carefully he pulled it open on its hinges. It swung towards him and he beheld a pale, beautiful woman.

Just as he got his heart to calm down to its normal pace, her eyes flashed open and she vanished in a wake of grey smoke. He felt her breath on his neck and he disappeared into the air and reappeared behind her. She turned around and hissed, her fangs gleaming.

The left coffin's lid creaked open. The man within stared at Shadowolf as he stepped down to the landing. At first his expression was one of shock, but his mouth curled into a smile soon enough.

"It's ok, Mirelda," Nellice said, his aVampeyer face shining softly. His two canine fangs glinted from his rosy lips, the dust falling from his long, maroon coat. "Shadowolf is no threat."

"Not to you anyway," Shadowolf smiled and embraced Nellice in greeting. Mirelda closed her lips over her fangs and smiled apologetically. "What on earth are you doing here?"

"Well, I told you that I was the last of my kind here." Shadowolf nodded. "I needed a place to hide from the sun, where I could feed without anyone noticing."

"What have you been feeding on?" Shadowolf asked, looking around for any animals.

"You forget," he replied, pointing to the roof of the warren, "there are orcs, centaurs and other wonderful meats in the Dark Boundary."

Shadowolf laughed, and then looked at Mirelda.

"Oh yes," the aVampeyer said putting his arm around her waist. "Meet my wife. Well, not in the sense that we had a formal wedding, but you get my meaning."

"Did she know it was for eternity?" Shadowolf jibed.

"I can speak, you know," Mirelda said, looking from one to the other.

"Our meeting wasn't a romantic one," Nellice said.

"Not at all," she giggled. "I caught you drinking from my horse."

"But the moment I saw her...," he started.

"We knew it was meant to be," she finished.

Shadowolf coughed.

"Oh, sorry," Nellice said, and he could have sworn he saw the aVampeyer blush a little. Then it was his turn to frown. "What exactly are you doing here, Shado? Not that I mind the company."

"I came looking for the mer-Kingdom. I couldn't find them in Sea's Reach."

"Ah, you wouldn't," Nellice replied. "They've gone to a place even you would be hard put to follow."

"Where?"

"The Straits of Malakov," he replied, and saw the realisation dawn on the human's face.

"You're right," Shadowolf said, "that will be difficult."

***

She walked down the sloping hill. Clouds had formed in the sky during the course of the day. Chenesia pulled the warm top tighter around her body as the promise of rain in the wind chilled her neck and her arms.

The items protruding from the grass lay at the bottom of the hill. A hundred or so tombstones commemorated the lives lost in the Battle for Eldor's Forest. The slabs were grey and rotund, ghosts sitting in the greenery surrounding them.

Covering the graves from above was a fine, green elvin cloth. It was supported in the four corners by strong, wooden frames and poles. The cloth was high enough to clear the roof of the cubical building in the centre of the graves. It was to this monument that Chenesia strode.

On either side of the closed archway were tigroyne statues. Their snowy tiger bodies with black stripes were standing in a fierce stance, their teeth glinting from between the marble lips. Their white wings stretched gloriously up from their backs, black stripes dancing along the top in the same patterns as on their bodies. Tigroys were the guardians of Bontu's haven, just as the statues were protecting her father's resting place.

When she was close enough, the two tigroyne heads moved, the marble dust falling from the necks onto the grass. Their wings stretched and a deep growl erupted from their throats. Her mother's words returned to her mind:

Wait for the hidden tigroy to appear...

The two tigroys did not attack, but merely watched that she did not proceed further. The doorway to the monument shimmered slightly before transforming with a soft light into another, larger tigroy. The feline approached her, sniffing the air and then her hand.

...and then etch your fairy sign on its forehead.

She still remembered the fairy signature given to her by the fairdievells of the Fairiwell so many years before. The black patterns on the tigroy's forehead shifted to form a white space for her to trace her fingers in. Carefully, she touched the marble, her nails etching the design she had been taught, the image of it forming in her mind with every curve, line and dot.

When she was done, she withdrew her hand. Feint fairy lights rose from the marble and the feline's eyes turned from white to blue. The tigroys purred comfortably and their marble skins changed to orange fur. The black stripes remained to compliment the patterns on the feathery, white wings.

The majestic tiger turned and led her to the now open archway. It waited by the archway to allow her to pass and, once she was through, it tucked its wings neatly back and guarded the entrance.

It was beautiful inside the monument. Candles that her mother lit every time she paid a visit hung on the walls. Embroidered red cloths, curtains and drapes dressed the interior on all sides. And in the centre of the room was the sarcophagus, with tigers drawn on the exterior.

She heard the patter of rain hit the elvin cloth outside. Slowly she walked up the three steps to the coffin, unsure whether she was ready to face his corpse. She touched the lid lightly with her fingertips, moving it to the golden rail that was used to move the lid.

She breathed heavily and then shoved the rail away from her. It moved with difficulty at first, but once her muscles had set into the task it slid over. When it reached the edge of the opposite side it did not fall onto the floor. Strangely, it hung in the air above an invisible support.

Chenesia stared down, her face unchanging. Her father's face was serene and the body perfect. His beard flowed from his jaw to his chest where his hands were tucked together neatly above his solar plexus. It was as if he was asleep, his body refusing to decompose.

A tear broke from the corner of her left eye. She sniffed; the emotions welled up inside until she stretched her arm over his chest and cried into his stringy, grey beard. Her sobs echoes over the graveyard, but the sound was drenched away by the pouring mist of rain.

She gasped in alarm as something glassy touched her palm. She looked up at his sternum and saw a red object in her hand. Chenesia cleared her eyes and looked down at the gem.

It was the Heart of Tigers, the magical gem that Eldor had used to protect the elves from their enemies. It had appeared in her hand above her father's sternum: exactly where she had wanted to feel his heart beating. She frowned at it: was it the gem that was keeping her father's body from decomposing?

With that thought, she frantically tried to push the gem back into his chest. The skin became podgy and bruised where she rubbed it, and with a frightening realisation she realised that his skin was decaying.

"NO!!!" she shouted, and through the haze of water covering her eyes she tried beating the Heart back in. The thunder rumbled in the clouds, her cries joining the tumultuous roar, when the lid slid back of its own accord. She jumped back, the Heart still clutched in her hand, when she missed the step behind her and fell to the floor.

Her breath broke from her lungs as her back hit the floor. She felt the gem hit her left breast hard, but her body was in too much pain for her to care. She groaned and rolled over, hoping the Heart that had been such a bane to her family would fall away from her. She crawled onto her hands and knees, waiting for the strength to rise.

A tongue bent below her face to lick the tears away. She looked up at the majestic tigroy's face. She didn't have the will to greet it properly, nor to repair any damage she had done to the monument of her father. She rose from the ground and ran out into the rain.

Unaware to her, the majestic tigroy roared a command to the other two. They purred in obedience and ran after her, their fur returning to white marble and their wings lifting them up into the rain.

The remaining tigroy smiled in satisfaction. His eyes turned red for a moment. A wind passed through the building and the tiger became the door that sealed the monument once again.

***

The eagle struggled to maintain his flight through the downpour. The clouds had grown darker since he had risen from the grass of Asbec Island and, before he had passed over the southern-most city within the Dark Boundary, the rain had pelted down onto his feathers.

The Far Isles, namely the Isles of Bentley and Masara, appeared on the western ocean. His eyes made out the crops of land jutting from the water further south known as the Straits of Malakov. He knew that the storm beneath the waters and rising rocks was far worse than the meagre downpour from above.

Shadowolf flew from the land over the ocean and headed straight for the rocks. He could see the currents of water battling each other beneath the surface and the large waves crashing against the small islands. The eagle prepared for the transformation, his wings holding strong against the rain, when he dived down into the water.

Shadowolf transformed into water. The current pulled at his fiber, and his mind cried in pain as he forced his essence to remain intact. He moved further down to a gap between two of the six, lengthy islands.

A strong maelstrom hit him hard and sent him hurtling into a mountain of rocks. After the hard impact that sent his molecules dispersing in every direction, he became wind that travelled in the form of an orb through the water. The water and tense forces within the ocean flowed over his round surface, rolling him over and over but no longer able to separate his essence.

He found calmer waters at the base of the islands, but remained an orb of wind. The light that he used from his soul to guide him pulsed in the centre of the ball. He continued under the islands, using his ethereal sight to detect any presence of the mer-

Kingdom.

Suddenly the water became darker. It seemed as if the colour changed from midnight blue to deep purple. It was a subtle change, but it obscured his view. He swam through it, hoping to find something on the other side.

Yet the purple mist continued. No matter where he turned and how long he travelled in that direction, the mist seemed to get longer and longer. He was about to give up and try and find the way back when a smooth, gentle hand touched the orb of light.

Let me show you the way, a familiar, loving voice spoke to his mind.

Shedaaij? he asked, becoming human again, his hand falling into hers.

Yes, my love, she replied. *Your search is over.*

She pulled him along. It took several minutes, but when they emerged he saw Shedaaij's beautiful face shining in greeting. She swam into his arms, her scaly tail flapping beneath her and her uncovered breasts against his chest. She took another look into his eyes, and then gave him one long kiss.

Shadowolf smiled after the kiss, but soon changed his expression as he looked around.

Why have you brought me back into the ocean?

Shedaaij drew him away from the purple mist, further down to where the current was the softest.

Have you heard that Lellian died in the last battle?

Shadowolf gaped, and then closed his mouth as he choked on the water.

Blosom killed him, just before James grabbed the trident and smote her.

So, James is the new mer-King?

She nodded in reply.

You can't stay here, my love. James wants nothing to do with humans anymore. He will kill you should you attempt entry.

What happened to the old allegiance between mer-people and humans?

That was a pact made with the former mer-King, she replied sadly. *He will not have any alliance with men again.*

And you? he asked. *Your father was human.*

Yes, but my mother was a mermaid. James has accepted that I will leave again, as our child is on the land.

Shadowolf smiled fondly at the mention of their daughter.

She still needs a name, you know, he said.

We can sort that out when we return, she said, leading him back to the stormy current and the land.

Don't you need to notify James?

He will know, Shedaaij said. *He always knows what's happening in the ocean.*

HORLORN'S RUINS
CHAPTER NINE

They emerged from the ocean on the southern beach early that evening. Shedaaij had informed him how she had decided to visit the mer-Kingdom a few months before and how she had just been getting ready to leave for Avalion again.

James had alerted her of his approach and she had made sure that they left before James became hostile. Shadowolf still could not believe how anti-human James had finally allowed himself to become.

When Shadowolf had first met James in *Marsandil*, the merman had already shown his dislike for humans. Now that he wielded power, it seemed that he was even more prepared to separate himself from the terrestrial men.

Shadowolf couldn't really blame him. After the merging with Avalion, the mer-Kingdom under the leadership of Lellian had still not been strong enough to stop the sirens and Demon-queens of Le'Mar. The stormy waters of the Straits did indeed seem a better hiding place than the quiet warrens of Sea's Reach.

Shadowolf saw Shedaaij's tail change to smooth, human legs as they walked onto the beach. He realised that she was completely naked, and was about to ask about her clothes. She turned to him as he realised it wasn't completely necessary. Small, golden scales stretched from her skin over her breasts and lower waist.

"Don't worry," she smiled in the soft light of Sothos. "I haven't forgotten the lusts of men."

He watched her walk, her shoulders proud and her face serene. Shedaaij had become a woman in every sense possible, the maturity of her mind expressive in every action and gesture.

Yet, he knew the small cover she provided her body was hardly enough. He whistled deep into the night, the sound carrying on the wind to the stables beside Degron Castle.

***

The tunnel within the rising hill came to an end. It was dark with torches unlit, and Cerexus followed a trail Hargon could not see. Anuxis's arms fell over the dwarf's shoulders, holding the three-strapped reins that issued commands to the three-headed hound.

The tunnel came to an end. Ahead of them light broke into the cavern from the outside. Cerexus, however, had to walk around crumbled stones which seemed to have once been a wall.

As Cerexus passed the stones, Hargon looked in the centre and saw a large well which descended down into the mountain. Wind was blowing up from the well, and Hargon assumed the stones that now littered the passageways had once enclosed this hole.

When they passed a corner of two walls, the dwarf could barley discern a banner that lay broken on the floor. He tried to make out the design, but he only saw a sword before Cerexus led them on to the light ahead.

They passed a broken doorway to their left and a crossway of passages before they reached the air outside. They were standing on what was once called the Sky Tier of Horlorn's Gate. The platform stretched out from the mountain, the protruding edge forming a semi-circle to look down at the other two tiers below them.

The glory of Horlorn's Gate had fallen to ruins. The ends of the tiers had fallen down upon the others. The walls of the mountain had been scoured with fire in what seemed a distant past. The night sky only illuminated the destruction.

Yet, Hargon heard Anuxis sigh in relief. The dark being dismounted and stood closer to the tier's edge than the dwarf would ever attempt. Hargon dismounted and stood a far way behind him.

"You seem pleased," he said a little too loud, his voice carrying against the mountain side.

"I am," Anuxis replied in a soothing tone. He dropped the hood of his cloak and looked up at the crescent moon.

"Care to share the elation?" Hargon asked, rubbing his hand through his beard.

"There's no fog," Anuxis revealed and spread his scepter-free hand towards the land before them. "Behind Dwarf Mountains, there is no fog."

Hargon walked forward without realising how close to the edge he was. The crumbled stones created nice footing to prevent him from slipping. Hargon smiled in spite of his fears. There was indeed no fog upon the land.

"This is great!" Hargon shouted, and so did the echoes. "Why would there be no fog though?"

"I don't know this 'dark lord' as well as you Celenics," Anuxis replied and then turned to his hound. "Cerexus, see if Shadowolf is available."

Hargon followed Anuxis to the dog. The centre head's right eye began to glow a horrid red until its shape was similar to that of Mandy's. The eye grew dark and deep, with a soft red pupil pulsing within. Soon they both saw a land hopping up and down.

"I think she's running," Anuxis announced.

"Where to?" Hargon wondered.

His reply was received in the image of the eye. On the land appeared two people walking towards Mandy....

***

"Someone's trying to call me," Shadowolf said as he saw Mandy approach. He patted her mane when she reached them and then finally saw the cloak he had thrown on the beach earlier that day. "Here."

"Thank you," Shedaaij replied, catching the cloak and pulling it onto her body. Shadowolf took out his shirt and pulled it over his naked torso.

Soon enough, however, the mist of rain that had become a drizzle dampened the top and soaked the cloak with a silvery sheen.

Shadowolf's joggens were still drenched from the ocean and the rain continued to pour over them as he looked into Mandy's right eye socket.

"It looks cool there," Anuxis's image said. Shadowolf didn't recognise the dwarf next to him.

"The rain has turned down a bit," he replied. "Isn't it raining there?"

"No, the sky is clear," Anuxis said, and then his wolf-head grinned, "and so is the land."

"No fog?"

"Correct."

Shadowolf smiled broadly. He was immensely satisfied with the news.

"Don't be too happy yet," Anuxis said, and Shadowolf responded with the appropriate frown. "The place is torn apart. Most probably your dark lord's attempt at making sure it never gets used again."

"Probably," Shadowolf agreed, and shifted his eyes to see Shedaaij mount Mandy's back. The cold did not seem to affect her.

"If I may," the dwarf suddenly said, overcoming his discomfort of staring into the hound's eye. "My name is Hargon. Perhaps...."

"Oh, Hargon!" Shadowolf interrupted. "Chenesia's defender! I've heard a lot about you."

What could be seen of Hargon's face behind the beard became a deep red. His mouth creased into a foolish grin.

"Sorry," Shadowolf apologised. "Please continue."

"My lord Gallon resides with the dwarf masters in the mountains," Hargon continued, his confidence boosted. "If you wish, we could assist with reconstruction of Horlorn's Gate. After all, the dwarves did build it in the first place."

"That will be marvelously pleasant," Shadowolf said, constraining himself not to flatter the dwarf more than was necessary. It looked like Hargon's head was about to pop from pride.

"Very well," Anuxis said. "We will inform Gallon of the latest news and request the reconstruction. I will await further developments from the others."

Shadowolf nodded and Mandy's eye returned to normal.

Nighthale looked up from his supper. His wife was seated

beside him in the circular tower once known as the War Council, and for the first in a long time their two daughters were present.

It was none of these three women that had caused him to draw his mind from its thoughts though. Shadowolf strode in through the sole door of the dining room, his hair and face recently dried and new clothes on him. From behind entered Shedaaij in a light emerald dress. She smiled in greeting at the others while her daughter yawned in her arms.

"Glad to see you've returned," Nighthale said.

"At least we didn't have to wait another two years," Karla jibed as his sisters jumped up to embrace him.

"Jesie and Marla," Shadowolf whispered, "how I've missed you."

"What, between the blood and blades?" Jesie said, slapping his chest. "What longing could we attract between those two?"

"Ok girls," Nighthale said, and then indicated two vacant seats. "Shado, Shedaaij, please."

"I'll go call for more food," Karla said and made to leave the room.

"So what do our ocean friends have to say?" Marla asked as she finished what was left in her plate.

"Well, James was very...."

"James?" Nighthale interrupted.

"Lellian died in the last battle against the sirens," Shadowolf continued. "James has taken leadership. He wasn't very hospitable when I reached the Straits of Malakov."

Nighthale frowned but decided not to ask.

"I have, however, heard of a place where the fog is absent," Shadowolf said, and bowed his head slowly in preparation. He placed himself in the presence of Bontu, ready for the reaction he knew was coming.

Nighthale lowered his fork softly onto the plate and looked at his son. Shadowolf could hear the muffled footsteps as his mother stopped by the door of the room. He heard his sisters swallow their food, waiting in abated breath.

"I thought you were in the ocean?" Nighthale asked and Karla sat beside him, holding his hand.

"I was," Shadowolf conceded, looking up at him, "but I did not return from uPendus alone."

Nighthale stared at him. Shadowolf could see his father's anxiety, his fear written in the irises of his eyes. However, he continued.

"Horlorn's Gate is free of the fog."

"And why would that concern me?" Nighthale asked.

"Because we have a chance to...."

"To what?" Shadowolf had never seen his father's eyes so cold. "To fight? Why on earth would we want to fight when there is no reason to?"

"Maybe to rid the world of the evil that has plagued the land for so long," Shadowolf's voice started to rise, his power burning within his soul.

"Shado..." Nighthale started, his temper boiling too, when Karla interrupted.

"Have you named your daughter yet?"

Shadowolf looked at her in shock, and then smiled when he realised she was trying to abate the argument.

"Yes," he replied. "We thought of how she loves your precious stones so much."

"You've named her Precious Stone?" Jesie asked, and even Nighthale couldn't help but smile while Karla laughed.

"No," he said. "We've named her Crystal."

"Ah, I've always liked that name," Marla said, looking dreamily at the roof.

"Anyway," Shadowolf said, standing up. "I am heading to my room. I'll ask that they bring the food there."

Nighthale nodded and they all greeted each other as Shadowolf, Shedaaij and Crystal headed for the door.

"What is the state of the Gate?" Nighthale asked as Shadowolf made to close the door.

"It is in ruins," he replied, "but the dwarves have offered to rebuild it."

Nighthale looked up, shocked more than ever and wondering how his son managed all this while in the ocean. But he closed the question on his mouth and simply nodded.

"I will explain everything in due course, I promise," he said, and left the dining room.

***

"Chenesia?" Larnesia said as she knocked on the open door and entered. Even though she could only see her daughter's back bent over the bed, it was obvious from her movements what she was up to. "Are you leaving?"

"My time is running out," Chenesia said. Her mother could hear that her emotions were cut off. She walked up to her and gently turned her around.

"There is no shame in mourning your father," she said.

"I know," Chenesia replied and walked to her wardrobe to collect a few more things, "but I have spent too much time crying when I need to be searching for the Butterfly Pendant."

Chenesia packed her last things and closed the carry-bag. She slung it over her shoulder and walked out the room to the open courtyard of the Sanctuary. Genewiu greeted her in the sunlight and kneeled as she mounted.

"Won't you need a weapon?" Larnesia asked.

"Le'Mar doesn't know I am here," she replied. "Like you said, the war doesn't exist anymore. The only thing I will need is an arrow."

"Wait," her mother said and ran off into one of the corridors. After a few minutes she returned and passed a bow, a quiver of arrows and two dwarven throwing axes to her.

"Thank you," Chenesia said, strapping the bow and quiver to her back and tying the axes to a belt on her pants. "Guard the Vale well, mother."

Chenesia didn't look back once as she took the skies and headed for the Fairiwell.

And, unknown to her, two tigroys followed on the arid land below....

A PHANTOM AND A POEM
CHAPTER TEN

Lucian turned his head from the entrance and looked at Trimistus. The reptilian man's eyes glowed red in the tunnel, a thin line forming whenever he moved his head.

"Do you think this is the place?" Lucian murmured. They had travelled long and hard, searching the depths of the mountain range and camping on the floor every now and again. They did not know how far they had travelled. It came to a point, however, where they had to leave horse and saurex in a small enclosure while they walked through thin and crude passages.

"I don't know," Trimistus replied. "It looks like every other place we've been."

Lucian agreed with him. From what he could tell in the complete darkness, it was just another large cavern within the mountain. The two crept into the hall, hardly daring to breathe. Even their scuffle on the floor was kept minimal, not allowing the darkness to fool their awareness.

Trimistus suddenly lurched forward. He spread his arms out, but instead of hitting the floor below his fall was abruptly halted. Where his hands connected with the object, he felt large scales. He ran his fingertips over the surface and then backed away slowly.

"I think we found her," Trimistus whispered once Lucian had joined him.

"The ancient dragon?" Lucian asked.

"A dragon."

"How will we know?"

"Same way that we found the way down here," Trimistus replied. "We ask. Not sure we're going to get a warm welcome though."

"Let me guess," Lucian said, still looking around, his sarcastic smile lost in the dark, "this one is not under your control either."

"Like I said, Celenic dragons do not fall under my command. And if the rumours are true, then this is the first of the Celenic dragons to walk the earth."

"You are correct," a gruff voice said. As they jumped and landed on the floor, Trimistus and Lucian felt the weight in the atmosphere change as something large rose in the chamber.

"Oh!" Lucian exclaimed as torches flared on the walls. What they had thought to be a large cavern suddenly became a vast hall.

Everywhere on the floor behind the dragon were an immense amount of treasures. Gold, sapphire, aquamarine, aventurine and every other gem and trinket worth collecting were stacked to the high roof. Four obsidian obelisks stood in line, randomly studded with ruby stones.

The dragon was the largest either of them had seen. Even Trimistus as the DragonWourd had not seen one as large as the one before them. She stood on her hind legs and spread her wings from one wall of the chamber to the other. She let out an almighty roar that shook dust from the top onto the visitors.

She was dark emerald in colour, with patches of red. The right wing had two talons cropped together mid-way along the top, but the left wing had a stump where the talons should have been. As she landed on her fore legs she tucked her wings in and circled the strangers. Her red, blood-stained teeth shone at them as a deep growl rumbled from her throat. Smoke rose from her nostrils. Lucian prepared to become wind should fire erupt from her mouth.

"What business do you have here?" she enquired. Lucian was reminded of his mother when he was a youngster waking her up in the middle of the night. Despite his fear, he had to constrain his laughter.

"We have heard tell that you were of the time of Bentley," Trimistus attempted. The two turned round and round as they watched for any sign of attack from her. "Fereya, as the others call you."

"That is my name," she conceded, "and that was my time."

"We have come in search of an ancient artefact; one that we believe befell you so long ago."

Fereya stopped and snapped her head before his. The growl

grew louder, but Trimistus held his ground, the Dragon Blade shining in the torch light.

"You're one of those DragonWourds," Fereya stated more than asked. "*Wisoum*, I believe the ancient term is."

"That I am," he replied.

"You believe you have power over me like those weak fools!" she screeched at him. "Dragons fall under no one's will!"

"You are right," he said, holding his palms up defensively. "I am under the service of the dragons, as ever."

Trimistus knelt on the ground, holding the edge of his sword back from his leg as he bowed his head.

Fereya studied him cautiously as if waiting for his devious plan to be revealed. Yet, he remained kneeled, unflinching even in her glare.

"We do not need servants," the dragon replied, yet Lucian could tell she was subdued. "Rise, and tell me of this artefact."

"We are looking for an ancient dagger," Trimistus said, standing up, "one that was lost when the range of Bentley Strip was created in the fury of Bentley and Malherin."

Fereya charged forward and roared in their faces. Lucian held his arm up to shield against the warm air. He was getting tired of her mood. Before she could reply to his question, he walked past Trimistus and faced her.

"Do you know of such a dagger?"

"Hu hu ha ha ha," she gave out deep laugh, filled with pity. "Yes, I have such a dagger with me, but I am afraid I cannot give it to you."

"Cannot, or will not?" Lucian continued. Trimistus whispered his name, pleading quietly that he alter his tact. Yet Lucian stared up in defiance at the old dragon, not relenting his glare.

Fereya rose on her hind legs again. Lucian and Trimistus watched as a red pulse broke through her scales. The emerald faded away as the ruby red became stronger, the heart of the dragon becoming ever more visible.

Finally, they could see a shadow of what was contained within the heart. A man, curled in a ball, was lying within the beating heart. He didn't move, but lay as if in a deep slumber.

Within his hands he held an object. Lucian was reminded of a baby holding its rattle. As the man turned unconsciously in the blood of the glowing heart, he could see the definition of the object and realised it was the dagger.

"Malherin does love his toy so," Fereya said as she dropped to her fore legs. "But you will have to get through me to obtain it."

Trimistus drew his Dragon Blade while a sword of wind appeared in Lucian's hand. Fereya roared again and began to charge them, when several noises erupting from above froze them in their tracks.

Hundreds of miniature dragons fell down upon them, breaking from several holes in the walls. There was something odd about their appearances, as if they should have been as large as adult dragons. Yet the largest was the size of Lucian.

"Oh, but they do so love their parents," Fereya said sweetly before charging to the attack again, her fangs falling upon them.

Lucian rose into the air and slashed his blade through the first scaly neck he could find. The head and body fell to the floor and Trimistus jumped over Fereya's furious maw onto her neck. He took the opportunity to drive his blade into the back of her head, but he knew his actions were premature. Before the sword could sink home, three dragons hit him off to the ground.

Trimistus sheathed his blade. His black sockets that held the small, red pupils became flaming torches of fire as he transformed into a dragon.

"That doesn't help!" Lucian shouted, dodging two dragons and stabbing a third. "How must I tell the difference?"

In reply, Trimistus's green scales became bright blue. A soft, white aura surrounded his body as he flew after several of the dragons, avoiding Fereya's fangs.

"That's better," Lucian said. He became wind as a small set of fangs made for the back of his neck. He twisted in the wind and materialised again, swinging his sword into the beast's belly.

Lucian twisted again as Fereya attacked him. He travelled as wind down her scales to the pulsing heart. His wind sword drew back to pierce the scales, but Fereya slapped him with a wing towards the wall.

Trimistus bit into a neck, held the head and throat with his talons and ripped it apart. A dragon plummeted into him, sending them falling in circles. He pulled the jaws apart, roared fire into its throat and let the body fall on its own onto Fereya's head.

Fereya crouched down and then launched into the air. Trimistus turned in time to plant his hind legs on her lower jaw and hold her lowering upper jaw up with his fore legs. His tail swished as he felt the heat rise from her throat.

"Oh no," he murmured, but choked as a gale of wind whipped him out her mouth when the fire erupted. Lucian and Trimistus landed on the ground, the small dragons already making their way down.

"I need you to distract them," Lucian said to him.

"It's a lot to distract," Trimistus replied, his voice rumbling deeper than usual in his dragon state. "What are you going to do?"

"Something only a Windfarer can do, but wishes he never has to."

Trimistus frowned but didn't have time to question. He flew up into an onslaught from the dragons, using his fangs, sword and claws to draw death and dodge danger. Some dragons fell upon Lucian, but he became a whisper in the wind and vanished.

Fereya noted his absence and became instantly suspicious. The flying *Wisoum* was the last thing on her mind as she whirled her bulk around in search of the *Enodhim*.

"Urh, you elementalists drive me mad!" she shouted and flew around the cavern looking for any hint of him. Her dragon senses honed in on any powers being used, but she could only detect Trimistus killing her younglings.

The air stirred the dust softly on the ground and settled again. Another breeze blew before dying down. Fereya landed on all fours, desperate to find him. Finally, she detected a transparent aura blanketing Lucian. She flew up in his direction, butting Trimistus out of her way.

The cave became very humid as the air escaped it. Trimistus coughed as he struggled to breathe. The dragons also stopped their fighting, clutching their throats as they choked for air. First one by one, then more, fell to the floor, unable to keep air in their lungs.

Fereya struggled to glide through the air now, her vision blurred. She breathed fire at the place she thought he had been, but the fire died the moment it left her mouth, having no air to burn on.

She yawned due to lack of air and fell to the floor. The cavern quaked as she slid across, her head stopping by a wall. Lucian materialised and landed near Trimistus. He placed his head near the reptilian mouth and felt his breath against his cheek.

He had to act fast. They weren't dead, only sleeping. Lucian approached the belly of the dragon, feeling for the warm bed of the heart. Slowly, he pushed his hand of air between two large scales. He pried them apart, feeling for the heart. He not only felt it, but he saw the light glow against his face, the tip of the dagger protruding through the wall of the heart.

Lucian grabbed the sharp tip and pulled. The dagger edged out, the hilt approaching the muscle. Finally the dagger emerged, but he still had to pull it out through the scales.

When the steel of the dagger made an appearance, he knew something was wrong. The scales started to widen of its own accord and he realised there was a hand holding the handle. Lucian planted a foot on the belly and pulled the dagger hard. A man fell through the scales and onto the floor.

Malherin was ethereal in form. His ghostly image drifted up, his eyes blank and his expression plain. His hands were held over his lap as he recited words during his ascent through the roof of the cavern:

"From disobedience I have obeyed
to the keeping of the sought.
Alone in time I have slept
for releasing the seed of evil on the world.

"The weapons of light must now
take its toll on the elements.
For by nature they were entrusted
To be removed from the seed's essence.

"Once removed, the world of man changed,
Vehement void becomes mystical mist.
The gates of Heaven again sealed with a softened light.
The deceiver razed; the deceived released."

As the phantom of Malherin vanished through the mountain, Lucian sighed.

"Wish I had a parchment to record that," he said, cut short from laughter when Fereya snorted in her slumber. He picked up Trimistus and left the chamber.

PART TWO

STAFF OF FALGAR

RELIC SANCTUM
CHAPTER ONE

The dry sand shimmered softly in the dull fog as the pegasus's wings soared through the air. Her hooves landed on the land, the air stale on her tongue. Genewiu glanced around, searching for the entrance to the Fairiwell.

Chenesia dismounted. The wind was blowing the sand up off the ground and she had to shade her eyes against it. She walked around looking for the entrance when her feet stepped on something hard, different from the arid soil.

"I found it," she said, and Genewiu walked to her. Chenesia removed the bow from her back, clearing the metal circle beneath her with her foot. It was a wide circle, one that Genewiu could comfortably stand on, with two long lines etched on the surface. One line was long and wide enough for a dwarven axe, while the other was short and thin enough for the head of an arrow.

Chenesia notched an arrow and held the head by the smaller line. She released the arrow into the line and stood on the circle, joined by Genewiu. The disc descended into the ground while the sound of gears turning filled the tunnel. Chenesia stepped off first as the tunnel was only wide enough for them to walk single file.

It wasn't walking abreast that worried her as she stared ahead. Three footsteps ahead of them the tunnel had collapsed, creating a barrier to the Fairiwell. Rocks and earth filled the tunnel. Chenesia leaned over the lower rubble, trying to find a gap to look through.

"It seems like it's blocked for quite a distance," Chenesia said, turning to Genewiu.

"That's strange," the pegasus said. "The earth didn't look collapsed from the surface."

Chenesia looked thoughtfully at the ruined path and the walls surrounding it. The curved walls of the tunnel were unscathed, and the floor beneath was still smooth.

"This can only be the work of an earth elemental," she finally said.

"One of Le'Mar's *Goudlems*?"

"If he has any," Chenesia replied. "I wouldn't be surprised. Now I wish Shado was here."

"I could always kick our way through," Genewiu joked, but Chenesia was still too much in thought to laugh. "How long do you think it will take us?"

"I have no idea," she sighed. "But we will have to make a way. Either that, or enter through Le'Mar's Forest on the other side."

Genewiu lifted her head, her eyes wide.

"That's a brilliant idea. Why don't we do that?"

"Because we risk drawing the wrong attention."

"I am sure we can make it through without being detected," Genewiu continued to persuade her.

"I don't like that idea," Chenesia said, frowning hard. "Is there no way we can get through here?"

Genewiu let the girl search through some of the rubble, but it was obvious they were not going to get through, unless they had an elementalist with them.

"What do you think are the chances of us making it through Le'Mar's Forest to the other side of the Fairiwell?" she asked.

"I guess we'll just have to find out," the pegasus replied, already walking back to the disc. Chenesia looked at the rubble one more time before turning and heading out.

***

"There are riders approaching the Gate," a dwarf scout said as he entered the meeting hall within Horlorn's Gate. Anuxis looked up from his deliberations with Hargon and three other dwarf captains. His wolf-head shifted its gaze to Hargon.

"Lord Gallon might have sent someone with a message," the dwarf replied, standing to leave the hall.

"They are not dwarves, Hargon," the scout informed them. "One is human and the other is reptilian on a beast I have never seen in my life upon earth. Much like a dragon, but without wings."

"It must be Lucian," Anuxis said and joined Hargon in leaving the hall. He placed the hood of his cloak over his head; it was a habit he chose not to forego.

Cerexus caught up with them before they had left the exit tunnel that opened up on the rolling hills leading to Dwarf Mountains. The sun played beautifully upon the luscious lawns, uninhibited by the fog that could not be seen behind the steely mountain range to the south. A plethora of moans escaped his abdomen as the strong sunlight hit Anuxis's robes, a darkness collecting around his body like a cloth over a table.

Lucian saw the light reflect off the wolf-man's sceptre and the axes strapped to the dwarves backs and sides. Lancenat's hooves echoed against the valley's coarse landscape, muffled only by the pounding of Trimistus's saurex. Wherever the saurex's claws dug into the earth, disrupted sprays of grass and soil indelibly left evidence of its passing in its wake.

The two travelers halted their mounts before the waiting hosts. Cerexus walked forward, unencumbered by fear, and sniffed the saurex. The beast growled softly at the three-headed hound, only to find itself ignored by the dark dog.

"It's nice to be out of the fog," Lucian greeted, visibly feeling refreshed.

"Welcome to Horlorn's Gate," Anuxis said formerly to Lucian's travelling companion. "Lucian, this is…."

"Hargon; yes I recall from my brief visit to the Vale some time back with Chenesia. This is Trimistus, but I will explain on the way inside."

The group listened intently to Lucian as he told them about the parchment concerning Bentley, giving them only brief details concerning their acquisition of the dagger. They arrived at the meeting hall, but Lucian lingered at the entrance.

"Why all that effort for a dagger?" Hargon asked, looking up at Lucian, who was at least twice his height.

"Ah, little man, that I will let Shadowolf tell you," the Windfarer replied, and then looked at Anuxis significantly before leaving the dwarves and the hall. "Only he can regale the importance of the weapons like no other."

"Excuse me, master dwarf," Anuxis said, following Lucian. For some reason unknown to Hargon, Cerexus didn't follow his master, but watched from the dwarf's side.

"I'm not little," Hargon groaned softly and entered the hall to eat from the freshly prepared meals laid out on the tables.

Anuxis and Lucian entered a door in one of the corridors to the left. The passage they entered snaked slightly before they entered another room. The only apparent entrance or exit to this room was the one they had just vacated. The other three walls were solid, ostensibly impenetrable.

Lucian remembered Shadowolf's instructions regarding the elemental quarters. From the room's immaculate appearance, he deduced that the same beings that had destroyed Horlorn's Gate had not bothered to search beyond this room. For that, he was grateful in some small measure.

He moved to the left wall and placed his palms on it. Calling the power of earth, he forced it from his soul through his arms and into the wall. The wall started to fray, pulling away from Lucian's hands in the form of roots and vines until a door was open to them.

They entered a room that once housed the water elementals of Horlorn's Gate. The room was still as it had been before the Gate was abandoned, untouched by the scourge of the dark lord's soldiers. But Lucian spared no time inspecting the room. Ignoring the wall to the left that would have led him to the former Windfarer room, and the wall of the right to the Mindwatcher room, he walked straight across to the opposite wall.

Repeating the same procedure he opened another door. They entered an elemental courtyard that was in the very centre of the five rooms surrounding it. A large forest terrain, with oak and maple trees and orange autumn leaves upon the grassy floor, filled the room before them.

Lucian looked around the room. They had walked for about the third of the room before he stopped.

"Here's good," he told Anuxis. He pulled his shirt out from his pants and removed the dagger that was hidden on his side. He closed his eyes, lifting the sword above his head and calling the air around him until it became a rush of air.

The dagger glowed in response to Lucian's power. Anuxis watched as it became vague, starting with the outer edges until the dagger joined the wind and vanished into the air.

"It is done," the Windfarer said, patting Anuxis on the shoulder and leading him back out to the Gate.

TALES OF FALGAR
CHAPTER TWO

Even though the sun shone on the outside, softened only by the pervasive fog on the land of Avalion, the candles flickered in the medium-sized personal study that belonged to Nighthale Degron.

Despite the large castle that belonged to his tribe name, the expansive dining hall that welcomed all from the city, the large guest quarters, the massive barracks and military yards, and the enormous courtyard where the children loved to play, Nighthale was a man that loved simple pleasures.

This could be seen in the small tower room that was once a war council, but became a private dining room. It could also be noted in the simple rooms that he, his wife and children frequented. And, despite having a large library in the south wing that measured two floors high and was five times the square area of the study, Nighthale insisted that he have a personal study that was quaint and homely.

It was in this quaint study that many of Eldor's parchments and manuscripts were kept, passed down to Nighthale over the years. It was also in this homely study where Nighthale kept the document that Eldor had handed him before the elves had left Le'Mar's Forest for the Far Isles. And it was in this candle-lit study that Shadowolf now sat, perusing the document.

His father kept the curtains drawn in the study most of the time to avoid some of the older parchments from being damaged by the light. The curtains were made of a soft material that permitted only the necessary light to find the way around the room and light the candles.

Shadowolf's eyes went over the document carefully. As he began, he knew that it must have been the right document, as it bore a resemblance to the one explained by Lucian. The top of the scroll was torn off, continuing where the former had ended. As was Shadowolf's habit, he started off reading in his mind but gradually the words formed on his lips and he was reading it aloud:

Shadow of the Father

In the light of his father's righteous victory, and with the last words of Saldheron on his mind, Mikinos changed his ways to that of his father Bentley. He obeyed the will of his father by marrying his sister Shardenel, and staying within the Nether Region.

But in the shadow of his father's bitter defeat, Temelrin watched as the legacy of the elves were defiled. He watched from the forest as his father Malherin dropped to his death by the blade of Bentley. Hatred arose in him, fuelled by the same darkness that had taken his father. Yet, Elhorin his sister beseeched that he belay the darkness inside, and take her as his partner and keep the bloodline of their father. Temelrin agreed never to taint his father's blood, but in his heart the darkness promised to exact revenge on the blood of man.

Seeds of Light and Dark

With the passage of time, children were born to these lovers. From the line of Mikinos and Shardenel were born many children, each pure in their own ways. Yet none were as pure as Falgar, who was said to be a reflection of his ancestor, Bentley.

From the line of Temelrin and Elhorin on the Isles were born many elves that passed down to many families. The three of note were their two sons, Selhorin and Melnirion, and their daughter Mehorin. They were all pure and fair as only elves could be, basking in the light of their mother and growing in the strength of their father. In the absence of the humans, and surrounded by the love of his family, Temelrin almost forgot about the death of his father, and the darkness was but a mustard seed in his heart.

Matters of the Hearts

As Falgar became a man, his heart longed to see more of the land. His father Mikinos had often told him of the elves, and there were times, when he spoke of Elhorin in Shardenel's absence, that Falgar could see the ancient fondness return to the old man's eyes. It was a fondness Falgar felt for none in the Nether Region, thus further compelling his will to leave.

On the Far Isles, Melnirion watched as his sister Mehorin grew distant. She often spoke to him of her will to return the elves to the land of man. The Battle of Bentley's Strip was taught to all the elves, but she could see the pain in her mother's eyes at every mention of Mikinos's name. She could not confide in her oldest brother, Selhorin, for he seemed to share the same dispassion for men as her father.

Finals Decisions

In the end, Falgar decided it was time for man to leave the Nether Region. He would be the only man in his time to do so, for no other wished to leave the dying sanctity of the forest. His father regarded him, wondering if it was the will of Bontu that Falgar followed. He could not detect any hint of the darkness that had nearly consumed him all those years before. He bade his son farewell, and Falgar left the Nether Region.

The same reasoning occurred to Mehorin, now stricken with the desire to return elves to the land of man. Melnirion debated with his mother, informing her that if Mehorin were not permitted to leave, she would find a way to defy them. But Elhorin knew Temelrin would never permit it, and so advised Melnirion to take her to the lands undetected. And so they travelled across the seas by light of night, unaware that Selhorin had witnessed their departure.

Return of the darkness

When Selhorin informed his father of their betrayal, Temelrin was angered. The mustard seed that was once sleeping within the pit of his heart grew in the rays of his anger, watered by the hatred of man. It consumed his heart once more, returning memories of the night he lost his father.

He turned to his son and instructed him to hunt them down and kill them before they ever had the chance to return to man. Selhorin was shocked and refused to commit such a deed against the will of Bontu. Temelrin hit his son across the room and left the Isles in search of his defiant children. Elhorin watched with tears in her eyes as she lost her husband, and as Selhorin pursued him in a desperate attempt to stop him.

Ancient Love Rekindled

Falgar travelled many days and nights, looking at the land's animals and landscapes, heading ever east past the River of Light. He found a dry landscape. The grass was yellow and dying for many fields ahead. He knelt down and inspected the earth.

Before the two elves reached the Nether Region, they had spied a man travelling east. It amused them that man was leaving the forest and so they pursued. Mehorin's excitement grew the closer she got to this strange man.

Falgar listened intently on the wind. He could sense someone approaching and turned to watch the two strangers approach. When he realised they were elves due to their pale green shade, he almost fell on his knees. He had heard of them but never seen them before. But his jubilation subsided when he saw the face of Mehorin, and she stared in awe at this handsome man.

The Wrath of Bontu

Melnirion caught Mehorin's arm as she proceeded forward to him, but she jerked it out of his grasp. When she reached him she ran the flat of her palm gently over his cheek. The love Mikinos and

Elhorin felt for each other were once again born in the hearts of Falgar and Mehorin. He felt the desires of his father, but it was washed away by the purity of her mother, and all that was left was love.

It was upon this moment that the sand stirred, the grass swayed and Temelrin landed heavily on the dry land. Mehorin tore her gaze from her love's face to witness the fury of her father approach them, his staff of power in his right hand. Falgar stood up, relaxing his arms on his side. He saw darkness in Temelrin's eyes that he had never seen in any before and for but a moment he was terrified.

"I will not have my blood tainted with the silt of man," he told them, his power rising in the air.

"Bontu runs through my spirit," Falgar replied, his confidence returning. "Do not make the same mistake as your ancestor."

"How do you speak of my father?!" Temelrin raged. Selhorin stopped by the River and watched the gathering.

Mehorin hid behind Falgar's back. Temelrin looked at Melnirion, disgust evident in his eyes.

"You would betray your own blood like this?"

"Our blood was tainted by your father before you," Melnirion replied.

"You will die for your deception!"

Temelrin moved to attack his son, but Falgar used the wind to move before him. Temelrin struck at him with the staff as if he was swiping an annoying bug, but Falgar grabbed the staff in his hand. The elf tried in vain to remove the staff from his grasp.

Power erupted around them as the land started to quake. Their auras broke into sharp light. Melnirion, Mehorin and even Selhorin fell to the ground as the light grew stronger. Falgar clutched harder on the staff, the wind building up around them as he stared at the darkness in the man before him.

But within him, Falgar felt that Bontu was angered by their battle. The ground beneath them started burning from the amount *of power surrounding them and soon they were engulfed with flames. Yet, neither Falgar nor Temelrin would relinquish the staff.*

An amazing light broke over the land. Falgar and Temelrin were thrown apart, the land laid to waste. The staff fell down on the burning soil. But neither would let this fall stop them in destroying each other....the light wanted to destroy the dark, and the dark wanted to extinguish the light.

Falgar and Temelrin both used their powers to attempt the staff, and the elf laid claim to it first. He raised the staff above his head and brought it down like a whip towards Falgar's skull. Falgar twisted and grabbed the staff, pulling it out of his grasp. The staff became a rod of fire in his grasp as he turned and thrust it through Temelrin's heart.

Exile

The power died down and the light faded as the elf fell to his knees, blood breaking from his mouth onto the soil. The only noise that could be heard outside the raging fire was the voice of Selhorin shouting for his father. Falgar escaped the fires and headed north. Mehorin looked once more at the fire before making a choice and joining Falgar.

Melnirion approached his brother. Selhorin was kneeling by the fire, looking into it for any sign of his father. Tears welled on his eyes, his gaze shifting to his brother. Melnirion stared back in shock as he saw the same darkness that once lived in his father take over Selhorin.

"I don't want you or her back on the Isles," Selhorin said. As he rose, the grief left his face to be replaced by intended murder. "If you ever step foot on the Isles, I will kill you."

Selhorin left the land of man, never to return to it ever again.

Tranquility

In the aftermath of the battle, Falgar and Mehorin settled to the north of the desert, in the land that would become known as Carmel.

Melnirion visited them on occasion. When the elves learnt of the battle, many of them left the Isles and travelled to the land of man, including the forefather of the elves, Saldheron. But Melnirion felt that Saldheron deserved a proper home, and so constructed the forests in the mountain ranges in the east that would become known as 'Saldher's Forest'. Elhorin later left her son Selhorin and lived within the forest.

The elves remaining on the Far Isles, under the rule of Selhorin, never tried to make contact with Mehorin and the land elves. The island elves have since considered themselves superior to the other elves in all lore and magic, claiming to maintain the bloodline of the elves.

Shadowolf closed the parchment and sat back in the chair. Everything that he had read was relaying into images in his mind. There was no actual mention of what had happened to the staff, except that it had turned into fire. He rubbed his fingers over his tired eyes.

Yet, Masara and Elmerion had known that T'Mar had found the staff. Had he searched the entire desert for it?

"Sorry," a voice called from the door. A girl entered the study with a tray carrying tea and food. Her black hair with hints of red fell on her shoulders, soft freckles touching the bridge of her nose and complimenting the jade of her eyes. "Your mother was worried."

"She usually is," he smiled, taking a closer look at the girl. "I know you, but I've never seen you with a tray before."

"Oh," she blushed, putting the tray on an open place on the table. "I'm Deihlia, Lastgorn's...."

"Sister, right," Shadowolf finished for her. "I haven't seen you since you were ten. That's almost nine years ago. Sorry, I'm not being rude I'm just...."

"I'm here with Lastgorn," she interrupted rather quickly. "He came to see how you are. It's been.....hard for him since Gwyn's death. That's sort of why I offered to bring the tea in. To find out how long you might be." Deihlia laughed and then dipped her head down, fiddling with her hands on her dress. "Now I'm being rude."

"No it's alright. I've just finished and I wouldn't mind the company. I tell you what, why don't you invite him to the study. It's more private here than in the presence of my parents."

Deihlia frowned at the last comment, but nodded and exited the study. Shadowolf was left in the shadows of the dying day, placing himself in the presence of Bontu if only to calm his throbbing veins. The ghosts of Sny-Ten and Gwyn haunted his mind momentarily as he waited for the survivor of the trio that had fought so valiantly in the Battle for Eldor's Forest.

The door creaked open, and the silhouette of the torn man stood against the light that lit the passage beyond. Lastgorn closed the door and approached the table.

On the outside, Shadowolf could see that Lastgorn was taking care of his health, or at least someone was. He suspected that it was Deihlia.

His face still shone with the rugged handsomeness that he had always been blessed with. The once, light brown hair had turned to a shade of blond, possibly from a lot of time in the sunlight. Its length had been cut in line with his eyes, but parted to each side. The muscles he had acquired through years of fighting were well hidden beneath the tan shirt which he wore.

But when Shadowolf looked in his eyes, he could see the torment that Lastgorn still went through every night. Only his eyes showed proof that the man still grieved for his friends, especially the woman that he had been so close to.

"You know," Lastgorn disturbed his observations and took a seat, "when you look at a person like that it feels like you're looking into their soul."

"Shedaaij reminds me of that fact constantly," Shadowolf offered a wan smile.

"How is she? I haven't seen her, but your mother says there's a wedding on the way."

"We've been talking about it," Shadowolf replied. "I can't really imagine my life with anyone else."

"You've got a really beautiful daughter. She was with your mother when I arrived. Congratulations."

Shadowolf contemplated Lastgorn for a moment longer, and was about to approach the ghosts of their past when Lastgorn offered a different topic.

"I see you're quite busy," he said, looking at the books and pages that littered the desk. "Might I ask what you're investigating?"

"Just old history notes," Shadowolf said. "I wanted to brush up on the origins of Celenic Earth."

"I know you better than that, Shado," he replied, looking a little insulted. "Your father might disagree with you on taking any action, but I deserve as much vengeance as you."

"What makes you think any action on my part would be based on vengeance?"

Lastgorn remained silent, looking down on the desk instead of at Shadowolf. The hand that lay on the desk was clenching and unclenching, working furiously to contain the frustration. And then, his hand went calm and he looked straight into Shadowolf's eyes.

"Whatever you're planning, I want to be part of it," Lastgorn finally said. "Please don't deny me my request."

"I won't. I would never deny you that."

Lastgorn's face contorted slightly before he regained control of his emotions. But for all his strong will, he couldn't control the anger and hatred that he felt within. Tears broke on his face and he let his head drop onto his arms that were now resting on the desk. The sobs broke out into the study, but Shadowolf could feel that Lastgorn was trying to hold them back.

Shadowolf leaned forward and placed his hand on the top of Lastgorn's head. Warmth flowed from it into Lastgorn's torn spirit, and in a moment the loud sobs calmed as the man lay serenely and breathed deeply.

IN A DARK DEEP WELL
CHAPTER THREE

Before his parents were awake, before the farmers woke to tend to the meagre crops and ample animals, even before the sun touched the rim of the horizon, Shadowolf arose to prepare for his departure.

Shedaaij stirred sleepily beside him while Crystal slept in the cot by the wall. He shook his head from the cobwebs of the night and walked to the bathroom. There would be no time for a bath, so he quickly washed by the basin before approaching the wardrobe.

He donned a dark green top with strings in the v-neck collar and leggings that was of similar fashion, with the strings on either side of his ankles. He put on a pair of boots and then grabbed his grey staff.

"Leaving so soon?" Shedaaij asked, holding the blanket over the top part of her body. She looked at him through narrow eyes, trying to adjust to the fading darkness of the morning.

"Yes," he replied, not offering more.

"Can't you wait till Crystal wakes?"

"I dislike saying goodbye to her," Shadowolf said, but moved to the crib and laid a soft kiss on her forehead anyway. "I will try to be back by tomorrow night. I don't know how long this will take."

"Please don't take another two years," she jibed.

"I won't," he said, and leaned down to give her a farewell kiss.

"What will you do if Le'Mar is there?" Shadowolf stopped by the doorway.

"I can't fight him," he replied, looking back at her, "at least not yet. It will ruin everything I've planned. But I'm not leaving there until I have my brother back."

***

"I thought it was here," Genewiu said. The morning was becoming day as the sun started rising. They had eluded most of the dark lord's soldiers during the night, after having flown between the mountain's peaks and landing in a forest of trees. But the trees were desolate, bearing no leaves to cover their ride over the desecrated land.

"It's different trying to find the exit from the other side," Chenesia replied. "The last time, elves opened the ground and aimed arrows at our heads."

She still had a vague recollection of those two elves that had rudely welcomed them into the forest and escorted them to Eldor's throne. She wished that they were still in the forest, assisting them in finding the exit of the Fairiwell.

Someone grunted near them. Chenesia turned to see a grey-hued Ma-Wreth standing behind them, its eyes puffy and its face set in a demeaning leer. It lifted an arm and pointed at them and grunted again, obviously unable to pronounce any words.

"Run," Chenesia instructed softly but firmly. Genewiu ran as fast as her hooves could carry her away from the sluggish giant. She tucked her wings in under Chenesia's legs just as the Ma-Wreth began charging after them. They were both glad its legs weren't as fast as its lightning-fast arms.

The dwarven throwing-axes on her side were clinging together, frustrating her further as they charged south. It was the general direction that Chenesia remembered the exit being, but she wasn't sure. As far as she could recall, there was no visible evidence of its existence from the outside.

"Chenesia!" Genewiu shouted, and the girl turned her head towards another giant. Riding towards them from the left was a Froth Hun. Its white skull with black sockets was burning with large, blue flames. Skeletal hands in black, leather gloves held the reins of the black horse that was akin to that of Shadowolf's.

The Froth was enough ahead of them that he would shortly intercept them. Chenesia removed the bow and notched an arrow, rising to stand on Genewiu's back. She watched the Froth's approach through the trees whipping passed them, hunching on the pegasus's back and waiting for the right moment.

The Froth Hun watched the pegasus ride forward, and calculated its attack. It removed a dagger from its side and threw it at where the girl was hunched. As the dagger reached the white horse, it passed over her back where the girl should have been. The Froth's skull contorted into a sneer when Genewiu halted and watched him.

The girl's legs appeared in the air above the pegasus. She released the branch that she was swinging from and, while in the air, released the arrow. When she landed on Genewiu's back, the arrow hit the skull with a crack and the flames died. Chenesia and Genewiu continued forward, the Froth Hun falling off the side of the horse.

It wasn't long until dead forest was filled with the sound of other hooves. Chenesia looked around frantically, but as much as she looked she couldn't see any riders approaching. Genewiu picked up the pace, looking around for any sign of the Fairiwell.

"Get ready to fly if we need to," Chenesia said, not willing to take any chances. The hooves got louder, but still she saw no sign of the cause. She tried to look for the Fairiwell too, but the search was constantly hampered by the sound of approaching riders.

Finally the enemies revealed themselves. The air shimmered far ahead of them. A cloud similar to the fog formed and grew until it became flames and brimstone. Out of the fire the riders broke out, racing to meet the girl on the pegasus.

"Up!!! Get us up!!" Chenesia shouted, but Genewiu had already unfurled her wings.

The group ahead consisted of a variety of the dark lord's army. There were five Dra-hu'Mar in the rear, their blond hair and fair faces fierce in the fires that they were now leaving behind. Their bows tilted on their backs, only awaiting the command to be transformed into swords.

Six Froth Huns complimented by two Ma-Wreths were ahead of the hu'Mar, equally rallied to kill the girl. Above the heads of these beasts were a small company of fletchlings. They were a little larger and more rotund than fairies, with bat-like wings upon their blue bodies to keep them in the air.

Two humans led the packs. One was a female, unfamiliar to Chenesia, on a brown steed that seemed very unnatural as if it had been summoned from the earth itself.

The man, however, was very familiar to Chenesia if only by reputation. His bald head shined with the light of the fire that burned within him, a hazy image compared to the flames that raged from the staff in his left hand. What shocked her more than his presence was that he was riding a black pegasus with wings that shimmered with the darkness of an abysmal night; it was similar to the one Le'Mar usually rode on.

"It's Darcwulf," Chenesia said, more to herself than Genewiu. "And he's riding a pegator. If you're planning on getting us out of here, now…"

"Give me a moment!" Genewiu retorted and kicked up in the air as a fireball from Darcwulf's staff exploded on the ground beneath them. But Genewiu's balance and speed had been miscalculated in the panic and her hooves hit the ground again. Genewiu ran right, riding between clumps of trees to evade the company.

Chenesia and Genewiu's screams filled the forest as the earth gave way beneath them. Chenesia fell off Genewiu's back and hit the ground, sliding into a clump of vines. The pegasus rolled onto her hooves again, stretching the wing that had been scarred by the fall.

"This is it!" Chenesia exclaimed. She touched the vines, looking through to the passages beyond. "And it's also blocked."

She looked up at the earth they had just fallen through, fear rising in her gut despite herself. Chenesia and Genewiu's breathing ceased for a moment as they heard the army stop above them. Soon enough, the two were backing into the vines, and Darcwulf and a few of his minions dropped into the hole. The unknown lady watched from above.

"Who sent you?" Darcwulf asked. "Why are you here?"

"I…..I…," Chenesia's brain was working hard on a lie, "I was looking for the elves."

Darcwulf's eyes erupted into flames. He growled deeply, anger distorting his face.

"You'll have to do better than that," he said. "Everyone knows the elves have left."

Darcwulf walked to and fro, studying her face and then looking at Genewiu. A sudden realisation took him, his burning eyes widening.

"Oh," he finally said, looking up at the woman. "Guess what, Sona?"

"You've slept with her too?" the lady joked snidely. Darcwulf sighed.

"This is the girl that took Shado away just as our lord was about to kill him," Darcwulf replied, grinning in satisfaction when Chenesia gasped involuntarily. "So my guess is that my brother has returned once again from his grave."

Darcwulf grabbed her wrist in a fluid movement, leaving a trail of smoke in his arm's wake. "Where is he? Why has he returned?"

"He's given up," Chenesia said with a straight face, not thinking about the consequences. "Just like all the other cowards on the earth."

Darcwulf let out a howl of laughter letting her go. He turned away from them, his arms clutched behind his back.

"You honestly want me to believe that you are more valiant than him?" he laughed again. "Shado, the hero of the world, leaving it in the hands of a pathetic girl with no powers?"

"Darcwulf," Sona murmured, and then nodded in their direction. He turned around.

Chenesia and Genewiu were on the other side of the vines. Before them, behind the entwined roots, was a young elf staring defiantly back at him.

"So," the *KariemsaPh* growled, "you're the one who has been killing my beasts and stealing from the stores."

"That's right," the elf replied. "Took you long enough to work it out though, although your earth elemental friend provided the perfect cover." He tapped the vines with his fingers.

"I can just as easily remove them," Sona replied.

The elf did not bother replying. Instead he held his palm out and muttered ancient elf runes. The atmosphere in the chamber where Darcwulf stood grew humid and then warm as fire tore through it. The beasts cried out in pain and writhed behind Darcwulf, who simply walked through the fire to the vines.

When he reached it, he only barely managed to see them retreating through the tunnels to the Fairiwell. He called the flames behind him into his body and turned to exit the chamber. Ignoring the smoking bodies still twisting in agony on the ground, he rose in the air to join Sona, a tail of fire following him.

"Aren't we pursuing them?" Sona asked as he mounted the pegator.

"No," he replied. "I have a special surprise for them. Besides, I have a feeling I should prepare for a visit from my brother."

***

Anuxis sat quietly in the darkness of the room, his mind calling out. His cloak lay on a table by the wall, his scepter before his folded legs.

After three hours of meditation, his spirit stirred. The souls within his abdomen moaned softly. He opened his eyes, his wolf-face serene.

Anuxis stood and donned his cloak. Grabbing his scepter, he left the room and whistled for Cerexus. Hargon frowned as the wolf-man raced passed him on the hound through the west tunnel that led to the Scourge and Dwarf Mountains. When Anuxis broke out the hill into the sunlight, he flipped the hood of his cloak over his face.

Hargon walked passively to the opening of the tunnel. The grass waved lazily in the wind, a mirror of the calm that had settled in the dwarf's heart.

Then he noticed movement. He looked at an outcrop of small hills and saw a man leap on his horse and ride north. Dust disturbed his study of the man, and soon he was gone.

Hargon rushed back inside, eager to send a message to Gallon that they were being watched.

CONVERTED SERVANTS
CHAPTER FOUR

Shadowolf rode calmly up the mountain side, the sun setting behind him in the west. If it had been any other stallion, he would have had to leave it behind, for the southern mountain slopes were tedious to ride and there were no clear paths to travel. If Eldor's elvin protection was still surrounding the forest, he would have had an even harder time.

But Mandy walked the mountain as if it took only a small amount of energy to do so, her rank breath rising in the fading light like coils of brimstone. Her face was serene, her eyes pulsing softly in the dark pits of the eye sockets. As for the forest, it seemed to Shadowolf that Le'Mar hadn't bothered placing any protection upon it.

Shadowolf kept riding as far up the mountain side as was necessary. He waited until his head cleared the fog so that he could use his power to travel faster. Yet, as he often reminded himself, perhaps that wasn't such a good idea either; he had known Le'Mar to use a Semeri crow before to spy for him. Shadowolf tugged the hood on his head again, making sure no part of his face was revealed.

Mandy stopped between clumps of bushes. She stood still, surveying the area, before jumping over a medium-sized bush and continuing on a different track. The density in the air became less, the fog starting to clear, and it wasn't long before they breached the ceiling of the fog and rode in the clear air of the night.

Mandy snorted softly, reminding Shadowolf that someone was still following him. He patted her neck in appreciation. He had waited for them to break free of the fog first before he acted. He wasn't sure if he needed to use his powers on the stalker, but wanted to make sure he was able to when the time came.

And so, when they rode passed a protruding rock on the mountainside, Shadowolf and Mandy became part of the air. All sound of the mare's hooves vanished as if she were never there, the scent of brimstone gone into the wind.

When the girl on the stallion passed the same rock, she panicked. She looked around frantically trying to find any sign of the elemental. Kicking the stallion into a run, she kept her eyes on the track for any signs of Mandy.

Suddenly her horse stopped and reared. She lost her grip on the reins and fell off the back of the horse. With an exclamation she hit the rocks that waited in the bushes below her, but it took only a moment for her to twist her head in fear. She watched all around her, waiting for the cause of the horse's fright.

"You are a very foolish girl," Shadowolf's voice said. Out of the air he and Mandy materialised, and he held his hand out to Deihlia. "I thought your brother had taught you better."

"I don't take lessons from Lastgorn," she replied, offering her hand so that he could pull her up. "And you promised to include him in everything you do."

"I promised I would not deny him his revenge," Shadowolf corrected her as she mounted her stallion. "That time has not yet come. Now why don't you head on home."

"No, I think I quite like this road," she said haughtily, looking at the landscape below her. "It serves as a becoming view."

"I don't have time for games," he said, putting his hood back up and riding forward again. "Go back before I make you go back." Mandy snorted in the stallion's face, which promptly caused it to retreat a few steps.

"Sure," she said, a sly smile creeping on her lips, "Should I tell Lastgorn it was you who left me to ride back on my own?"

Mandy stopped as Shadowolf tugged the reins. He looked up at the sky, which was meant for Bontu, and groaned.

"Very well, Lord," he said, and then turned his voice to Deihlia. "Just don't get in my way. Now get over here."

Deihlia was too excited to remark on his abrupt command and urged the horse beside them. He held her hand.

"Close your eyes," he said softly, and she complied.

The wind built up and surrounded them. Like a sheet falls softly over a bed, so wind covered them. And, like a broom sweeps the dust off a tiled floor, so the air swept them off the path and up into the air. They travelled over the peaks to the other side of the mountain, dropping down on another path that led directly down into the forest.

When they rematerialised, Deihlia gasped out loud as if she had been holding her breath. Her hand came to her neck as she rubbed it, looking up at Shadowolf and then the land below. She saw the tower of Le'Mar's Throne in the centre of the forest that once belonged to the elves. The topmost part of the tower just broke the fog that also lay over the forest.

"Why didn't you travel like that sooner?" Deihlia asked. Shadowolf answered with his silence as Mandy led him into the fog once again. "Oh; right."

She followed, her eyes watching for any sign of the dark lord's soldiers.

***

The barn-house was filled with men and women who felt freer than they had in a long time. The lights of the building shone brightly through the windows onto the rough, gravel road outside that led to a meagre village to the west.

The lights from the small village formed a small cluster on a hill that rose up to the dark lord's camps. Vast tents, barracks and camps spread for many fields in all directions between the village and the castle. Only the slightest din rose from the snores of the creatures that stayed within them.

And beyond these camps and the village with the barn was Le'Mar's castle. From there Le'Mar's highest officials stood guard. They looked beyond the cliff that fell to the Alcove of Light, watching for any signs of trouble within the fog, or for any approach to the castle.

Anuxis dismounted from Cerexus's back and bid him stay until his return. He left the scepter strapped to the hound and covered his head with the hood. His steps led up the grass to the barn and only when the light from the barn touched his toes did he slow his pace.

He walked into the huge doors that were taller than most homes he had seen. One or two of the fifty people in the barn looked his way; the rest chose to ignore him or were so busy dancing or drinking that they never had the chance to pay him notice. He saw a bar on the one side and chose a stool.

"What would you like to drink?" the barman asked.

"I'd like essence of Bazanah," Anuxis replied snidely.

"Uh...," the barman replied.

"Just give me a Bloody Petri," he said and the barman hopped away to make the drink.

"Haven't heard of Bazanah before," a man said beside him, taking the vacant chair. "As a matter of fact, I don't think I have seen you around here before. Are you a spy for our masters?"

"And which masters would that be?" Anuxis replied from beneath his hood. The drink arrived and Anuxis transformed his snout into a human mouth.

"Who are you?" the man asked, frowning deeply.

"I'm looking for someone," Anuxis said, licking his lips after taking a sip. "Someone the Crethans call a Creth-Angel."

The barn went silent. His voice had been soft, yet somehow the title has shaken them all to silence. Anuxis withheld a growl as he felt tension rise in the barn. His snout returned beneath his hood as he waited in edgy patience.

"If you're not a Crethan, then you have no business being here," the man said, walking back to join the crowd. Anuxis was now alone at the bar, his back to them. Even the barman had joined the others.

"I didn't know this was a private club," he replied, drowning the drink down his long mouth and licking his teeth from the taste.

"Why do you search for the Angel?" a woman asked.

"I have a business deal for her," he replied.

"Kill him," another man ordered.

Anuxis heard a growl behind him and a rush of steps. In the short time it took for the Crethan to reach him, Anuxis's thoughts were working in his mind. His mind was not on the Crethan that was now charging to kill him, but rather on another matter.

The Crethan jumped, his claws almost upon the back of

Anuxis's hood, when he turned in the stool and grabbed the man around his neck. The man hung in the air, his claws ripping the space between them.

"I see you have managed to control the curse that holds you," Anuxis said, frowning. The man's face had become a wolf's, his teeth trying to bite the arm that held it. The man's hands had also become paws with sharp nails, but the rest of his body remained human. "But you're not from my world; you're Celenic Crethans."

Anuxis dropped the hood from his head. The Crethans gasped and retreated to the far wall; even the struggling man in his grasp went still. Anuxis put him down on his feet as the man's appearance became human again.

"I don't understand," another man said. "Why haven't any of us changed into wolves? It's obvious you're a Creth-Demon."

A woman cried out, followed by a few others, as Cerexus entered the barn. Anuxis glared at him and the hound lay down on its belly, sulking.

"What you refer to as Creth-Demon on Celenic Earth is called *Haniegke* in its original form. The curse that holds you is called *Hieragke*."

"But who are you?" a lady asked.

"My name is Anuxis. My faithful hound and guardian of the Underworld that I rule is called Cerexus."

"So the dark lord employed you to...."

"NO!!" Anuxis shouted, and then constrained his anger. "Somehow, without my knowledge, my *Haniegke* betrayed me and took some of their *Hieragke* with them. By biting into Celenic humans, they put their essence in your blood. I guess they named you Crethans to distinguish between Celenics and *Hieragke*."

"What about the Creth-Demons, our masters?" the lady asked again.

"Those are the *Haniegke*," Anuxis replied, deep in thought. "Only I can make them. Those are the ones that betrayed me."

"So...," the barman began, "does this mean that you can take this curse from us."

The others started to murmur as the realisation dawned upon them.

"Your salvation comes at a price," Anuxis said carefully, "only to be negotiated with the Creth-Angel."

"My name is Angelicus," the lady that had spoken before said, stepping forward. "Why should I negotiate any terms with you, when it is your horror that stripped us of our freedom?"

"Because Shadowolf told me that you are the only one that would understand," he said, satisfied that the name made her eyes go wide.

"What are your terms?" Angelicus asked, looking Anuxis straight in the eyes.

"We seek one duty of you and the Crethans, and then I will free you of your curse."

"Let's go," Angelicus said, reaching for her few possessions. The other Crethans milled around getting their things also.

"No," Anuxis said. "You misunderstand me. In order for you to fulfil your duty, I need you to remain here."

THE BUTTERFLY PENDANT
CHAPTER FIVE

Chenesia stirred in the bed. She had just woken up, with no idea of whether it was night or day. The underground trees swayed in the air current that somehow flowed through the large Fairiwell. She stared blankly at the two ledges that both rose from the centre of one wall; the one led to the former entrance of the Fairiwell and the other to the exit to the forest.

The young elf that had rescued them earlier had left them to investigate the other entrance. Without a further word of welcome, he vanished up the long ledge, leaving Chenesia and Genewiu to wander the Fairiwell alone.

It hadn't been long before they both decided to rest for a while. Chenesia had barely laid down on the comfort of a bed she had found in the hollow of a tree trunk when she had passed out into a deep sleep.

Now that she was awake, she wondered just how long she had been out. Her body felt rested and her mind fresh, so she assumed that it had been a couple of hours. She stretched her limbs and yawned before leaving the comfort of the bed and making her way to a lovely looking fire.

"Hello there," she greeted the elf, thinking for the hundredth time that he looked familiar. "Do you know what time of day it is?"

"I would say it is three hours after midnight," he replied, offering a smile and a basket of fruit. "You slept for most of the day and all of the night."

"I was a little drained," she admitted ashamedly. "Has Genewiu risen yet?"

"Yes. I saw her go to the water holes for a drink and a wash."

"That reminds me. I will need to take a bath too." Chenesia

looked at him again, dying to place a name to the young elf's face. "Sorry for being so rude, but I'm sure I know you from somewhere."

"Yes," the elf smiled again, "our time together was but small, but I do believe I saved you from a heavy downpour not some four years ago?"

Chenesia screwed up her face, her mind racing back to that time, before enlightenment struck her.

"Sinor?" she moved closer to inspect his face better.

"That's right," the elf replied. "At least you remembered my name."

"My, how you've grown into a strapping lad...uh...elf," she corrected and then laughed. "Where have you been all these years?"

"Well, living in the forest most of the time," he replied, stoking the fire. "I was there during the last battle too, in Lard's Den. I saw you for a moment before the battle started, but I didn't get a chance to greet you."

"I'm sorry I didn't come looking for you," she said, dropping her head.

"That's ok," he said boyishly. "I heard that you had been kidnapped by Le'Mar, so I kinda figured you were busy once you escaped."

Chenesia sat quietly for a moment before something bothered her.

"Wait a moment. Why are you here, Sinor? Why haven't you left with the other elves?"

"How can I?" Sinor said, throwing the stick in the fire with a sudden outrage. He stood up, looking deep into the flames. "This is our forest. We should never have yielded it to that monster. And of all places, Eldor decided to return to the Elders."

"The who?" Chenesia asked, leaning with her arms on her knees, shifting herself on the uncomfortable log. She vaguely remembered Eldor's son, Lesan, mention that name sometime before to her.

"The Elders," he repeated. "It's the term used for the Eastern Elves on the Far Isles. They believe that they are mightier and holier than us."

"That's strange," she interrupted. "I never knew the elves were separated in that way."

"Why are you here, Chenesia?" he asked, looking at her. "The last I heard, you had vanished through a portal with that man."

"Shadowolf," she told him.

"Yes, him."

"Well," she said standing up beside him, "he's kind of the reason I'm here."

"I don't understand."

"I'm in search of something; well, someone really. Her name is Sorceress and she carried a pendant around her neck in the shape of a butterfly."

"The one with the pale blue skin?" Sinor said, and continued when she affirmed with a nod. "Yes, she was here after the war for about a month or two, with the few remaining members of what they called the Shadow Clan.

"But then, once they saw that Shadowolf wasn't coming back, they decided to return to their homes. All of them, except for Sorceress of course."

"Why didn't she return home?"

"There was a unicorn with them...."

"Ursula," Chenesia said.

"Yes, Ursula," he said. "She asked Sorceress to keep the pendant safe. There was a place that she asked her to go, in a forest on the beaches by Le'Mar's castle."

"The Alcove of Light," Chenesia said. Sinor got lost in thought.

"I seem to have lost touch of the things of the world down here," he said, looking around the Fairiwell. "Maybe it's time I leave. Would you mind if I joined you?"

"Of course you may," Chenesia smiled. "It would be an honour."

"Not much of an honour," Sinor said, looking down at his hands. The elf seemed repulsed by his own presence.

"Sinor," Chenesia broke his grim mood, "what happened to the fairdievells?"

"The fairies followed the pendant," Sinor said. "This was one of the reasons that Ursula asked Sorceress to travel to the Alcove. Apparently the forest was cut off from the fog and was better defended than the Fairiwell."

Chenesia nodded her head, glad to know in which direction she should head. She spoke again when a thought occurred to her.

"What were the other reasons?"

"She said that we should await Shadowolf's return," Sinor replied, his gaze vanishing between the flickering flames of the fire. "That's the only real reason that kept me in the Fairiwell for so long; it's because I had already refused to join the other elves that Ursula asked me to keep watch."

"Well," she said when he finished, and patted his back, "your purpose here is done then."

"Yes. It is time to move on."

Sinor threw the stick into the fire and left Chenesia alone. After a few minutes of his absence it became clear to her by the noise emanating from one of the abodes that Sinor was packing something for his departure. She remained by the warmth of the fire for a moment longer before she decided to find a pool to bathe in.

It wasn't difficult for Chenesia to find one of the pools. The warm moisture created by the rising vapour from the waters led her through clumps of trees and a dip in the floor. When she cleared three trees that stood close together, she saw that the ground sloped at a slight angle to a pool below her.

Once she reached the bank, she looked around for anyone that might have been able to see her. Even though it was only Sinor and Genewiu in the Fairiwell, she still felt inclined to make sure that no one else was there.

She gently pulled the shirt over her head. Her breasts tugged on the fabric for a moment, but fell back into place as she got it passed them and over her arms. While she removed the rest of her clothes, she indulged in looking at her breasts. It had been a while since she had just relaxed and took note of her body, but it seemed to Chenesia that they had grown in the past year. After mentally chastising herself for her silliness, she threw the clothes in the warm pool and walked in.

The water ran over her body like a smooth salve. She moaned softly in relief as the icy pains and aches of tension she had developed in the last few days seemed to melt away. She bent her knees and let the water cascade over her face and hair, running her fingers through the strands.

The dirt and grime swept off her body, staining the light blue of the water momentarily before draining away to an unknown place. From the perimeter of the pool, water flowed into the bath through various slits along the circumference. The water was warmer along these edges than in the centre of the bath where Chenesia now swam.

As was usually the case in the Fairiwell's pools, she needed no soap or shampoo for her hair. As she drifted on her back in the water, the surface just covering her body, the dirt and sweat were washed away into the water. She opened her eyes now and again to check the top of slope, in case Sinor or any unexpected person arrived.

It was on one such occasion that something caught her eye. It was indistinct and small and she had to stand in the water to make sure she had seen correctly. The water fell off her shoulders and breasts as she stood and she shivered slightly in the temperature change, but her gaze didn't leave the spot in the sand that had moved.

Chenesia turned her gaze to the right of the hill as a similar movement shifted the sand there. Even in the calm of the pool, she became fretful. The soil of the slope was shifting ever more, and soon sand started toppling into the pool. Chenesia grabbed the clothes she had intended to scrub clean and donned them quickly, the material sticking to her body. She ran up the slope, sand rolling over her feet and making them muddy.

When Chenesia returned to the fire, Sinor and Genewiu greeted her with bewildered frowns. She accidentally stepped on a small piece of red coal that had fallen out the fire and cursed loudly.

"Where are your shoes?" Genewiu asked.

"I must have left them at the pool," she replied. "What's happening, Sinor?"

"I don't know," he said, waiting for an assault, "but I would wager my life it's from that *KariemsaPh*, Darcwulf."

The sand shifted beneath them and Chenesia hopped about. The ground broke open in some places and black, worm-like bugs sprang out and crawled with unnatural speed towards them.

"What on earth are those things?!" Chenesia shouted, retreating to the fire.

"Leeches," Sinor replied, watching the fat slugs approach. "But they shouldn't be moving so fast. Whatever you do, don't....CHENESIA, WATCH OUT!!"

She had no time to turn. From the flames of the fire, three leeches rose and attached to her shoulders. Where they sucked into it, the shoulders became blue with lines spreading out like tainted veins under the skin.

Sinor ran forward and pulled them off hard. Chenesia's cries rang up into the Fairiwell, the pain striking her nerves and sending a stinging chill up her spine. When the sensation reached her neck she collapsed forward, Sinor barely stopping her from falling into the fire.

Genewiu trotted forward and Sinor pushed her onto the pegasus's back. He jumped up behind her slumped form, a shoulder pack strapped to his back. As Genewiu ran for the ledge that would lead them out, Sinor placed his elvin hands on Chenesia's shoulders. He spoke soft runic words, a green light pulsing from his palms into the bite marks.

The blue stains retreated from her spine back to her shoulders and gradually faded. Chenesia groaned as she sat up and rubbed her head.

Hardly a word was said when they reached the ledge. Leeches had broken out from the walls and were crawling over the walkspace of the ledge.

"Ride over them," Chenesia said sleepily.

"Or we can fly," Genewiu replied, and spread her wings from out under Chenesia's legs. She turned away from the ledge and began picking up speed. Leeches formed in their path, and Chenesia waited for Genewiu's hooves to trample on them.

When a hoof connected with a leech, a soft explosion sent her head into the trunk of a tree. Chenesia groaned again, her eyes unwilling to open where she lay slumped against the tree. Her ears rang softly as she pried them open. Fires were spreading through the Fairiwell and she squinted to see into the sharp light.

She watched carefully as one of the fires hit a leech. The leech cracked open into pieces with a soft bang. She watched the pieces fly to various spots; she watched the segments hit the ground; she watched as each segment mutated into a fresh, fat leech.

To her left Genewiu lay on her side, her wing trapped under her unconscious body. Sinor had gotten up already, and held a blue orb of power in his hand. Chenesia raised her palm in warning and was about to shout, but it was too late. Sinor hurled the ball of power at several leeches that were racing to feed on him.

Fire and explosions erupted as the ball killed the leeches. Sinor fell back as the leeches broke in many directions, the fires falling onto the closest leaves and trees. Every piece that hit the ground transformed into a new leech, just as hungry and deadly as the original bugs.

Chenesia ran over to Genewiu, joined shortly by the elf. The pegasus stirred and rose onto its legs.

"Can you fly?" Chenesia asked.

"I think so," she replied. "Get on."

They mounted her and she turned to run down a path between young trees. Leeches were breaking out from trunks, roots and soil in an attempt to feed on them. Genewiu tried to pick up speed but was severely hampered by the leeches on the ground.

"Hold on," she warned them. Chenesia held onto the mane of white hair, while Sinor grabbed her soaking waist. Chenesia screamed as Genewiu jumped into the air and landed hard on several leeches.

The resulting eruption sent them up into the air. Genewiu almost fell back to the ground again but manage to regain her balance and flapped her wings hard. They rose up in bounds until she could maintain a settled flight. After some minutes, they landed on the highest point of the ledge by the Fairiwell door.

Chenesia quickly dismounted and etched the fairy design given to her four years before by the fairdievells. Even though she had not done this often, the design appeared to be written in the archives of her brain. The door slid open, and they left the ruined Fairiwell to the explosive leeches. As the fire touched them, they exploded into many more fires and leeches, bangs resounding in the massive cavern that the three left behind.

Chenesia was sure that, if she ever returned to the Fairiwell, there would be nothing left of it.

PEGASI AND PEGATORS
CHAPTER SIX

Hargon's scruffy beard swayed lightly before his eyes as he studied the rough map. His short hands leaned on the table that was standing on the Sky Tier of Horlorn's Gate. Beneath his feet, a chair held him up high enough to view the layout of the landscapes on the scroll.

The map took up most of the table's surface. The corners of the map were held down by various weights. These weights comprised mostly of coffee mugs, breakfast plates and juice glasses.

Lucian rubbed his eyes from the morning's sleep, looking up behind Hargon and staring at the horizon. The dwarf with them joined his gaze and saw the sun rise over the low peaks of Dwarf Mountains to the east.

Soon enough, Anuxis joined them at the table. His eyes scanned the remaining food on the table and, seeing nothing fit for his appetite, decided he would find more appropriate food later.

"When did you get in?" Lucian asked, his eyes returning to the map.

"Sometime in the morning," he replied, yawning with his maws wide open and ending it in a soft, dog-like whine. His only attire was a belt that covered his thighs and groin with a cloth, and a large pendant that lay between his bulging pectoral muscles.

Trimistus walked from behind Anuxis and sat beside Hargon. His deep, black sockets betrayed no tiredness, but the red pulsing orbs within them were bleak compared to their usual flare.

"So have you had any deliberations as yet?" Trimistus asked.

"Well, I've marked certain areas," Lucian said, and everyone got comfortable around the table as he pointed with a pencil. "Before Chenesia left the Vale of Tigers, she informed me that she had spoken to her mother. Apparently Larnesia will be setting up a meeting shortly with the town captains and then with the villagers. If all goes well, we could have them moving to Horlorn within a month or two."

"That's cutting it close, Lucian," Anuxis said. Hargon and Trimistus looked at them questioningly.

"Close to what?" Hargon asked.

"How far is Horlorn to being equipped to hold the cities, Hargon?" Lucian said, trying to steer the conversation in another direction.

"We can be done within a month or two," Hargon replied. "Just in time for the......" The dwarf's eyes went wide as a realisation hit him. He remained silent, not sure if he should utter his thoughts. Trimistus looked at them, but Lucian returned to the map.

"I need it done in two weeks," he said, tapping the map with the back of the pencil.

"I'll go meet with the others," Hargon said, but waited for the Windfarer to continue. Lucian's pencil moved to Carmel.

"At some point we're going to have to meet with Carmel and the surrounding villages. Shado and I knew some elementals from there, and he was hoping we could rally some more fighters."

"I can do that," Trimistus replied. Lucian scribbled something in Carmel's area before continuing.

"The only other area of concern is Avalion," he said, tapping on the area. "I don't think Shado has broached the matter with his father yet, otherwise we would have heard about it by now. Let's hope the Degron stubborn will doesn't get in the way."

"Why would his father refuse?" Trimistus asked.

"I don't think Nighthale will want to instigate another war after our defeat in Eldor's Forest," Lucian replied. "He almost lost Avalion. I hate to say it, but if Le'Mar had held out his victory a little longer, Avalion would have been destroyed."

"I disagree," Hargon countered. "I have a feeling they held back deliberately."

"Why would you think that?" Lucian asked, his expression betraying his bewilderment.

"If Le'Mar destroyed everyone, who would he rule over?" Hargon said. Lucian thought on this a moment, his face blank.

"Think about it; he only wanted the elves out of the way. Now that they are gone, who can stand up to him?"

"It's a valid point," Lucian replied. "But then why attack Avalion at all."

"To show them that he does hold power over them too," Trimistus guessed. "Maybe to put Nighthale in exactly his current state of mind, in case the dark lord's victory over the elves wasn't daunting enough to stop Avalion from attacking."

Their thoughts drifted through their hazy minds while they stared at the map. Not even the dwarven footsteps behind them bothered Lucian until he was tapped on his shoulder.

"Your horse needs you," the messenger said.

Lucian got up from the seat and left the others. He walked to where Lancenat was being kept and saw that its face shone with a soft, white glow. He looked into Lancenat's eyes that were swirling with minute, purple stars and saw Chenesia's face. Lancenat's mouth moved with Chenesia's voice.

"Lucian, we've discovered where Sorceress might be," she informed him. "I can't talk long, as I think Darcwulf might be following us, but…"

"Darcwulf?" Lucian interrupted her. "You entered the forest?"

"We had no choice," she replied defensively. "The way was blocked by the entrance to the Fairiwell."

"What did you…"

"I don't have time to explain," she said quickly, looking left and right. "Someone is following us. I'm heading for Carmel and then the Alcove of Light. Listen carefully; there are pegators in the forest. I will contact you again if I run into trouble."

Before Lucian could stop her, the image faded, the glow dissipating from Lancenat's face and its eyes becoming brown again. Lucian stormed out of the stable chamber, pulling the stallion's reins behind him. It trotted to keep up.

"I'm leaving," he said, mounting Lancenat's back as Trimistus, Anuxis and Hargon turned to look at him.

"Where are you going?" Anuxis asked.

"Back to uPendus," he replied. "I have information for the pegasi."

"Oh!" Hargon jumped off the chair and ran towards him. "May I join you please?"

"Sure," Lucian said, pulling him up by his hand. The agreement was more in favour of not wasting time than the glittering ambition in Hargon's eyes.

The Windfarer spread his palm before him and summoned the wind. The air shimmered and burned before Lancenat, twisting into an elliptical portal. When the image of a snowy land was stable before him, he dropped his arm and raced Lancenat through to the other side. The portal vanished....

"It's.....very.....cold....here...." Hargon said after five minutes in uPendus, his teeth clattering beneath his beard.

"I thought dwarves were a sturdy lot?" Lucian laughed, shivering slightly.

"Doesn't mean that we're impervious to snow," Hargon retorted gruffly. He peeped from behind Lucian's back and looked at the land that they were entering.

They were riding between brown tree trunks that glistened from the snow on the ground. White leaves above their heads held flakes upon them. Hargon turned to look back, but he could not see anything but the surrounding forest. From the light in the sky he guessed that the sun was many leagues south.

The trees were not very high. It would have taken four men standing on each others shoulders to reach the top of the highest tree. Lucian had to duck sometimes to miss an overhanging branch, ones that lightly touched the tip of Hargon's head. Soon the dwarf forgot the cold embracing him, his eyes steadfast on the land so that he would not miss anything.

A movement to his left caught his eye. He twisted his head quickly, scanning the snow carefully. He narrowed his eyes and, just when he thought he could make out a shape in the snow, a sound to his right made him spin his head that way.

The wolves were large. Hargon was almost certain that the animals could comfortably rest their heads on Lancenat's back. The sky blue eyes shone from their white heads, their bodies barely discernible from the snow beneath them.

Then the forest opened up. The trees fell back and revealed a wide, flat land. From the top, the trees ringed the glade in an elliptical form. There were more wolves closer to them, but Hargon ignored them as he saw the pegasi on the other side of the field. Their immaculate coats shone as brilliantly as the snow. Some were stretching their wings in laziness while others waded around the snow-covered grass.

He easily recognised the white tigers. Their backs were covered with black stripes with a strange green hue to them. But there were other feline creatures he did not know the names of, and several large plump beasts with bulky ears.

"This place is wondrous," he finally breathed.

"Maybe Deyton can show you around while I speak to the queen," Lucian said.

"That would be wondrous," he replied, to which Lucian chuckled. They were approaching the herd of pegasi on the other side of the field. The horses became jittery the closer they came, but Hargon saw that they settled down once they realised it was Lucian.

"You spent two years here?"

"Most of it," Lucian replied. "The other times we spent doing research."

"Is this where you found Anuxis?" Hargon asked as Lancenat took the last few steps to the main pegasus before them.

"That is an entirely different story," Lucian said and dismounted, helping Hargon off. "Treya, queen of pegasi and fairest of horses; I salute you."

"Oh come now, Lucian," Treya replied, spreading her vast wings and curling them back at her side. "I think you've stayed long enough in our company to forego formalities."

"You know it's always an honour," Lucian said.

"Isn't that horse too large for a dwarf?" she asked.

"Dwarves don't ride much where I come from," Hargon said, and then added shyly, "your majesty. But a horse is quite uncomfortable for our height."

"Well your bravery has been told of by the camp fires that Chenesia, Shado and Lucian entertained us with for many a night," she said, looking down on him. He looked up at her face, only realising now how large she was. But the pride that swelled up within him made him feel taller than even Lucian. "You deserve your own mount. Cavella!"

From outside the pegasi herd a feline shape walked towards them. Its features were very similar to a tiger's, but he could tell from small differences that it was not one. It was thinner than most of the other felines, but he could tell by its muscles that it was not hampered by its lack of weight.

"Yes, your highness?" the female cat said after looking the dwarf up and down.

"This is Hargon," Treya said with significance.

"I am honoured to meet you," the cat purred. "I am Cavella, one of the few remaining jaguars on this earth."

"Show him around, get him acquainted with our land," Treya instructed. Cavella nodded and sat on her hind legs.

At first Hargon was unsure the feline would be able to hold his weight. He slowly approached Cavella's back, her head reaching just over his. When he was in position, she stood and he rose on her back. Suddenly the fear of his weight vanished as he felt the hard muscles of her back and legs that held him up. To her, he was as light as a grain of sand on a mountain. Lucian watched as Cavella left to introduce him to the animals he had never seen before.

"I take it you didn't come here to show him around, though," Treya said, leading him to a small groove between the nearby trees. Fireflies dangled from the tips of the branches, bearing an eerie light to the queen's den.

"No," Lucian replied gravely, sitting down on a clump of blankets that he and the others had used during their stay. He was glad they hadn't removed them yet. "I have received news of pegators in the dark lord's land."

"Singular or plural?" Treya asked.

"I'm not sure how many," he said. "Chenesia was very brief, but she was adamant that I bring the message to you. I wouldn't be concerned if she wasn't."

"I don't see the need for Le'Mar to keep the pegators in his land," Treya said, pacing up and down. "In his eyes, he has won the war. Unless....."

"Unless?" he asked when she didn't answer immediately.

"Unless he has offered them a haven in the forest," she

completed. "The land they lived in was stale and barren, not offering much in sustenance."

"Do you think Le'Mar will help them in attempting uPendus?"

"It's a possibility that has crossed my mind," Treya replied. "How far along is Horlorn's Gate?"

"Hargon has promised that they will try to complete it in the coming weeks."

"We're running out of time," Treya said meditatively. "But if we can have it done in the next two weeks it should give us some lead time to prepare."

"Let me return," Lucian said. "I will let you know when you can go to Horlorn."

They left the shelter of the den just as Hargon returned on Cavella. Lucian began laughing at the dwarf before he got a chance to open his mouth, for his eyes were large with excitement and his mouth was set in a huge grin.

"You should see all the animals!" Hargon lifted his hands to count them off his stubby fingers. "Cheetahs, tigers, pumas, wolvarynes, rhinos, elefronts...."

"Elephants, Hargon," Lucian laughed, "They're called elephants."

TAINTED THRONE IN
A FORSAKEN FOREST
CHAPTER SEVEN

He sat in his throne chair, staring out into the forest. His eyes scanned the ground below him. Could it be Shadowolf was in the throne already, after him or something else?

"I don't care how you do it," the man said, turning in his chair to look at the elementëls. "Find him and bring him to me."

***

Hargon rode onto the Sky Tier through the portal, followed closely by Lucian. The dwarves that were walking about turned their gaze upon him; they weren't sure if they should look at him in awe, or at the jaguar with caution.

Anuxis and Trimistus patted Hargon on the back, but the congratulations were short-lived as a dwarf scout ran onto the Tier from within the Gate. He gasped a few breaths before giving his warning.

"There are five riders approaching the Gate," he said. The others left their mounts behind as they raced for the tunnels.

When they reached the exit of the hill, the riders were almost upon them already. Three of them were men, their wavy hair glinting in the noon sun. Two were women, one with short hair and the other long.

Anuxis strode forward with his scythe to call them to a halt, but Lucian ran passed him when one of the faces became clearer. Trimistus soon joined Lucian, leaving Hargon and Anuxis frowning in the background.

The travelers jumped down and soon they were all embracing Trimistus and Lucian. Laughter erupted as the group of seven walked back to the Gate, leading the horses by the reins.

"Anuxis, I want you to meet some old friends of ours," Lucian said, pointing as he introduced each person. "This is Theroy from the college I once taught at. He was one of the best Feniseraat students I had, unrivalled in the art of the fire element.

"This is Lanel, Harmony and Nashela. They were all Aegledaele students in my Wind classes. Lanel and Harmony usually caught up to mischief with Shado."

"Well," Harmony said, blushing, "more Lanel than I."

"And this is Lord Treville," Lucian finished. "He was the custodian of the Gate during the last war."

"Pleased to meet you all," Anuxis greeted. "I am Anuxis and this is Hargon."

"Goodness," Nashela said. "We've heard tales of Hargon the Brave in the Blue Periwinkle, but I never thought I'd meet you. I thought you were just a myth that Simnab like to spread around."

"Your legend precedes you, little man," Lucian ruffled the dwarf's hair as they all began to walk inside.

"I'm not little," Hargon moaned silently, but chose to ignore it in light of his new fame.

Once they had passed all the familiar corridors and entered the meeting hall, Anuxis asked the dwarves to prepare a small meal for the travelers.

"You mentioned Simnab?" he asked Nashela when they finally settled down to drinks.

"Yes, he's staying at the Blue Periwinkle with his wife," she replied."

"Oh, he got married?" Lucian asked, smiling.

"Yes, to the landlady of the Periwinkle."

Lucian's face dropped. Images of Telgar buffeted his mind for a moment, although to him it seemed like several minutes. When his brother had introduced Lucian to his new wife, he and Telgar had had secret feelings for each other ever since.

But Lucian had already married, and when his brother had died it had been that much harder for Lucian to show his commitment to Kailan. Yet he had always managed to make sure Telgar was well and taken care of. Her loss for her husband had always outweighed the minute love she held for Lucian, and it had never amounted to anything solid.

He was glad she was married again, but a strange sadness took his heart. While the others told Anuxis more about Simnab, he realised it was because the duty of protecting her no longer fell on his shoulders, as abstract as it had once been. But another thought occurred to him, and he realised she needed protection now more than ever.

"Isn't Simnab a Crethan?" he asked, interrupting something Lanel had been saying.

"He's still human," Nashela said defensively. Lucian looked at Anuxis.

"Not really," he said. The former students frowned.

"Why not?" Harmony said. "Just because he has a curse....."

"It's more than that," Anuxis said. "Simnab was a general in my army of the Underworld. He was greater than what you call a Creth-Master. He held powers that held many envious, powers so great they almost rivalled mine."

"So, he's not from this world?" Treville asked.

"No," the wolf-man replied.

"That's why you knew about him when we first met you," Hargon said, thinking back. Anuxis nodded his head.

"Then why is he affected by the Creth-Demons?" Lanel asked.

"I heard rumours that he was going to start an anarchistic order," Anuxis said. "Many believed that Simnab could overthrow me and become the new lord of the Underworld. I sought him out and crushed him, taking away that power which I had given him. He was left under the control of one of the *Haniegke*."

"You say that with sadness," Lanel noted. "Did something go wrong?"

"Long after some of my *Haniegke* started vanishing with their servants did I find out that Simnab had never planned to overthrow me. All of his so-called disciples had merely created a fad and hoped that he would liberate them. Simnab, however, had proclaimed his loyalty to me and had refused to lead any such order."

"What did you do then?" Nashela asked.

"When I discovered the truth, I sought him out again," Anuxis replied, anger growing in his wolf eyes. "That's when I discovered that, not only was he not in the Underworld, but neither were my *Haniegke* or their *Hieragke*. It took me several Underworld months to find out where they had gone."

"And that's how you ended up here," Trimistus said.

"Luckily I met someone named Elgoth first. He led me to Shadowolf, who explained everything to me."

"What is your purpose here?" Lanel asked cautiously.

"To reclaim my servants," he stated simply, but Lanel could tell there was more.

"I don't care what you do with the Crethans," Harmony said, standing up and leaning towards him threateningly. "But we all love Simnab and we won't let you take him."

She stormed out of the hall towards the Sky Tier. Anuxis watched as the other new-comers glared at him and followed her. Anuxis then looked at Lucian. The Windfarer stood and patted him on the shoulder.

"Welcome to Celenic Earth."

***

It had been easy enough for Shadowolf to leave Mandy behind on the fields. The Froth Huns would mistake her for one of their mounts and not bother. If they did bother, they would quickly become suspicious of her odd behaviour and refusal to be led away from the other horses.

Deihlia's horse, however, was a more difficult matter. There were hardly, if any, normal horses around and it wasted Shadowolf an hour trying to find a group to put it with. Deihlia's apologies were muted once they entered the throne that once belonged to Eldor, partly in awe and partly in fear.

The trees ran in circles around the throne. There were mixtures of tall, thin trees and short, wide ones. In the centre rose a magnificent oak, stairs spiralling around the trunk to the top and various other trees in the near vicinity.

In the vacant land not occupied by trees were many of the dark lord's creatures. Pits of lava that were never there before boiled through onto the corrupted soil. Vines and ferns which looked hideous to touch or smell choked the remaining elvin foliage, leaving nothing of the ancient heritage.

"How are we going to get in there?" Deihlia asked despairingly. Her eyes marked each of the beasts either slumbering or doing something in some of the few tents that were staked to the ground.

"Sometimes I wonder what the point of his conquest was," Shadowolf said, ignoring the question. He leaned on his mottled staff. "They aren't building a meaningful civilisation for themselves like in the Dark Boundary. They just sit here, waiting to die."

"Perhaps these are the reserves in case you return," she offered.

"I'm not that important," he replied, looking for a way in.

"Oh, then why are we here?"

He looked at her sarcastic expression. Her arms were crossed and she tapped her left foot in mock seriousness. He laughed and shook his head, peering once again into the woods.

"It's time to announce my presence," he said after a moment.

"What!?" she exclaimed, and he held his hand over her mouth. "After we just spent a day moving with stealth?"

"Well, we can either waste time fighting through this lot," he pointed at the beasts, "and announce our presence anyway, or we can travel on the wind through the fog and get there faster."

She stared at the creatures one more time before nodding. He moved closer and held her in his embrace. His arms locked around her waist and hers moved around his neck.

"I could get used to this," she said, looking naughtily into his eyes.

"Behave," he said sternly as the air shifted around them. Their bodies became transparent as they drifted into the breeze that carried them into the fog above the beasts and camps. He twisted around the trunk of the tree, making his way up the throne to one of the openings....

The man watched as the window before him became obsidian black. An image of a breeze moving through the fog up the throne oak appeared on the glass.

"Come to me, dear brother," Darcwulf said. "I'm waiting for you."

They blew through the crack of one door and materialised on the inside of the tree. Deihlia let go of Shadowolf as she squinted down the dimly lit corridor.

"Don't these guys need light?"

"Not when they have a *KariemsaPh*," he commented. He noticed that the glass cups along the walls held flickering white flames, fires that he knew would not die unless commanded by the Firephoenix that had created them; or if he was killed.

They walked down the corridor, Shadowolf's eyes alert for any movement and his aura sensitive to any powers being invoked. His energy was kept to a minimum within the core of his soul, ready to be pulled out like a whip from his gut.

He stopped when he sensed power from one of the rooms above them. He looked at the ceiling of the corridor, eyeing it warily.

"What's the matter?" Deihlia whispered. She coughed softly as her throat tightened from tension.

"Let's move," he replied, leading her around a bend in the passage and passed several doors. When he turned at the last door to their left, she saw that a yellow light flickered from his pupils. "This one."

His eyes returned to normality as he jerked the door open. Within was a staircase that rose up, turned left, then continued up to the next floor. They ran up, Deihlia barely keeping up with his broad steps, and entered the door to a large dark room.

Deihlia held her hand before her mouth, trying not to vomit. Shadowolf's eyes flared open, his aura burning blue around his body, as he walked to the table at the end of the room. The sheet of the table was covered in blood, and a strange insignia was painted with the blood on the wall above the table.

Two dead candles stood on either end of the desk. Shadowolf placed his palm above one. The candle had not been lit for at least a month. Deihlia looked at the blood runes on the side walls, becoming more desensitised to the horror as she spent more time studying it.

Shadowolf stepped back, his eyes narrowed on the symbol, when the heel of his foot dropped below the floor level. When he turned to look at it, he saw that there was a pit falling through the floor. The square pit was rimmed by blood crusts where it was joined to the wooden floor boards. It was only then that he noticed the blood trails leading from the table to the pit.

"I don't understand," he thought out loud. "Neither Darcwulf nor Le'Mar showed any tendency to this kind of evil."

"The last time I felt these chills were when Lastgorn explained demons to me," Deihlia said, turning to him and staring at the hole.

"Of course," he said, "demons. That must be it." Suddenly, Shadowolf's staff vibrated softly in his hand. He frowned. Deihlia interrupted his thoughts.

"Do you......."

Shadowolf looked up at Deihlia's sudden silence. She was coughing soundlessly into the air, holding her throat with her hand. He realised the air in the room was getting thinner, but because he was a Windfarer it hadn't really affect him. *Enodhim*'s automatically compensated lack of air with the element created from within their souls.

He ran and caught her as she fell back, his staff knocking on the floor as he dropped it. Without thinking he put his lips by hers, breathing the air from within him into her. His lips were so close to hers he could almost taste them. Shadowolf put his palm on her right breast and felt her heart beating. Moving his hand to her abdomen, he felt the rise and fall of her breathing.

He looked at her, but could sense the air still becoming thinner. Just when he thought that she had fallen into a sleep, her lips moved.

"It's....getting...cold.....," she shuddered and crawled into his arms, her head resting on his chest. Her skin became pale before it took on a blue tint. From Shadowolf's body, warmth rushed against her. Fire burnt from within his soul until it provided enough warmth to return the colour to her skin.

"Come on, Deihlia, stay with me," he whispered, looking around for the source of the power. He knew Darcwulf was a *KariemsaPh*, but not a *Sadgi*. Was it the dark lord? Had he finally find him?

He looked with shock at Deihlia as her head tilted back and her breath came out in rasps. The skin above her lips became white as her body dehydrated. A tear that had formed rolled down to her ear and evaporated.

Shadowolf plunged his lips onto hers, opening them wide. Slowly, he let fresh water trickle from his soul, through his tongue and into her mouth. She gasped, her eyes opened wide in panic. She put her hand on his cheek and sucked gently on his tongue, letting the water nourish her dry body.

Just when he thought it was over, he watched as the skin on her body started to peel away. The pupils of her eyes turned white as she slumped back once more. Her body turned brown and then dark red as the skin pulled back in on itself. Shadowolf looked around desperately for the enemy, pushing some of his power into his eyes.

Four elementël beings stood by the wall of the door staring down at them. Each one's ethereal, man-like form consisted of their element and power flowed from their outstretched palms.

Shadowolf looked at Deihlia. He could feel the pulse of her heart weaken. He could return the earth back to her body and restore her, but he wouldn't have been able to fight them and hold off the elementëls' powers.

"Forgive me, Deihlia," he said. He closed his eyes and the blue of his aura became white, bursting into the room. Within a fraction of a second, the light vanished and only Deihlia lay on the floor. The power in the room simmered as the elementëls became visible. They floated over to her body. Her eyes sprang open.

The elementëls stumbled back as she rose. In a fluid motion, she somersaulted over Earth and wrapped a coil of water around its neck. Twisting her body she flung Earth into the wall. The elementël splattered against the wall, leaving stains of soil and dents off rock in its demise.

Power thrummed into the room again as the elementëls powered up. The room shook slightly as fire blazed from Fire, water broke out to flood the room from Water and Wind erupted into a hurricane.

Deihlia became air and flew through Fire. Her hand passed into its abdomen, her body rolling over the floor with the elementël. Power surged through her arm into Fire. With an unnatural howl of exploding flames, Fire cried out as the air filled it. At first the flames flicked higher, raging out of control. But, as the wind slowly overpowered Fire, the flames simmered down into nothing.

Water smashed into Deihlia's head from behind, wrapping around her body. Deihlia turned on the spot and sank into the water, becoming liquid herself. When she reached Water, a sword of metal erupted into the elementël. Water stepped back, writhing in pain, as the sword became a twisting tornado of earth and metal. Water shred apart, molecules of liquid flying across the room and down the pit until Deihlia stood from within its death and watched Wind with a malicious grin.

The elementël vapourised into the air, moving for the door. Deihlia moved straight into Wind, her body flaring with fire, as she ripped the air apart. Brimstone floated down the staircase, the elementël's hoarse rasp echoing into the stairwell.

Deihlia moved back to where she had lain, and gently lay down again. She closed her eyes and her aura glowed softly. Shadowolf emerged from her skin, shining for a moment before becoming solid.

"I guess we can rest for now," he said. He faced his palm to the door. The door closed hard and became part of the wall. When he was done there was no door, but only the four walls. He sat down and checked on Deihlia. She was fast asleep, but healthy. Putting his head against the sidewall, he looked at the bruises on his arms and abdomen.

"Ah well, the wounds will heal," he murmured as he closed his eyes, picking up his staff that lay beside his leg. "Just like they always do, hey Nelnar?"

TROUBLE AT THE PERIWINKLE
CHAPTER EIGHT

"This should be interesting," Chenesia commented as the trio passed through Carmel. The sun was setting in the west, but they could not see it behind the peaks of Bentley Strip. The road they rode on was already dark, only illuminated by the home and shop lights that they passed.

Genewiu walked calmly to the stables of the Blue Periwinkle. The stableboy, one that Chenesia didn't recognise from the last time she was there, stuttered greatly when he saw the pegasus and the elf. Genewiu made her own way to one of the stables where stacks of hay and a trench of water were.

"Will you come in later?" Chenesia called. "You know Telgar doesn't mind."

"I'll greet them in the morning," Genewiu grumbled, her lethargic voice barely carrying to Sinor and Chenesia's ears.

Chenesia and Sinor entered the Periwinkle. The tavern didn't hold many customers that night, and the few that were there seemed very bored. But Chenesia knew that the tavern would fill up once the night had settled. The entertainment only really started two hours after sundown when the band played and the evening waitresses arrived.

From a bar opposite them Simnab waved, holding a mug and drying rug in his other hand. His smile was the broadest she has seen in a long while and she strode in to greet her old friend.

"So," he said, "I see you bring the elves with you on your return."

"Not quite," she replied. "This is Sinor, an old acquaintance of mine that once saved my life."

"Ah, we all have need of those," Simnab joked and shook

Sinor's hand. "I'm...."

"Simnab," the elf said, looking around cautiously. "Yeah, I know."

"Relax, Sinor," Chenesia said, feeling the tension fall from her shoulders as she visibly became more relaxed, "Telgar's establishment is one of the best on Celene. Speaking of which..."

Telgar put down the dishes she had been holding and rushed over to greet the girl. They embraced each other for a lengthy moment before Chenesia introduced her to Sinor.

"So I take it by your return that....uh...," Simnab spoke softer, "that those who left with you have also returned?

"Yes," she said, noticing secretly that Telgar's face lit up in joy. "Everything is well, although you might want to start packing."

"Why!?" both of them exclaimed, before Telgar ushered them away from the customers. "Go wait in the house so we can speak in private."

Chenesia and Sinor left the glaring stares of the customers and exited the tavern through a back door. They crossed a patch of land and entered Telgar's home. Chenesia found some matches on the window sill and lit a few of the candles and lanterns. Sinor meanwhile busied himself observing the three-room cabin.

"Have a look at this," he said. Chenesia joined him in looking at a hand-drawn picture of Telgar and Simnab's wedding. Simnab stood on the left, holding Telgar's hand. Her right hand held a bouquet of flowers.

Their observation was disrupted when the door opened. They both jumped, fearing that it was Darcwulf. Chenesia sighed, her hand on her fast beating heart, as Telgar put some plates and warm drinks on a low table.

"You two are jittery," she said, sitting down on a single sofa. They sat in a double seater adjacent to her. "Mind sharing what you've been up to?"

Chenesia told her everything that had happened to her since returning from uPendus. Telgar listened quietly as the girl regaled her with the tale, only interrupted by Sinor at short intervals. The only details Chenesia left out were the Heart of Tigers and what their plans were.

"Do you think anyone followed you here?" Telgar asked, sipping her tea.

"I'm not sure, but I would keep a look-out," Chenesia replied.

"What of the elves, Sinor?" Telgar asked. "Do you think they will return?"

"I have serious doubts, unless Shado can convince them somehow," he replied. "If Elgoth was with them in uPendus, then I don't think it would be too much hassle."

"Why do you say that?" Chenesia asked.

"Elgoth is still given high appraisal among the elves," Sinor replied. "He is Masara's son, after all."

"I heard what happened to Masara," Telgar said. "Simnab told me Le'Mar killed him and trapped his soul in that staff of his."

"It was horrible," Chenesia concluded, her hand shaking and causing the tea to spill. She took a cloth and wiped the floor clean.

"Well, we've been talking for hours now," Telgar said, standing up. "Why don't you get some rest while I help Simnab? The tavern should be bustling with people now."

"Telgar," Chenesia called, and she looked down at the girl. "At some point in time, someone from Horlorn will be coming to Carmel to recruit warriors and elementals for a battle."

"A battle?" Telgar asked, sitting again. "I thought there might be more to this than you looking for Sorceress. Why will we be fighting again when Le'Mar hasn't been bothering with us?"

"Can you honestly live like this for the rest of your life?" she asked, and then leaned forward to bring the matter closer to home. "Can you let your children grow up in this world?"

Telgar thought about it carefully, looking out the window into the darkness, knowing that part of that darkness was the fog.

"Oh, you sly little girl," she smiled. "You're right. But can we afford another loss?"

"We won't lose," Chenesia said. "Not if I find the pendant. The question is, will Simnab join us or stay here and protect his family, especially since...."

"Since he is a Crethan," Telgar finished the silence. "I reckon Simnab will want to be at Horlorn, to assist in the fight and to stay away from me. Whatever he decides, so will it be."

Telgar rose and left the cabin without another word. Chenesia was lost in thought, her words and those of Telgar still playing in her mind until a picture on the far wall caught her attention.

She rose and walked to the picture. It was in an ornate pine frame and Lucian's graphitic face stared up at her from it. Chenesia's stomach felt odd as she held it, emotions building up inside her.

Those emotions were not for the Windfarer, but rather for someone she still held dear in her own heart. She turned to look at Sinor, almost wishing it was that person. But the elf frowned at her and smiled, and Chenesia put the picture back. She would see him again, even if she had to kill every orc in the land to do it....

Later that night, while the light linen blanket laid over Chenesia's soft skin, beasts moved towards the entrance of the tavern. Chenesia's mind was deep in sleep when the orcs shoved the doors of the periwinkle open to allow the *Goudlem* in.

Sona Nelma surveyed the late customers with a smirk on her face. The purorcs followed her in. Unlike the hurorcs, which Le'Mar had created by mixing dead humans with orc blood, these orcs were as pure as they came, unadulterated with human DNA.

They slumped and walked forward awkwardly. Even though Le'Mar's reign had lasted two years, they were still unaccustomed to walking into a human settlement without their heads being lobbed off. They hissed and snorted at the men and women that sat at the tables, their fear retreating and hauteur increasing with each step.

"I believe," Sona said to Telgar once she reached the bar, "that a girl entered your tavern with an elf and pegasus."

"I don't know who your source is," she replied sarcastically, "but no such girl came by here."

"Oh really?" Sona asked and turned to one of the customers. "Have you seen an elf or pegasus tonight?"

"Elf or pegasus?" the man scoffed. "And here I thought I had too much too drink."

The crowd laughed. Sona smiled appreciatively and tilted her head to the side. As the man saw her hand become a rock, Sona smashed the back of it into his face. The man soared over two tables and crashed into one by the wall. The other clients near Sona stood up and moved away from her.

"Someone tell me where they are," she said, her voice as dangerous as her eyes, "or I will destroy this tavern."

No one said a word. Their loyalty to Simnab and Telgar rose above their fear of Sona. If she did not tell her, then neither would they.

A crash sounded from outside the tavern in the direction of the cabin. Telgar tried not to react, but her anger betrayed her.

"What are you doing to my home!?" she shouted, moving around the bar to face Sona.

"Worried are you?" Sona asked, putting her face against Telgar's. "Hiding something are you?"

"No, but I don't want my home destroyed!"

The men in the tavern moved forward, picking up chairs and smashes glasses to use against the orcs. The purorcs unsheathed their rusty blades, moving towards the men. Sona closed her eyes, calling upon the earth, and they all stopped as the ground shook.

Vines broke through the floorboards and hit the men back. Dust from the ceiling fell over them as thorny vines rolled over the outside and wrapped the tavern in its tight embrace. The walls began to creak inwards, the planks cracking.

A growl flew over the bar and Sona landed hard on her back. She stared up at the drooling, white teeth of a wolf, his human body pinning her to the floor vines she had summoned.

"Release this tavern," Simnab growled, "or I will kill you right now."

"You don't scare me, Crethan," Sona said calmly. "I hold the power within me to control you."

"You have earth, but you don't have fire," he replied. "I still serve the dark lord, and so this establishment serves him."

Sona still looked into his face without betraying any fear.

"Remove the vines now," Simnab said, bringing his teeth closer to her face.

"They're not anywhere in the back or in the cabin," an orc voice said to her from the rear door.

Sona sighed and focused her power. The vines pulled back into the earth, releasing the tavern from her grasp. Simnab stood up and let her rise, his face becoming human again.

"If I find that you are aiding the girl in any way," she said as she led her orcs out of the tavern, "then I will return and have your head for supper."

Telgar ran out the back and made for the cabin. By the door were two dead orcs, their heads lying further down the grass. She checked the cabin and saw that Chenesia was indeed gone.

"Are they safe?" Telgar asked as she emerged from the cabin into Simnab's arms.

"I don't know," he replied, "but I can smell their trail heading west. My guess is they heard the commotion and left for the Alcove."

"Ok good," she said and left his arms to enter their home. "Please close the tavern. I'm going to bed"

She looked down at the orc corpses by the door and then at Simnab's mouth. There were black stains on his lips.

"And brush your teeth before you come to bed."

ALLIES AGAIN
CHAPTER NINE

Deihlia stirred, her eyes opening slowly to the gloomy darkness. The lids felt heavy and sticky as if she had walked into cobwebs of honey. She rubbed the tips of her fingers over them and cleaned away the residue of sleep.

They were in a kitchen of some kind. Marble basins and steel tables, one of which she was laying on, furnished the room. Rusted cooking instruments hung from their hooks on the rails. There were three windows on the far wall opposite her, but the other walls were closed by racks of herbs and strange spices she had never seen before. Between two racks on her left was the sole door to the kitchen.

Shadowolf stood by the central window, looking out on what she assumed was the forest. His hands were clasped behind his back and from the angle that she saw him it appeared as if his thoughts were elsewhere. She moved softly from the table, trying not to alert him. Shadowolf, however, turned before her feet even touched the cold tile floor.

"Sleep well?" he asked her, smiling comfortingly.

"How long have I been out?" she asked.

"Give or take five hours," he replied. "I think we are well into the early morning hours."

"Did you get any rest?" she said as she joined his side.

"I woke up moments before you."

She looked out of the window he had been staring through. There was no forest or outside view, but rather a dark passage that her sight could not pierce. She cupped her hands on the glass and tried to make out any objects, but the effort was fruitless. Darkness and two walls gazed back at her.

"What did you do to me back in that altar room?" Deihlia asked him, not daring to look into his eyes.

"It's called transmigration," he replied. "The technical definition is the ability of a spirit or soul to transfer bodies."

"Says who?" she wondered out loud.

"Elgoth," he said. "If you practice hard enough, your soul can take your body with it."

"I don't really understand," Deihlia said. "I don't really remember much of what happened though. It felt like a dream."

They stared out the window in silence until Shadowolf approached the topic that had been on his mind.

"Do you now understand why I wanted to do this alone?"

"Not really," she frowned looking at him. "Was I that much of a problem?"

"I couldn't fight the enemy without worrying about you," he said. "It's just easier when the only one I have to worry about protecting is myself."

"Well, life isn't that easy," Deihlia said. "Besides, you got to kiss me."

Shadowolf had opened his mouth to reply to her first comment, but closed it upon the second. In small ways, Deihlia was how Shedaaij had been in the beginning, finding ways to be close to him. While he was in thought about the matter, she smiled at him patiently and he realised that she was being facetious.

"Why hasn't Darcwulf attacked us yet?" she said.

"I think he is waiting for me in the throne room," he replied. "He probably has something prepared for me there."

"Alright, so should we go find him?"

"Yes and no," Shadowolf replied. "You can come with me until we get to the throne room, but thereafter I want you to find a place to hide. What I must do, when I confront him, must be done in isolation."

"Alright, dear mystical one," Deihlia laughed. "So let's go."

Shadowolf nodded and led the way to the door. They entered the passage and walked around the kitchen until they were on the other side of the three windows. A small flame sizzled from the top of his staff, breaking the intimidating darkness.

The walls were streaked with trails of green blood. Shadowolf sniffed the air, narrowed his eyes and then continued forward.

"What is it?" Deihlia asked, whispered despite the lack of enemies.

"Smells like orc blood," he replied. "But why would he kill his own soldiers?"

"Traitors?"

"For whom?" Shadowolf countered.

They reached the end of the tunnel and found a door. Shadowolf gingerly turned the knob and it opened freely. Curtains rose before them to a vast ceiling above. Wooden beams and worn supports creaked, shivering dust down on the large stage that they entered.

Memory flashed across Shadowolf's eyes as he looked down at the broken sheets littering the stage. This was where Lord Eldor once kept meetings with the high elves of his forest. Lower down, beyond the stage, the elves used to gather and have their meals and chat away while the higher elves planned and discussed the dark lord.

Now all that was left of the congregation were the sheets that once were the tents of the elves. There had never been one speck of dust or any crack in the walls to mar the immaculacy that personified the elves. What Shadowolf saw before him could only be an example of the neglect that humans practised upon their homes.

"Deihlia," he finally said, his face not betraying his anger, "remind me to clean my room when I return to Avalion."

"What?" she said, and stumbled as she following him down the stairs from the stage.

They left the hall and entered more passages. From past experience, Shadowolf knew that the passage to the left led out of the tree. They walked right, following a tunnel lit by his staff. Deihlia saw the sconces on the walls that once lit the way, but that now lay dormant on the wood.

They entered a circular courtyard. The perimeter was laid with stones and brick, surrounding yellowed grass and a single apple tree. Shadowolf had seen such a courtyard in one of the elvin villages before, where a unicorn statue had stood in the centre. But the tree was real and the apples whole.

Deihlia stood amazed, looking at the tree. Her eyes sparkled as she stepped forth her hand raised to grab one of the apples. Shadowolf watched her, feeling that perhaps the tree wasn't as good as they would hope. He struggled against his will, his aura visibly shifting from yellow to deep purple and back to yellow again.

"Deihlia," Shadowolf muttered. But his word was lost on her as her fingers lightly teased the skin of the apple. She pinched the meat of the fruit. It felt strong, healthy, and her desire to taste the apple overcame her. She grabbed the apple, pulling it down.

Shadowolf had been a moment from ramming into her with a tackle when she disappeared from his view. He fell on the grass and was up in an instant wielding his staff. Swords crossed by his neck. He slowed his breathing, his heart racing less in his chest, and searched for Deihlia. She was being held by a wall to the right.

And the apple was swaying from side to side, still attached to the tree.

"Do not eat of that tree," someone said in a grating voice. "It will poison your body, and corrupt your soul. It feeds on the darkness."

Shadowolf saw by the wan light of his staff that something crawled within the trunk of the tree. The cylindrical shapes moving under the bark looked like serpents, and a soft hiss confirmed his suspicion.

"Reveal yourselves," Shadowolf said.

Three men and four women stepped forward. Deihlia was being dragged before one of the women towards him, but Shadowolf still didn't know who was behind him. As the group drew closer, their human skins become grey and hard, soft cracks replacing the wrinkles.

"I don't believe it," Shadowolf said. "Is Dren with you?!"

"You knew Dren?" one of the men said.

"Once upon a time," he replied, staring at the gargoyles. "I didn't know there were so many of you. My name is Shadowolf."

Some of them widened their eyes, while others audibly gasped. The bulkiest of the group grinned joyously and motioned for the swords to be removed.

"You've returned?" the gargoyle asked uncertainly.

"Dren?"

"No," he replied sadly. "Dren was my brother. I am Glasden. Come, join us."

The gargoyles walked out of the courtyard, and the further they walked from the light the more human their appearance became. Deihlia stared from Shadowolf's side, watching them leave.

"What do we do?" she asked.

"We follow."

As they passed the tree, Deihlia looked at the apple again, but Shadowolf gave her such a hard tug on the elbow that she didn't have a choice but to continue.

They eventually reached a quiet den within the tree. It was more pleasant there than in any of the other places they had been. A fire burned softly in the enclosure, and Shadowolf and Deihlia sat upon logs eating the rations they had been handed.

"Food is hard to come by in the forest," Glasden informed them. "But we would rather not leave the forest at this point."

"Why not?" Deihlia asked. "The fog will surely protect you from the sunlight."

"It doesn't," he replied. "The only thing the fog is good for is controlling the people's powers and making sure they are not abused."

"So why do you remain here?" Shadowolf asked, not completely convinced.

"Where shall we go?" he asked in return. "Do you know of any suitable accommodation from the light?"

"Dren had many...."

"That was Dren," Glasden said, a tone of anger deep in his voice. "Haven't you noticed yet?"

Glasden turned his back, and Shadowolf saw that it was smooth. There were no wings protruding from his back, only the muscles that bulged from the stone.

"I don't understand," he said. "Fornoren, Masnen and Dren all had wings."

Some of the gargoyles around the den stopped what they had been doing and stared at him. One woman's eyes filled with tears before turning away from his gaze.

"They accepted who they were," Glasden told them. "We refer

to them as the superior gargoyles. We, however, never accepted this curse placed upon us."

"How did you become cursed?" Deihlia said, resting her chin on her palm, her elbow leaning on her leg.

"That is a tale I do not wish to tell at the moment," he sighed. "But if we had accepted the curse sooner and become like the superiors, we would have been able to assist in the Battle for Eldor's Forest."

"How so?" Shadowolf asked.

"While you were in the land of the dragons," he said, "Dren came to us. We were skulking around in Lasglow, not wanting to accept our fate and remaining in our homes. Many of the villagers became suspicious about our habits, not answering the doors at day and awake at night. They began to fear that we were aVampyere.

"Dren approached us one night and showed us the Lapis Pin that he wore. He told us that Masara could provide us with a means to travel during the day with that pendant. So I asked him what the catch was.

"Dren said he was on a quest to find you. I don't know how long he searched, but we denied his request. What did we care about a boy lost to the dragons?

"But he nevertheless approached us again, before the Shadow Clan entered Eldor's Forest. I believe you were in Lasglow at the time. He told us everything that had happened and asked us to join you."

"And you refused," Shadowolf stated, wondering why he hadn't noticed Dren's absence.

"What could we do without wings?"

"You have arms!" Deihlia jumped up. "My goodness man, look at your strength!"

The shade in Glasden's face drained. Shadowolf pulled her down gently onto the log beside him. The gargoyle hid his face in his stony hands, his shoulders shuddering.

"Glasden," Shadowolf said, "if I were to offer you all a chance to fight at my side, would you accept it?"

The gargoyles went silent again, but this time gathered behind Glasden's back. He lifted his face from his palms, streams of water rolling down his cheeks. His muscles creaked as he rose, his chest standing out in pride.

"We will fight," he replied, clenching his fist in the air. "We will fight!"

"Good," Shadowolf said, hearing Deihlia giggle in excitement beside him. "Then I want you to leave the throne today."

Glasden dropped his fist, and the other gargoyles similarly dropped the joy in their expressions.

"Where shall we go?" one of the woman asked.

"Just north of Dwarf Mountains there is a large structure built in the hill known as Horlorn's Gate. Do you know it?" After they all nodded their heads, he continued. "Speak my name to anyone there, and they will provide you with a home."

"Very well," Glasden said, and indicated that the others prepare. "Till we meet again."

"Till we meet again," Shadowolf agreed, but then stalled him. "I have one favour to ask before you leave."

"Anything."

"Keep Deihlia safe until my task is done."

"What?!" she jumped up again, looking down at him. "You said I could go with you!"

"I told you I must face Darcwulf alone," he replied.

Shadowolf rose and looked her straight in the eyes.

"Wait here until I return with my brother."

THE GUARDIAN OF THE STAFF
CHAPTER TEN

Shadowolf approached the entry to the throne room, lowering his power so that it could not be detected. He blinked calmly, breathing at slow intervals as he played with the air through his fingers for a moment.

Someone sat in the black swivel seat behind the ornate table, looking out the window over the forest. Shadowolf couldn't see any part of the body except the arms that rested on the arm rests, and the hand that held the staff.

"I've been waiting for you," said a very familiar voice. Shadowolf looked around for Le'Mar, but there was no sign of the dark lord. Shadowolf stopped by the desk, leaning on his staff.

"I hope I am well received," he replied candidly. Darcwulf spun in the chair and faced him. His eyes pulsed red and his expression was blank.

"So the mighty hero has returned," Darcwulf said, flaring his arms out in mock glory. "Do you like what we've done to the world?"

"It lacks a certain dignity, I'll give you that," he replied, pretending to be impressed.

"I'll take that as a compliment. Tea?"

"No thank you."

"So tell me, why have you come to visit your dear brother?" Darcwulf bore into Shadowolf's eyes with his own, but Shadowolf kept his soul closed.

"Well I thought that, once you're done with this façade, you could come back home with me and prepare for the war against Le'Mar."

"You speak boldly of your plans," his brother replied, a frown creasing his bald forehead. "You have no fear that he will hear you?"

"I fear none but the Lord," Shadowolf said plainly.

"Ah yes, of course," Darcwulf spat on the table, "ever the vindicator. When do you ever remember me having any regard for Bontu?"

"Possibly the reason Le'Mar could take you so easily," he remarked.

Darcwulf calculated him, looking him up and down.

"I know you want the staff," he finally said. "I've known for a long time. Le'Mar told me someone would come for it one day."

"I don't need the staff," he said, his eyes filled with sincerity, "I only need you."

"So I am to be just another pawn!" he shouted, standing from his seat and walking around the desk to put his face near Shadowolf's. The two staves were close to each other, curls of lights twisting around the timbers as they repelled each other. "Just another member of the infamous Shadow Clan."

"The Shadow Clan is no more," he said, wiping the spit off his face. "And rather a pawn for good than evil."

"Matter of opinion," Darcwulf said. "So take the staff."

"I don't want the staff," he said again. Darcwulf tried to shove the staff into him, but Shadowolf stepped back. Darcwulf stared at him and then the staff, confusion covering his face.

"Well if it's really me you want," Darcwulf finally concluded, "come and get me."

He stamped the butt of the staff on the concrete floor and a wall sprang up. The wall pushed Shadowolf back. He stepped back, waiting for the wall to stop and watching it turn in circles. When it finally came to an end, he realised that he was standing in the passage he had used to enter the throne room. The door was before him again.

"Why does it always have to be this hard?" Shadowolf muttered to himself, and opened the door. He walked into a circular corridor, facing another wall before him. He turned to the left and walked around, hearing pounding footsteps from behind and ahead of him.

Shadowolf knew, before the full body of the beast entered his view that he was in for a big fight. The three Ma-Wreths stopped and watched him as the two behind him slowly caught up. His staff vibrated in his hand.

"No, not yet," he said to it as the beasts charged for the attack.

As the lightning-fast fist plummeted down on him, he jumped back and landed on his hands. He flipped over and let his feet land on one of the arms that were swiping at him. The arm was about to retract and if he had waited a second longer would have fallen to the floor. He twisted and smashed the staff into the beast's face.

The Ma-Wreth wailed in pain falling to the floor with face in hands. Another fist came down upon him and connected with his cheek, sending him sprawling across the floor. With the elegance of an eagle, he curled his feet beneath him and stood up in mid-sprawl.

It was easier now that the five were ahead of him and not surrounding him. He started running towards them, fire building around his skin as he ran up along the wall. Shadowolf twirled the staff on his left, the wall beneath his feet, when the first Wreth smashed at him. The wall collapsed where it made contact, and Shadowolf landed on the floor smacking the flaming staff into the Wreth's backs.

Leaving the beast roaring with a black line on its back, he ducked under a heavy blow and dodged another. He caught an arm in the centre of his staff and danced around, twisting it into an awkward angle. The passage resounded with the snap of the elbow and the beast howled out.

He released the elbow, but not in time to stop another blow. The fist hit the fiery chest and Shadowolf flew back again, his head and back slamming into a wall. He groaned and stood up, killing the fire raging around his body and become water instead.

Shadowolf raced up again, and this time he let a fist hit him. Water sprang out his back, but he twisted his body around the arm and yanked the shoulder out. The Wreth's head crashed into the wall. Its body collapsed into a heap, the life failing it as blood trickled down the hole in the wall from its neck.

Instead of sending the others running away in fear, it only enticed them more. His staff vibrated again, but he ignored it, focusing rather on the Wreths. He ran straight into one of the beasts, the water soaking its chest and face.

The Wreth held its arms out, inspecting the water. The liquid became boiling hot, and soon fire broke out on the skin. The beast screamed and cried, dropping to the floor to try and roll the fire out. But the fire burnt relentlessly, turning the skin into char as the Wreth died and wailed its last note.

The fire rose from the body and became human again, the staff held firmly in his right hand. The Wreths breathed deeply, considering their next move. It seemed to Shadowolf as if they weren't contemplating retreat as much as how to kill the man.

The three Wreths attacked at the same time. Feet and arms slammed into him, his feet dragging on the ground as he slid backwards but refused to fall. Shadowolf stopped and struck the end of his staff along the wall. A wave of rocks and vines slid long the wall and exploded when it was by them. They held their arms up helplessly as the rocks broke over them, the vines clinging around their wrists and pulling their arms apart.

When the dust subsided, Shadowolf walked forward. The beasts were hanging by their arms from the walls, struggling against the constraints. They looked down at him fiercely, but he offered them a soft smile.

"Maybe next time," he said, walking through the hole in the wall created by the Wreth that had smashed it.

He entered another circular passage, facing another wall. He could tell by the angle of the turn that the circle was smaller, and guessed that Darcwulf waited for him in the centre. Walking forward, he placed his palm on the wall, ready to break it out, when something in the wall disturb him.

Shadowolf stepped back. The wall was bubbling profusely, joined by the floor beneath his feet. He steadily backed away, waiting for whatever it was to emerge. The staff rattled again, but he shook it.

"I said no," he said, eyeing the bubbles carefully. "It's not time yet."

Leeches broke out of the floors and walls. They moved crazily for a moment, seemingly blind, but then crawled at incredible speed towards his feet. Shadowolf summoned a rock and threw it at one of the leeches.....and then was flung back as a huge explosion rocked the passage.

He groaned again, lifting his head to watch the massacre. Fire was raging everywhere, but he noticed that as one flame touched a leech, the bug would explode into many fragments. He moaned in desperation as each fragment became a fresh leech that exploded in the fire to repeat the cycle.

Leeches broke out of the fire and raced towards him. The remaining leeches remained in the fire, breaking into hundreds of pieces that chased after him also. Shadowolf ran in the passage, thoughts and options passing through his mind. The bugs were catching up though, and soon the light of the fire was reflected on the walls ahead of him. Leeches left the fire to chase him from the front.

An idea entered his mind. He became wind and floated into the air, rising above and beyond the fire to land on the other side. As the leeches entered the fire, they exploded and blew the walls out on either side. Shadowolf lurched on his feet as the ceiling gave in, stones and wood falling on his head.

When the passage stabilised, he saw the leeches charging for him again, but the fire was out. The roof and wall had fallen over it and extinguished it. The leeches, however, were still strong in numbers. Shadowolf cursed under his breath and ran along the wall again. The bugs followed, crawling at a speed that was unnatural.

When Shadowolf reached the breach in the wall, he jumped and formed a rock in his hand again. He turned in the air, became wind, and hurtled the rock at the first leech he saw. The leech exploded, fire raging out behind it as the other leeches erupted, and the inner wall burst out in a large avalanche of rubble.

Even in his wind form, Shadowolf was thrown through a wall and crashed in his human form against the entry door. Shadowolf shook his head, almost losing consciousness, as the fires raged from the inner circle to the outer. The Wreths suspended to his left cried out as the fires consumed them. Shadowolf closed his eyes, the fire surrounding his body.

He leaned on his staff and stood in the raging blaze. There was not one part of the throne room that was untouched. He watched as fragments of leeches spurted all over the place, but the fire was so hot and wild that they exploded before they could form again.

Something rose from the centre of the room where he had thought Darcwulf would be waiting. It was burly and tall, taking up the space from the floor to the high ceiling which was at least triple Shadowolf's height. As it emerged from the fires, he could see horns above its head and eyes that stank of the deepest brimstone. It roared out loud, it huge mouth revealing stalactites for teeth. Its mane was rippling with fire, coursing like veins over its brown body.

"I'm impressed," Shadowolf said. "You demons get uglier every time I meet you."

He whipped his staff around and stood in a fighting stance. The demon stamped towards him, fury emitted from its eyes and mouth. The staff rattled harder than ever in his hand and Shadowolf sighed.

"Alright then!" he shouted and threw the staff before the beast. "You handle him."

The staff transformed in the air. The mottled wood became fur and twisted into an animal shape. Teeth and eyes were borne from it, the grey fur mottled with white clinging to the strong paws that landed on the fiery floor. Nelnar growled deeply at the demon, baring its teeth in a deathly grin.

The pet that grew up with Shadowolf was much huger than when they had last been in the forest. Its shoulders met with Shadowolf's shoulders. He had been glad that he no longer had to bend down to nuzzle his neck into Nelnar's, and he could stand up straight to look into its eyes.

Shadowolf watched as Nelnar jumped into the demon's belly, ramming it down to the floor. They rolled on the ground fighting furiously as he walked passed them to where he assumed Darcwulf was.

Darcwulf walked out of the fire with the staff in hand. His body was made of fire too, preparing to face his brother in combat. Shadowolf turned his body into wind, untainted by the billowing fire around them.

"I thought Nelnar was dead," Darcwulf commented, anxiety evident in his voice.

"Apparently, a Wolvaryne is not that easy to kill," Shadowolf said. "When I reached uPendus, he was waiting there for me."

"Interesting," Darcwulf replied. "You know, I'm not as ignorant as you believe."

"What do you mean?" he replied as they circled each other.

"I know you still have Ruben-Willow inside you," his brother said, and Shadowolf smiled. "You would never forsake your sword."

"There are too many things you don't understand yet," Shadowolf said. "I will not fight you with Ruben-Willow."

"Then how will you defend yourself?"

Shadowolf let the fire curl into his right hand. It formed into the shape of a sword. He added some earth power to the element, hardening the blade until the steel glinted in the light.

"Oh, but you are resourceful, aren't you?"

The staff became a sword of fire in Darcwulf's hand, the flame complimenting his burning pupils. He charged forward and attacked.

Shadowolf deftly stepped to the side and blocked the blow. He moved as swiftly as the wind, sliding the blade along his own and kicking Darcwulf's leg down every time he lunged forward with it.

When Darcwulf plunged the sword directly at his heart, he curled his own sword around it and twisted it onto the floor. The staff-sword clanged on the ground and it transformed back to its original form. Shadowolf let his blade return to the fire and raised his palms in a bare-handed fighting stance, smiling softly.

Darcwulf attacked. Shadowolf curled his hand to grasp his wrist, but Darcwulf smacked it down and pinned his hands around the back of Shadowolf's neck. Pushing his head down, Darcwulf smashed his knees into Shadowolf's face, ramming it hard the fifth time for good measure.

Shadowolf stumbled back, his mouth bleeding despite his wind form. The ceiling crashed onto the floor behind him as his brother approached him again. They exchanged a flurry of blows, each receiving some damage before another hard crash resounded behind them.

They looked around and saw the demon and Nelnar rolling towards them. Looking at each other, they both raced for the window that had blown out a long time ago. Darcwulf held his hand out and the staff flew to his hand. They made the window and jumped, Nelnar and the demon plummeting over them to the ground far below them.

Even while falling, Darcwulf attacked Shadowolf. Shadowolf panicked as the staff neared him and ducked, careful not to let the wood touch him. He opened his hand and his own staff appeared into it. Distantly, they heard the demon crash onto the forest floor.

Staff clanged against staff as the two battled, the owners not bothering to resist against the pull of gravity. Fire and wind twisted around each other, blow raging against blow. Darcwulf flung violently at his brother, and when Shadowolf ducked his arms flew out wildly and out of control.

Before the staff could return, Shadowolf struck his windy hand into Darcwulf's heart. His brother cried out as Shadowolf's aura flared out in a white, blinding light that lit the dark sky of the morning. Deihlia gasped from the forest floor where she waited with the gargoyles as the ball of light fell to the earth.

Darcwulf passed out and the fire dwindled. The light pulsed through Shadowolf's arm into Darcwulf's heart. He looked passed his brother's body and saw the ground not so far below them. With a quick expulsion of energy, wind broke into the earth and the ground exploded around them, forming a bowl of sand above which they floated.

Shadowolf let them float to the ground, holding his brother in his arms. The staff of Falgar fell out Darcwulf's grasp to the floor.

"Darcwulf," Shadowolf called softly. "Darc, are you alright?"

Darcwulf's eyes fluttered a moment before opening. He stared around the bowl for a moment and then looked up at Deihlia and the gargoyles at the top of the rim.

"Talk to me," Shadowolf pleaded. "Let me know you are ok."

Darcwulf looked into his eyes, guilt and anger still foaming beneath the surface. But when Darcwulf smiled, Shadowolf knew that he was just fine.

"Nanoo nanoo."

PART THREE

HORN OF MASARA

THE MIGHT OF THE AXE
CHAPTER ONE

Lucian stared down upon the land below the Sky Tier. There was nothing in particular that interested him about the green fields, but his mind drifted over the months to come. He could almost see the warriors shedding blood over the lawns, the glint of steel in the light of torches and the bodies falling from the force of the elementals.

His thoughts were momentarily disturbed when hands closed on the rail's edge beside him. Lucian looked up into the canine eyes of Anuxis, which held the same blank, meditative gaze. Lucian looked at the fields again, trying to envisage a glorious victory.

"How long before they arrive?" Anuxis finally said, the morning sky becoming a soft orange as the sun approached the horizon.

"They should be here within minutes," Lucian replied. "It would have been quicker through a portal, but Treya felt they should rather fly in."

"Perhaps they wanted to warm their wings up," Anuxis offered. "The temperature differs tremendously from uPendus."

"Valid point," he replied.

"When will the others from uPendus be arriving?"

"In a week or two, once Treya is satisfied with the arrangements," Lucian replied, and then smiled. "She can be very picky."

"I'm just glad that the dwarves finished the Ground Tier so quickly," Anuxis commented. "A week and a half ahead of schedule."

"Hargon mentioned something about Gallon sending the remaining Vale's dwarves and the one's within the mountain here," Lucian said, frowning. "We will have to place them on the Ground

Tier too."

"Because of their inability to jump from the higher tiers?" Anuxis jibed.

"Yes," Lucian replied, "that, and its practicality. The armoury there is sufficient for all their weapons and mechanics."

Something stirred behind them and they turned simultaneously. The air started to shimmer in an elliptical manner and a portal appeared. Lucian grabbed the staff leaning on the rail and Anuxis summoned his scepter into his hands.

The portal became more concrete and fire broke out around the centre until a whirling vortex of flames raged before them. Out of it walked Darcwulf, black staff in hand, his bald head shining in the light of the flames. His old serpent sword hung faithfully at his side. His eyes were also burning, his hands gripping his staff tensely.

"So, this is what you were planning?!" Darcwulf shouted, baring his teeth out at them in defiance. Lucian waited in anticipation, raising the wind slightly. Cerexus ran around the portal, sliding on the tier until he stood beside Anuxis.

Darcwulf's expression changed as he blurted out with laughter. The fire of his eyes died until he looked at them through his natural green eyes and stepped away from the burning portal. The fire of the portal also died to be replaced by a soft blowing breeze.

Shadowolf stepped out of the portal with an apologetic grin on his face. Lucian and Anuxis relaxed uncomfortably as he was followed by a girl unknown to them, Mandy and a few men and women.

"I told you they wouldn't be impressed with your humour," Deihlia said, crossing her arms and shaking her head.

"Sorry," Darcwulf said. "It's been a while since I had a reason to laugh."

"You better get inside," Shadowolf said, seeing the sun's upper rim breaking the horizon. The men and women nodded and entered Horlorn's Gate.

"Who are they?" Anuxis asked

"They are gargoyles," Shadowolf said, and pointed at one of the men. "That is Glasden, Dren's brother."

"Unbelievable," Lucian muttered and then frowned. "I thought they had wings?"

"So did I," Shadowolf said, then looked up past Lucian's head at the sky. "Now that's a beautiful sight."

Darcwulf, Anuxis, Lucian and Deihlia turned as one to look at the rising sun. Winged creatures flew across the diameter of the light. Their silhouettes crowded into the sky until the sun was blotted out from their sight. Shadowolf gaped in awe at the army of pegasi.

Someone on Ground Tier was waving to the flying horses. The pegasi broke off the formation, with the exception of the leader, and Shadowolf had to raise his hand briefly from the returning sunlight.

Treya landed on the Sky Tier and tucked her wings in. Lucian introduced her to the others, while Shadowolf introduced Deihlia.

"Excuse us," Shadowolf said. Lucian nodded in understanding as he and Darcwulf left the crowd. The others made for the dining hall for breakfast while the two brothers slipped away to the elemental quarters.

Shadowolf parted the walls until they reached the elemental courtyard. The artificial light shone upon the trees and leaves, a soft wind beckoning to Shadowolf's call. They walked through the courtyard until he called a halt.

Darcwulf lifted Falgar's staff horizontally on his up-turned palms. He focused his energy into it and the staff broke out into flames. The fire roared softly until the last of the staff vapourised into the air with it.

"It is done," Darcwulf said, turning to Shadowolf.

"Do you need another staff so long?" he asked.

"No," he replied, unsheathing the serpent blade. "It's about time I get properly acquainted with my old friend. Which reminds me; where is Ruben-Willow?"

Shadowolf smiled at his brother, but chose not to answer. He turned around and they walked across the courtyard together in silence.

"…and then there was this large explosion and we eventually saw Shadowolf and Darcwulf falling from the throne!" Deihlia was saying in exasperated tones when the two finally joined them in the hall.

"Where was Le'Mar?" Lucian said, having waited for their return before chancing the question.

"He is not on our earth," Shadowolf said, sitting down and helping himself to a plate and dishing scrambled eggs, sausage and toast. Darcwulf followed suit.

"That explains how you travelled by portal from the fog without causing alarm," Lucian commented. "But where has he gone?"

"He mentioned a conquest with the Gemetrashef," Darcwulf informed them, pouring a warm drink. "He's been away for three months now. He also cautioned me to watch out for my brother, in case he decided to make his traditional biennial return."

The group laughed around the table. Shadowolf's smile took on a sad undertone as he realised that he missed Nelnar sitting by his feet waiting for food. He thought fondly of the staff now strapped to Mandy's saddle.

"How is Crystal?" Lucian asked suddenly, and Shadowolf's face shone again.

"Crystal?" Darcwulf asked after swallowing his mouthful.

"My daughter is well, as is her mother," Shadowolf replied, realising that Deihlia must have told them about her.

"Shedaaij is back?" his brother asked, forgetting his food for the moment. "You have a daughter?"

"We have so much to catch up on," Shadowolf laughed.

"I knew she was pregnant, but I never heard any news," Darcwulf said, staring at his plate. "Even during the times I visited your father's kingdom on Le'Mar's orders, there was never any mention."

Darcwulf went into an uncomfortable silence, staring at his food still. Shadowolf turned his gaze upon him, chewing the eggs with a deep frown.

"What's the matter?" he finally asked when Darcwulf's face went pale.

"Fransiska," he replied. "I never found out what happened to her."

"Oh," Deihlia said, reaching over the table to hold his hand. "Don't worry. She's on the Far Isles with Ursula apparently."

"That can't be. The elder elves never allow a human to live among them on the Isles; except Masara of course."

"It has something to do with a siren power she has," Deihlia said, reaching for her glass. "Lastgorn explained it to me, but I didn't really get it."

"It probably caused problems in Avalion," Shadowolf said. Darcwulf started eating again, lost in thought.

"Well, well, well," someone said behind Shadowolf, and he turned to look into Lanel's face. His mind swam with excitement as he jumped up to embrace his old school friend. He greeted Theroy, Harmony and Nashela with just as much joy.

"Mourna must be sleeping still," Shadowolf said, referring to the girl that had always been part of their small school group. But Lanel and Nashela looked at each other before replying.

"Mourna got married," Lanel said, and Shadowolf almost dropped the glass he had picked up. "She met some guy in Lasglow and they hooked up."

Nashela gave Lanel a supportive smile and twined her fingers in his, giving him a kiss on the cheek. Shadowolf sat down, not sure how much news he could take all at once.

He knew Lanel had always been protective over Nashela since her home had been destroyed in Shenama, and even when he had met up with them again in Horlorn's Gate two years before he had sensed something between the two of them.

But the reality of it still shocked his mind. Lanel, Nashela and Harmony were now questioning him about his travels, but he decided that he did not wish to go over it again. He was about to say just that, when Deihlia cut him short.

"Well, you see, it began when we travelled the tumultuous mountains of ...." Shadowolf let her regale them with their adventures. He excused himself and indicated silently to Lucian and Darcwulf that they follow him to the tier outside. He spied Trimistus rising from a far table and joining them on the way out.

"Good to see you again, lord Danaka," Shadowolf teased when they were standing on the tier.

"Good to be back," Trimistus replied. "What are your plans?"

"I will be heading back to Avalion in a moment," he said, turning to Darcwulf. "You can stay and rest if you wish."

"Not a chance," Darcwulf replied. "I'm with you."

"Alright. Lucian, how long before the quarters will be ready?"

"Gallon said that the Avalion quarters will be ready within the week," Lucian replied. "Lanel will be heading with lord Treville back to Carmel to recruit more warriors. The Carmel quarters should be ready by the middle of next week."

"I haven't met with Treville yet," Shadowolf said, looking down.

"Don't be overly worried," Lucian said, noting the concern. "Treville has told me that he has no desire to reclaim his rule of the Gate and leaves it in our hands."

"That's good to know," Shadowolf nodded. "And the Vale?"

"Chenesia's mother sent us an eagle," Anuxis replied. "She agreed that their warriors will join us within the next two weeks. We can have quarters ready for them by the end of next week."

"Is it a good idea to take all the defences away from the cities?" Darcwulf asked.

"Le'Mar has no reason to attack them," Shadowolf said. "If, however, he is such a coward, then I will challenge him myself."

Darcwulf went silent, seemingly contemplating something, but Shadowolf interrupted any commentary.

"I need to leave," he said, and then put his hand on Lucian's shoulder. "Don't forget...."

"I haven't forgotten," he replied quickly. "Once things have settled down here, I will be on my way."

"Very well. I..."

This time a different noise interrupted him. The sound of coarse wheels grinding against stone and rock came from the entrance within the Gate. The group ran from the tier and joined Deihlia, Lanel and Treville at the end of the corridor, almost bumping into a wheel-barrow.

"Oh, my apologies," a dwarf said, and pushed passed them. In his barrow were coal and iron. He walked until the tier and then sighed, walking back to them. "Wrong tier again."

Lucian frowned and walked to the entrance tunnel after the dwarf, followed by the others. A quarter way down the widened tunnel, they found a rough door frame on the left wall. They stared down the hole and saw the dwarf push the barrow up a ramp into a large, steel bucket.

"Wait!" Lucian shouted as they ran down the passage to the bucket. "Where did this come from?"

"What?"

"This?!" Lucian indicated the bucket.

"Oh," the dwarf said, looking around. "Lord Gallon instructed the dwarves to construct rail systems to all the tiers. It helps us transport all the material in order to get the work done faster."

"Can we have a look?" Treville asked.

"Of course."

The group of seven climbed into the bucket tentatively, afraid they would rock it down the rail. Yet the bucket was stable, flinching not for a moment. When they were seated on the rough, wooden benches along the sides, the dwarf released a catch and the bucket rolled down the rail.

Even when the ground levelled out, the momentum of the bucket kept it running through the passage. Other passages branched off from the one they travelled through, but the air whipped through their faces as they continued straight.

The dwarf pulled back on the lever slowly and the bucket slowed down. When it was once again at a standstill, the dwarf leaned over the side and turned a vertical crank. They watched as the rail they had just ridden on broke off from the passage they had left and slotted onto another track heading off into a passage on the right.

"They never cease to amaze me," Treville said, shaking his head.

The dwarf knelt down and fiddled with a catch on the floor of the bucket. He pulled it up and a steel rod lifted up with two handles. When the mechanism was in place, he held the two handles and turned them over and over.

As he turned the handles, the wheels starting moving back the way they had come, but towards the right passage, gaining momentum until they were rolling down the track again. The dwarf pushed the rod down again until all that was visible was the catch on the floor.

It didn't take them long to reach their destination. The bucket came to a halt again when they were by the Ground Tier. Shadowolf and the others climbed out the bucket, swaying slightly on their feet as they approached the room before them.

At first, they shied away from the heat that was breaking through the entrance of the room. All concerns fell away though when their eyes beheld its contents. Furnaces and dwarven mechanisms churned away as axes were made. Steel edges glinted in the furnace lights and wood was being lathed along the sides.

Axes of all shapes and sizes, even axe-blades fixed atop long staves, lined the walls on all sides. Dwarves perspired and hammered away at steel. It took a long moment before Shadowolf saw men working towards the rear of the chamber. The one man he recognised crossed the room, joined by Hargon and the jaguar Cavella.

"It's been a long time," Mannius Saphin said. "I heard you looked after my cousin quite well."

"Skywolf did her fair share of fighting, believe me," Shadowolf laughed. "I see they managed to get you to help with the weapons."

"We wanted an elemental 'punch' added to our axes," Hargon replied. "It's become obvious that the war will be based on the elements."

"So when Gallon asked Hargon if he knew anyone," Mannius continued, "he thought of the infamous Shadow Clan and visited your father."

"And he directed them to you," Shadowolf finished.

"Well after your father saw the effect of Ruben-Willow, he decided it would be for the best," Mannius replied, looking on Shadowolf's waist for any sign of the sword.

"So show me around your workshop," Shadowolf said, deliberately ignoring his prying gaze.

DISPUTE IN THE FAMILY
CHAPTER TWO

It was by mid-afternoon that they were finally able to leave the Gate. Amidst several farewells, Shadowolf opened a portal to Avalion. With Darcwulf and Deihlia by his side, he rode through the portal to Saphin Vale so that Deihlia could return home.

Darcwulf brooded in silence as they rode through the Vale to the main road that would take them up to Degron Core. Darcwulf stopped when they reached the road, however, and looked at his brother through squinting eyes.

"Do you feel like ale?" his brother said, raising his hand to shade his eyes from the sun.

"Sure," Shadowolf smiled, entering the road. "We can get some in the Banqueting Hall."

"I was hoping we could visit a pub here," he replied, nodding to one past Shadowolf in the Vale. "Once we reach your father's castle, I know you will hardly have a moment to yourself."

"Very well," Shadowolf frowned, and turned Mandy to follow him to the tavern down the hill. Several of the Vale inhabitants looked up at Darcwulf in consternation, their fears only assuaged when they realised that Shadowolf rode beside him. They dismounted at the stables behind the tavern and then entered the establishment.

Applause surrounded them as they walked towards a vacant table. The crowds cheered the musicians on the stage who were dressed in beautiful, dark suites similar to those of the aVampyere. The lead singer wore a beautiful midnight blue dress which sparkled in the dim light from the windows.

At the back of the stage was a drummer with a set of drums and cymbals. There were two guitarists, one holding a type of guitar he had never seen before. Another two had violins, and a few around the stage had other instruments he had also never seen before.

"That must be one of the largest music groups I have seen," Shadowolf said, sitting down and ordering two Periwinkle ales. Darcwulf considered them for a moment under a deep brow before commenting.

"This one has become quite popular," he said, twining his fingers on the table before him, "and I think they're called 'Evorcent'."

"What a name," Shadowolf replied. He felt an energy surrounding the stage, and it took him a moment to realise that it was elemental in nature. "They're using the elements? I thought it was forbidden in the fog?"

"You forget," Darcwulf smiled, "in Le'Mar's absence, I was the governor of powers. You must see what this band is capable of. It really is unheard of."

Shadowolf raised his brow, but humoured his brother with a smile. The ale arrived just as the crowd went silent. The singer, whom he picked up was called Emily from the dying cheers, drank water and placed the glass on an empty chair before walking to the edge of the stage.

Everyone went quite and the musicians had their instruments at the ready. Shadowolf was entranced, waiting for the moment that they would start. The atmosphere shimmered with tension, and he wasn't sure if it was from the elemental powers on the stage or the crowds' excitement.

An additional musician walked up on the stage and sat by a long, narrow instrument that Shadowolf couldn't see properly.

"It called a fingerboard," Darcwulf said to his frowning expression. "Delivers a sound….well, you'll hear."

Shadowolf felt the power rise from the fingerboard musician as it passed through his hands. When the musician's fingers landed on the keys, sound broke out around the tavern in a way that Shadowolf had never experienced.

Shadowolf attuned his hearing and tried to work out how such a small instrument could deliver an amplified sound like it did. It seemed as if the power of the elements carried it out to the audience. The sound was like a chord he had once heard from a guitar and, as the musician lifted his fingers, the remnants of the chord resonated along the walls until it finally died out.

Still, the crowd waited in silence. They waited for Emily to begin singing, and even Shadowolf couldn't deny that he longed to hear how her voice would sound from the amplified atmosphere of the stage.

"They call it 'elementicity'," Darcwulf told him in the small intermission.

Her voice broke in several, short moans as the musician played notes from the fingerboard. Her voice carried well as his fingers slid elegantly from key to key. The drummer dropped the tips of his sticks on the drums as the song began, and the crowd cheered again.

In the verse leading up to he chorus, the song played out in a mellow manner. She sang of how the world grieved, lost to the darkness that they could not forsake. Along the soft sounds that the amplified guitars now added, her words told of many that had tried to save them and failed. As they neared the chorus, the drums grew softer until it was almost inaudible; and then the chorus broke over them like a thunderstorm.

Shadowolf felt the power stream over him. It electrified his nerves and it felt like he was going to explode with the energy he kept hidden in his soul.

She sang high, of how the world was waiting for the one they would call their leader. The guitars played with fury unheard of, and the guitar he didn't recognise played deep bass notes. Even when the chorus flowed into the second verse, they continued singing with passion and anger, alternating with sadness and omens where necessary.

She sang the last chorus, pleading that heaven send them a hero, that light break away the darkness that held them. And all at once, all instruments stopped as she ended her last note.

The crowd tore the silence with their shouts and joy. Shadowolf turned to Darcwulf, his nerves excited and shocked at the same time.

"What do you think?" his brother asked.

"It's....new," Shadowolf said, unsure of how he felt. The excitement and tension rode his veins like eagles tearing a river open to catch its prey. But he could not deny that the song held appeal to him.

"That song has become a favourite," Darcwulf said.

"It's called 'Saviour'," the waitress commented as she refilled their ale.

"Listen, Shado," he said as the band played a gentler song. "I know there are things that can't be forgiven, but..."

"All things can be forgiven, Darc," Shadowolf replied.

"Be that as it may," he said, looking him in the eyes, "I know my previous servitude to the dark lord does not permit me to ask..."

"Just ask me."

"Ok," he said, leaning back in the chair, "Why did I have to unite the staff with the chamber, and why are you planning this war against Le'Mar?"

Shadowolf calculated Darcwulf with his gaze, considering how much of an answer he should offer.

"There are several answers," he finally replied, deciding to give his brother only as much information as he thought necessary. "The first I can give you is that I have discovered that I have to kill the *Sadgi* in Le'Mar before I can confront him."

"I don't understand."

"You don't need to," Shadowolf replied bluntly, and was not dismayed by the hurt he saw reflected in Darcwulf's eyes. "When I battled you in the forest, I could have killed you, brother. But I chose to save you instead. That is the difference between Le'Mar and I."

"Ok I think I know what you mean," Darcwulf nodded. "But you're not really answering my question."

"Maybe if you clarified the question," Shadowolf replied, trying not to sound sarcastic.

"At the Gate, you told them that if Le'Mar attacked the cities you would challenge him yourself," Darcwulf said, leaning forward again. "Why prepare such a large force, when you can just fight Le'Mar yourself?"

"There are things you don't understand about a *Sadgi*," Shadowolf said. "If Le'Mar and I expended our powers in battle, we could destroy this world."

Darcwulf kept his gaze steady, waiting for a better answer.

"Say I manage to defeat him," he said, trying a different tact, "what happens to the orcs and Ma-Wreths that are left behind. They will not join us. They will not live among us."

"Won't they?"

"Will they?"

"I believe that they would," Darcwulf replied honestly. "I believe they want peace just as much as we do. They don't want to die."

"And how do I separate the sheep from the goats?" Shadowolf said, resting his arms on the table. "Who says another dark lord won't rise or be delivered by the Gemetrashef to lead the dark armies against us once again?"

"What aren't you telling me?" Darcwulf asked. Shadowolf stood and dropped some coins on the table.

"We will be taking this world back from Le'Mar," he said staring down at his brother. "And that is my final say in the matter."

Shadowolf knew before Mandy brought him through the Degron gates that the discussion with his father was going to be a lot more difficult. Darcwulf rode silently beside him, and he wasn't sure if it was through anger or his own personal thoughts.

After stabling the horses and making their way through the castle, they found Nighthale in the courtyard below the bedrooms. He sat on a blanket with Shadowolf's mother, Shedaaij and Crystal on a separate blanket. Shedaaij was speaking to his parents while they ate biscuits from a basket that also held some cheese and jams.

The scene was so placid and only disturbed when Shedaaij arose from her blanket in joy and ran into Shadowolf's arms. Crystal waltzed over in a small run and he lifted her up in his arms.

"This is your uncle Darc," he said in a child-like tone. Darcwulf smiled politely and then watched as Nighthale and Karla approached him.

"Welcome back," Nighthale said, shaking his hand in greeting. Karla did the same, and Shadowolf could see they were uncomfortable with their adoptive son. Darcwulf gave them soft smiles, but he more than any of them felt the most uncomfortable.

They all walked to the blankets, Shadowolf joining Shedaaij and his daughter while Darcwulf chose a marble bench in the shade of a tree behind Nighthale. Shadowolf helped himself to a few biscuits and Crystal helped herself to the same before it reached his mouth.

"I half-expected Le'Mar to be hot on your heels," Shedaaij said.

"Apparently Le'Mar isn't here," Shadowolf replied. "He is off on another conquest."

"Oh, that's interesting," Karla said.

"So we're free?" Nighthale asked.

"Define 'free'," Shadowolf replied snidely, and then smiled apologetically when his mother reprimanded him with a stern gaze.

"Le'Mar will return shortly," Darcwulf warned them. "It won't be long before Sona notifies him of my absence."

"Sona Nelma?" Nighthale asked.

"One and the same," Darcwulf replied. "It was only once I had met her in the forest with the dark lord that I learnt that she had lived in New Avalion under his orders while the Shadow Clan travelled the earth two years ago.

"He was hoping for some news on Shado, but Shado had only visited Avalion once that time."

Shadowolf reflected on this briefly then looked at Shedaaij.

"Do you think you can convince James to join us in the northern oceans above Horlorn?"

"Why would you want him there?" she asked, and then continued when he didn't reply. "You will have to give me a plausible reason; otherwise I won't be able to convince him."

"Ask him if he wants to hide from the sirens forever after we have conquered Le'Mar," Shadowolf replied. Nighthale looked at his wife. "I will assist him in getting rid of the sirens if he joins us."

"I will try my best," she said. "When would you like me to leave?"

"Today," Shadowolf replied, and she gaped. "If you don't mind. I will look after Crystal while we move to Horlorn's Gate."

"Ok, that's enough," Nighthale said, standing up. "I have had enough of this foolishness. No one is moving to the Gate."

"Father," Shadowolf said, standing too after passing Crystal to Shedaaij, "I will not argue with you, but know this.

"Carmel and Vale warriors will be moving to the Gate within the next two weeks. The pegasi from uPendus have recently moved in and their companions will be joining them shortly. Anuxis has his Underworld servants on standby as we speak.

"There will be a war, make no mistake," he continued, and even though his body quaked with anger, he held his voice relatively calm. "I will be taking as many Avalion warriors with me as are willing to fight. It will be your decision whether or not you want to join us."

Nighthale stared at him with the deepest resolve, but then lowered his glare to the grass. Words that were biting at his nerves fought to fly out his mouth, but he held them from being spoken.

"Dada," Crystal said beside Shadowolf's leg, hugging it as she looked up at him. He picked her up, and the men forgot their anger and disagreement. He looked at her face and flashing blue eyes, and returned the smile.

"How would we all get there?" Nighthale finally said. "Hyperportal?"

"No," Shadowolf said, forcefully removing his gaze from Crystal. "I don't have the ability to do that at the moment, and Horlorn isn't quite ready for us. I will borrow some ships from Malkius and the other lords. If need be we can summon some."

"Just answer me one thing before I agree to join you," Nighthale said. "Why don't you just confront Le'Mar? Why do you feel the need to bring the whole world to war?"

Shadowolf sighed. They were all going to keep asking him this. He finally decided that a partial answer would suffice.

"Le'Mar's ambition was to destroy Masara," he said, and Darcwulf lifted his head from his silent contemplation. "He didn't face Masara until the end, did he? He chose to destroy everything Masara cared about to bring him out."

"Is that what you're doing?" Karla asked.

"In a way," Shadowolf said. "I need to give Le'Mar some incentive to fight me. But it's more than that.

"I can fight Le'Mar, and there is a chance that I could win, and maybe not. But in the end there is one truth that Masara realised that has become very clear to me in the past two years."

"And what is that?" Darcwulf asked.

"That this world is not mine to fight for alone," he said. "I don't feel I have a right to take that chance away from the people of this earth. They have every right to fight beside me should they so wish, and reclaim their home. I am giving them that chance."

"Very well," Nighthale said, seemingly satisfied with the reply. He walked up to his son and grasped his free hand firmly. "I am with you."

LE'MAR'S AWAKENING
CHAPTER THREE

Genewiu flew towards the distant alcove of water. The two parts of the continent held the large bay within its embrace, and the light of the sun shone brightly upon its fogless surface. On the south-eastern banks of the Alcove of Light, below the very lip of the bay, rose a vast forest.

Just north of the forest various estuaries broke out from the Alcove, meeting to form the Dark River that flowed east. They could see from their height that the crystal clear water of the Alcove steadily became the murky water of Dark River.

"Why don't I ever remember a forest being here?" Chenesia shouted over the howl of the wind and Genewiu's flapping wings.

"There never was," Sinor replied, his green elf head resting on her shoulder as he looked towards the forest. "That was created by Sorceress."

"What?" she asked. "That looks like the work of an elf!"

"I assure you she had assistance from the fairies," the elf replied. "But she has become a powerful *Goudlem* in the past time, despite her former lack of elemental mastery."

Chenesia marveled at the forest below her, which seemed to repel the fog. The trees glistened with various shades of green, interspersed with amber and golden leaves between. An aura of yellow light glowed dully around the perimeter of the forest, and Chenesia wondered what it would take to enter it.

The aura was complemented by the fluttering of butterflies, insects and small orbs of lights around the tree tops. This activity stretched with the forest around the southern coast of the alcove.

"Has anyone attempted the forest?" Genewiu asked.

"I have no idea," Sinor replied. "But it still stands, so I have hope."

Genewiu banked down to the grasslands and landed gently on the earth. Chenesia and Sinor dismounted respectfully and gazed around them. All seemed quiet and, despite the activity from the animals of the forest before them, it appeared unoccupied.

The forest was long enough along the coast to house two cities full of creatures. The Vale of Tigers could easily have sat within its depths, and the top of the Jin Tai Sanctuary would not come near the tall tree tops.

"I am really surprised that Le'Mar's bears the forest's presence," Chenesia frowned. "Are you sure Sorceress resides here?"

"Last time I checked," Sinor confirmed. "Maybe he overlooked it."

As hopeful as that sounded, they all knew that the dark lord overlooking the forest was improbable. Perhaps some power held him out, like the Heart of Tigers once held him out of Eldor's Forest. Or perhaps, Chenesia realised as she stepped forward, Le'Mar had no need for the forest. After all, he had done what he came to do – killed Masara and conquered the world's mightiest heroes.

Genewiu turned away from the forest and looked into the sky behind them. She narrowed her eyes.

"Someone's coming," she said and her two companions stared up above. "A pegator rider."

Chenesia knew who she was before the woman came into view. It had been the same earth elemental that had pursued them with Darcwulf in the forest. It was the same woman they had spied in Carmel before they had left the Periwinkle. And the pegator beneath Sona Nelma was similar to the one Darcwulf had ridden.

"Run!" Chenesia said when she saw that Sona was accompanied by fifty fletchlings. The blue, chubby creatures raced past the pegator to meet them. Their wings audibly polluted the air with their beatings, their fierce faces and tarnished teeth falling down to the trio.

Chenesia, Genewiu and Sinor entered the forest at the same time, running with rich lengths beside each other. Wings flapped all around them and passed them into the forest, the beasts turning around to face them again. Genewiu looked back to see Sona land with the pegator upon the grass of the forest, unperturbed by the aural surrounding.

When Genewiu looked forward again, a glint of steel caught her eye as Chenesia tossed one of the dwarven axes ahead of them. The twin edges of the axe sang through the air, slicing fletchling wings and heads on its way to be embedded in the trunk of a tree.

The other fletchlings ignored the demise of their companions and flew to bite and scratch the trio. What they all missed was the tree swinging a branch to slap the axe aside. Sona, however, felt the energy of the earth vibrate through the forest and rode in carefully.

Sinor threw his palms open to the flying attackers and balls of elvin energy coursed into them. He lifted his arms in time to cover his face from fangs that bit down upon him, and then exclaimed when they lifted him in the air. Chenesia pulled the bow off her back and loosed several arrows above Sinor's head.

By the time three arrows had claimed their victims, Chenesia was thrust to the ground when a ball of ten fletchling hurtled into her belly. Sinor deftly swung his legs up and kicked the four beasts that still pulled him up. As he fell back down, he leaned to a tree trunk and ran down it on all fours like a squirrel.

Genewiu tried to reach Chenesia, who was still on the ground being barraged by the blue beings. But she had a line of fletchlings to get through first, daring her to try. She flapped her wings out, rising on her hind legs as the wind picked up and blasted them back into trees. This time, the pegasus saw the smaller branches swing to slap or kill the fletchlings.

Sona had also noticed and rode faster to engage the enemies. Sinor jumped from the tree, did a back somersault to avoid a ball of power from Sona that just scraped the bottom of his chin, and landed with his feet on either side of Chenesia's body on the ground. The fletchlings scattered and flew away to regroup.

"Get on!" Genewiu shouted. Sinor climbed the closest trunk and began running along branches and jumping from tree to tree. Chenesia mounted Genewiu as the remaining thirty fletchlings surrounded Sona like a cloak of water. She raced the pegator towards them, the fletchlings swaying behind her as they struggled to keep up.

Genewiu jumped without warning over roots that broke through the earth to stop them from going further into the forest. Her wings spread out, and she glided back to the ground and ran away from their pursuers again.

But the pegator manoeuvred through the forest with greater agility and was gaining on them. The fletchlings were lost from view, their sharp cries of pain echoing through the forest as nature destroyed them.

Chenesia turned on Genewiu's back and notched an arrow. She loosed it on Sona, the arrow whistling through the air before the *Goudlem* slapped it aside with the back of her hand. Sona thrust her palm out, sending an orb of rock pulsing with power at them. Chenesia threw her last dwarven axe at the orb.

A bang resounded through the forest as the axe cut the orb in two. The halves hurtled to the sides, sending sprays of sand and stone into the air as they exploded. The pegator jumped through the chaos, landing on the grass again and racing forward. Its muscles bulged as it strained to catch them, perspiration beading down its neck.

Three arrows crossed the air before Sona was settled on her mount after the explosion, and one entered her right shoulder. She exclaimed, pulling the arrow out in pain. She glared up furiously at the girl, and saw another four arrows approach her. Her skin became rock, and the arrows bounced off her body harmlessly.

Once her skin returned, Sona's eyes shone a deep green. The power filled her eyes so much that even Chenesia could see it from Genewiu's bouncing back. Sinor came into view above her, traversing the branches with the skill of an elf.

Sinor was lost from view as the grass was uprooted below them and a sand storm engulfed her. Genewiu reared up as a stalagmite rose below her neck, and Chenesia fell to the ground. The storm swirled around them, Sinor's voice calling from somewhere above.

Chenesia choked on the sand that hammered her face, despite her best efforts to close her mouth. She felt stones and blades of grass bite at her skin, but even in her turmoil she looked up when a thud hit the earth behind her. Genewiu had been pushed aside, her wings looking worse for wear the longer they stayed within the tornado.

Suddenly the tornado whipped out of control. Like clay warping from side to side in the hands of a potter, the sand swayed frivolously as if to the beat of nature's tune. The sand and grass collapsed around them into odd shapes. Chenesia and Genewiu watched as they became sand creatures neither of them had seen before.

Their sandy faces reminded Chenesia of eagles with large beaks. Their bodies were similar to the tigers she was so fond of in the Vale, but the tail split into two that ended in snake heads. The snakes hissed at them to remain where they were, but the eagle heads glared at Sona.

Sinor landed beside Chenesia as the sand beasts attacked Sona instead of them. They were entranced by the beings, the sand shifting in the form of muscles as they bound forward to a very perplexed *Goudlem*.

"How did you manage that?" Chenesia asked, looking at Sinor.

"It wasn't me," he replied, and she looked at Genewiu as the pegasus shook her head in denial. All three then looked around the forest for the creator of the sand creatures.

Sona jumped off the pegator, landing in a fighting stance as a staff flared into her hands from her soul. The staff was similar to aventurine in colour, the glossy green sparkling in the light that managed to break through the tree tops. As the first beast descended upon her, she swung her staff in circles and sprayed the sand into the air.

Chenesia turned her gaze away from the fight as hooves pounded against the earth. She saw the pegator moments away from her, ready to ram its head straight into her breasts.

A pristine white coat smashed into the pegator, their necks locked as they contested strength. The two rose on their hind legs, their necks straining against each other. Chenesia ran to assist, but wings spread out around the pegasi as they rose into the air and lashed out with their legs.

"Genewiu!" Chenesia shouted with concern etched in her voice. She watched helplessly as the two soared above the tree tops and out of view.

"Let's attack her while we have the chance," Sinor whispered in the din of the battle. He ran to the sand beasts, jumping over one of the snapping snake heads and rising in the air for the attack.

Sona whirled her staff in time to hit him across the abdomen and he flew back across the grass. He rolled onto his feet, slightly dizzy from the impact. Sona then ran back as the sand creatures glared at her and she raised her free hand.

Power thrummed into the air as her eyes burned green again. Words incoherent to Chenesia escaped Sona's lips and the sand beasts groaned inwardly as the sand changed again. Their physical attributes disintegrated and grew vertically into the air until each of the five beasts looked like women.

Grass sprouted on their heads and turned the black of hair. There were no eyes or ears or any other facial features. Their bodies were naked sand streams, breasts with no nipples and hands with no nails. They floated above the ground in a ghostly manner, their bare feet just brushing the top of the grass.

"They're beautiful," Sinor murmured and walked forward in a daze.

"Sinor!" Chenesia ran before him, placing her hands on his shoulders. His eyes were glazed white, his pupils gone. She shook him furiously, but he pushed her aside and she tripped over a root onto the floor.

"I've always wanted a wife," the elf said as he smiled merrily. The five women floated over to him, their hands caressing their own bodies in seduction.

"Sinor, they're sirens!" Chenesia shouted, rising to try and stop him again.

"On no, my dear princess of the Vale," Sona smirked, "they're more than that. They are from the deepest pits of darkness, bred from the demons that lurk in the night. Where they come from, these demons are called Succubi."

Sinor fell to his knees one step away from the foremost succubus. He groaned inwardly much like the sand beasts had done at their transformation. Chenesia wept silently as she watched his pain, not knowing what she could do to assist him. But when she saw the confusion on Sona's face, she realised something had gone wrong for the *Goudlem*.

A bright yellow aura burst out from Sinor in floods as he screamed, his arms stretching out around him. His pupils returned to his eyes as he stared in disgust at the demons before him.

"No one traps my soul," he said and jumped into the air from his kneeling position. Pulling a dagger hidden in his sash around his waist, he slit the first succubus's throat and landed behind her. As the blade traced her neck, yellow light flared out against it and the demon wailed out in pain before disintegrating to the grass.

Sinor once again made for the branches. The remaining four succubi ran along the air in pursuit of the tree-bounding elf. Sona turned her angered eyes upon Chenesia, who could feel the air thrum once again with power.

"Now it's just you and I," the *Goudlem* said, tapping her staff against the earth. Chenesia picked up the bow beside her and notched an arrow, but both fell to the ground just as quickly. The vines yanked her off her feet, twining around her ankles in a deadly grip. She clawed the grass as she slid on her belly to Sona.

Another two vines broke the sand before her and gripped her wrists, pulling her vertical in the air. They stretched her arms and legs wide and she screamed as the joints almost snapped out of place.

"Such a pretty girl," Sona said, lazily walking around her with a knife in hand that Chenesia had not seen on her before. She ran the tip of the knife over the bridge of Chenesia's face. "I wish I hand your freckles. They look so…appealing."

Sona ran the blade down her cheek laden with tears, down her neck soiled with sand until it rested on her shirt between her breasts. The few freckles there were stained with the soil and grass of the tornado. Mixed with those was the blood running from a cut above her right breast.

She cut the top of the shirt open and it tore down the centre to her belly where she stopped. Chenesia wriggled in the grip of the vines, then cried out in pain as her shoulder dislocated. Her breasts almost fell out the shirt as her head lolled forward from the agony, sweat falling from her brow to the ground below.

"Do you want me to end the suffering?" Sona teased. "I can give you the darkest pleasures you could ever imagine. Just tell me why you've returned, and I will make the pain all go away."

Chenesia raised her drenched face, looked deep into Sona's eyes and spat in her face. Sona recoiled and wiped the grime off her face in disgust.

"Then you shall join your father," Sona said and drove the knife into Chenesia's heart.

Chenesia gasped as the cold knife entered. She almost passed out from shock, her head spinning, but she frowned as Sona stepped back with the knife in her hand. The blade was crooked as if she had thrust it against a rock. Chenesia looked down at her now exposed breast and saw the Heart of Tigers shining from beneath the skin.

"What on earth?" Sona said, and then cried out as an arrow entered her back. Lights crashed around them as two tigroys and a blaze of fairies snapped the vines and Chenesia fell to her knees. Hooves entered the area as centaurs arrived with bows and swords.

Sona turned around to face the centaurs. There were hundreds of them. She dropped the knife in defeat and turned to flee. Chenesia rose from her knees instantly and planted her fist up into Sona's chin. Sona's head snapped back. She tripped on a root and, as she turned to stop the fall, hit her neck hit against the trunk of a thick oak. A crack sounded into the air and Sona's limp body collapsed.

Chenesia held her top closed as the centaurs, tigroys and fairies surrounded her. She studied the tigroys carefully; she was sure they looked similar to the ones guarding her father's grave. Before she could speak, Genewiu and Sinor landed beside her defensively.

"I think they're friendly," Chenesia said, and looked at the centaurs. She remembered how Millon and Kentaur had looked when the Shadow Clan had fought in the Battle for Eldor's Forest. These centaurs were similar, but lighter in complexion. Where Millon and Kentaur's faces had once reflected their servitude to the dark lord, these centaurs held beauty upon theirs. The fairies circled their bald heads like angelic wreaths.

From the rear, a centaur rode through the others with a rider upon its back. Chenesia gaped in joy when she recognised his elvish face. He strode majestically upon the centaur, his chest protruding beneath the tunic with might and his sword dangling from his hip in glory.

Lesan dismounted from the centaur hastily and ran to hold

Chenesia in his embrace. The girl nearly collapsed in his arms, but his strong chest supported her frail head and she clasped her arms around his body.

And then she did what she had waited too long to do. With the last of her strength, she looked up at him and lovingly kissed the prince of the elves.

***

Above the Alcove of Light, behind the sky-tearing mountains, stood the dark lord's castle. It was situated on the northern cliffs that dropped down to the oceans and a breeze blew against the stone walls lazily.

The throne room looked similar to the one that Darcwulf had occupied. Le'Mar had changed Eldor's throne to reflect his to give the dark brother a sense of authority in the forest. The circular walls were only interrupted by the domed glass that looked out upon the sloping hills, allowing him to see over the vast earth.

The dust of the room lay across the tables and books. It had been unoccupied for nearly a year since the dark lord's departure, and none of his servants had dared enter.

The solace of the room was interrupted by a shimmer along the wall. The bricks pulled back and a purple portal opened up in the gap. Le'Mar's black boots stepped through, followed by his black pants, red shirt and cape. A golden sword blinked on his side, and his brown staff slapped against his back.

Le'Mar lay down his weapons and cloak and circled the table to look out the domed window. The fog still covered the earth, and from the cliffs the castle stood on he could see the fog better than those within it.

He walked away from the window and traced his fingers along the brick wall. The dust vanished as if it had never been there, sweeping silently across the floors out of the vents along the walls. He breathed the clean air, glad to be back from his recent victory, and then cowered down as the window crashed all around him.

He rose and saw the pegator bleeding on the floor. He had crashed against the table, sending timber all across the room.

"I would have appreciated it if you had knocked first," he said to the horse. The pegator breathed hoarsely and spoke in a deep, wounded voice.

"They.....they're back," he said.

"Who's back?" Le'Mar asked, waiting patiently for the answer from the dying beast.

"Chenesia," he said.

Le'Mar frowned and looked out across the earth.

"And Shadowolf?" he finally asked.

"We don't know," the pegator replied. "Sona is dead."

"What!?" Le'Mar shouted. "Who killed her?"

The pegator didn't reply but closed its eyes instead. Le'Mar ran over and yanked its head up.

"Tell me who killed her!"

"Chen......chen....."

But his voice faded as he died, and Le'Mar dropped its head. He walked to the window and teleported to the throne in the forest.

His body rematerialised in the room that Darcwulf was supposed to occupy. The walls and floor were burnt, and the room was on its side. He walked along the ruined walls until he met with a gaping hole. He exited the room onto a field in the forest. He whistled for the nearest orc to approach him.

"What happened here?" he asked the kneeling orc. He looked up and saw that the room had snapped off from the trees and had crashed through its branches until landing on the earth. What remained of the topmost branches was blackened by the fire that had caused the destruction.

"It was Shadowolf," the orc said. "He returned for your high servant."

"And where is my 'servant' now?" Le'Mar asked, already assuming the reply.

"With Shadowolf," the orc grunted. Le'Mar lifted his knee up into the orc's face and teleported back to his castle.

TALES OF MASARA
CHAPTER FOUR

In the early hours of the morning, the tribe lords and their warriors boarded the twenty ships that waited in the harbour of Lowle Village. Half of them had to be summoned by the earth elementals of Avalion, which bothered Shadowolf. That much power would not go unnoticed if Le'Mar had returned, but he knew it would take much longer had they hand-crafted the ships.

After he made a request to his father, the ship Shadowolf chose to sail on was affably named "The Windfarer" after the ship that had carried him while he was still in his mother's womb. Soon, he and his family and the few close Degron warriors on the ship were joined by familiar faces.

Skywolf and Angelia boarded the ship first, their faces gleaming with joy as they embraced him in greeting.

"It's been a long time," Skywolf said. The sun glinted off her left hand and he looked down to see a ring.

"You and Dredwolf got married?" he exclaimed excitedly.

"Yes," she replied. "And that's not all."

She turned around to her husband walking up the boarding plank. Upon his shoulders sat a boy about a year younger than Crystal. His eyes were fixed on the large sea vessels, his hands clasped in his father's.

"And you?" he asked Angelia after Skywolf, Dredwolf and Tailan left to find cabins below deck.

"I'm not really into the love-game at the moment," she smiled. "I'd rather wait until the right man arrives."

"Good for you," he said in mock sincerity and she laughed at his silliness. After a moment of friendly chatter, she left his side and Heula walked up to him.

"Good to see you're going with," Shadowolf said. "Will you be up for a fight after giving up your dark powers?"

"I have other skills," she teased and walked passed him. He placed his hand on her shoulder to stop her.

"Just because you don't call yourself a witch anymore doesn't mean you can't use the powers Bontu has given you," he said.

"It's the way I used my powers, not what I was called," she smiled back. "The only difference between a saint and a witch is which side you're fighting for, right?"

She left him frowning, having never pondered that before. His thoughts were cut off though when Lastgorn and Deihlia joined him and after a brief greeting they joined the others in finding accommodation.

And, when the ships set off for the River of Light two hours later, Shadowolf left Darcwulf's side to check on his daughter for the hundredth time.

***

The sunlight shone passed the trunks, wading between the roots, and upon the woman that lay against the tree. She breathed deeply, her mind still lost to sleep, as a hairy tongue licked her faced.

She opened her eyes slowly, her body aching with defeat. Sona Nelma leaned on her elbows and saw the aged root that had cracked when her shoulder had collided with it. Her neck was swollen and blue from the impact. She crawled to the black tiger that had heeded her summoning and climbed its muscular back.

Sona drew power from the earth as she commanded the tiger further into the forest.....

***

Shadowolf rested his feet on the stern of the ship, the scrolls held firmly upon his lap. The flaps of a large umbrella blew in the wind above him. Deihlia stood to one side under the umbrella, holding Crystal in her arms and pointing at the greenery on either side of the River of Light.

Despite the shade of the umbrella, the glare of the evening sun still irritated his eyes. He squinted at the documents of Bentley and Falgar and then sighed, looking out at the ships that followed.

There were three other Degron ships with the flag of his father hoisted on the main masts. On the ship immediately behind The Windfarer, Mandy and the war horses were being kept with all the provisions necessary for cooking, cleaning and other domestic tasks.

Following the Degron ships were four ships per tribe. The Saphin flags blew wildly in the wind, followed by those belonging to the Lowle, Watre and Orion tribes. Like the Degron ships, the second one per tribe carried the provisions and mounts.

Even though the tribe lords had set out from the harbour on their primary ships, Malkius, Jasnon, Sjedwolf and Lucian's wife Kailan had joined the foremost ship by the time the sun was at its noon apex. Shadowolf had thanked them, his father, Nowles and Franklin sincerely for joining him before leaving them to their tribal deliberations.

"Your mother says supper is nearly ready and you should bring Crystal in before the night wind picks up," Darcwulf said as he grabbed a reclining chair and raised his feet on the stern.

"It's ok, I'll take her," Deihlia offered and Shadowolf nodded in gratitude.

"What's with all the papers?" Darcwulf asked, grabbing the scroll concerning Bentley as Deihlia left them.

"Elgoth shared some more secrets of his father with me while I was in uPendus, and I'm trying to piece them all together."

"You mean there's more to Masara than Eldor told us in Lard's Den?"

"Not so much more as what was left out," Shadowolf replied, handing his brother the Falgan scroll.

"Do you ever wonder why they don't tell us everything?" Darcwulf sighed and paged through the documents.

"Elgoth said that Eldor only told us what was relevant to the battle," Shadowolf said as he stared at the river water.

"Ok," his brother said, returning the scrolls. "Give me the synopsis."

"Elgoth told me I would need these scrolls to fully understand what he told me," Shadowolf said. "It seems that all this trouble really started at the time of Bentley."

"But we mostly know what happened in history, don't we?"

"You see that's the problem," Shadowolf said. "Our schools only taught us briefly of Bentley as the father of humans, and then we were taught from after the time of Falgar."

"So these scrolls go further back?"

"That's correct," he replied. "But I will highlight the key elements of the tale; you can read it yourself later."

"How charming," Darcwulf joked.

"Well, as we know it all started with Bentley meeting the elves in the Nether Region," Shadowolf said, his brother listening carefully with his eyes closed to the setting sun. "He and his wife made love and gave birth to Shardenel and Mikinos."

"As is the natural order of things," Darcwulf murmured.

"Then they make mention of the first elf Saldheron's granddaughter, Elhorin," he continued. "Apparently Mikinos really fancied the elf daughter, despite the fact that Bentley wanted him to court his own sister."

"That's disgusting."

"It's either that or his mother, Darc," Shadowolf stated.

"Ok, I get your point."

"They mentioned that he 'lusted' for her, but later they say Mikinos referred to it as 'love'," he said. "But even her father, Malherin, would not permit it.

"So one night this guy decides he can't live without her anymore and he tries to meet her secretly. She, of course, denies him because of her father and then he tries to forcefully persuade her. And then her father walks in on them."

"Ooh, now you're in trouble," Darcwulf laughed.

"So the battle between the two of them is discussed, and how Malherin was going to be the first to commit murder. However, Bentley steps in in order to prevent this. Malherin goes mad and tries to now kill Bentley.

"In the end, Bentley uses Malherin's own power in the form of a dagger of wind to kill the elf, thereby taking the first murder upon himself."

"Interesting," Darcwulf commented.

"Now, Elgoth told me that it was a darkness that was born of Malherin's hatred that Bentley tried to destroy," Shadowolf said.

"What kind of a darkness? Like a cloud?"

"Almost, but one that clouds your soul and judgement so that you no longer care which is right and which is wrong," Shadowolf said.

"Like the end justifies the means?"

"Precisely. Elgoth says that Bontu recognised this evil with Malherin as His long time enemy, and wanted to remove Bentley from the continent. The scrolls say that Saldheron took his elves and journeyed to the Far Isles too, but I think they went to the Isle of Masara."

"What happened to Mikinos and Shardenel?"

"They obeyed the wishes of their father and got married," he replied and Darcwulf screwed up his face, in spite of his earlier understanding.

"Elgoth says this darkness needs a host to survive," Shadowolf continued. "After I read the scroll concerning Falgar, it became obvious that it passed from Malherin to his son, Temelrin."

"Why do you say that?"

"The scroll talks about how Temelrin saw his father's death and a hatred for man lived in him forever. Apparently Elhorin, who was by now his wife, asked him to 'suppress the darkness'. He eventually did, but circumstances called it up again.

"One of Mikinos's sons was Falgar. Both he and Temelrin's daughter Mehorin wished to act against their fathers' wills."

"Like children often do," Darcwulf smirked.

"Falgar wanted to leave the Nether Region and she the Isle. Eventually they did so, and as fate would have it they met each other and fell in love. Of course, the son of Temelrin told him of her departure...."

"And so the darkness rose again," Darcwulf guessed.

"...and he left for the continent, but had to face Falgar. The two battled and Falgar used the elf's own staff and power to destroy him."

"I see there's a pattern developing here."

"And guess who saw his father die."

"His son?"

"You got it," Shadowolf said. "Selhorin witnessed the whole thing, then banished Mehorin and his brother Melnirion from the Far Isles. Melnirion took the elves that followed him to what we called Eldor's Forest, and they let the ancient elf Saldheron rule."

"And Falgar and Mehorin lived happily ever after."

"They established Carmel," Shadowolf confirmed. "The elves were now separated; Selhorin named the elves on the Isle the Elder Elves."

"Even though the darkness started with them?"

"Selhorin believed in keeping the elf blood pure from the taint of human blood," Shadowolf said. "And that's where the scroll ends."

"Selfish idiot," Darcwulf commented. "So now I ask the obvious question; where does Masara fit in the tale?"

"Permit me to tell you," a voice said behind the two.

"Elgoth!" Shadowolf exclaimed, almost falling off his chair.

"You didn't think I would let you fight without me, did you?" the saint smiled. "After all, I did save your life last time."

Shadowolf laughed and they let him sit down.

"You don't mind if I continue, do you?" Elgoth asked politely.

"Not at all," he replied. "After all, you know it better than I."

"It is important to note," Elgoth said, carrying on from Shadowolf as if he had been telling the tale from the start, "that we all now carry some stain of the 'darkness' within us. In some way, we have all been affected by its sting.

"But through Selhorin, the demon that required his soul as a host still lived strong. Unlike Temelrin who had his good wife to help him suppress the urges of the demon, Selhorin exercised his anger whenever he had the chance, denouncing man as the harbinger of death.

"And so it was that Melnirion had two sons, Eldorion and Elmerion."

"Now it's starting to sound familiar," Darcwulf said, remembering Eldor's lecture in Lard's Den.

"When Saldheron passed away, as he was no longer on the Isle that sustained his life, Eldor became the ruler of the Eastern Elves. Selhorin had many children, but to one he passed the knowledge of his father's death; Seimarion."

"Let me guess; the demon needed him as a host?" Darcwulf

asked.

"Yes," Elgoth confirmed. "Selhorin's age held him well, but with it came repentance for his life's failures. Selhorin slowly began to see the error of his ways and confessed it to his son. Seimarion, however, standing at his father's grave, grew angered with humans, and repeated the vow that Temelrin once made."

"To exact revenge on the blood of man," Shadowolf said.

"Seimarion's method was different to his forefathers," Elgoth continued. "He decided to take a human as his wife from the continent."

"What!?" Darcwulf exclaimed. "Even after Temelrin had promised never to taint the blood of the elves?"

"Yes. His reasoning was that, through a human, he would obtain their downfall. But it was the demon inside that wanted to taint the souls of humans, Bontu's most precious creation.

"But the Elder Elves found out about his actions before he wed, and banished him from the Isle. Instead of choosing a new leader from among them to rule, they decided it best to institute the Circle of Elders to rule together."

"Where did he go?" Darcwulf asked.

"To a place no one ever thought he would," Elgoth said sadly. "A place considered sacred to the elves; the Alcove of Light."

"So that's where Le'Mar got the castle!" Darcwulf realised.

"Seimarion lived a long, good life with his wife in that castle. He realised, too late, that although he had wedded a human, it was not from the pure line of Falgar which he had so desperately hoped for. Yet he stayed with her nonetheless for love did grow between them.

"Eventually, the demon became disturbed by lack of chaos. Their hybrid son, T'Mar, was growing strong and wise in the ways of his parents. He learnt the ways of the humans and the lore of the elves. The darkness simply waited for the right time to transfer hosts.

"Concurrent to all this, Falgar and Mehorin had many children. The two of note were Morlen and Falara, but we will focus on Falara for the purpose of the tale. It was Falara that fathered Namara...."

"Who was the father of Masara," Darcwulf interrupted. "It's all starting to fit together now."

"Seimarion passed away, his elvin age failing him," Elgoth said. "This worried T'Mar, knowing fully well that elves lived longer than his father had. At that time, Saldheron was still alive, and he could not understand why his father was taken from him.

"But the demon passed through to T'Mar, and it was during this time that Elmerion was teaching Masara the history of the demon."

"So Masara always knew about it?" Darcwulf asked.

"Yes," Elgoth replied. "It was the reason that he forbade his mother to marry T'Mar after his father's death. But Levon considered his omens as a child's protectiveness over his mother. She married him, and upon Le'Mar's conception the demon had what it wanted; a tainted child from the blood lines of both Falgar and Selhorin.

"That was one of the main reasons Masara sought to keep Le'Mar from his father. He knew that upon T'Mar's death, the demon would seek to claim the child as its rightful heir to the throne of darkness."

"And in the end, Masara killed him," Darcwulf said.

"Yes, but as was his nature, Masara tried to save him first," Elgoth said, and Darcwulf looked at his brother. "But the demon overcame T'Mar's will to repent. In the end, when they were both battling in the waters of the Scourge, T'Mar used his last energy to try and kill Masara. Masara trapped T'Mar's final power within his staff and then drove the staff through T'Mar."

"As with the others, killing him with his own darkness," Shadowolf said.

"When he realised that Ursula's horn had been lost, he transformed the staff in his hands and healed her with it and the power of earth," Elgoth said.

"Which became the butterfly pendant," Darcwulf vaguely remembered. "But where is it now?"

"Chenesia should be obtaining it soon, hopefully," Shadowolf said. "But do you understand now why Ursula wanted her old horn back, and why her power was diminished?"

"Of course!" he exclaimed. "There was still some of T'Mar's energy within the new horn."

"Yes," Elgoth confirmed. "The tainted power-sack within her

horn would not permit her to grow to her old potential, and when she got the old horn back she was powerful enough to expel any remnants of the darkness within the sack.

"The demon should have died with T'Mar. That's the reason that the waters became so dark. Its spirit cried out in fury, crying out as the chains of hell sought to claim it. But Le'Mar, like the others, had witnessed his father's murder and the despair he felt allowed the demon to enter him. Everything Masara had taught him about Bontu vanished in that moment."

"So that's why Masara didn't want to kill Le'Mar in the forest?" Darcwulf asked, unsure of his thoughts.

"Masara was pure to a fault," Elgoth admitted. "He believed he could save Le'Mar by destroying the demon. He always blamed himself for not being strong enough for what needed to be done."

"But Masara never faced Le'Mar like Bentley faced Malherin, or Falgar faced Selhorin," Darcwulf commented. "Not until the end."

"You've read how the previous battles affected the earth," Elgoth said. "He tried to avoid that. And mostly, Eldor held him back."

"Why?"

"Masara had almost died against the darkness before," Shadowolf said. "Eldor knew another confrontation would kill him."

"He was right," Darcwulf thought aloud. "And so the Elder Elves protected him, and Le'Mar set the world at war to bring him out."

"That was Le'Mar's reason," Elgoth corrected. "The demon wanted to show his power and give the heir to his darkness a kingdom to rule. He wanted to make sure he would always have a host."

"So that he could remain here for all eternity," Darcwulf concluded. "This darkness wouldn't by any chance be called 'Gemetrashef' by others, would it?"

"No," Shadowolf said. "But the demon is one of the Gemetrashef's high demons. When the demon that ruled Trimistus's world was eventually destroyed, the Gemetrashef sent Le'Mar. This was when Le'Mar first realised he could use some of the Gemetrashef's armies to assist him here on Celenic Earth."

"Although that was probably the demon thinking," Darcwulf realised. "Le'Mar's purpose was Masara alone, while the demon's was the entire earth."

"And so in the end Eldor felt that, although Le'Mar sought to kill Masara, it was the world's responsibility to be rid of the darkness and not his alone." Elgoth said, and Darcwulf looked at his brother.

"And it's not your responsibility alone, either," Darcwulf finally said, looking down at the waters that were becoming dark as the sun set. "I understand now why we must face him. But how do we destroy the demon without losing Le'Mar?"

Before Darcwulf looked up, Elgoth gave Shadowolf a meaningful look, and Shadowolf nodded.

LIGHTS OF THE ALCOVE
CHAPTER FIVE

Shedaaij saw the Straits of Malakov ahead of her. Her mer-sight allowed her to see deeper into the waters than Shadowolf could have, guiding her path between the roots of the six islands as she entered the watery maelstrom.

She used her scaly tail to drive her forward, turning her body at the correct angle to avoid being thrown into the rocks. She opened her lips minutely and emitted ultrasonic sounds. Soft vibrations returned against her skin, and she turned to avoid swimming into the crag before her.

When she left the maelstrom, she entered the purple mist that surrounded the mer-Kingdom. Her ultrasonic signals warned her where the tiger sharks were and she twisted her tail to swim further down. She eventually felt power pass over her as she neared the exit of the mist and called out with her mind to them.

It's me; Shedaaij.

The power softened only slightly as they awaited her entrance. Her body broke through the mist and entered the shining light of the mer-Kingdom.

Barely past the mist were seven mermen with crude coral swords in their hands. They relaxed their stances as they realised it was indeed her and let her pass. She swam slower through the calm waters, enjoying the warmth that the city radiated.

The mer-Kindgom was situated between the roots of two islands. A round ball of yellow light around the city held it dry from the waters of the ocean, thereby allowing the mer-people to walk freely. From the bottom dome of the ball sand rose up until the centre.

Upon the sand were the coral buildings. Although she knew

them to be marble white in colour, from her viewpoint in the flowing waters the city was a yellow blur in the distance. She could just make out the vague shapes of the homes that surrounded James's throne.

Before she entered the ball and landed on the beach sand she transformed her tail back into her smooth legs. The other mermaids often envied her of this ability, but as she was the only one whose father had been human they knew they would never be able to change their tails at will. As soon as water touched their legs, they would fall upon the scales of their tails and thereby be vulnerable to any attack. It was the sole reason that they never pursued their dreams of living on the continent.

The power of the trident in the hands of the mer-King often provided them with a replica of terrestrial life. Although the sun never shone in any of the mer-Kingdoms she had lived in, there had always been coral to reflect the light provided by the trident.

She reached the perimeter of the ball and placed her foot on the beach, stepping through. Water fell down her hair and skin, off her bare legs and onto the sand. Her gills closed beneath her ears and her lungs took over. The only coverings she wore were the glimmering coral plates over her firm breasts and the coral armour around her waist.

The other mermaids wore even less, if any, fabrics. Most waists were covered by soft cloths made of seaweed while their breasts were left bare. The mermen were not burdened with the same lusts as humans, and therefore the mermaids never feared any of them.

Shedaaij reflected that when a mermaid and merman chose each other as mates, they would stay with their partner until their last breath. In the history of the mer-Kingdom, it was unheard of that a mermaid would seek another mate after his death and vice versa.

Due to the past battles with the sirens, there were many widowed mermaids that would never bare children again. This was one of the main reasons that James decided that they would separate themselves from the world. Too many losses had been counted, and almost half the mer-Kingdom had already been widowed.

Shedaaij walked passed many mer-people on her way to

James, receiving friendly greetings from each of them. She had never told any of them about Crystal with the exception of James. Even he had agreed that Crystal should not be allowed beneath the waters until the ripe age of seven. If they were right and the girl had obtained her mother's nature, Crystal would be able to travel the waters as well as any mermaid could by that time.

The ground rose steadily up a hill to the centre of the ball where the throne stood. She had to admit, it was not the most attractive throne she had ever seen. It broke from the rock like a stalagmite to the sky, towering above the city to the very top of the ball and tapering to a thin point. And at the wide base of the throne was the entrance.

Her body had dried by the time she entered the throne and walked up the spiral stairs. The warmth radiating from the tower drove any moisture still clinging to her hair away. Shedaaij entered the large throne hall and waited to be called forth.

James was discussing trivial matters with a few of his warriors. They lay relaxed in coral beds, his being the biggest of all with his recent mate sleeping with her head on his chest. A pearl ring hung from a chain around his neck, signifying his partnership with the naked mermaid in his arms.

James smiled at something one of his men had said, dimples flashing on his cheeks and his eyes gleaming. The smile faded slightly without vanishing as he saw Shedaaij waiting at the stairwell. The men turned in their beds, covered only with coral cloths around their waists, and then looked to James for instruction.

"Leave us," he said calmly, not losing his happy demeanour. The mermen left obediently, greeting Shedaaij as they passed. He slipped out from under his mate and indicated silently that she follow him to the floor above.

They climbed the stairwell and entered a small dining room with a washroom attached on the side. He grabbed a shellbrush with fine hairs and used dentifrice on it to clean his teeth. He spewed the paste out with water and finally looked at Shedaaij.

"You left without saying goodbye," James said. He sat down by the dining table and indicated that she join him.

"You know why, my lord," she said politely.

"It's ok, you don't have to be so formal," James smiled

encouragingly. "And yes, I detected his presence. How long has he been back?"

"Not long before his arrival here," Shedaaij said, and then added quickly. "He didn't know the new rule against humans and I thought it best to warn him."

"Well, I wouldn't have minded telling him myself," he said to her surprise. They turned to the stairwell as they heard footsteps. His mate arrived and asked him if he needed anything. Shedaaij spied a similar pearl ring resting on her sternum. "A nice, warm cup of segwik-tee, please Murladia. Shedaaij?"

"Yes please," she said and waited for the mermaid to vanish to the kitchen. She said her next words carefully. "Shadowolf asked me to return to speak to you."

"Oh, indeed?" James said, frowning as he continued. "The trident informs me that there are several ships travelling the River of Light."

"They're heading for Horlorn's Gate," she said. "Most of Avalion, that is."

"What on earth for?" he asked.

"We're waging a war against Le'Mar," she said bravely. Murladia walked up the stairs and Shedaaij saw that the anger James was about to release was held back. The nude mermaid settled the mugs on the table before heading back down the stairs.

"Is he out of his human mind?!" he finally exclaimed softly, flexing his left hand as if he could just reach out and throttle Shadowolf. "The world is lost to darkness. There is nowhere they can go where Le'Mar cannot find them. Why do you think we moved to the Straits?! It's the only place the sirens are too afraid to follow."

"Please James, just listen," she said, and he sat back hard against his seat.

"No, that was Lellian's problem," James said. "He always had time to listen to that boy's nonsense."

"James, please," she said and placed her hands on his. "I have seen the determination in his eyes. I have no doubt that he will fight this war, and I believe that he will win."

"Of course you would; he's your mate."

"It's more than that," she said, her eyes looking far away. "I have felt Bontu within him. What's more is the armies of the earth are joining him in this war."

"Good for them!" James shouted, before looking worriedly at the stairwell.

"Don't you understand, James?" she pleaded with her eyes. "When Le'Mar is destroyed and his forces annihilated, all that will be left to be taken care of are the sirens. Do you want to live in the Straits forever?"

James went quiet as he considered this.

"What's the difference if we fight the sirens now or wait till our forces are replenished?"

"Because by the time we have bred enough warriors, who knows what evil the oceans will hold," she replied. "You know evil has never lain still before."

"They haven't bothered us these last two years," James retaliated, uncertainty clouding his expression.

"But with Shadowolf challenging the dark forces of the world, they might rise again," she said, and then sweetened her voice. "James, this could be our chance to take back the seas before it's lost to us forever."

He looked away from her seductive eyes and stared out the window. The yellow wall of the city shimmered softly, with soft waves of current rolling on the outside. He closed his eyes, breathing deeply.

"What does he want us to do exactly?" he said, but she could see that he had not given in just yet.

"To travel to the northern oceans above the Gate," she said, knowing full well that this revelation was going to make it harder for the mer-King to make a decision.

"That's far," he said, calmer than she had expected.

"I know Shadowolf would not send us up there unless he has a plan."

"Us?" he said, smiling again. "He's letting you fight alongside us?"

"Yes," Shedaaij said, and her expression made it clear she was unhappy with the idea.

"I will only send the warriors who have lost their mates," James said as he stood, a huge smile appearing on her face. "Don't get too happy; I haven't decided yet."

He left her in the dining hall and summoned the mer-Kingdom to a council.

***

Chenesia woke up late that morning. The forest whispered softly around her as the others walked about and prepared the breakfast that they would eat. The tigroys that had been secretly following her since her departure from the Vale lay quietly nearby with their wings tucked upon their sides. Despite their marble exterior, one of them was licking its paws.

She didn't move, but instead kept her eyes closed. Chenesia needed a few moments alone for her thoughts, without the invading concern of the others upon her. She took a deep sigh, keeping her ears pitched for any sound of feet approaching her and let her mind dwell.

Her body still ached dully from the battle with Sona, despite Lesan's healing hands. The comfort of the prince's embrace and love went a long way to emotionally soothe the discomfort, but in the solitude of his absence the wounds that pulsed deeply reminded her that she had nearly lost her life. She was just glad one of the centaurs had volunteered to search for her axes.

To this reflection was added the image of the Heart of Tigers that had glowed from within her own heart. She tried unsuccessfully to recall when the Heart had slipped from her hands at her father's tomb. All she could remember was falling back and then looking around for the gem.

Chenesia shivered when she realised again that she had nearly died. Sona had been overwhelming and even Lesan's powers would not have brought her back had the Heart not stopped that evil blade.

"Oh, you're awake," Lesan said, a broad smile on his face. Chenesia had not realised that she had opened her eyes during her thoughts, but she smiled back at the prince. She stretched and then allowed him to pull her up from the coat she had used as a bed.

"Where's Genewiu?" she asked, looking around for the pegasus. Elves were sounding the breakfast bell while mounts were being led away.

"There's a river further in," the prince replied. "She went for a quick drink and swim. Do you wish to eat?"

Chenesia nodded and he led her to the area where the elves ate. She rested her back against a protruding root that was half as thick as the tree it belonged to as Lesan got her some breakfast. She had expected him to stay to continue the frivolous chatter from the day before, but he surprised her with a smile and left.

She finished her meal and drowned it with some warm tea, before setting off to find him. Her bare dirty feet waded through the ankle high grass as she listened for any sound of his presence. All she heard however was the river she was approaching and the rustle of hooves somewhere to the left.

Chenesia stopped suddenly when the trees around her vanished. Before her was a vast open area surrounded by the forest. It was filled a light so bright that she had to narrow her eyes until they became accustomed to it. Fairies flew all around the open glade, filling the sky with their bounteous lights and powerful presence.

She realised that, not only was the glade filled with the fairdievells from the Fairiwell that she had grown used to, but with other species of fairies too. Where the fairdievells had all looked similar in size and varied in colour, the fairies of the Alcove were minutely larger in size and brighter in light. There seemed to be only two different colours in their group; cyan and yellow.

Chenesia pulled her observations away when she saw the river that flowed away from rapids to the right. Where the water was relatively calm, she saw a splash break the serene surface. Lesan drew his hands over his face to clear the water, his light green back muscles bulging as he drifted.

Chenesia walked through the haze of light. It felt like she was dreaming and the lights from the fairies were warm. She reached the bank of the river and undressed. She quietly entered the refreshing river, the water rising on her skin until it just covered her breasts.

She sank under the water and kicked against the bank. She swam until she could see Lesan's legs before her and swam between them. He jumped in shock, but settled down when he felt her hand rise upon his legs and her head broke the surface.

"You gave me a fright," he said, trying to keep his eyes locked with hers so that they did not drift down over her submerged body. Chenesia giggled, paddling her feet to keep her head above the water. The river was a bit deeper in the centre than on the banks. Lesan held her hands in his to keep her floating, too shy to hold her in his arms.

"How long before we find Sorceress?" she asked, her laughter dying down as her longing for him arose again.

"Another day," Lesan replied. "She's at the other end of the forest. You and Genewiu can go ahead if…"

His words died down as she gave in and swam into his arms. Her lips locked with his again, savouring the taste of his lips as her hands held on to the back of his neck. Lesan slipped his hands onto her bare back, more in support than in desire, but he returned the kiss lovingly.

Even in the chill of the river, her body grew warm for him as the kiss deepened and she locked her legs against his waist. Lesan almost choked in shock and then swam back before her embrace became more permanent.

"I can't," he said, dropping his head.

"Why not?" she asked kindly, frowning as she tried to subdue her passion for him.

"The time isn't right," Lesan said. "There is something I must do first."

"What's that?" Chenesia said. She crossed her arms over her breasts to keep herself from shaking, but it was not the river that made her shiver.

"Chenesia, I have known you since you were born, and even then I was old in human terms," he said, looking her straight in the eyes.

"If this is about age difference then…"

"No, no," he interrupted her and placed his hands on her shoulders. "It's more than that."

He looked down into her eyes, sadness welling up in them as his mind seemed to travel to another place.

"I thought I had lost you twice," the elf continued. "Both times I thought my life would fail me. If I ever lose you again I…."

She waited to hear what would happen to him but the single tear running down his cheek was all the answer she needed.

"I'm not leaving your side again," she said, stroking his face and running her thumb in the wake of the tear.

"I know," Lesan replied. "Chenesia, I want to marry you."

Chenesia swam back for a moment, almost drowning as her head slipped under the water. Lesan reached out and caught her body, holding her up as she looked up into his wet eyes. She gaped briefly, almost forgetting to breathe.

"I understand if the thought of marrying me…"

"Yes!" she exclaimed, and plunged her lips on his again. "Oh yes, I want to marry you."

She held him tight, her head resting firmly on his shoulder as tears of joy trickled down her face and the lights of the fairies played on their backs.

THE DARK LORD'S WRATH
CHAPTER SIX

Lucian walked into the dining hall and saw Anuxis feasting on some meat for lunch. Cerexus sat behind him chewing a large bone. The *Enodhim* sat opposite the wolf-man and tapped his fingers on the table as he surveyed the hall.

"Growing anxious?" Anuxis asked before biting into his meat again.

"A little," Lucian replied. "I must still head to Philagus at some point for Shado, but there's so much to be done here."

"You might have to wait before you start that trip," Anuxis replied. "I have a little errand of my own that I have to run."

"Trimistus is here," Lucian said.

"Still, Shado entrusted us…"

Anuxis pulled his face away from the meat and stared through the walls of the hall. Lucian frowned, wondering what the wolf-man was doing. Trimistus entered the hall and sat down beside Lucian.

"Good morn…."

"Shhh," Anuxis said, holding up his hand. Even Cerexus stopped chewing and sniffed the air as it stood.

"What's the matter?" Lucian asked.

"I think Shado's in trouble…"

***

Shadowolf walked across the deck of the Windfarer, stretched and then leaned against the port railing. It wasn't long before Deihlia joined his side, a soft smile greeting him.

"Missing Shedaaij?" she asked.

"Yes," he replied. "Mostly because I still have to get used to my parental duties. Luckily my father has a knack for such things."

"Don't worry, she'll be back soon," Deihlia said encouragingly. Then her mind drifted off.

"How is Lastgorn?"

"He is well," she said. "He's just glad to be part of this expedition. It means a lot to him, but I can see how much Gwyn's death has affected him."

"In what way?" Shadowolf asked, although the sombre difference in Lastgorn was palpable.

"He used to treat journeys like these as epic adventures, a tale to tell his children one day," Deihlia replied, and Shadowolf laughed softly. "But now it's all about exacting revenge and expelling an anger that's been hiding in him for years."

"You know, I was thinking of writing about all of this in a book," Shadowolf said, staring blankly at the trees on the banks of the River of Light.

"You might have to write more than one," Deihlia teased. "I don't think one will be enough."

"Well, I'm not sure I'll be able to write it," he said. "Only a madman could possibly write about everything we've been through, and even then the readers would be hard put to believe it."

"It's not that bad," she laughed.

"Maybe I'll travel worlds like Le'Mar and get someone else to write it," Shadowolf mused, "a place where I can thrill the people with my story. I can see the title now: 'Shadowolf Degron: Eons before Time.'"

"Now you're just being ridiculous," she laughed again and slapped him on the back playfully as she left.

Shadowolf laughed at his silliness a moment longer and was about to leave the railing when something on the western lands caught his attention. For a flicker of a second it seemed as if the fog shifted, coalescing into shapes he could not yet discern.

"Hey bro," Darcwulf greeted, and then looked at the land. "What the..."

"Call my father."

Soon he was not the only one watching the scene before him. The people on the other ships also watched as lines and lines of orcs, Froth Huns, Ma-Wreths and Dra-hu'Mar formed on the land.

"That's ironic," Nighthale said beside his son. "This is almost the same place where the original Windfarer ship was destroyed before you were born."

"That's a comfort," he replied. He looked ahead of the ship and saw the junction of the River of Light and Shadow River approaching. "I guess Le'Mar's back."

"What's that?" Lastgorn asked, his sharp Blue Falchion in his hand.

They all looked at the army and saw creatures they had never seen before. They were larger than the Froth Huns, but a few hands smaller than the Ma-Wreths. What appeared to be black hair fell down in locks from their heads. Their skins were pale grey and their faces seemed scarred.

Despite their height, their bodies were thinner than those of the Ma-Wreths. Their clothes consisted of basic leggings and tunics, with fur coats hanging from their shoulders and large metal spikes sticking out from the skin of their lower arms.

The only other features of the beasts that stood out were the hands. Each hand consisted of two stubby digits that were connected to the wrist and a thumb below them attached to the base of the palm. These hands held axes larger than those of the dwarves, and it reminded Shadowolf of the Axehorn weapon that had belonged to Sny-Ten.

"Shriekers," Darcwulf informed them. "Nighthale, let the other ships know that only elementals should go up against them. The swordsmen need to stay on the ships."

"What do you mean?" Lastgorn asked as Nighthale left to send the message.

"Their cries sting your nerves and bring you to your knees," Darcwulf replied. "This gives them time to swing those lovely blades through your skull."

"What a pretty picture," Deihlia commented.

"Because elementals can surround their bodies with their elemental auras, it defends them in some way by softening the blow," he continued.

"We should tell the others," Lastgorn said and left to join Nighthale.

"There isn't time," Shadowolf said, although Lastgorn had

already left. "Let's go."

He rose into the air as the first flight of arrows flew towards the ships. Shadowolf stopped his flight and focused on the wind. A gale rose up from the land and caused the arrows to rise higher than was intended. The arrows landed harmlessly in the water on the other side of the ships.

Shadowolf could hear the transformations happen behind him. Wind, water, fire, earth and spirit elementals flew passed him to land on the western banks of the river while the swordsmen stayed to defend the ships.

Even Shadowolf was shocked to see how many elementals were present on the voyage. They lined the beaches in vast numbers, and he estimated about six hundred. Yet, even this army of elementals was small compared to the vast numbers that were marching towards them.

"And so we begin," Shadowolf said as he descended down into the crowds on the beach. Darcwulf landed by his side, a blazing body of fire with his serpent blade in his hand. They both looked up as the land grew dark. Clouds were covering the sun and the land was covered in shadows.

"That's odd," Darcwulf said. "Le'Mar doesn't have creatures that are cursed by the sun anymore."

Darcwulf's comment was lost to Shadowolf's sentience as it became absorbed by the battle. He drew just enough power from his soul as he felt necessary, surrounding his body with the aura of Bontu and completely immersing it in His presence.

Elemental orbs crossed the distance to the orcs from the frontline. The beasts were flung back and killed where contact was made. The orcs panicked, realising they still had a field to cross to get to them and broke the formations.

They ran back into the hands of the Shriekers, who deftly lifted them up by their necks and threw them towards the elementals again. Ma-Wreths cracked whips, forcing the orcs to march. It was then that Shadowolf realised that there were no hurorcs in the army, only purorcs.

The elementals ran forward with staves and elemental swords in hand, their powers burning around their bodies like blankets of rage. Orbs continued to assail the dark lord's army as the beasts hastened to meet them in melee combat.

The two armies were moments from colliding, their weapons shining despite the clouds, when a white portal opened up between them. The elementals stopped, the orcs tripping over their own feet, as everyone watched the portal.

Cerexus raced through the portal with Anuxis on its back, golden scepter flaring in his hand. They crashed through the front orcs, followed by the windy form of Lucian on Lancenat's back.

Shadowolf waited for the portal to close, but gaped in astonishment as the gargoyles raced out and drove their stony fists into the opponents. Trimistus exited the portal just as it closed, his Saurex biting furiously into any orc that crossed its path.

After a moment's hesitation, the chaos arose again as orcs finally raised their crude swords and shields in battle. Froth Huns rode forward to engage the newcomers and the elementals ran into the battle to assist.

Shadowolf dodged an orc blade, twisted the orc's arm until the blade fell out its hand and snapped its elbow. He twisted the orc around until its back fell onto another's orc thrusting sword. Before the sword-wielding orc could remove the blade, Shadowolf became wind and blew up behind the beast, snapping its neck.

He turned in time to block a Froth's blade with his staff. The impact of the long, two-handed blade should have broken the staff in two. The skull of the beast frowned down from its dark horse as the second half of the staff became coils of red-hot chains that spun around the blade. Shadowolf yanked the sword out its grasp, twisted the chain around his leg and kicked the sword through its skull.

The staff reformed and Shadowolf ran it around his body in circles, slapping six orc swords away from him. He bent backwards as a sword passed over his stomach and chest, almost clipping his chin. He moved around the blade as the orc tried striking again. When the tip of the blade swiped horizontally, Shadowolf hit it with his staff and sent it back the way it had swung. The orc's arm twisted and the tip cut across the beast's neck.

Lucian removed his elemental sword from a Dra-hu'Mar and held a fretful Lancenat at bay as a Shrieker stomped up to them. It drew in a huge lungful of air and a cry broke out from its throat.

Waves of shock broke against him and the nearest elementals. The aura of wind around his body dissipated slightly as the sound stung his nerves and Lancenat fell to its front knees, neighing fiercely.

The cry stopped and Lucian looked up with blurred eyes. He could barely make out the dark form of the beast approaching, its axe swinging around for the slaughter. Another grey-shaped body suddenly crashed into the giant and, when his vision cleared, Lucian saw it was Glasden that was driving the beast's own axe through its chest.

Shadowolf killed another two orcs and saw several elementals get slaughtered by a Ma-Wreth as the orc bodies fell from his staff. He ran forward to face the beast when three Froth Huns raced down on their black mounts to fight him. As they bore down on him, he concentrated the power he required into his back.

Their massive swords dropped to kill him and his *Wisoum* wings snapped out from his back. The dragon-scaled wings pulled him up as he hit two Froth's off their mounts and plunged his feet into the chest of the third. Before the Froth had fallen off the rear of his horse, Shadowolf's skull had turned into a dragon's head. He caught the falling Froth Hun by the collar of its coat and bit into its blue-flamed, skeletal head.

Fragments of bone fell on the grass as Shadowolf spun around in mid-air, his wings beating hard against the wind. He growled deeply, his sapphire dragon-eyes burning up as Mandy appeared out of the wind and he dropped on her back. The two mountless Froths turned in fear and ran into Skywolf and Angelia's elemental blades.

He turned Mandy back in the direction of the Ma-Wreths, his face becoming human again as he tucked his scaled wings behind his back. Trimistus's Saurex was running around feasting on the orcs as its rider was flying around with his own set of dragon wings, slaughtering Froths where he could.

Shriekers formed a line before him and Mandy reared up as he pulled the reins hard. Shadowolf became wind just as the first Shrieker ripped the air with its cry. The wind of his body rippled in the air like fire being blown by a gale.

Mandy twisted beneath him and he was about to regain composure when a second Shrieker sent waves of tension through his body. The wind died around his body and he bent over as his nerves sang with the nail-biting pain.

He heard the stomping of large feet as another Shrieker ran to drive its axe through him. The stomping sounds were swiftly by the imploding, cracking sound of fire. Shadowolf's recovering vision saw walls of flames all around him as the Shriekers ran around in agony and Darcwulf flew up into the air. One by one the Shriekers fell, their corpses stinking of burnt flesh. Shadowolf saluted in thanks as his brother left to join the other elementals.

Shadowolf strapped his staff to Mandy's mount and used the wind to pull one of the Shrieker's axes up to him. His right arm bulged as he held the long stem of the axe and raced forward to the four Ma-Wreths in his sight. The Froths and Dra-hu'Mar he passed were too preoccupied with Trimistus and Lucian to bother facing him.

The first of the four Wreths turned and saw him approach. Its arm pulled back for what he knew would be a lightning-fast strike. Shadowolf waited for the right moment and rode straight into the Wreth's embrace.

Its two arms struck at Shadowolf eight times in one second. He and Mandy became wind, the arms making the slightest of whispered noise, as the horse turned and lashed out with its hind legs. The giant lifted off its feet and landed with a quake on the ground. Shadowolf rematerialised and flung the axe into the chest of a second Ma-Wreth.

The third and fourth Ma-Wreths watched Shadowolf cautiously before running with big bounds towards him. Shadowolf unstrapped his staff, swinging it in circles on his right-hand side. His power seeped into the staff as the Wreths' arms prepared to bring him down. Shadowolf threw his staff forward and it transformed into Nelnar. The large wolf collided with the surprised Wreth at the same time that Cerexus bit into the other one with all three heads.

"I was wondering what had happened to him," Nighthale said as he removed his wind blade from the chest of a Dra-hu'Mar. Shadowolf smiled at his father as he turned Mandy.

The fog became dark again and the remaining soldiers of the dark lord vapourised into it. Their forms shimmered as they disappeared. Only two Dra-hu'Mar remained behind, and their limp bodies fell to the grass as Nellice and Mirelda removed their aVampyere fangs from their necks. Shadowolf smiled at them and nodded in greeting. They jumped into the air and became two wisps of smoke that travelled to the nearby Shadow Lake.

"Do you think we upset him?" Darcwulf said, smiling broadly beneath his fiery face.

"I don't know," Shadowolf said as Nelnar jumped in the air and became the staff as he caught it. He looked north towards Le'Mar's castle as if addressing the dark lord himself. "But I hope he knows that this is just a taste of things to come."

Shadowolf turned to return to the ships, but stopped in his steps. Among the elementals and men returning stood two lone figures staring lovingly at each other, words barely escaping their lips. And then Lucian moved forward and embraced his wife.

CHANGE OF HEART
CHAPTER SEVEN

They finished boarding the ships and set off again. Once Lucian had taken the gargoyles and his family back to Horlorn and the clouds had pulled back from the sunny sky again, Shadowolf and Anuxis had boarded the plank to the ship together. Mandy was taken to the Degron supply ship again, but Cerexus followed in its master's wake.

The ships rode the current of the river, heading for the Scourge to the north. They would pass Carmel to the right and Philagus to the left before they reached their destination, but it was already agreed by the tribe lords that they would not stop at the Carmel port.

"Dada," Crystal muttered in Deihlia's arms. Shadowolf walked up to them and took his daughter in his arms.

"Thank you," he said. She smiled politely and left to attend to her brother. Crystal looked up at the wolf-man with apprehension. Anuxis looked down at the girl with just as much uneasiness.

"She won't bite," Shadowolf joked, and Anuxis smiled. His daughter's gaze turned to Anuxis's scepter and he twirled the shaft between his fingers and thumb sportingly. She giggled as the head of the scepter turned and turned.

"How did you guys get here so quickly?" Shadowolf finally asked.

"I sensed a great shift in the fog," he replied, and Crystal became temporarily aware of his fangs again as he spoke. He offered her a smile which seemed to ease her a bit. Then she looked down.

"Puppy," she said gleefully. She reached out her hands to Cerexus, Shadowolf holding her back.

"It's ok, Cerexus is good with children," the wolf-man said. Shadowolf raised his brow in uncertainty and then put Crystal down. She quickly moved over and started patting the central forehead of the hound. It wasn't long before she became engrossed with the task of attempting to pat all three heads.

"Le'Mar will summon more creatures from other worlds," Darcwulf said as he joined them. "This won't be his last attack. We just weakened his pawns."

"Let's hope he holds off long enough until we're ready," Shadowolf said.

"Which brings me to another matter," Anuxis said. "I need to head to the Underworld. Make sure things are in order."

"Very well," Shadowolf said. "Ride safe."

Anuxis nodded and whistled softly to Cerexus, who sadly left Crystal and let his master mount him. The hound jumped onto the port-side railing and bound over into the water. Anuxis held the reins tight as they rode onto the land.

A large black portal with lava innards opened up. Anuxis gave one wave, with Crystal replying comically with her own, and they jumped through as the portal vanished.

Shadowolf headed below deck and smelled the first scent of supper being prepared. He passed his companions, greeting them in turn until he reached his father's cabin.

"Mama," Crystal said, pointing over his shoulder.

"Don't worry," he patted her back, "Mama will be back soon."

She muttered the word one more time as he entered the cabin. Only his father was present and Crystal smiled broadly when she saw her grandfather. Nighthale was perusing small eagle-scrolls in his hands.

"How many losses?" Shadowolf asked as he sat down beside him.

"Thirteen dead, seven wounded," he replied and Shadowolf could tell by the expression on his face that, although this was minor, it still plagued him to lose any lives.

"Our battle with Le'Mar will cost us dearly," Shadowolf commented.

"Which is why I wanted to prevent it in the first place," Nighthale said. He leaned back in his seat, sighed and appraised his son with his gaze.

"I know, dad," he replied, kinder than any of their past discussions on the topic. "But have you seen how eager the others are?"

"You're right," Nighthale said. "I have never seen them fight like that in ages. I thought the two years of peace would have rusted their reflexes, but apparently I was wrong."

"This is their first time waging war against the dark lord," Shadowolf continued, glad that his father was talking so openly. "In the past we've just defended, but now we're taking the war to him."

"I thought you were bringing him to us?" Nighthale smirked.

"Well…yes, I guess you're right."

"What about the elves, son?"

"I'll have to go see them," Shadowolf said, looking down at his daughter's face. She had fallen asleep, "for more than one reason."

"How so?"

"They have something I need," Shadowolf replied. "Something that might help me….what's that?"

"What?" Nighthale looked at the table and smiled when he saw the drawing. "Oh, one of the Orion children drew this. Jilian Asmuth if I'm not mistaken."

"Any chance she's related to the philosopher?" Shadowolf said, taking the drawing in his hand. Depicted on it was a man throwing his staff forward. The top half of the staff was a wolf's head, and he suddenly realised that this was when he had summoned Nelnar. Rough drawings of orcs surrounded the two, but he and the staff were very clear.

"She's the granddaughter of Philgarn," Nighthale said. "The girl's only thirteen and she was able to draw that while watching from the Costen ship."

"What!?" Shadowolf exclaimed, frightening Crystal awake and causing her to cry in alarm. After he managed to calm her down, he looked up at his father again. "I was quite a distance from the ship if I remember."

"It seems to be one of her gifts," his father replied.

"And it was her grandfather that had had the prophetic visions," Shadowolf said, his face set in awe.

"Must have skipped a generation, for her father claims not to have the ability. Her father was more interested in martial combat than sensing."

Shadowolf studied the drawing again, and only then realised that there were words scripted at the bottom:

Setting free what he had loved and lost

"Very literate, isn't she?" Shadowolf laughed.

"Quite."

There was a knock on the door and Nighthale asked that the person enter. Darcwulf walked in, smiling to both in greeting.

"Shedaaij's here," he told his brother.

"Oh," Shadowolf said, panicking silently as he realised that Crystal had just fallen asleep again. His father carefully took the girl from his arms and Shadowolf dashed up to the deck.

When he breached the deck, Shedaaij had just climbed the last rung of the starboard ladder. Her body dripped with the river's water and her coral armour's light dimmed. She smiled at him as they embraced, holding him tightly in her arms.

"Come, let's get you dry," Shadowolf said just as Deihlia came over with a towel. He walked with her to their cabin and closed the door, pushing the lock closed. Shedaaij dropped her coral armour to the floor and sat on the bed in the towel.

"How was the journey?" he asked. He put a blanket on the floor beside a make-shift fireplace made of bricks that lay in a circle. He quickly threw twigs and small logs in and with his hand lit it a fire. Shedaaij moved down beside the fire on the blanket.

"Where is Crystal?" she asked, ignoring his question.

"With my father," he replied and then waited for her answer.

"Well, the oceans are surprisingly quiet," she said. "No evidence of sirens, although James says they're abundant."

"And how did my old friend take my request?"

"Better than I thought he would," she said. "At first he was against it like your father, but somehow I managed to convince him of the importance of the situation."

"So he will join us?" Shadowolf asked, astounded.

"Yes, but you should have the seen the mer-Kingdom's reaction."

"Let me guess; they were not too keen."

"Actually," Shedaaij said, looking up at him, "they were overly eager. James stood there, silenced by their shouts of joy. They had kept quiet for so long only because he had expressed his anger at the humans and forbid any to enter the kingdom.

"But the mermen and maids that had lost their loved ones have been aching to strike back at the dark lord and rid the seas of the sirens. Even the ones with companions wanted their children to live freely in the oceans."

"Nice to have a consensus," he said, relief flooding him.

"What about you?" she asked. "Everything turn out alright?"

"Well, we had a bit of a skirmish today," he said as her face took on panic. "Lost a few good warriors, but I think Le'Mar's losses count into the hundreds."

"Did he appear?"

"No, he just sent some beasts through the fog," Shadowolf replied. "Nothing too serious, but I see we have some new ones to contend with."

"I bet he'll have much more by the time we fight him," she said thoughtfully. "How soon before Ringos appears?"

"The Masaran Phenomenon is only a few weeks away," he replied. "We're cutting things really short."

His thoughts were stopped when she leaned forward and kissed him. Her hand stroked the back of his neck and his hand fell under the towel around her and pulled it away. She lay down as he moved over her, their kisses deepening as their love for each other woke again. He clutched his fingers in hers, pinning them to the ground above her head as he bit into her neck, when suddenly a knock resounded on the door.

"Crystal's looking for you," his father's voice sounded. Shadowolf dropped his head over Shedaaij's shoulder, sighing as she kissed his forehead.

THE BLUE UNICORN
CHAPTER EIGHT

The centaurs and pegasus ran at their own leisure, unhastened by the riders that they carried through the forest. The sun had set two hours before, but Lesan had advised Chenesia that they were so close to their destination it would be fruitless to set camp.

Behind them, on the far north-eastern horizon, Sothos the moon broke out and lit the earth with its fractural light. More to the north, where the travelling group knew Le'Mar's castle to be, the minute light of the planet Ringos blinked in the blanket of the night sky.

Chenesia spared but a moment watching the soft pulsing light that would either be their omen of doom or glory. It would not be long before the planet was close enough to disrupt their hours and bring about the phenomenon that occurred every four years.

The Masaran Phenomenon will awaken his power.

He is the Windfarer, the DragonRider, the Sadgi.

How little she had known about what was truly happening when it all had started. In ignorance had she left the Vale of Tigers against her father's will and despite his ill-health to search out Eldor and request a better defence for the Heart of Tigers. In innocence had she being captured and held as ransom so that the Heart could be delivered to the dark lord to enable his victory over the elves.

Yet, after everything, Le'Mar had still prevailed and taken what he wanted. Elgoth had encouraged her so many times in uPendus, ensuring her that all she had done had not been in vain. Yet the world was lost to darkness; the forest had been taken; her father had died.

She became self-conscious as she realised how serious her thoughts had become. Still staring ahead, Chenesia wondered how silly she looked with such a stern expression and eyes that reflected despair. Yet, as she turned her gaze slowly to the others, she saw that she was not the only one wallowing in thought.

Lesan's head drooped slightly, his eyes unblinking. The centaur on whom he was mounted kept a steady pace, his eyes focused on the path through the forest. She heard the tigroys running behind her, the other centaurs spread out on either side of them as far as she could see.

Despite the approach of winter, the night air was slightly warm in the forest. Not only could they see by the dim light that the rising moon provided, but the barks of the trees seemed to emit soft auras of pale blue light. It added an eerie essence to the ride, accentuating each clop that the hooves thundered upon the leafy terrain and sensitising her vision to a point where she could almost stare her way to her destination.

Something in Lesan's behaviour brought Chenesia out of her reverie. He looked slowly to each side as if to ascertain that they were in no danger without alarming the others. She could see in the steel of his eyes that he was disturbed by something she could not see, that he heard of things that she could not hear.

The prince of the elves sighed deeply, his chest rising and sagging as he looked at Chenesia. He smiled at her, reassuring her with that simple gesture, before looking ahead again. She looked ahead too, Genewiu's long mane teasing her neck and her wings tucked beneath the girl's inner thighs.

The pegasus also turned her head for a moment, causing Chenesia to become more alarmed than before. She turned on Genewiu's back, looking at the swaying forest behind her. The trees glowed beautifully, the branches hung limply in the light breeze, but still there was no sign of what was bothering the others.

"Are we almost there?" Chenesia dared to ask. Lesan looked at her and replied, but she couldn't hear what he said. At first, she thought he had not spoken loud enough, but suddenly she realised that she couldn't hear anything.

There was an omnipotent silence in the forest that overrode everything else around them. The centaurs and Genewiu stopped and turned around as the power thrummed in the air.

The silence was so dense and the pressure in the forest so heavy that Chenesia's vision began to blur. She groaned inwardly as the power vibrated through her. She was sure that, if it didn't end soon, her bones would crack.

Chenesia screamed as the sound exploded all around them and her ears ached. She closed her eyes and held her palms over her ears as the forest came alive with noise and the earth shook beneath them. She only opened her eyes when sprays of sand hit her legs.

Monsters were rising from the forest floor before them. They were far enough ahead that Chenesia and the others could still flee. She slowly removed the hands from her ears and watched as the beasts raced forward.

Chenesia suddenly feared that Sona had returned. The monsters were made out of rock and soil, grunting in hoarse noises she did not recognise.

As if in answer to her fears, she saw Sona at the rear of the rushing army upon a tiger made out of obsidian. It had no eyes, ears or any external features that normally characterised a living being. Yet its perfectly polished shape was that of a tiger, with a dark, cloudy tail protruding at the back.

"Chenesia, get out of here," Lesan ordered. The girl looked up at him with trepidation swimming in her eyes.

"I won't leave you," she said, forcing defiance into her voice.

"You need to find Sorceress," he continued, raising his voice over the banter of the approaching army. "She can stop this. You need to do it now!"

"No!" Chenesia shouted, the mounting tears cracking her voice. She drew her bow and notched an arrow. "I will die with you this night if I must."

"Heltaur!" Lesan commanded, and the elf nodded in Chenesia's direction. She hardly had time to protest before the centaur pulled her off Genewiu's back and clutched her in his arms.

Chenesia screamed and shouted, unable to see what was happening to the others. She didn't hear the pegasus's hooves running alongside them. She didn't see the prince's face looking down at her encouragingly. She twisted and resisted the centaur until she heard the clash of steel and the flight of arrows. Numbed by her helplessness, she closed her eyes and sobbed.

The earth shook again and Heltaur lost his footing. The centaur had almost fallen on top of her, but she rolled in time and ran back in the direction of the battle. Heltaur had already carried her a distance from the battle and it was going to take her a few moments to back.

She looked up and saw two monkey-like creatures swinging through the branches to the prince with wooden pikes in their hands. She drew her bow, notched two arrows and split them into the air together. The arrows struck the monkeys in their sternums, and Chenesia continued to run.

She didn't look back, but knew from the loud thumping and the vibrations on the ground that Heltaur was in pursuit of her. She jumped over logs, dispatching more arrows as the centaur gained her.

Then something caused both her and Heltaur to stop. Sand blew up in the area beyond Lesan and the centaurs. Rocks clustered together to form a massive, ugly brute that towered as high as the trees. It roared and stretched as if from eons of sleep, and then started slumping towards them.

Chenesia loosed three arrows after each other at the brute's head. It simply flew through, strange shifts in the sand being the only evidence of the arrows' attacks. The giant became enraged though and pulled at the closest oak. The tree itself was at least six times wider than Chenesia, but the brute clutched the uprooted tree in its hand and hurled it at them.

"Oh dear Bontu save us," Chenesia whispered as the trunk flew right through the earth monsters, Lesan and their companions and finally to Chenesia and Heltaur. She stood there, not knowing what to do, when the centaur picked her up and somehow threw her into the air.

She held her arms out for balance and as the trunk rolled under her she ran on its surface and jumped up further. She folded her knees and rolled when she reached the ground. By the time she stopped rolling, the arrow was already notched and she let it soar through the air. The arrow hit a rock in the brute's arm and it bounced off harmlessly.

Chenesia ignored this however as she struck an arrow across a monster's face, kicked it to the ground and used the bow to send the arrow into its back. The beast howled before melting into the earth.

Anxiously, she searched the forest for Lesan. She panicked when she saw some of the centaurs struggling to rise from the tree that had hit them. Others were dead with their corpses lying in awkward positions. Ignoring the sand creatures around her and unaware of Sona racing towards her on the dark tiger, she went through corpses and rubble for any sign of Lesan.

A centaur landed hard beside her and she stole a moment's glance to find that it was Heltaur. Frantically, she started to search again when his gaze into the tree tops made her look up. The sand giant was trying to swat an elf that was jumping and flying around its head and with sudden elation she realised it was Lesan.

He landed on the side of a trunk and kicked away again as the large fist slammed against the spot he had been. He ran along its arm, his elvin sword shimmering in his right hand, his left hand glowing with power that he was calling. The giant swung the arm back to its side and Lesan jumped away to another tree and ricocheted higher towards the beast.

Chenesia's focus was forced away as Heltaur threw her aside. Two sand monkeys collided with the centaur, sending him rolling with them through the forest. Chenesia got up from her knees and released arrows at the growing horde around her.

Lesan finally landed on the broad shoulders of the giant and ran behind its neck onto a large hump atop its back. He saw the giant's hand rising to hit him, but he quickly drove his sword, now livid from power, into the base of its neck.

The earth began to swirl but the beast cried out and landed on its right knees, fists clenched from pain. Lesan's arms pulsed from the energy he drove into the beast and the giant roared louder, its guttural voice echoing like a lion in fury.

Chenesia grabbed a deceased centaur's dagger, which to her was as huge as a human's sword, and plunged it into an earth monster's abdomen. As much as she loathed the weapon, Elgoth had been right: she would one day be grateful that he had taught her how to handle weapons in uPendus.

She yanked the sword out and twirled it around into the neck of another monster. She chopped off another's leg and then kicked its head in before standing up straight to face Sona, who was not far before her.

"This time your prince won't take my prey," Sona said, dismounting from the obsidian tiger. Chenesia faced her with a blank stare, sword in hand and bow on her back. She knew there was nothing she could do against Sona's elemental abilities, but she would not submit to her.

The giant twisted the hump on its back and the sword cracked from within it. Lesan stared dumbly at the sword in his hand for a moment, the broken teeth cutting the air mid-way up the blade. He threw the remains to the forest floor and started running down the beast's right shoulder as thorny vines and raving felines rose from the giant's back in pursuit of the prince.

The giant arose and in a movement that belied his bulk, it rushed its back against a line of trees in an effort to squash Lesan. The prince grabbed a vine hanging from one of the trees, swung around its trunk as some of the felines got crushed, and landed back on the beast's hump.

With a mighty yank the vine broke from the tree and Lesan pulled a dagger from his boot and wedged the vine with the blade into the hump. He grabbed the vine hanging from the dagger and ran over the beast's shoulder, jumping into the air and letting the vine swing him around the neck and back up the other shoulder.

The beast was about to react when Lesan swung around the trees it had rammed into. It grappled for the small vine with its huge finger, unable to get a hold of it under its thick chin. Lesan quickly swung around the neck to the other shoulder again, making sure the vine held on tight.

The prince jumped to the forest floor and pulled with all his might. Blue arcs of lightning flared around his arms and he pulled and the giant roared. The tree trunks began to crack as Lesan pulled, the veins in his upper arms pulsing with the light of his power as he bore his face in a grimace. The beast held its one hand up and slammed its fist down on its throat in a final attempt to break free.

"Let me guess," Chenesia said with a wry smile, "You're going to tie me up and beat me like a defenseless child."

"Oh, you want a chance to prove that you can defeat me?" Sona replied in return, but it was plain to Chenesia that she had intended to do just that. Then Sona held her arms out in mock supplication. "Please, do try."

Despite feeling that it was hopeless, Chenesia charged forward with rage in her. She held the sword steady, careful only to strike at the last moment in order not to give her intentions away.

Yet, even when she struck in a fluid, fast motion, Sona kicked her wrist aside and drive a fist up into her chin. Chenesia's jaw slammed up and she fell onto her back on the forest floor, the sword falling to the side.

"Revenge can be sweet," Sona said, smiling satisfactorily and summoning the centaur dagger into her own hands. She held it on Chenesia's sternum, the tip teasing blood out of the skin. "Pity I am the only one that will taste it."

The giant struggled limply against the tree trunks, its arm trying sluggishly to remove the vine. Lesan's power waned as he held on tight, the elvish dagger holding the vine tight into the beast's hump.

Suddenly Lesan lurched forward as all the trees supporting the giant snapped and the beast fell backward. Lesan fell on his hands and quickly turned to see the giant rise weakly, yet with anger scrawled over its face. Cries of centaurs and earth monsters in battle permeated through the forest, yet Lesan only heard the creaking of the forest beneath the giant's huge feet.

The vine still dangled from the dagger lodged in the giant's back. In a desperate hope, Lesan rose and pulled on the vine, but the beast laughed sickly and yanked the vine. Lesan flew up into the air, forgetting to let go. He had no strength to change course, no more power to expend teleporting out of the way. In defeat, he let the giant catch him in a rocky fist and leer down at him.

As if pulled by the same puppet strings, Sona and the giant turned their gaze away from their victims. Even the earth monsters that had been so riddled in battle with the centaurs remained motionless. The tiger sniffed the air, watching the tree trunk that the giant had originally thrown into the forest.

Over its upper rim the tigroys pounced. They glided with their wings down to the forest floor and charged towards the enemy. The obsidian tiger itched to face them in battle, but something else disturbed him. A light rose over the fallen trunk in the wake of the tigroys, and then the tiger growled in warning to Sona.

The dark *Goudlem* removed the sword tip from Chenesia and backed away carefully. Hordes of fairies rushed over the plains towards them, but that was the least of her worries.

In the wake of the light that trailed in their flight a unicorn appeared. Sona had Ursula's name on the tip of her lips, but then realised it could not be. She never remembered Ursula having a blue coat, with a deep purple horn.

Chenesia turned in her position on the floor and saw the unicorn. She smiled softly and whispered Sorceress's name. She laid on her back in relief. Sona became infuriated suddenly and drove the sword down upon Chenesia.

Before Sorceress's arrival, Chenesia would have let the blade strike her. But now, her appearance inspired renewed energy as she rolled out the way and swept Sona's legs with her feet. The *Goudlem* fell to the ground and Chenesia grabbed the sword to plummet it through her heart. Sona sank into the earth and rose again further away from the girl.

The giant pulled it attention away from the approaching fairies, tigroys and unicorn and growled at his fist, but Lesan was gone. He stood on the floor, tucking his dagger back into his boots before running towards Chenesia. The giant was bewildered, but as it tried to walk its legs gave way. It cried out as the sand of its body collapsed into the earth below and became part of the world again.

In a short time, the fairies cleared the forest of the remaining earth warriors and surrounded Sona and the tiger.

"Leave," Sona said simply, and the tiger looked at her and then turned and fled.

"Get that tiger," Chenesia instructed the tigroys, and they ran in pursuit as the girl faced the *Goudlem*. Lesan joined Chenesia's side shortly.

The unicorn walked up slowly and transformed. A sparkling green dress covered her as she became human, a hood drawn over her pale blue face. The butterfly pendant sparkled on her sternum as she pulled the hood down and stood between Lesan and Chenesia. There were no obvious signs of weapons upon her.

Sona reacted faster than Lesan or Chenesia expected, but Sorceress seemed to have sensed the silent rising of power. As Sona's arms flew out towards them with the power of the earth and spirit, Sorceress simply raised one palm. The gesture was as simple as breathing, yet Sona fell to her knees and clutched her throat.

Her body began contorting as skin became sand. Sona's eyes went wide as she began losing her internal organs. Chenesia watched in horror as Sona attempted to fight the change. The sand became skin momentarily again before turning to sand and ash.

Sona crawled into a ball as her flesh appeared beneath skin. She coughed as the flesh melted into the earth and her bones glowed dully in contrast to the leaves around her. A sigh escaped into the wind as the remains of her body became one with the pile of ash. The dust floated up into the wind and was spread over the forest floor.

"Come," Sorceress said, lowering her power as if what she had done had just been a thought. "We have much to discuss."

SEPARATE WAYS
CHAPTER NINE

The images of the last battle with Le'Mar's horde still played in his mind as he bathed in the sunlight on the deck of the ship. Crystal was on her hands and knees trying to retrieve toys from her mother's hands. The ship was active with daily duties and wandering crew.

He watched everyone move around him, not shifting his head but simply gazing ahead of him and watching them glide across his vision. He felt them stir around him, their voices and footsteps nudging his attention from the surreal peace of the day and the absence of any malice.

Shadowolf spared a glance over the ship's port rail to the far Dwarf Mountains. The peaks behind which Le'Mar's castle was tore the sky as much as the dark lord's tyranny tore at Shadowolf's soul. Yet, despite his feelings, his spirit remained calmed and the soft wind teased the hair from his face.

The time would come when Le'Mar would face his judgement. Shadowolf narrowed his eyes and growled softly.

"Is everything ok?" Shedaaij asked, but he didn't have a chance to answer.

"And here is the saviour of the world," Darcwulf commented snidely as he fell into a reclining chair.

"Whoever said I was going to save the world?" Shadowolf replied, turning his gaze from the castle to them.

"Well let's see," his brother replied, counting them off his fingers. "There is the prophecy, which clearly says you're going to destroy him. And the fact that you've been putting the spanner in Le'Mar's plans since the beginning."

"First of all, the prophecy made no mention of me facing

Le'Mar, so I don't know why everyone assumes I will. Secondly, it's not my fault he chose idiots for champions."

"Hey, what's wrong with you?" Darcwulf asked, a deep frown caressing his forehead.

"I don't know," he replied, trying to relax. "I guess I'm just a little frustrated that's all. I've been thinking about how we've all been fighting this war for years, but somehow everyone now expects me to just take on Le'Mar without their involvement."

"What are you talking about, Shado?" Darcwulf said, sweeping his hands around him. "We're all coming with you."

"Yes, but most of them don't really appreciate how important this is," he said grumpily. "I only half convinced the tribe lords, and I have no idea what the others feel."

"My love, you're being silly," Shedaaij interjected. "Did you see the passion that the men had when we fought his army? They were driven to destroy those beasts."

Shadowolf took what she said in, bowing his head in thought.

"Look Shado," his brother said, "I know this is difficult. The men have been looking for a reason to fight, to take back the land, but they never knew what they should do about it. To them, Le'Mar had won.

"But you've given them new hope. You seem to have a plan, and that's enough reason for them to pick up sword and bow again. The mere fact that you brought me back from the dark lord's power was daunting enough."

"We can't dispute that you've stirred the men to battle," Shedaaij said, "nor that they look to you now for leadership and salvation. But that does not change the fact that this is what they have been waiting for for so long."

"Thank you," Shadowolf smiled at them, and they nodded. "But in the end it is not I that will save them."

"What do you...," Shedaaij began to say, but then she and Darcwulf both frowned as Shadowolf's expression went blank.

He sat still, his eyes not blinking as traces of fire, wind, earth and water swept like a ghost across the blue irises of his eyes. When they had blown past, his pupils glowed purple. He blinked, and his eyes returned to normal.

"I need to go," Shadowolf said and stood up.

"Why, what's happening?" Darcwulf said alarmed as he and Shedaaij arose.

"The elementëls are summoning me and I must leave," he replied and turned to go.

"Wait!" Shedaaij called and picked Crystal up.

"No, love," he turned around, his outstretched hand forestalling her. "Not with Crystal. I'm heading to where the fake portal in Lasglow took us."

Shedaaij stood still, understanding written across her face.

"She could leave her with Deihlia," Darcwulf offered.

"No, he's right," Shedaaij said. "Crystal's been alone for too long with neither of us around. One of us must stay with her."

"Well, I'm going with, whether your stubborn heart will allow it or not," Darcwulf said. "Let me just get my sword."

Shadowolf bid Shedaaij and their daughter farewell and then used the wind to fly over to the ship behind them. He reached Mandy and looked deep into her dark eyes until the mist formed within it and he could see Lucian on the other side.

"Shall we go together?" Lucian said before Shadowolf could speak.

"Yes," he replied. "Bring Trimistus with you."

Lucian nodded and the image in Mandy's eyes cleared. He turned around at the sound of feet landing on the deck and saw that Darcwulf had not returned alone.

"Where are you going?" Nighthale asked, the other tribe lords looking at him expectantly. Shadowolf assumed that Darcwulf's haste for his sword must have alarmed them.

"Perhaps it is best if you see for yourself," Shadowolf replied, a warm smile appearing on his face.

Shadowolf noticed that there was someone unknown to him with the tribe lords. He deliberately frowned in the man's direction and Nighthale obliged by introducing him.

"This is Salinos, Shado. He's from the Orion. Kailan appointed him to stand in for her after she went with Lucian to Horlorn."

"Pleased to meet you," Salinos said and extended his hand in greeting. Shadowolf shook it while studying the man. Salinos was at least ten years older than him, but his fair tanned face was nowhere as aged as the other tribe lords. Shadowolf trusted Kailan enough though to know she would not just appoint anyone.

The air began to tear around them as a portal started to form. Their hair blew and their clothes flirted with the wind as the portal appeared behind Malkius, Sjedwolf, Jasnon, Nighthale and Salinos. They moved away as the portal became more solid, twisting and whirling into a grey vortex.

Lucian stepped through the portal followed shortly by a bemused Trimistus. The group of nine greeted each other and began to talk amongst themselves as the portal closed. Shadowolf went quiet, letting the wave of voices and sounds drown over him as he calmed his spirit. Darcwulf simply watched his brother and saw a dim light cross his closed eyelids.

The air thrummed again with power, sparks of lightning tearing a new hole before them. Men and women from across the ship followed the sound until they saw the swirling portal flare with lightning before the small group. Shadowolf opened his eyes and then walked through.

He waited patiently on the other side for the others to cross over. The portal was gentler now, only the occasional spark breaking the serenity of the fields around him.

"I didn't know you could summon portals to other worlds," Darcwulf said, clearly amazed.

"I can't and I didn't," Shadowolf replied, washing his brother's face from awe and sullying it with confusing.

The portal closed and the group looked out on the glorious fields around them. Flowers of various, bright colours dotted the landscape and many insects were busy with their floral duties. The air blew sweetly over them, soothing their taut nerves.

"Welcome home, my friend," Shadowolf said, laying his hand on Trimistus's shoulder. The reptilian face changed drastically as it dawned on him. He turned around in circles at the fogless world around him. The wind was gentler than he ever remembered it being, and the landscape was not as barren as it should have been.

"It can't be," Trimistus said softly. He ran further down the land, ignoring a rising cave to his left. Shadowolf and the others walked slowly in his wake and soon Trimistus vanished from sight as he ran down a hill. Shadowolf turned to the large cave, leaving him to discover his home planet by himself.

Shadowolf entered the mouth of the cavern, leading the other six behind him. Darcwulf walked beside him, watching the cave walls carefully as if he suspected the earth to reach out and attack him.

"I see they haven't bother changing the inside," he commented. Shadowolf nodded, continuing down the tunnel. He felt ill at ease, the soft sand beneath his feet an echo of the moist tension that ran through his veins. They reached the area where they had met the elementëls previously, the small raised ledge before them as empty as the rest of the cave.

The tribe lords held back, letting Lucian, Shadowolf and Darcwulf remain at the fore to await the arrival of the elementël angels. Darcwulf spared a moment to look at his brother's face, which was placid and void of emotions. He simply stared before him at the dais, his eyes sparkling softly in the dim light that seemed to be part of the walls.

The air shifted slightly and became warm. The light grew slightly sharper and Darcwulf groaned as a fire broke out from his skin. He relaxed when he saw that fire also rose around Shadowolf and left their bodies. The flames flickered and merged as they reached the dais.

A green mist rolled off Shadowolf's skin next, flowing towards the disc and folding into shape beside the fire elementël that now waited on the ledge. Shadowolf dropped his head and his brother watched with concern as a tear rolled down his brother's cheek.

The tear dropped to the ground and flowed rapidly to the stage, joining the other elementëls. Darcwulf's concern continued unabated as he saw the sadness in Shadowolf's eyes. The wind stirred up from both sides of him suddenly as Lucian and Shadowolf's bodies emitted rushes of air. The four elementël angels were now fully formed before them.

"You've brought quite an audience with you, Shado," *Enodhim* said, the air stirring through her form like ripples across a silk sheet.

"I wanted to remind them what we're fighting for," Shadowolf replied, "to show them what we're trying to regain."

"We have some news on Le'Mar's forces," *KariemsaPh* said, the fire crackling in his voice. "He has done as was predicted."

"He's rallying more forces from the Gemetrashef," Shadowolf assumed.

"Correct," *Merlandsi* said, the silver sheen of the water glistening in the light from *KariemsaPh*'s body. "What type and how many, we're still unsure of."

"Do we stand a chance against an ever-growing force?" Nighthale asked boldly from the group of tribe lords.

"Gemetrashef will not easily dispense his armies for Le'Mar's cause," *Goudlem* said, his rocky surface bulging and shifting with each word. "For one reason, he is currently using them to conquer other worlds. For another, he feels Le'Mar's rule is incontestable. To all appearances, the Celenic Earth armies cannot stand against the force he already has."

"Well, the armies he knows about anyway," Shadowolf smiled softly.

"Le'Mar has ensured one contingency though," *KariemsaPh* said forebodingly. "He has obtained one of the prince demons from the Gemetrashef's throne. This Saemnati is the best summoner of the Governor's court."

"Is he powerful?" Shadowolf asked.

"You remember that demon I cast against you in the forest's throne? The one Nelnar battled?" Darcwulf said, to which Shadowolf nodded. "The Saemnati is a thousand times its size and that much more powerful."

"I'm sorry, my son," Nighthale said and walked up behind them. "You brought us here to see hope, but I only see despair. Let's rather avoid the wa...."

Nighthale went silent as his son jerked his head to look at him. A sharp, glistening light flashed across his eyes warningly and Nighthale stepped back.

"Shado," *Enodhim* was before him as he looked forward again, his jaws clenched in anger, "this war will test you in more ways than we can ever prepare you. Are you sure you're ready?"

"Yes," he said confidently. "Bontu will give me the strength I need."

"Very well," *Merlandsi* said as *Enodhim* floated back to the ledge. "Then there is only one other matter left."

KariemsaPh moved down from the ledge and drifted before

Darcwulf.

"Trust him," Shadowolf said. "We need to purify you."

Darcwulf's face was fretful as he nodded. *KariemsaPh* dissolved into him and Darcwulf groaned as his skin exploded with fire. He rose into the air, stinging the vapour with his nerves and purging the cave with his fiery essence.

Shadowolf remained as the others stepped back from the pervading heat. Celestial lights broke out like a corona around Darcwulf's body, rivers of fire flowing out like solar flares from his skin. His contorting face and tense jaw relaxed as he opened his eyes. Suddenly, Darcwulf looked the happiest anyone had ever seen him, his spirit calm and his heart content.

The fire slowly died down as he floated back to the ground. The flames pulled back into his skin and his unscathed clothes settled back onto his body. Darcwulf looked up at the four elementëls, his calm smile not leaving his face.

"Thank you," Trimistus's voice suddenly echoed through the cave. "Thank you for restoring my home."

"It is time you returned," *Enodhim* smiled sweetly at them all. "Bontu bless you all"

The four angels became wisps of light in the air, melding into one glowing cloud that drifted before them momentarily and then melding slowly into a soft, humming portal....

The ships drifted in the current of the River of Light that flowed from the Scourge. They had disembarked and finally reached the banks opposite Dwarf Mountains, leaving the ships stranded in the waters. The Scourge's waterfall was too powerful to attempt crossing safely into Dark River.

When they reached the bank, they saw the concrete bridge that the dwarves had constructed. The centre rose up gently towards the sun above them, and rolling down again over the waters to the other bank. It was wide enough that several people could walk abreast with mounts and equipment.

Shadowolf let everyone else proceed over the bridge to the newly constructed tunnels that would lead them faster through the mountain range to Horlorn than the past tunnels had.

Darcwulf and Shedaaij stayed by his side, Crystal watching

silently from her mother's arms. Shadowolf caught a glimpse of Skywolf's blond hair glistening in the sunlight as she and her family crossed the bridge. It wasn't long before Lastgorn and Deihlia broke Shadowolf's observations by appearing before him.

"Making sure the last ant crosses over?" Deihlia said sardonically. "Or are we headed somewhere else?"

"How are you holding out, Lastgorn?" Shadowolf said, ignoring her.

"Ready for a fight," he replied, and Shadowolf could see the resolve and cold ambition in his eyes. The blue hilt of his sword shimmered as a reflection of his expression from behind his left shoulder.

"I'm heading to the Far Isles to see the elves," Shadowolf told them. Shedaaij lowered her head thoughtfully beside him. "I'd appreciate it if you prepared yourselves in Horlorn."

"The lone warrior, hey?" Deihlia commented.

"The elves won't be very accommodating," he continued to persuade them. "I don't know what reception I will receive."

"So let us c...."

"Deihlia, stop it," Lastgorn said, and she looked at him with painful emotions. He walked up to Shadowolf and placed a hand on his shoulder. "Good luck with the elves. We'll see you on your return."

Deihlia gave one last scolding glare to Shadowolf and walked beside her brother, bickering and complaining up to the bridge. All Lastgorn offered in reply was a deaf ear.

Shadowolf saw Nighthale walk up on the bridge with Mandy's reigns in his hands. His mottled staff glistened in her saddle-belt. He turned to Darcwulf and Shedaaij.

"Let's go."

THE GUARDIAN OF THE HORN
CHAPTER TEN

Chenesia stirred in Lesan's arms, turning her head off his elven chest and onto his arm that held her. The night air blew softly through the drapes at the entrance of the rough tent they slept in. The nightdress that Sorceress had given her tingled against the skin of her legs as she quietly moved from the prince's embrace.

The opening revealed to her the quiet forest that stood all around them. A vast canopy consisting of the tree tops twined together hid the night sky from her. She could hear the trickle of the river that ran somewhere close to the tent as she wandered further away.

Chenesia quickly looked up as she heard a twitter from one of the lower trees. Even though their bodies were dark and the night hid them well, she knew that the fairies were there. She swiftly moved on, attempting not to wake them or trip over one of the roots that littered the forest floor.

Though Sorceress had sounded adamant that they should talk, Chenesia had not seen her since they had left their last battle with Sona. The centaurs and fairies had guided them to this resting place and she had waited anxiously for Sorceress's return.

Chenesia looked up, trying to find a space between the tree tops where she could see the night sky. There were tiny gaps and narrow slits, but as she turned and walked she could not get a better view. Without warning, a root caught her toes and she fell cursing to her knees.

Lights flared up above her as the closest fairies awoke and dropped down to her shoulders. She stood up steadily, brushing the dirt off and looked around. The lights were bothering her sight and she squinted. As if they had read her mind, the lights of the fairies drifted down her slender arm to her fingers, adorning them like beautiful jewel rings.

She could now make out the vague floor beneath her. She followed the sound of the river carefully, knowing that they would probably be the best place to view the sky from. It took her several moments before she could smell the river, and a few more before the bank of the river was before her.

The shallow river's water hobbled over the rocks on the bed. The water would take her up to her knees, but the width of it belied its depth. She reckoned it would take her at least twenty steps to reach the other bank, if she could negotiate the rocks properly.

She looked up past the tree tops that hung above her head. Soft clouds drifted overhead, hiding most of the stars from her. She hugged her chest, folding her arms over to retain the warmth of Lesan's arms that were now but a memory to her body.

"Come on," Chenesia said, starting to shiver slightly. "Just a glimpse."

The clouds floated at its own slow pace, not giving her much of a view. She looked further north, carefully watching the sky for any view of the planet that was the harbinger of death.

And then it caught her eye; an amber pulsing object a little bigger than the largest star in the sky. It was too far away to see the rings that cluttered its surface or the different hues and contortions that marked its appeared. She had no doubt though that it was Ringos making its slow orbit to the earth.

Chenesia heard footsteps on the leaves behind her and quickly spun around. The fairies left her arms and drifted to the unicorn's blue head, floating around the horn briefly before landing softly on the long mane that ran along the neck.

The unicorn transformed. It reared up on its hind legs as the coat pulled in and became soft, blue skin. A purple dress dropped down her lovely, slender body as the forelegs became arms. Her hair dropped down over her shoulders, the fairies shining like bright crystals in her hair.

As beautiful as she was, Chenesia could not help but turn her attention to the pendant on her chest. It shimmered from the light of the fairies on a silver chain in the shape of a multi-coloured butterfly. Sorceress smiled at her observation and joined her on the bank of the rivulet.

"Is it the pendant that helps you transform?" Chenesia asked conversationally.

"It used to be," Sorceress replied, her blue face glowing eerily by the light of the fairies. "But since I've managed to learn the way of the earth from the fairies, I can maintain that form for much longer."

"Ringos is getting closer," Chenesia said, switching to her concerns.

"I take it from what I've seen lately that we're on our way to a war again," the elemental said.

"Yes," she replied, dropping her gaze to the river. "we're gathering all the forces we can to take back the earth. But it's more than that."

Chenesia looked up at the pendant again and then into Sorceress's eyes. Sorceress lifted her hand to touch the butterfly softly and then walked to the edge of the bank and sat down. The water just touched her toes.

"If it wasn't for Sinor and Lesan with you, I might not have trusted you so readily," Sorceress replied. "We've been hidden all these years quite comfortably. And in all that time Ursula has only visited us once."

"Well, if you still have doubts....."

Chenesia moved to the nearest tree and traced her hands along the bark. As the tips moved in a pattern, a soft glow lit its wake until her fairy signature was complete. The tree groaned softly, swaying when she stepped back. The fairies twittered from Sorceress's hair.

"We never really discussed what Shado sent you to me for," Sorceress said once Chenesia had returned to the bank. "I assumed it was the pendant, but do you know why?"

"Except that it is vital for the war, no," Chenesia replied. "He and Elgoth have been secretive about the matter."

"So, should I hand it over to you?"

"You'll be joining us in the war, won't you?" Chenesia asked, suddenly concerned. Sorceress remained silent, lifting her one knee up into her arms. "We'll need all the help we can get, Sorceress. The fairies and centaurs...."

"Can join the war without me," she finished for her.

"Sorceress," she said, sitting down on her knees, "we need more warriors like you with us. I saw you fight in Eldor's Forest."

Sorceress turned her head away at the mention of the place.

"I've heard of your Orion skills," Chenesia continued.

"I sense there is more to this war than you're telling me," Sorceress finally said, looking up passed Chenesia to Ringos in the sky. "I can't be that important. Are we heading to a war of the *Sadgi*?"

"I promised Shado I would return with you," Chenesia said, standing up again. "Right now, you're more important to him and I than that pendant around your neck."

Sorceress frowned. She clutched the pendant again, the lights in her hair dimming as the fairies fell asleep. Footsteps made Chenesia look around at Lesan approaching them.

"Think about what I said," she said and left Sorceress alone at the bank.

Chenesia hooked her arms into Lesan's, hugging his warm body close to hers. She could smell the sweet scent that drifted so naturally from him and laid her head against his muscular arm.

"Will the elves help us, my love?" she asked, trusting his footing through the forest better than her own.

"My father's elves will follow me," the prince replied. "Whether or not my father will join us is another question."

"And the Elders?"

"They will be stubborn," he replied. "I don't know if I will be able to convince them, but I will be heading back to the Isles tomorrow to report to them everything that has happened."

Chenesia stopped and looked up at his face. Lesan returned a sympathetic smile.

"Would you by any chance like to join me?" he asked her.

"Why are you only telling me now?"

"I've been meaning to return since yesterday," he replied and took her in his arm again as they continued walking. "I was not sure when the best time was. But with Ringos getting so close and signs of the dark lord presence on the earth again, not to mention Shado's return...."

"Chenesia," he stopped this time, turning to face her. "we all thought Le'Mar had put an end to it all."

"All what?"

"To the prophecies," he said, "to everything that had been foretold. To any sign of hope. What is Shado up to? Is Sorceress right? Will we be seeing the *Sadgi*?"

"All I can tell you, my dearest," she said, offering him a comforting smile, "is that this will be the war the world has been waiting for. Everything that has transpired since the birth of that power node and the prophecy concerning it has led to this point.

"Le'Mar did nothing to stop that which must still come," she continued, and then touched his cheek gently. "Trust me, all he did was delay the inevitable."

"Are you sure?" Lesan asked, frowning deeply. "You put a lot of faith in Shadowolf."

"My faith lies in Bontu," she said, leading him back to the camp again and resting her head on his arms. "But yes, I trust Shadowolf with the fate of the world."

PART FOUR

BOW OF CELENE

THE WHITE WOLVES
CHAPTER ONE

The moon shone beautifully in the sky overhead. In the valley of Bentley Strip, in the northern folds of the land, lay the small group. The cool air remained still and the few trees and bushes stood speechless as the humans slept; all except for one of them.

Shadowolf turned his head to look at Shedaaij and Crystal cradled beside him. He slowly pulled his left arm from under Shedaaij's neck and rose. Darcwulf lay a small distance from them, caught up in the web of his dreams.

He left them in the embrace of the land, alone to their solitude and unencumbered by solicitude. His soul was restless and, no matter how hard he tried to soothe it or ease the burning turmoil in his mind, the elements raged within him to be released. He clenched his fists and closed his eyes, letting his other senses guide him to a place in the fields where he could meditate.

The mountain became a shadow behind him and he stopped. The grass rustled softly beneath his feet and between his toes; he could feel a strong amount of energy exude beneath him from the earth. He sat down on the grass, his legs crossed beneath him and his hands gently resting on his knees.

Shadowolf let his spent energies and chaotic spirit slowly drain from him. The elements remained quiet around him; even the air was as still as stagnant water. He sighed deeply as emptiness filled him, the last of his energy draining into the soil of the earth below him.

He lingered a moment longer, his head swaying with dizziness and his eyes opening to the world around him. As the earth renewed his energy, he took in the fields and the night sky. He heard the twitter of birds somewhere close by and even tasted the taint of the fog on the land. The ground shivered beneath his body, ready to release to him his rejuvenated powers.

He knew he could not instantly draw them into his body; such an act would either kill him or drive him insane. Instead, he used a trick that Elgoth had taught him in uPendus. He reached into the top hem of his pants and tore a well-placed stitch there. Five stones fell into his hands and he played with them between his fingers before laying them down on the grass.

Controlling the energies, he slowly drew them from the earth with his mind. They stirred in the earth and the amethyst, citrine, jasper, agate and unakite all lit up with their respective hues. The stones rose up in to the air before him, ready to heed his call.

The blue agate floated away from the group and began to dissolve into water. The liquid rushed around him like a whirlpool, cleansing the other stones with his power and drowning him in its wonder. He let his mind think only of Bontu and the miraculous wonder of water as it slowly seeped into his body through his skin, flowing into his spirit through his aura.

The red jasper moved next, Shadowolf's eyes crystallised with a brilliant blue light. The jasper melted down into vapours of smoke and eventually burst into an inferno that roared around him like a maelstrom of fire. He thought of Bontu and the glorious wonder of fire, the flames raging into him like sulphurous vapours.

The unakite shifted before Shadowolf's raging, amber eyes. Its grainy exterior broke into soil and vines, the earth twisting around him until he could not be seen inside the cocoon. The sound of uprooting trees crashed all about him, the smell of earth and grass filling his senses, the feeling of nature's warm, tender love caressing his skin. Bontu and the almighty wonder of earth filled his heart, and the earth drained into his body and soul.

The yellow-tinged citrine swirled before his green, opulent eyes. His fondness for wind made him long to reach out and grab the stone, but he stayed his hand as the citrine became wisps of wind that stirred the stale air around him. The hurricane broke out, untainted by any of the grass or soil beneath him, and as he thought of Bontu and the auspicious wonder of air, it blew into his being.

The wind picked him up into the air and his legs dropped down beneath him as he floated. His head dropped back and his body went limp as his spirit dropped back down to the earth below.

The aura of his hand reached out and clutched the amethyst as it got to the peak of its spin. A bright light broke out as it exploded into him, his aura burning up with white, preternatural effervescence. He rose up into his body again, the light cracking out the pores of his skin into the dark night around him.

Shadowolf slowly drifted back to the ground again, his head drooping forward as the light subsided. The air rushed around him causing his hair to blow wildly around his face. Fire started arcing up from his arms and face, eager to be released. Water trickled from his chest down his stomach and his fingers became rocks of rubies and emeralds.

"No," was all that Shadowolf muttered, and everything went quiet. His hair fell back down on his face and the fire died. His body dried and he flexed the skin and muscle of his hands. His spirit was silent.

He walked back to the group, making sure that his soul was at rest. When he first neared the area, he frowned. A soft light was pulsing in the distance. As he got closer he relaxed when he saw that it was Elgoth standing beside a portal.

"The Elders are ready to receive you."

*****

The wolf tribes settled down in the dark interior of Dwarf Mountains, their tents lit only by the torches that stood on the perimeters of the encampments. The few dwarf escorts wandered around, their axes gleaming dully from their backs and hips.

Nighthale looked up from his thoughts, the fire before him reflected in his eyes. His muscles were throbbing from all the latent stress that was building up inside of him. If his wife had been with him, she would have soothed the taut nerves with just a stroke of her fingers or a gentle whisper in his ear.

But he had left her and his daughters in Avalion. The further he travelled from them, the more he feared for their safety. They had left the city defenseless, despite the few warriors he had instructed to stay in the castle.

Nighthale cursed as he realised he was gnawing his teeth again. He massaged his jaw as he rose from the log on which he sat, and made his way passed Mandy to the other tribe lords.

The horse groaned softly as he passed, the ghostly mane swaying softly in his wake. She glared around her thoughtfully, inspecting the dwarves that crossed her path. She walked slowly to one of the tunnels that led to Horlorn and turned her side so that the staff strapped to her saddle faced it.

The mottled staff slid out of the belt and started to transform. Ancient wood became sacred fur, the topmost sanctified tip becoming the large face of the nelmurian wolf. Nelnar gave one shake as he completed the change and then charged into the tunnel.

"Alright," Hargon said as he stopped at the table in the Horlorn dining hall. "Most of the quarters are complete."

Lucian smiled and crossed his arms over his chest. Trimistus, Lanel and Harmony sighed deeply in relief.

"Maybe we should send the Avalion ships to the Carmel port for them," Lanel said.

"There's no need for that," Trimistus interrupted. "Mynisna will be here with the dragons later today. We'll be able to get the Carmel and Vale warriors here within the day, if they followed our instructions."

"And then it's only a matter of time before Le'Mar starts his attack," Harmony said, bowing her head. "It's not like he can miss hundreds of dragons carrying people across the skies."

"I wonder what's going through his mind right now," Lucian commented.

The table went silent as they all contemplated the thought. Lucian lingered a moment longer before he rose from his seat and left the hall alone. The morning air was chilly and the stars burnt beautifully across the sky.

In his solitude he thought of the arrival of the Carmel warriors. His nerves twitched as he thought of seeing Telgar with Simnab. He had heard good things from Lanel about him, that the Crethan gave her a certain happiness that had been void in her life since

Lucian's brother's death.

The wind bit into his eyes gently as his mind raced back to the first time he had seen Telgar. Lucian had been one of the dreaded Sandrihelin, the four elementals that had served Mercius during his reign of terror as the Windfarer. It was during their attack on the Degron tribe so many centuries before that his subservience to Mercius had changed so drastically.

He closed his eyes as the mental images of that battle flashed through his mind, as it had done so often over the years. The only creatures they had fighting for them at that time were orcs, and they were raging all around him into Avalion. Where necessary, Lucian had summoned the wind to assist him destroy Degron warriors. Fire arose constantly from the maniac Malferus, who was ever so keen on proving a point to Mercius.

Then someone had caught his attention amongst the throng of the defending army. His brother Durial was wielding a water staff, hardening the tips into spikes of ice against the orcs that surrounded him. Lucian frowned hard, wondering what his brother was doing so far from his home in Iceland.

Lucian's heart pounded hard in his chest. In that surreal, frozen moment in time no one had approached him or attacked him. He had stared dumbfounded ahead at Durial, conflict causing his vision to blur. The orcs were starting to overpower him, and Lucian spared a glance to see where Mercius was.

In the moment it took Lucian to become wind, the air around him exploded with fire. Lucian fell back to the ground and saw a few Degron elementals running his way, their elements burning on their arms.

He had wanted to plead with them, beg them to let him save his brother, when a cry resounded over the bloody fields. Lucian bit into his teeth and erupted into a hurricane of wind. Before the Degron elementals could react, he had already blown past them and emerged in time to catch his dying brother's body.

The orcs around them retreated a few steps, smart enough to know not to attack further. Durial choked on his blood, the gaps in his chest and abdomen from the orc spears crying red rivers onto Lucian's legs. Lucian's eyes bled tears over his brother's face, but his cries of torment went unheard over the fields amongst the din;

except by one person.

Dark clouds of wind coalesced behind them as Durial let out his last breath. Lucian kissed his brother's wet forehead as he stood to face his master. Mercius growled deeply as he walked up to his Sandrihelin.

Focus on the battle, Mercius had said. *There's no time for trivial sympathies now. You abandoned them, remember.*

Those words rang through Lucian's heart now as the images continued to play. He had been about to unleash the growing anger burning inside him, the wind rising to sting the back of the Windfarer, when another cry reached his ears.

He had turned around and saw a woman cradling Durial's lifeless corpse. It took him a brief glimpse to see the wedding bands on both their hands that made him realise how much he had missed of his families' lives.

One of Malferus's stray fireballs arced across his sight towards Telgar and Durial. Without thought, Lucian had become wind and had grabbed them, teleporting them to the river alongside Carmel. She had looked up at him, her eyes extremely moist. He had offered her a comforting smile, and teleported back to Avalion.

The emotions from his brother's death quickly shifted into confusion. Saphin warriors from the neighbouring city had arrived and had begun destroying most of the orcs on the outskirts of Avalion. Lucian searched for the other Sandrihelin members and saw them all staring in the same direction.

Mercius was on his knees, hands being shackled by elvin chains with Eldor's outstretched palm on his forehead. There was a shimmer in Mercius's appearance, Eldor's fingers cracked with lightning and the Windfarer groaned. One by one the Sandrihelin had vanished into their elements, the last being Lucian.

Lucian opened his eyes suddenly as he heard someone walking up to him. He looked over the morning fields from the Sky Tier and let the wind dry the few tears strolling down his face. Kailan turned him to face her.

"You know that trick doesn't work with me anymore," she said, using her fingers to gently dry his damp skin. "What's the matter?"

"Durial," Lucian said, and she nodded in understanding and laid her head on his chest.

"Does it have anything to do with Telgar arriving later?" she asked carefully. He smiled. She knew him so well.

"It's hard seeing her with someone other than my brother, I admit," he said, avoiding the matter of his own feelings for her. "But if he truly brings her happiness, then I am glad."

"Try not to be too awkward around her," Kailan advised. "She still needs you for support. It will mean a lot to her."

"I won't be here when she arrives," he replied and she looked up into his face. "There's a matter I have been putting off, waiting for Anuxis's return, but I can't wait anymore."

He looked up at the sky, but Ringos was no longer visible.

"Lucian......" Kailan's voice trailed off as she pointed to the fields.

He narrowed his eyes on the Ground Tier far below. A large wolf stood behind the black iron gates that had been constructed that week. The dwarves were pulling the mechanisms that made the gates grind open.

The single wolf remained where it was as the gates came to a halt. At first Lucian thought the fields immediately behind the walls were covered with snow, but soon the shapes shifted and moved. The dwarves circled around Nelnar, cautiously walking to the shapes.

White wolves as large as Nelnar watched them all carefully. Nelnar stood regally with his tail up in the air, its face proud and strong. It heaved its chest out and gave one almighty howl that resounded eerily into the morning air and against the mountain walls. Nelnar's cry was joined by the other nelmurian wolves, and Lucian's heart beat with confidence and strength.

RISE OF THE DRAGONS
CHAPTER TWO

Lucian, Hargon, Lanel, Harmony, Nashela, Trimistus and Treville gathered later that day at the foremost gates that allowed entry into Horlorn from the east. The nelmurian wolves were still outside in the fields and lifted their heads curiously as the gates opened. A few sniffed the air as the jaguar Cavella followed behind Hargon, but then simply lowered their heads back onto their paws.

The little sunlight that was visible through the high clouds seemed to glint off the white fur of the wolves as it would off pure snow. As the group waded between the resting animals, they could see the daunting shades of grey, blue and green shimmer from their eyes.

They continued through the hordes of wolves until they reached an open expanse of land. Trimistus turned to face Horlorn as the others walked past him and did the same behind him. There was a low thrum coming from behind Horlorn's hill, and they waited patiently for the magnificent beasts to break the crest.

The entire rim of the hill was filled with the sight of the rising dragons. There were so many of them that even their wings were barely discernible from the floating bodies beside each of them. Not one of them led the horde, showing neither rank nor rulership. As one, their green and grey faded scales shone dully in the shallow rays of light that managed to escape the clouds.

The group that waited upon them felt the ancient power of the dragons grow stronger the closer they came. A few nelmurian wolves in their near vicinity moved out of the way as the three hundred and sixty dragons landed on the fields. Not one let out a roar or made any sign of greeting. Asgorna the former dragon king simply watched as Mynisna approached his DragonWourd.

"We are ready," the dragon king grumbled deeply. There was a fondness on his face, and the dragon bent his head down to let Trimistus greet him. The *Wisoum*'s arms complimented the scales of the dragon's head, in the same way that Trimistus's rimmed skull complimented the dragon's horned brow. He nuzzled the dragon's face for moment before Mynisna raised it to face the group.

"I will provide dragon's for any o..."

"No, that won't be necessary," Lucian cut off his offer politely. "You will need as much carrying space as possible to move the Vale and Carmel quickly. We're committed enough here at Horlorn as it is."

"I would like to go with," Harmony said suddenly. Mynisna turned his head to look at her. "I've always wanted to ride a dragon."

The dragon king looked at Trimistus, who nodded in response. Mynisna turned to look at one of the smaller dragons.

"This is Beliva," Mynisna said once the dragon had walked up to them. Harmony used the wind to rise up to the bottom of Beliva's neck. Trimistus's dragon wings broke out from the top of his back and he flew up to mount Mynisna.

"Have a good journey!" Lucian shouted and waved as the dragons lifted off the ground. Mynisna led the dragons south to the peaks of the Dwarf Mountain range.

Once the last of dragons dropped out of sight in the direction of the Vale, the remaining group headed back between the wolves to Horlorn. Lucian slowed his pace without letting the others notice.

While they talked away and laughed, Lucian became part of the wind and floated up to the Sky Tier. He materialised on the concrete surface and made his way through the interior to the passages that led out of the hill.

When he reached the western entrance, he greeted the gargoyles waiting with Lancenat. Silently he mounted the saddle and took the reins from Glasden.

"Don't you want to wait till the sun sets so that we can join you?" Glasden asked.

"No," he replied. "Le'Mar will be watching all the activity happening with the dragons, which will be the perfect cover for me. That's why I asked you to prepare Lancenat. If Le'Mar even senses through the fog what I am up to...."

The consequences of his actions vanished into the air as his lips drew to a close. Within his heart, he knew that facing Telgar was another reason he chose to leave now. The dragons' journey was mere convenience.

"I hope you find what you are looking for," Glasden said in farewell.

"Not what," Lucian said as he kicked Lancenat into a sprint, "but whom....."

***

Le'Mar felt their power in the air. It was unmistakable and so palpable to his nerves. He sat in his throne chair in the castle above the Alcove of Light, his eyes closed to the world but his senses wide open. He could feel the immense throng of them travelling in the air to the Vale.

He rose from his seat and walked forward towards the window that was engulfed with images within the fog. As he stepped into the window, his feet landed on the soil of the forest that had once belonged to Eldor and his elves. The fallen tower that Darcwulf has forsaken still lay in ruins in the centre of the valley.

His beasts and creatures stirred. Orc eyes and Ma-Wreth heads turned to watch his stride through the forest at a slow pace that they were all too familiar with; calculating, restraining his angered will.

He found it hard to remember the last time a decision had been so hard to make. Ever since he had watched Shadowolf vanish through a portal to who knows where, he had been battling within himself whether he should be a coward or control his impulsiveness.

He clenched his fists at his side as he continued further south into the forest. The wails of the creatures he was searching for were growing closer. Even while he was arguing the dilemma in his mind, he knew he was taking the coward's route.

Never before had Le'Mar felt so helpless. He had no idea what Shadowolf was up to, except getting a strong enough force to challenge him. The only place that Le'Mar could guess the portal took him was the Far Isles. Gaining the elves' assistance would help the earth greatly, and it was a move that Le'Mar was powerless to prevent.

Yet the opportunity to stop the dragons collecting more warriors was in his grasp. With Shadowolf gone, Le'Mar could hamper them from making Horlorn stronger.

As that thought crossed his mind, he wondered once again what Shadowolf's plans were. It would take nothing less than the dark lord to stroll into Horlorn with his existing army and smite them with the might of the *Sadgi*. But that action was premature, and Le'Mar had a sinking feeling that Shadowolf had a contingency just in case Le'Mar did indeed decide to do that.

His knuckles turned white with frustration. Even Masara had not put so much doubt into his mind. It was not fear, he kept reminding himself mentally; it was just the frustration that Shadowolf seemed to have the upper hand and Le'Mar had no idea what he was waiting for.

He reached the pits that held the wyverns. They were like dragons in appearance, with their lengthy bodies, their expansive wings and their long tails. But where dragons had scales, the wyverns were leathery to touch and deep charcoal in appearance. Where the dragons were bulky, they were slender and streamlined.

They clung to the extreme dark recesses of the pits, their brimstone stenches mingling with the acrid vumes exuding from the craters below. Their cries echoed out between the jets of vapour that erupted spasmodically from the broken earth.

Le'Mar rose upon the wind and flew over to the central hub. There the majestic queen, largest of them all, lay amongst her five mates coiled around her like snakes.

When Le'Mar reached them, the males jumped up and hissed defensively. Their necks stretched out to him, challenging him to come closer if he dared. Le'Mar's eyes flared with power, his right palm extending out to them with a sharp, violet light.

The males hissed again and recoiled from his power. They twisted under the queen that rose from the pit and levelled with his face in the air. He floated there, the air rushing around him calmly as she smelled his scent.

"Mynisna is here," he said to her, and she growled and then hissed a horrendous cry that reverberated throughout the pits. She extracted herself from the males and released her wings. Le'Mar floated to her inviting back and sat upon it as the other wyverns gathered like cloaks of darkness around them.

Sometimes being cowardly is the best way to prevent defeat, he decided.

***

There were very few people left within the Vale of Tigers's walls by the time Mynisna and his dragons landed on the dry ground. The clouds weren't as thick above the city, and the humidity was streaking across the Vale's warriors as they waited.

There were a few dwarves amongst them, but not as much as there had been in the years before. The dwarf king Gallon had moved almost all of them within Dwarf Mountains after Chenesia's father passed away.

Trimistus wiped his brow as he jumped off Mynisna's back, his dragon wings spread so that he could glide to the ground. Chenesia's mother waited for his approach with the other leaders of the Vale.

"Everyone ready?" Trimistus asked, nodding to the group in greeting.

"Yes," Larnesia replied boldly, not letting the DragonRider's appearance daunt her, nor the mighty dragons' presence sway her. "The elementals will assist the warriors mount."

"Very well," Trimistus said. "Let's begin."

It did not take as long as Trimistus had estimated it would, but it was still too long for his liking. He assisted where he could, but when he had moments to brood by himself, his hands on his sides, the anxiety bit into heart and he waded around watching the skies for any sign of the dark lord.

They managed to get all of the warriors on the dragons with fifteen dragons to spare. The families that stayed behind watched from the gates, the children waving at their fathers and mothers sitting astride the beasts like heroes.

The clouds moved along and the sun caught them magnificently as they rose into the air and soared towards Horlorn's Gate. Shouts and cheers echoed from the ground as they left the Vale defenseless. Eventually, the dark shapes became too small to distinguish from the peaks of the mountains.

The remainder of the Vale turned around and walked back into the city when the sound of rushing wind broke over them. Long beasts swept above the city in a hail of speed that stirred the dust and sand from the ground. The people screamed in terror, thinking they were being attacked.

The dragon-like creatures kept flying passed them in the direction that Mynisna had gone. It was several minutes before the last of the dark cloud of beasts flew over them and then there was immediate and utter silence.

Trimistus watched calmly as they rose up to the peaks. He gripped the scaly back of Mynisna's neck, his nerves pulling within him. The flapping of the dragon's expansive wings beat to the same rhythm as his heart.

Trimistus turned his head with Mynisna as they felt the primordial power approaching them from the back. Screams rose like horrendous cries in the darkest pits as the beasts attacked the rearmost dragons.

Mynisna twisted around instantly with the other dragons, the Vale's elementals struggling to prepare their elements on the other dragons; fighting while flying was not something that they were accustomed to. Trimistus hoped they would learn quickly though, as it was a weakness they could not afford to have.

He disengaged himself from his dragon and used his own wings to carry him, removing his dragon blade from the belt on his side. He saw the largest of the wyverns carrying a man on her back, but was distracted when one of her beasts rose up to challenge him.

Trimistus swirled in circles and dropped down to avoid the snapping, elongated face of the wyvern. His wings picked him up as he drove his blade into one of the beast's legs. The wyvern cried out in pain and Trimistus removed the blade, preparing to either strike again or parry an attack.

A tail from a different wyvern smacked him sideling into his chest and he soared backwards, the first wyvern flying towards his sailing body. Trimistus did a back somersault and flew with fierce determination towards his assailant.

The beast's eyes flared up and it made two, short sneezing

sounds. Two jets of fire flew towards him and it took a lot of his strength to adjust his flight and miss the comets of flame. With speed that Trimistus had not made provision for, the wyvern slammed its head straight into his chest and sent him spitting blood towards the earth.

Trimistus flapped his wings hard, the scales glowing white with power. He turned up to face the wyvern again and saw that it was almost upon him. His eyes burned orange as he gathered flame within him.

He flew up hard, readying his blade beside his leg. At the last possible moment, he swerved from the beast's claws, drew the tip of his sword into its belly and spat fire from his mouth as it tore its skin open. The beast cried and he pushed the blade deeper as he flew up and the wyvern fell down.

Its wail ended when he removed the blade to let it fall to the earth. He tried to find the man he had spotted earlier, but more wyverns were heading his way. Elementals were soaring in the air, throwing their powers where they could without hurting any of the dragons and the warriors mounted on their backs.

Then a dragon's cry sounded in the air and Trimistus looked to see Asgorna falling from the sky. The queen had hit his side near his heart and he had been struck by many smaller wyverns in the same attack.

Trimistus could feel the dragon's power waning as he tried to reassert his flight. Trimistus flared with power and stretched his wings to its full length, watching as the man on the queen's back spread his palm out and arcs of lightning travelled up his arm.

A silent shout in defiance choked in Trimistus's mouth as the lightning broke from the man's fingers, reaching into the air to Asgorna's failing body.....

"AHHHH!!!!!" Shadowolf shouted and fell onto his left knee on the grass. Elgoth rose from the fire he had been tending and Crystal cried beside his mother on the blanket.

"What's wrong?!" Shedaaij shuddered in panic, running to him. A long line of blood formed under his shirt and, when he lifted the top, she saw a long bleeding wound running deep from his stomach up to his shoulder.

She found no words as she reached him, her fingers trying not to touch the wound, but her instincts wanting to assuage his pain. She looked up into his face, but the face she saw was not one that she recognised.

His eyes were burning with a light so bright and effervescent that she could not see anything else within them. His pained expression had changed to an expressionless one and his *Wisoum* wings were stretched out from his back. She retreated as the wind ripped around them and he was gone.....

.....and held out his right palm. The lightning hit into him hard, but he did not sway. The blue bolts arced and coiled in the air into his hand, but his wings kept him aloft and his eyes burnt wildly as the dark lord's power passed into him harmlessly.

Le'Mar stopped and gaped. Somewhere below, cries and flames rent the air. A sickly sound erupted as teeth ripped flesh, as blood fell like rain to the earth and corpses hit the earth. The dark lord spared a moment to look down.

The five mates of the queen lay sprayed somewhere in the valley of the mountain. The queen wailed and left Le'Mar alone to challenge their murderer. Asgorna was rising up furiously to meet her, their red death plastered like paint on his jaws.

Le'Mar wanted to speak, wanted to utter his rage, but he found no words. Shadowolf was still burning with power; his eyes still alight with supernatural light and his wings still keeping him afloat. Yet, to Le'Mar, it seemed like Shadowolf held no power at all, as if he were a mere husk floating upon a breeze of energy.

"Recall your beasts, or force me to act against Bontu's will," Shadowolf said. "The choice is yours."

Le'Mar almost choked on the audacity of this child. For all the centuries he had lived, no one had ever challenged him like this. His pride knocked hard against his temple. Inside him, his spirit recoiled against this impetuous elemental.

Le'Mar flew forward on the wind, striking hard at Shadowolf. He only used minimal power, rousing some wind within him and fire along his arms. The little power he used should have thrown Shadowolf back, or injured the hands he was using to defend himself.

Yet Shadowolf kept turning his blows aside without attempting a strike himself. It seemed like it took no effort on his side to block and parry the dark lord's attack.

Le'Mar did not hold his anger in check and was completely riled by Shadowolf's actions. He threw his hands in for more attacks, striking with his leg and letting fire slash out towards Shadowolf's face. Before the fire touched his skin, Shadowolf crouched down and slammed the back of his open hand into Le'Mar's ribs.

The dark lord bent over from the attack and did not see the fist as it struck him hard in his temple. Before he could open his eyes from the pain, Shadowolf's foot lashed out like a whip into his abdomen and he soared back away from him.

Le'Mar righted himself and let the wind flow calmly around him. During the attack, he had felt the power rise within Shadowolf, but now that he was done it seemed like there was nothing within him again. Someone had taught him well.

"I must say, I am impressed," Le'Mar commented. "Whoever taught you did a good job."

Shadowolf did not reply. His gaze stayed fixed on Le'Mar, despite the fighting around them and the elementals summoning their powers. Le'Mar smirked. He wanted to see Shadowolf's power, to see how much he had grown since they had last faced each other.

The wind started stirring more around them as Le'Mar called his power and Shadowolf vanished. A wyvern flew into the space Shadowolf had been and Le'Mar cursed. His beasts were interrupting them. Shadowolf reappeared a moment later, his eyes still fixed on him as if he had never left.

Suddenly the battle stopped around them. Silence filled the mountain peaks except for one, shrill cry that sent shivers down everyone's spines. Shadowolf and Le'Mar looked down and saw the queen rolling down the mountain, her back broken and body disjointed from her impact with one of the peaks.

Everything became dark as the wyverns left their quarries and chased after Asgorna. The dragon twisted in the air and flew down the mountain side between crags and cliffs. Le'Mar looked up as Shadowolf vanished again.

The dark lord expected Mynisna and the other dragons to

pursue the wyverns and assist Asgorna. He looked up at Trimistus, who was not far away from him. There was a pulsing, white mist in the sockets of his eye that disappeared after a moment.

For reasons that Le'Mar could not fathom, Trimistus returned to Mynisna's back and retracted his wings. The dragons turned and continued to Horlorn's Gate, the elementals returning to their backs among the other warriors.

Le'Mar's frown blurred his face and gave him a headache. It seemed to him that Shadowolf gained great pleasure in confusing him. He relaxed his power and became one with the wind.

The air slid off Asgorna's soft back as he raced down the mountain with a tail of wyverns hunting him. As large as the mountain was, he knew he was going to run out of vertical space soon. He twisted his body up and flew along the side of the mountain towards T'Mar's Scourge. He spared a glance back and saw that the fastest of the horde were catching him quickly.

Shadowolf reappeared out of the wind, his wings flapping hard as he braked in the air and landed on the foremost wyvern. Water coursed and froze up his arm and a sword of ice entered the back of the wyvern's neck.

As its body fell down, he kicked up and twisted in the air. He reversed his hold on the ice blade so that it was level with his arm and cut the edge along the length of the next wyvern's neck. Two wyverns curled under the dying corpse. Shadowolf gripped the one's neck in his arm, slit its jaw open, and spun around with the blade fully extended. The tip of the ice cut across the second beast's eyes and, before it could cry out in pain, the sword pierced its chest.

As fast as he was, he could not dodge in time to avoid a wyvern's fangs biting into his left arm. He ground his teeth together as the pain travelled up his arm and the wyvern began to swing him with its jaws. He became wind and slipped out of the teeth, travelled like a mist under its belly and around it side, and reappeared with the ice digging firmly into its ribs.

Another wyvern caught him off guard and slashed into his side with its claws. The welt that Shadowolf had received originally from Asgorna's injuries burned open again, but the beast's victory was short-lived as Asgorna slammed through the wyvern's surrounding him with tremendous speed and bulk.

Shadowolf grabbed weakly at the tunic he was wearing and ripped it off. His muscled abdomen and chest heaved up and down with exhaustion and the blood tricked down his skin. He looked around at the situation desperately, contemplating teleportation, when a dark mist coalesced before him and Le'Mar's fist struck his face.

Shadowolf's body rushed through the air and he groaned loud when his back struck the mountain side hard. He pushed his hands weakly against the sand behind him, letting his wings pull back into his body. His eyes went wide as he felt the power, and he rolled away and jumped up into the air as the fireball exploded on the spot where he had been.

Le'Mar hit at his face again, but Shadowolf grabbed the wrist, turned in the air and threw him at the mountain. The dark lord planted his feet into the earth, knelt down with the air pushing against gravity around him and flew straight back at Shadowolf. He gathered his power into his arms, grinned as it filled every vein and nerve, and lashed out with his arms.

Empty air greeted him as Shadowolf vanished. Le'Mar felt him materialise behind him too late and groaned as Shadowolf kicked him in the spine. Shadowolf vanished again and reappeared into Le'Mar's path of flight and hit his fist up into his chin.

Le'Mar felt him vanish and reappear again, but this time the dark lord did the same and appeared above Shadowolf. Le'Mar grabbed him hard by his hair and twisted, throwing him over his shoulder towards the mountain. Shadowolf screamed in agony, trying hard to focus on the elements.

Before he could recover, Le'Mar became a flaming ball of fire and flew into his aching body. The two of them crashed with tremendous force into the mountain just as Shadowolf gained enough strength to become wind. As fire and air, they twisted and fought, elements burning through the rock and scorching the earth with their battle.

Mynisna and the dragons landed on Horlorn's hill and looked back at the power they felt within the mountain. Nighthale and the wolf tribes of Avalion turned back from their entry into Horlorn and looked up at the peaks of the mountain too, feeling a power that they had never sensed before.

Nature's songs and the earth's noises became soft as the power grew greater. With an explosion so sudden that several on the fields nearly fainted, a great crater broke out of the top of the mountain. Rocks, soil and grass fell from the skies as Le'Mar and Shadowolf emerged in each other's grasps, blood falling like rain from their bodies.

Shadowolf grabbed the collar of Le'Mar's broken coat and threw him towards the earth, vanishing from the scene. Le'Mar allowed gravity to pull him down, watching with every one of his senses for Shadowolf's approach. He raised his power within him, waiting patiently.

Le'Mar twisted to the left as he felt the man's powerful attack, but he had been tricked. Shadowolf slammed into his body from the top, fire and lightning burning around him. The others on the field watched as the two hurtled to the earth in a raging chaos of powers, and then fell down as the powers exploded upon contact.

A great orb of power burst up from the place where they had landed and a second explosion broke out over everyone. Sand, water, fire and wind crashed over them and their screams went unheard in the tumult of the powers. Nighthale lay quietly for a long time, waiting for the land to calm down and finally rose to his feet with the few that had the strength to do so.

If anyone expected to see a crater in the earth from the impact, they were sorely mistaken once the dust had settled. The earth was ripped along the surface, jagged edges breaking the land where fine grass had once been. They saw two silhouettes on the land facing each other from a distance, standing strong as if they had never battled.

"Our time will come," Shadowolf told Le'Mar, and then disappeared into the wind.

Le'Mar brought his powers down and relaxed his arms at his side. For several moments, he stood there in view of Horlorn's men and beasts. And then he looked up at the sky.

"Of course," he said to no one in particular. Even with the sky lit up with the sun's rays, he could see the dim shape of Ringos heading southwest in a gap between the clouds. "The Masaran Phenomenon; that's what you're waiting for."

The sand shifted in the wind, and he was gone.

Little Jilian Asmuth completed the drawing. Graphite wyverns covered most of the page with a single man slicing his sword into one of them. There was a large dragon fighting in the background, and the man and the dragon had the same wound on their sides. At the bottom of the page was a neat inscription:

As one with his dragon, he fears none

TALES OF CELENE
CHAPTER THREE

Lucian stirred from his rest. He was sure he had heard something that time. He stood up again and moved down the dark corridor. The walls were warm from the hot springs and lava that still stirred within this part of the earth.

He had never personally been in the caves of Philagus and he hoped that he was still moving in the right direction. Shadowolf had told him of the Butcher of Philagus, the centaur king that had ruled from the depths of the earth. Lucian sincerely hoped that no one had taken Kraakis's role as the new king of the centaurs.

Lucian had decided to leave Lancenat on the surface. The entrance to the underground caverns had been utterly destroyed and there were no signs that anyone had entered them since the Shadow Clan's battle with the centaurs. Even if he had dared use his powers to assist Lancenat's entrance, the corridors were too jagged and narrow in places to allow any horse to travel comfortably.

This made him wonder once again how the centaurs had managed to travel through the caverns for so long. He squeezed his body through a very suffocating wall-space, a feat he could not imagine a bulky creature accomplishing. Unless they had powers he was unaware of, there was no way that any beast as large as the centaurs could travel these passages.

Lucian stopped. Soft murmurs were reaching his ears and he was sure they were voices. His legs became air as he drifted forward, careful not to disturb any rocks that might alert his presence. He edged closer to the voices until he saw a wide area lit only by one torch.

There were two centaurs speaking to each other, one of which was the bearer of the torch. As Shadowolf has described, these centaurs were very rugged and not pleasant to look at. Their bodies were bred for war and their muscles were scarred from battle. On their heads were cropped horns, with two lifting up higher than the others on either side.

Yet, even though these centaurs had obviously experienced war, Lucian could tell by the aged scars that it had been a while since they had fought. There were no fresh wounds or any recent bruises to indicate that they had served the dark lord in battle as they once had in the past.

Another thing Lucian noticed in his observation was that they had tufts of dark hair from the knee joints down to their hooves. As they talked, with their human arms crossed over their chests, their equestrian legs prodded the ground softly, almost as if they were anxious about something.

"I'm sure they also felt it," the torch-bearer said in his gruff voice. "There's no need to leave our post for that."

"But did they feel it down there?" the other centaur responded in a younger voice. "Millon said we were to report anything suspicious."

Lucian smiled. Shadowolf had mentioned that Millon had once been part of the Shadow Clan together with his comrade Kentaur. It was thanks to their allegiance that they had survived so many battles.

The *Enodhim* knew about what they were speaking now. He had already felt the great release of power earlier during the day. It had sent shivers down his spine and he had almost left the caverns to return to Horlorn. This task had been placed upon his shoulders though and it needed to be done before the war started.

Against his better judgement, Lucian made his legs whole again and entered the small area. He scuffled his feet purposefully and the centaurs turned in alarm to face him. He held up his hands to show that he was not armed.

"He's an elemental," the torch-bearer said to the other centaur. "Don't put any trust in those arms."

"You are indeed wise," Lucian greeted formally with a bow, "wise beyond my knowledge of centaurs."

"And you are a fool to be travelling these corridors on your own," the older centaur replied. "I have no doubt your happening here was deliberate."

Lucian held back a sarcastic retort.

"I am here to speak to Millon," he replied instead. "Shadowolf asked me to…"

He went silent as the centaurs looked at each other sharply. There was great consternation on the older centaur's face, yet excitement on the younger one.

"Does this constitute enough suspicion to call him?" the young centaur asked.

"Yes, yes, Mirentaur," the senior centaur sighed. "Go get your father."

Mirentaur left with glee on his face. A grey portal opened on the wall beside him and he entered through it.

"My name is Glamidon," the remaining centaur informed Lucian, and then indicated the portal with his hand. "Please, after you."

Lucian obliged by entering the portal first, followed shortly by Glamidon. They were in another corridor, but this once was longer and wider than any Lucian had passed through in Philagus. The only other distinct difference was that the walls were smooth and the floor was paved with bricks. Glamidon's hooves clicked beside him on the surface.

"He is such an eager foal," Glamidon said with a certain pride in his voice. "Millon could not have sired a better prince."

"Hang on," Lucian interrupted him. "If I remember correctly from what Shadowolf has told me, Millon did not have off-spring when he was with the Clan."

"You're correct," the centaur confirmed. "Mirentaur is only 14 months of age."

"My goodness," the Windfarer said. "You do grow fast, don't you? But where did he get those bruises? Have the centaurs been at battle recently?"

"We start at a very young age with training," Glamidon laughed. "If our arms are strong enough to hold a sword, then we're ready to fight."

"You mentioned that he's a prince," Lucian continued. "Does that mean Millon is the new centaur king?"

"He was chosen to lead us, but Millon refused. Some other idio… uhm, centaur is leading us now until Millon's son is old enough to take his place. Or until Seridon dies. Whichever comes first really."

"Does Seridon not have foals that will contest the sireship?"

"Seridon only has one son to stake that claim," Glamidon smiled, "and I am definitely too old to be thinking of ruling anyone."

Lucian stopped from replying when he saw that the passage stopped. The tunnel ended with a huge gaping mouth that led into the underground cavern via two ledges on either side. Lucian and Glamidon walked to the edge of the platform that overlooked the centaur camp.

"It's gorgeous," Lucian whispered in awe.

***

"How is he?" Shedaaij asked.

Elgoth turned to her and then looked back down the hill he stood on. The grass fell away from where he stood and ran up again to form another rolling hill. Shedaaij looked back to see Crystal bouncing joyfully on Darcwulf's knee before standing beside Elgoth.

"He is healing slowly," he replied. "By the time the sun rises again, he should be replenished. At some point during the night, you must wake him to feed him these."

"What are they?" she said as he handed her a small, transparent bag with round items within it.

"They're berries," he said. "Not really found on the continent so much as on the Isles. It will assist in regaining some of the energy he lost in battle."

"There was something I wanted to ask you," she said, looking up at the stars above them, "something I need to understand about everything that's happening."

"Ask away," he replied with a soft smile.

"Shadowolf has been telling me about the documents he has found," she said, "about the history of Celenic Earth and where this war stemmed from originally."

"Carry on," he said encouragingly.

"As someone from the mer-Kingdom, there is a lot I don't know about the terrestrial life after Masara. These past four years we've learnt a lot about your father and his battle with T'Mar and the darkness."

"Is there something specific you wanted to know?"

She remained silent for a moment to phrase the question properly before answering him.

"Not really something specific," she said, crossing her arms over her breasts as the wind blew passed them quietly. "More in the sense of what happened between the times Le'Mar left the earth and then returned to start this war."

"There is a lot to be told about that," Elgoth said, and then looked up at the hill as if he was expecting someone. "I think to give you a brief idea, I would have to tell you about the life of Celene."

"Ah," she smirked. "Somehow I had an idea it had something to do with her."

"How so?"

"Well, so far we've dealt with every person after whom the Ages have been named; Bontu, Falgar and then Masara. I knew Celene was going to pop up at one or other stage."

"Well, besides the political and essential linguistic changes that took place in society," Elgoth said, and then suppressed a laugh when he saw the frown on Shedaaij's face, "Celene's story has a lot to do with what we're facing today. It's minor in scale compared to her predecessors, but most definitely just as essential."

"Alright," Shedaaij said and then took a deep breath, "let's begin from when Le'Mar left the earth to serve the Gemetrashef. If the darkness was with him, then certainly it left with him?"

"Of that I am unsure," Elgoth said, dropping his head in thought. "To give you an idea of why I say that, I need to give you some perspective.

"You will remember that Falgar took the elf Mehorin as his partner?" he continued and she nodded uncertainly. "They had several children, but the one we focused on with regards to my father was Falara, who then had a son Namara."

"And that was your grandfather," Shedaaij assumed, and Elgoth nodded.

"That bloodline effectively ends with me," he continued. "Now, to tell you Celene's story, we need to focus on the second bloodline.

"One of Falgar's son's was Morlen, Falara's brother. From Morlen came Colene, and from her Cailene. Cailene lived during the time of the Battle of T'Mar's Scourge."

"Confusing, but I think I follow," Shedaaij interrupted.

"After the Battle, the elementals above the Scourge no longer had anyone to follow," Elgoth said. "Lucas and T'Mar were both dead, and Masara had vanished from the earth.

"In the end, there was a split between the people. The first group wanted to leave the northern lands and travel south."

"And the second group wanted to stay above Dwarf Mountains, right?"

"Correct. Cailene was part of one of the families that decided to head south and form what became known as the wolf tribe.

"Once they had reached the southern lands beneath Bontu's Wrath, there were arguments about who would lead them."

"Why did anyone have to lead them? It's not like they had rulers before."

"Precisely," Elgoth agreed. "It's a question my father and I have asked for many years. Nevertheless, they did split into further tribes, which eventually developed into the Degron, Saphin, Watre, Blue and Orion wolf tribes.

"A few years before I was born, Cailene conceived her daughter Celene. Celene lived in Avalion under the rulership of Derinwolf Degron, and it was no secret that she was inlove with his son, Nitewolf."

"Mmm, I see where this is going," Shedaaij said and looked back in the direction she knew Shadowolf was sleeping.

"We assume that during this time, the darkness felt restless again."

"Wait, hold on," Shedaaij stopped him. "I thought it left with Le'Mar?"

"I don't pretend to understand how the darkness works," he confessed. "But T'Mar did have another son before Le'Mar's time, one that stayed in the castle above the Alcove of Light. His name was Telmirion.

"Now, we don't know who Telmirion's mother was, but it was not my grandmother and we don't know what happened to her. Telmirion's existence was unknown to us until he left the castle during the time of the tribes."

"Why did he leave the castle?"

"Probably to find out what had happened to his father," Elgoth guessed. "In any event, practically the same thing happened as in the past. Telmirion wished to have Celene as his wife, but she was already devoted to Nitewolf.

"One day Nitewolf was walking along the beach and there was Telmirion, waiting for him by the waters. Telmirion was adept in the water element, but Nitewolf had not built an affinity towards any of the powers. It was Telmirion's one chance to gain Celene's love."

"You can't get someone's love by killing someone close to them," Shedaaij commented. "That's just absurd."

"Not in his view," Elgoth replied. "Anyway, Telmirion did use the ocean to try and kill Nitewolf, but Celene had not been far and had rushed to save him. She was just as adept, if not more so, with water.

"She saved Nitewolf, but continued battling Telmirion in rage. At some point near the end of the fight, he summoned a large liquid beast that rose high into the air."

"He was going to kill her?"

"His torment knew no bounds now. If he could not have Celene, then no one could. So it became his determination to take her from this world. But as the beast descended upon her, she called some of its own power to her. It was right above her, some witnesses had said, and yet she still continued to seep the power from its core into her spirit.

"When at last the beast engulfed her and drowned both her and Nitewolf, they could see a white light pulsing from the depths. Even in the waters that surrounded them, the beast tried suffocating her. Yet the light did not dim, and a single arrow broke the surface of the water.

"That arrow struck Telmirion in the heart. He dropped from the air where he had been controlling the beast and the water receded back into the oceans. Nitewolf coughed the water out of his lungs, but Celene stood there with a magnificent, blue bow made of water in her hands. There was a fine spray of mist from where she stood to where the beach of the ocean started."

"And that's where the Mists of Celene came from," Shedaaij

murmured, her voice rattling in the sudden chill of the night.

"Well, the power eventually did seep into the earth and when the forest grew, the mists became part of it," Elgoth affirmed. "Just one of the many mysteries, I'm afraid.

"To end the story, Derinwolf learnt from their mistake and had his son tutored in the way of the elements. Nitewolf and Celene did the same with their children, one of which was Shadewolf. Shadewolf made sure Nighthale learnt the ways of the elements...."

"And Nighthale sent Shadowolf to Asbec College of Elements," Shedaaij concluded.

"Do you understand now?"

"Yes, I do," she said, and looked up as a figure topped the hill before them.

The white unicorn trotted down the hill. Even though there was no rush for her to be with them, she longed for news and could not keep her anxiety intact. Before she reached them, she transformed into her human form and her blue dress fell down her slender body.

"Where is he?" Ursula asked.

"This way," Elgoth replied, turning and leading them to him. Darcwulf arose from the ground with Crystal and joined them.

Shadowolf was lying on a long blanket beneath one of the few trees on the grasslands. His hands held each other on his abdomen and his breathing was peaceful. There were moments when it seemed like his closed eyelids flickered with miniscule lights from beneath the skin.

"He wasn't supposed to face him just yet," Ursula whispered. "What happened?"

"He was defending his dragon," Elgoth replied. "We both know that if Asgorna dies, then so does the *Wisoum* within Shado."

"It's more than that," Shedaaij said, hiding her alarm at Elgoth's statement. "Shado loves Asgorna more than he is willing to admit, I think."

WHEN SAINTS GO TO HEAVEN
CHAPTER FOUR

He groaned and stirred in the pale morning light. His head was throbbing dully and his body still ached from his confrontation with Le'Mar. Shadowolf shifted on the blanket and stretched his limbs, his hand knocking a wooden object beside him.

He opened his eyes carefully and felt his staff. A wan smile passed his lips. It was often one of Nelnar's traits to somehow find his way back to Shadowolf, no matter how distant the location.

He gripped the staff in his hands and used it to rise from the grass. His legs wobbled slightly once he was up and he took a moment to let them become more stable before moving around. He could feel soft energy passing from the earth through his staff into his body. There was also a strange taste in his mouth that had nothing to do with morning breath.

Shadowolf called the wind and let the cool air wash over him, his hair waving out of his eyes. His legs wobbled again slightly and he released the summons on the wind; the air was now moving of its own accord.

"Good morning," Shedaaij said when he reached the group. She passed him a plate of food. "How do you feel?"

"Strong enough to make the elvin city," he replied, and nodded in greeting to Darcwulf. Crystal was still asleep. "Where is Elgoth?"

"With his mother over the rise of the hill," Darcwulf replied.

"Ursula's here?" he asked quickly. Darcwulf nodded and Shadowolf made to walk to them.

"No no," Shedaaij said and pulled his arm. "You will eat first, mister."

After a few minutes of silent eating, Shadowolf found that he did not have to wait long before Elgoth and Ursula returned to them.

She offered him a warm smile in greeting and he rose to embrace her. They held each other for a long moment before breaking free.

"Will we be heading for the city soon?" Shadowolf asked her.

"Eldor informed me that the elders are not too keen on you entering the city," she replied with a smirk. "We will be meeting with them in the auditorium on the outskirts of the city."

"Well that's just grand," Shedaaij said. "It's not like we've given them reason to distrust us. It is Shado, after all."

"Thanks love," he smiled and planted a quick kiss on her cheek. "Well, we might as well get started."

They packed up the few things they had and then joined Ursula and Elgoth at the top of the hill. Ursula tenderly raised her arm, her palm facing the south, and summoned a blue portal. It swirled in a long spiral and she lowered her arm when it was done.

Shadowolf let the others enter and passed through last. The bottom end of the staff clinked against marble on the other side. He looked around at the large structure before him and then at the cliff behind him.

Shedaaij and Darcwulf walked with him to the edge of the cliff and looked down at the magnificence of the city. A very sleepy Crystal opened her eyes and pointed with her left hand at the large buildings.

The city stretched far beyond their vision. On all points of the horizon, they could see large towers and spires rising to meet the clouds. As was the case with any elves that Shadowolf had known, forests of trees cluttered the base of these buildings, and he had no doubt that the homes of the elves resided within the large timbers.

Sparks of light and arrays of colour complimented the tops of the towers. Large bird-like creatures circled a few of them, while unknown terrestrial creatures spanned the few open lands that they could spot from the cliff.

It was a wonder that Shadowolf had not expected, even after having been in the glory of Eldor's Forest. Yet, his joy and excitement was suddenly clouded by a grim expression. The magnificence of the city proved only one thing to him; the elders had never seen or experienced war. They had been protected for far too long from the plight of the continent.

"Welcome," an elvin voice greeted them jovially from the

auditorium. The trio turned and smiled when they saw Eldor. His green-hued skin had grown darker since they had last seen him, and his exudiant power was more subtle to their senses. He was also not as skinny as they remembered.

"It's good to see you again, Eldor," Shadowolf said as they each shook his hand in greeting. "Are the elders ready to defy me?"

"I would not put it that way," Eldor laughed with him, "but they will hear what you have to say. After that interesting battle yesterday, I would think they are more than eager to talk to you."

"Well, I'm sure their reception won't be as warm as yours," Darcwulf said.

"It never is," Eldor whispered behind his hand, and winked at them.

"The eld...."

Darcwulf went silent as he saw someone exit the auditorium. Her black hair fell down on either side of her face, complimenting the beauty of her eyes, but neither of these competed with the wonderful smile on her face and the longing in her eyes.

Darcwulf left the group and walked up to embrace Fransiska. At first unsure, the two looked deeply into each other's eyes and then their lips touched. Their kisses became more passionate and warm as they held each other more firmly, and then Fransiska pulled away.

"I've missed you," she said, a smile fading slightly as she allowed a minute of pain to show through her eyes. "There's someone I want you to meet."

Darcwulf stepped back from her arms, panic rising within him. He had known that she could have moved on and found someone new while he had served Le'Mar. He would not have blamed her had she done so. But the reality that she had indeed found someone else still stung him harder than he had prepared for. She stepped aside and Darcwulf saw him.

The little boy grasped his mother's hand tightly, hiding in the folds of Fransiska's dress. The boy seemed to be the same age as Crystal. Darcwulf opened his mouth slowly and then closed it again, unsure of what to say.

"Don't you want to hold your son?" she asked, her voice sweet and inviting.

Darcwulf knelt down and reached out slowly to the boy. The boy slid behind his mother again before peeking out at the strange, bald man before him.

"It's ok, Tyler," she said to the boy. She put her hand gently behind his back and moved him closer to his father. Darcwulf took Tyler slowly into his arms at first and then held him firmly. The boy stood there, unsure of what to do, before looking up and staring at Crystal in Shedaaij's arms.

"Do you still have it?" Shadowolf whispered at Eldor's side, not taking his eyes from the scene.

"Yes, it's safe," the elf replied.

"Good," Shadowolf said firmly while the others cleared their wet eyes. "Let's go face the elders."

***

Lucian walked steadily between Glamidon and Mirentaur. He had slept well within the room that they had provided for him, and had slept longer than he usually permitted himself to.

Even though the buildings they walked among were crude, the magnificence of the camp was undeniable. In its own fashion, the odd designs and strange material lent a certain glory to the place that could only be associated with warriors like the centaurs.

The brown and red schemes of the warrior homes and tents, which were very similar to stables in many senses, resembled the same shade of the centaurs' lower bodies. In a human village, such a scheme would have been viewed as dull.

However, with the centaurs walking around the stone paths, and the wells and bridges specifically constructed for the lava rivers that flowed through the camp, any other scheme would only have taken away the sense of lordship that seemed to exude from the walls and floors.

They reached the second largest building in the camp and entered the main gates. The stony structure of the building loomed above them, and it stirred a sense of foreboding in Lucian. If Millon had not once been a friend to Shadowolf, he would have been particularly frightened to enter it.

Lucian shivered as he passed overhanging, dry fangs that were part of the decorum on the walls. He was not sure if they were indeed fangs or horns, but they were daunting enough. He tried his best to ignore them, hoping that whatever creatures wore those instruments of death were as far away from the camp as possible.

They did not have to go far within the building before they found Millon. He was waiting patiently for them with a serious, thoughtful expression on his face. His hands were behind his upper human back, comfortably resting on the equestrian part of his body.

"Good morning Lucian," Millon greeted. "I trust that you slept well."

"Very well," he replied. "The camp is well suited for humans, despite the lack of any."

"I have spoken to Seridon," Millon said, ignoring his comment. "He says you may do with the Tree of Life as you will. We have no need for it. However, there is another matter I have discussed with him, one that you have not requested."

"And what is that?" Lucian frowned.

"My allegiance has always been with Shado from the start," Millon replied. "With the centaurs that wish to follow me, I request that I join your army in Horlorn."

Lucian could not hold back the curious smile. This request was more than he had bargained for, but one that he knew he should not deny. The centaurs' aid in battle was one that would assist them greatly.

"How many will follow you?" Lucian asked before answering his request.

"Let's put it this way," Millon replied with a sly smile, "once we have left he camp, Seridon will hardly have any left to rule."

"Then why does he not come with?"

"My father was always stubborn-willed," Glamidon said, "even in the face of idiocy."

"You don't like your father very much, do you?" Lucian asked rhetorically.

"'Like' is a strong word," he said.

"Your allegiance will be appreciated, Millon," Lucian finally said.

"Yes!" Mirentaur exclaimed, and then returned to a formal stance after a meaningful glare from his father.

"My warriors are almost ready," Millon told Lucian. "My son will take you to the tree while the final preparations are being made."

Down brick paths they walked, passed enormous buildings and tents they went until they reached a small island surrounded by a river of fire. The lava spewed and bubbled softly as Lucian crossed the sole bridge that led to the grey tree in the centre of the island.

The tree was not much taller than Lucian. He traced his fingers along the bark and branches, trying to sense if there was any life left in it. It was very dry, and one of the branches broke off in his hand. It disintegrated on his fingers and he rubbed the ash together thoughtfully.

Lucian became part of the air and entered the tree. He travelled through the empty shell, using his mind to enter the spiritual realm. His sense of reality shifted around him until he was standing on a dark plain.

There were stars in the night sky and as far as he could tell it was the only source of light. Yet Lucian managed to see the barren landscape well enough and the richness of the brown soil. The wind picked sand up from the ground and twisted it in the air before letting it fall again. This seemed to happen at random locations throughout the land.

"What do you want?" a frail voice said behind him. Lucian turned around to see the aged man leaning on a weak staff. "You don't belong here."

"I was wondering if I would find you," Lucian said and walked up to him with joy on his face. "It's taken us months to...."

"Stay back!" the old man said. "Or I will be forced to hurt you."

He swayed on the staff and extended his right hand. Fire rose from his fingertips, roared softly in the air and then died just as quickly. He retracted his arm and stared at his hand in amusement.

"Masara, listen...."

"There's nothing left of me," he muttered and walked passed Lucian. "Even my powers have deserted me."

"Wait Masa..."

"She'll be here any moment," Masara said with sudden glee. "She's always been there when I needed her the most."

"Masara," Lucian tried again, walking up behind him and placing a hand on his shoulder, "Ursula won't be...."

Lucian went silent when he saw the unicorn racing towards

them. He had seen Ursula often enough to know that it was her; or at least it appeared to be her. Masara walked forward to embrace her, the staff falling from his outstretched arms. The unicorn began to transform and then fell as dust over him. The wind picked the sand up and sprayed it over his face and body again and again until Masara fell down to his knees and started sobbing.

"Masara, your son..."

"Elgoth," the old man said and turned on the ground to face Lucian. He was holding some sort of plastic doll in his hands the size of a baby. "My son still loves me. Don't you, boy?"

Lucian was lost for words. Masara had lost his sanity and he was at odds as to whether he should free the old man's spirit.

"Leave that doll alone, yer silly man," another voice said from behind Lucian. He turned sharply and saw another old man walking towards them.

"Masara?"

"Me name's Malanite, me boy," he replied and then walked up to Masara and slapped him hard in the face. Masara fell with his face in the sand and spat out the dust that collected on his lips. Malanite disintegrated into the air.

"Just five minutes rest," Masara cried softly. "All I need is five minutes rest."

Lucian stepped forward and then stopped. Two men were walking towards them now, eager smiles on their faces. He knew the one was Le'Mar, and he assumed the older man was his father T'Mar for they strongly resembled each other.

"That's enough," Lucian said and grabbed Masara's coat. He pulled him up and summoned his power. The two still walked at an even pace towards them. Lucian pulled Masara until they were looking into each other's eyes.

Lucian's eyes flared with light and a rush of power flowed from him into Masara. Their hair blew wildly in the gathering wind and Lucian's muscles went tight as his power filled him completely.

Soon enough, the light of his power shone all over his body and Lucian could not be seen. Masara groaned as the power coursed into him too and then they were gone.

The power settled down and the light fell away. Lucian stepped back from the ancient tree and watched as it crumbled to the hard soil of the island.

A white smoke arose from the ashes of the tree and the spirit of Masara formed before Lucian. He had a peaceful expression on his face as he drifted in the air.

"Thank you so much, my friend," Masara said. "I owe you so much."

"Well, there is one way you can repay us," Lucian smiled slyly. "It's a special request from Shadowolf himself."

"Name your price," Masara said as he began to fade into the heavens.

"Prepare the angels," Lucian said boldly. "We're going to war."

THE TRICHOTOMIC PROPHECY
CHAPTER FIVE

The auditorium was a beautifully sculpted glass building with white frames on the edges and between the panes throughout. The morning sunlight passed through the eastern and northern windows onto the green atmosphere within. The distant western and southern windows were covered with creepers, vines and an assortment of other greenery and flowers. On the outside of those windows were the rocky walls that the auditorium hugged against.

The floor was laden with grass and a few scattered shrubs. There were white wooden chairs randomly situated throughout the open areas with creepers and plants hanging overhead from the roof. Despite the pensive gathering within the auditorium, the scene still managed to lend to them a relaxing atmosphere.

Behind the rocky walls, a shape drifted down from the roof of an internal cavern and landed softly on a grainy rock tip. His sight shifted until he could see through the rock into the auditorium, albeit they were mere blue shades and lines to him. He adjusted his hearing until he could hear the wind softly whistle outside and Darcwulf's voice from the stage upon which he was seated.

"How long do you think they can stare at us?" he smirked. His new staff lay on the glass wall behind him and his serpent sword glinted on his side. He rubbed his right hand over his bald head and then cleared the perspiration onto his vest.

"Ugh," Fransiska said to his right and pulled a sash from the satin belt on her dress. She gave it to him and he offered her an apologetic smile in return.

"Here you go, Shedaaij," Ursula approached them and handed her an umbrella to shade Crystal with. The girl squinted up at the unicorn lady and Ursula smiled back. Ursula ran the side of her thumb gently across Crystal's forehead and minute starry lights flickered in its wake.

"When you're done brooding, you might wanna join the conversation," Darcwulf said to his left without shifting his head.

"I'll have my turn to talk when Eldor returns," Shadowolf replied with a half-hearted smile.

"What's taking him so long anyway?" his brother asked. "We've been waiting for almost an hou…"

Darcwulf's comment died away as Eldor entered the auditorium. Another elf was following him, but Eldor turned swiftly and waved him off the stage. The junior elf stumbled slightly and then walked towards the back of the auditorium, well hidden by the overhanging branches of a miniature tree.

It was not the elf though that kept Shadowolf and the others interested in him. On his crossed arms he carried a wide yellow pillow with braided knots hanging from the sides. And on the pillow was a crystalline, blue bow.

When Shadowolf returned his gaze to the Elders, he saw that not one of them had bothered to watch the young elf's short journey. Their attention was divided between Shadowolf on his seat and Eldor approaching the centre of the stage.

Eldor rested his hands on a wooden object that Shadowolf was not really familiar with, but seemed similar to furniture he had seen before. It rose up to Eldor's abdomen and had a level surface at the top like a table. Shadowolf could not discern the purpose of the object until he saw there were compartments beneath the top that held scrolls and parchments.

Eldor watched the Elders carefully as if calculating them with his mind. Darcwulf narrowed his eyes perplexedly as Eldor stood in silence above the council of elves before him, running his green finger tips over the wooden top tentatively.

"I have never found it easy to approach the council with any matters on my heart," he started. "You know my feelings on these matters, so I will not do much deliberation from my side.

"I am here to finally introduce to you a man about whom I believed the prophecies were about," he continued, and Shadowolf dropped his head and clasped his hands together thoughtfully. "He has a lot on his mind and most of the happenings on the continent now were brought about by his recent actions.

"Without wasting further time," Eldor turned and looked at him, "Shadowolf Degron."

Shadowolf stood up and calmed his spirit. Filled with a grace that Bontu was bestowing upon him, he walked up to the object that Eldor had leaned upon and faced the council.

He had not been able to see as much of the Elders as he could from the end of the stage. He noticed how much darker most of their skins were compared to the younger elves that had served Eldor so many years ago. A few were tinted in colours other than green, and he assumed that it represented those specific families or creeds.

"I believe Eldor has already spoken to you about his fears that the prophecies were false and should not have been heeded," Shadowolf said. "If any of you hoped that I had come here to convince you otherwise, then you are wrong."

The Elders began to murmur and questions arose from their lips in such a flurry that Shadowolf could not discern one sentence from another.

"Please give him a chance!" Eldor erupted with controlled anger. "I would not have called this council if I did not believe he had a good case. However, I also would like to hear why he has started this war and what he hopes to achieve."

Shadowolf breathed deeply as the Elders quietened down. He could feel his own temper rising, but he could not afford to lose his calm just yet. With as much composure as he could muster, he looked at them again.

"I believe too much hope was placed on the prophecy," he said carefully, deliberately not using the plural form. "And that, as one part of the prophecy was supposedly fulfilled, the next was expected to occur. To our benison, Le'Mar made the same mistake."

"Sorry for interrupting," an Elder raised his hand respectfully.

"Go ahead, Selgar," Eldor encouraged.

"What mistake is that, my boy?" Selgar asked.

"The belief that the one prophecy would be fulfilled in three parts and that one part would succeed the other," Shadowolf explained. "Tell me, why do any of you believe that any part of the prophecy has been accomplished?"

"Are we not dealing with three prophecies as foretold by Philgarn and the other Orion sages?" another Elder said, whom Eldor softly identified as Brigem. "Why do you keep referring to it as a single prophecy?"

"I believe the prophecy is one of three parts," Shadowolf confirmed, "but I believe that no part of it has been fulfilled. I do however believe the events portrayed therein will come to fruition."

"You're confusing me," another Elder by the name of Haligon said. "You don't believe in the prophecy, but you believe it will happen anyway."

"Haligon," Shadowolf addressed him directly, "do you believe it was fulfilled?"

"In a sense, yes," the Elder replied. "You destroyed Mercius four years ago and opened the node. It was foretold that only the true *Enodhim* would receive that power."

"Yes, but it was not in the prophecy, was it?" Shadowolf said, and the council fell silent. "It was an assumption, but one where only Philgarn knew the true extent of its truth. Where in the prophecy was the power node that I released even mentioned?"

Once again the Elders could not answer. He could see that some of them were thinking of the words of the prophecy to try and contradict him.

"What about two years ago?" Brigem asked. "You became the *Wisoum*. You killed Sonersaat and fulfilled the second part of the prophecy."

"Did I?" Shadowolf asked with a raised eyebrow. "Trimistus lived and is now DragonWourd of the dragons. Was the Dragon War or the events that happened in Eldor's Forest two years ago ever mention in the prophecy?"

"What are you getting at, boy?" Selgar leaned forward.

"That Le'Mar made the mistake of trying to fulfil a prophecy that was never his," Shadowolf answered. "He tried to force the words to be fulfilled, hoping it was about him, and thereby he created the events that happened."

Selgar sat back again, and it seemed to Shadowolf by the expression on the elf's face that the little he was saying was breaking through.

"Let's think back to when this all started," Shadowolf continued, encouraged by Selgar's reaction. "Does anyone remember how the prophecy came to be?"

"It all started with the power node," Brigem said. "The sages were summoned to try and unravel what it was."

"The power node was created when my father and his elemental comrades protected me," Shadowolf said bluntly. "All the elements were centered around me as a new-born baby, on the morning of the Masaran Phenomenon when the sun rose."

Shadowolf could tell by the new silence and the expressions that the Elders had never considered this before. He wondered just how little they had known about the power node.

"With such convergence of powers," he continued, "it is not impossible to believe that a node of similar power would have been created.

"But my belief is that when Philgarn touched the node to reveal its secrets, he did not see the future of someone that would save or damn the world. He did not see the future of the world and the outcome of the war. He did not see the one that you all have been waiting for and expecting."

"What is it that you think he saw then?" an Elder called Pendum close to Elgoth at the back asked.

"He saw glimpses of my future life," Shadowolf said. He let it sink in for a moment, waiting for either outbursts or expressions of affirmation, but he received neither. "More importantly, I think he saw my life at the culmination of the war."

"Why only that part of your life?" Selgar asked. Shadowolf found that with every question from this elf, he respected him more and more. In a way, Selgar reminded him very much of Masara.

"The power node was created at the height of all the powers and at the time of the Masaran Phenomenon," he replied. "I believe what he saw was a time when the powers would be reunited in me again at the time of the Phenomenon."

"But these last four years we've seen the release of the *Enodhim* and the *Wisoum*," Brigem said with consternation. Shadowolf could see he was going to have difficulty with this elf. Then the rest of the council murmured in agreement, with the exception of Selgar, and Shadowolf allowed himself to sigh.

"After Philgarn cryptically wrote down his thoughts on what he saw," he tried again, "everyone felt the power node was the key to realising the prophecy. When Le'Mar returned, he read about it and found himself a Windfarer to release the power node. But, as Ursula and Masara had already worked out in a way, no one but me could release it."

"Why you?" Pendum asked.

"Because the powers consist of five," Selgar assumed. "Shadowolf's spirit became part of the creation of the node along with the other elements. It recognised his spirit when he touched it, not Mercius."

"Exactly," Shadowolf smiled in relief. "But Le'Mar was unphased by the release of the node. Just like everyone else, he believed that only one part of the prophecy was fulfilled and that he still had a shot at the other two."

"Or that by fulfilling the next steps, he could stop you from becoming what he wanted the most," Elgoth said from the back.

"From becoming the *Sadgi*," Shadowolf affirmed. "That's why he sent Sonersaat to compete against me for the role of the DragonRider. He was not interested in that part of the prophecy; only in becoming the proclaimed *Sadgi* that everyone was waiting for."

"So by trying to fulfil the prophecy that was nothing but a vision of Shadowolf's life," Eldor said, "he only created the events that would lead up to what Philgarn saw would happen in the end."

"That statement in and of itself is both true and false," Shadowolf commented, hoping he did not offend Eldor. "Le'Mar came here with two goals in mind: conquering the world for the Gemetrashef, but mostly to avenge his father like so many before him."

Some of the elves' expressions went dark when he mentioned this, although Shadowolf noticed that Selgar seemed pleased that he had done so.

"But as you say, Eldor, had the prophecy not existed, Le'Mar would have continued his personal quest without concern over the power node and dragons."

"Would Philgarn not have made this clear in the prophecy if he knew it was you who would become the *Sadgi*?" Brigem asked.

"No," Shadowolf replied. "The one thing I had going for me throughout all these years is that Le'Mar never knew who the prophecy was about or that it concerned only my life. If he had known that it was about me..."

"He would have made every endeavour to have you killed from the start before you released that node," Selgar finished for him. "Philgarn was protecting you."

The Elders sat in silence for the hundredth time, contemplating the revelations that had been laid before them.

"This is a bit hard to swallow," Haligon said. This time however, fewer Elders murmured in agreement. "I need more than conjectures. It sounds like a nicely contrived theory, but is as much assumption as the prophecy is."

"Very well," Shadowolf said with a small amount of anger rising in his voice. "There is one way that I can convince you, and that is to ask that the prophecy be read in its entirety."

"I agree," Selgar said.

A scribe was summoned from one of the side mounts and he ran up the stage and politely reached passed Shadowolf to the scrolls. He pulled one small scroll and opened it on the wooden surface. Shadowolf could see elven language scrawled delicately on the parchment.

"That's it," Darcwulf whispered behind Shadowolf's back. "Rip the prophecy to shreds. Nanoo power."

Shadowolf tried hard not to laugh as the scribe read it loud enough for all to hear:

He serves none; he walks alone in the passages of time,
For he has bound his soul with another; their powers are one.
He rides upon the wind as if it were his own,
He rides the dragon as if he were its king,
To finally destroy all those before his throne.

He journeys the world; fear is the tool of his power.
His name spreads over the earth, and they tremble.
With bow, horn, staff, dagger and sword he will kill the Sadgi,
With fire, wind, earth, water and soul he will rectify.

He rules the phoenix by becoming one with his ensemble.
Earth, ocean, sky and mountain will be his command.
Yet, with these powers, the land will be his battlefield.
In the end, blood will run from his hands.
In the end, with victory he will leave the land,
With his powers as his conquest and shield.

The Masaran Phenomenon will awaken his power.
He is the Windfarer, the DragonRider, the Sadgi

Darkness comes; he wades across the fields of time,
For he has bound his soul with a dragon, and fears none.
Having commanded the wind under his soul,
He rules the dragon with only a word.
But a time of foreboded testing still comes.

He journeys the elements; for in the end he will be contested.
False claims to his name produce showers of confusion.
Yet, in the end his power will be not be denied,
All armies under his hand will be unified,
To destroy that which has always only been an illusion.

He will lose those he loves, only to set them free.
For the dragons he rules will demand a part of him.
Fear will drive his veins
Until it is fear that he tames.
Then the elements will reign in his kingdom.

The Masaran Phenomenon will awaken his power.
He is the Windfarer, the DragonRider, the Sadgi.

Light will prevail; his path lies within the nodes of time,
For he has found allegiance with the stars, their purpose
almighty
Thousands will call to his name, albeit unwanted
Thousands will raise him high, he remains humbled
For he only awaits his destiny

He journeys the void; within it, light will confront dark
Repentance will serve as death, exultation, eternal fire
The righteous will lie scattered in their salvation
The wicked will die burning in their putrefaction
And he alone will see it transpire

In victory, he will find his honour do him justice.
And the world he defends will no longer be his home.
For the sake of those he loves, he will leave
To journey with those he once deceived
But in a glorious light, he will return alone

The Masaran Phenomenon will awaken his power.
He is the Windfarer, the DragonRider, the Sadgi

The scribe walked away and left the scroll before Shadowolf. He tried hard to hide a sarcastic leer that was creeping on his face.

"Have any of you seen anyone rule a phoenix at the time of the Windfarer?" he asked the stunned gathering. "Did anyone see armies unified under my hand during the time of the DragonRider? Did...."

"This is a very intelligent debate," Selgar said, and this time Shadowolf was shocked into silence. Of all the elves that he expected to interrupt him, Selgar was the last. "But can you rightly assume that Le'Mar holds any value to the prophecy?"

Shadowolf frowned. He did not understand what the Elder was trying to tell him.

"He never showed that he wanted to partake in any form of what was foretold," Selgar continued. "He used his minions to play the roles, yet he continued on his personal missions and succeeded. Perhaps he used our belief in the prophecy against us.

"Be that as it may," the Elder sighed, "I feel that discussing this matter will only waste further time. Why don't you tell us rather why it is that you are really here?"

Shadowolf stood silent for a moment longer. Selgar was too clever for him and was calling his bluff. He had to tell them his purpose now before the Elders realised that Shadowolf did not hold much stock in the prophecy himself. Perhaps that was what Selgar was trying to prevent too.

"As you all know by now, we are going to war with Le'Mar," he stated. "Whether or not the words are true, it gives us some form of hope that we will succeed."

"We have no need to go to war," Brigem replied. "The choice to rally Le'Mar's anger again and raise armies on the continent was your decision, not ours."

"The elves are as much part of this war as the rest of the earth," Shadowolf countered, but he felt that he was losing their conviction. "It started with the elves right in the beginning, in as much as it did with Bentley's son."

Selgar looked surprised, as did several of the others. For once in the history of Celenic Earth, a human had confessed that as much of the blame fell on them as it did on the elves.

"We all have a responsibility towards the earth," he continued. "The dwarves are with us and the mer-Kingdom is joining us in this war. The pegasi and most of the warriors from uPendus are already rallied at the Gate. I even have soldiers from the Underworld fighting in this damn war!

"In the end," he said, calming down, "it will not matter to me whether or not the elves join us. But it will always be remembered that the elves were the only race who decided not to defend the earth."

With that said, Shadowolf stormed off the platform. Darcwulf and the others followed shortly. Eldor waved with his hand for the elf carrying the bow to join them and briefly saw Selgar shake his head almost as if in disappointment.

Eldor turned back to the stage however when he felt a strange power form. The other elves looked up, also feeling the elements build on the stage. It did not take long before *KariemsaPh*, *Enodhim*, *Merlandsi* and *Goudlem* were visible to their elvin perceptions.

The dark shape within the cavern moved away from the wall, unaware of the elemental appearance. He became a bat once more and flew to the roof to join the others that were waiting silently.

THE MISTS OF CELENE
CHAPTER SIX

The dwarf led the new visitors to Horlorn's Gate through the entrance tunnel. Hargon tried not to show his sense of position within the ranks of Horlorn, but with most of the key leaders gone from the Gate he could not help but feel important. And with the jaguar Cavella walking beside him, he felt equal to any task put to him.

Even the dwarf king Gallon and the Gate's former lord Treville seemed to give him plenty of leeway to organise the armies without them. They were constantly in the lower armouries, making sure the weapons were prepared perfectly in ways of stone and element.

With Lucian, Chenesia, Anuxis and Shadowolf away on their separate quests, it left only Trimistus to ensure that the deadlines were kept. Yet even the DragonWourd seemed very occupied with the dragons and the warriors that had arrived from the Vale and Carmel. Nighthale and the other Wolf Lords kept themselves busy with the Avalion warriors. The one key person who seemed to be keeping all these ends tied together, well at least in Hargon's opinion, was himself.

The smile and the proud, broad shoulders dropped down again in sadness as he looked behind him. Sorceress walked majestically in her human form in his wake. Above her head, flowing like a brightly lit coral veil behind her head, were the fairies. And on the ground behind her the heavy hooves of the Alcove's centaurs marched.

His eyes tried to pierce between the equine bodies of the angelic centaurs, but he still caught no sign of Chenesia. Hargon was quite sure that Trimistus had warned him of Sorceress's awaited arrival with Chenesia, but the princess of the Vale seemed to be absent from the gathering. He looked forward again as they reached the junction that led further into Horlorn and to the tiers.

Despite his feelings of authority and his new found ego, he realised that he would have to find Trimistus. He knew where the centaurs would stay until the war and the fairies would make their own home. He also knew that Trimistus would want to see Sorceress immediately.

When they reached the Sky Tier, Lanel turned from his observations at one of the tables and walked up to them.

"You must be Sorceress, if I remember correctly?" Lanel greeted. "We didn't have much of an introduction the last time you were at Horlorn. My name is Lanel."

"Pleased to meet you," Sorceress greeted.

"Is Chenesia with you?" Lanel frowned, also searching the large group for her.

"She went with prince Lesan to the Far Isles," the *Goudlem* replied. Hargon's expression of awe went unnoticed.

"Ah ok," Lanel said and turned to Hargon. "Would you mind showing the centaurs to their lodging on the Mountain Tier? I need to speak to Sorceress in person."

Hargon nodded and led the centaurs back inside to the passages that would take them below. Sorceress looked up at the fairies and the lights left to find their own place within the Gate.

Lanel led Sorceress inside in silence for a brief moment before she spoke.

"I thought you would place the centaurs on the Ground Tier?" she asked.

"That tier is already quite occupied," Lanel said. "Once everyone has arrived and we have a clearer indication of where…"

"They can stay on that tier," Sorceress interrupted. "The centaurs can jump to the ground if need be. I was just curious."

Lanel opened the walls that took them to the elemental courtyard. The forest within moved softly as if a fresh breeze had entered.

"I need you to release the horn," Lanel said once they stopped near the centre of the courtyard.

"Release the horn? Why?"

"I can't tell you why," Lanel replied. "I don't even know why myself. All I know is that the horn needs to be released to the courtyard. Shadowolf said you would know how to do it."

Sorceress frowned. She fiddled with the butterfly pendant on her chest thoughtfully before looking back into Lanel's eyes.

"Are you going to miss being a unicorn?" Lanel asked with a sympathetic smile.

"I can still take a unicorn's shape if I wished," she replied, her blue hands dropping back to her side. "It's the power and the abilities unique to a unicorn that I am going to miss."

Sorceress turned from Lanel and walked away from him. She pulled the chain off her neck and held the butterfly in her hand until it took the shape of a dried out horn. She closed her eyes. Lanel could feel power rise around the skin of her arms as the horn became ash and fell between her fingers into the soil of the courtyard.

Lanel smiled at her in comfort as they both left the courtyard. They walked in silence once more, quietly enjoying each other's company, until shouts could be heard coming from within Horlorn. Lanel frowned and the two broke into a run towards the entrance tunnel.

When they reached one of the exits to the tiers below, Lanel knew what the cause of the commotion was immediately. Lucian was standing on one side, confronting the centaurs that had arrived with Sorceress. Behind him, Millon was equally holding back the centaurs that had arrived with them.

The contrast between the two groups was stark. The Alcove centaurs held angelic faces, light brown in complexion and inspiring to look upon. No horns broke the crests of their smoothly groomed heads, nor did any marks mar the perfection of their equine bodies. Even in the absence of the fairies, faint flickers of light seemed to circle their heads like burning effigies of molecular stars.

As far as the Philagis centaurs were concerned, their heads were cropped with many horns and their complexions were darker, bordering on a deep red tan. In further contrast, their expressions were more demonic. Their coats were rather unkempt and most of them kept their chest manes braided.

Another noticeable difference was that the Philagis centaurs were more muscular than those from the Alcove. Veins ripped across their arms and chests, their abdomens rippled with knots of muscles. Thanks also to the scars riddling their bodies, it was clear to all present that they had seen more battles.

"So these are the traitors we've heard so much about!" one of the Alcove centaurs shouted. Mirentaur growled loudly and tried to ram passed his father, but Millon's arms held his son back. Glamidon joined Millon's side to keep the others at bay.

"Stop this behaviour!" Sorceress commanded her centaurs and they became visibly obedient and calm. Only their eyes betrayed that they still wished harm on the others.

"What are we going to do?" Hargon said quickly. "We can't keep them together."

"That's exactly what we're going to do," Lucian said stubbornly, and Millon turned around sharply to look at him. "This war is against the dark lord. That's why you've come here. You will learn to co-exist for the sake of the war. I will not have you guys tearing each other to shreds on the battlefield instead of the enemy!"

Lucian's glare was penetrating, waiting for anyone to contest him. He knew Millon would stand strong, and therefore his centaurs too, but he was not sure what the Alcove centaurs would do. He looked at Sorceress briefly and found that her stare at her centaurs was just as demanding.

The Alcove centaurs started walking down the passages again. Without a word, they followed her silent command to the Mountain Tier. Mirentaur and Glamidon stared at them as they left and, when the final centaur was out of sight, they led the Philagis centaurs down.

"Hargon, go with them and let me know when they're settled," Lucian instructed. "I have a few things I want to finalise on this tier first."

Hargon's initial expression indicated that this was a task he considered too heavy a burden at first, but he shifted his shoulders and headed behind the last centaurs with determination. Cavella walked beside him, a deep growl in her throat.

Lucian, Sorceress and Millon walked together to the Sky Tier. The air was very humid, and the sweat was trickling down Lucian's forehead. He summoned a small breeze to help keep his body cool, but found that the heat made it difficult for him to get a response. He called harder with his mind and after a few moments the wind started passing through the corridors.

"Have you been to the courtyard?" Lucian asked.

"Yes I have, but I'm still not sure what purpose it served," she replied, anxious to get answers.

"Shadowolf will tell us everything in due course," he promised. "For now, I am glad the horn has arrived."

As the trio walked out onto the tier, Trimistus rose up from a lower tier with his dragon wings and landed before them. He retracted his wings and greeted.

"Any news from the others?" Lucian asked bluntly.

"None," he replied, and then looked at Sorceress. "Chenesia was supposed to have return with them."

"She's on the Far Isles with prince Lesan," Sorceress repeated. "Lesan wants to speak to the elves about joining us."

"Well, that makes two of them then," Lucian said, and then replied to her frown. "Shadowolf is there too, trying to convince Eldor and the Elders."

"That should be pleasant," Sorceress said sarcastically, and then changed her tone. "Tell me Millon; is there anyone from the old Clan still here?"

Millon dropped his head. It was something he had thought of asking Lucian also, but every time he tried the words seemed to choke. Lucian walked up to Sorceress and laid his hand on her shoulder. The gesture was wasted however, for his expression was very strict.

"The Shadow Clan is no more, Sorceress," he told her. "Everyone in Horlorn is now your family and your loyalty should lie with all of us.

"Now," he continued and walked to the edge of the tier, "if you will excuse me."

Lucian became one with the wind and drifted out of their sight.

"I don't care what he says," Sorceress mumbled. "I'm going to find our Clan."

"Count me in," Millon smiled and followed her.

Lucian floated down to the Ground Tier where most of the human warriors seemed to be located. He drifted passed many of the Vale's warriors, including Chenesia's mother. He waded between men and women, elementals and swordsmen.

It took a few minutes before he felt her presence. He stopped in the air and became whole again, seeing her back and the hair that fell down from her head. Simnab was in discussion with her, but he looked up. His distraction caused Telgar to look around and she almost faltered. Her hand leaned against Simnab's chest as she stared at Lucian.

"Go to him," Simnab said reassuringly. "I won't hold it against you."

Without wavering, she left Simnab's company and ran towards Lucian. The Windfarer became wind and flew passed soldiers towards her, becoming whole in her arms again.

For long moments they held each other tightly, too afraid to let each other go. Finally, with a hard squeeze, Telgar pulled away.

"Come, it's been a while since you've seen my husband," she said. With a tight hold on his hand, she pulled him along.

***

Shadowolf sat down in the shade of the trees away from the others. The wind was toying with his hair across his eyes and he felt the scruff of his soft beard with his fingers. He would have to get rid of that again to keep the peace with Shedaaij.

He could see the auditorium from where he was seated on the grass, even though they were far from it. He was just beginning to wonder when he would hear from Eldor when steps on the grass behind the tree alerted him to the elf's presence.

"You always wander away from your friends without telling them?" Eldor smiled.

"It's an old habit I find difficult to shake," Shadowolf returned the smile. "So what have the Elders decided?"

Eldor remained silent for a moment, walking a few steps away from Shadowolf to stare at the auditorium in thought. He was unsure as to whether or not he should inform him about the elementëls appearance, and in that second he chose not to.

"They have not made a decision," the elf replied.

Shadowolf felt his anger rise again. He wanted to retort, to push his temper to the limits of his power. Eldor waited patiently for his reaction, perhaps expecting him to lash out. It was this patient expectancy that Shadowolf sensed that caused him to relax.

"I cannot wait for their decision Eldor," he replied. Eldor turned with mild surprise on his face. "The war is about to begin and I cannot wait on the elves before I return."

"Give them the day, Shado," Eldor said. "You can't expect them to make a decision right now. There is a lot to consider."

"While they think, the armies are gathering on the continent," Shadowolf said, standing up. "We truly will start this war without them if necessary."

"I have no doubt of that," Eldor said. "I wish I could answer for my elves, but I too must make this decision carefully. Know that my heart is more for you than against you."

"Once we've won, will you return to the continent?" Shadowolf asked.

"That is a question I have often asked myself, and one that the Elders have cautioned me about," the elf said. "You see, I've been told that, should I participate in this war without their consent, I will never be permitted to return."

"That's not such a bad thing, is it?" Shadowolf said without a hint of sarcasm. Eldor chose to ignore the question anyway.

"If per chance the elves do not join the war, there is something I want you to have."

Eldor reached to his belt and pulled out a red pouch with a string closing the top. He undid the string and put his hand within the bag. When his hand returned, it held a crystal blue egg on the palm. Shadowolf walked closer to inspect it.

"What is it?"

"When I was younger," the elf explained, his eyes momentarily happy, "I used to pay a visit to the Mists of Celene at the start of every spring."

"I remember visiting that forest every year myself," Shadowolf smiled fondly. "It always refreshed me."

"The Mists had a way of replenishing itself. I began to wonder if there was a way that I could store some of its power somehow. It took me a while, but my determination won out.

"No one ever knew about these eggs, except Ursula. Every

year I would collect some of the forest's mystical power in an egg and the mists would just replenish what I took within a few days."

"How many did you collect?"

"Just five," Eldor said. "I never found much use for them, but perhaps you will."

Shadowolf watched as Eldor returned the egg to the pouch. The elf handed it over to him.

"I do have one question though," Eldor said as he tied the pouch to a clip on his side. "Are you sure you want Fransiska to have the bow? Shouldn't you be the one to use it?"

Shadowolf smiled slyly and decided that it was his turn to ignore a question. With a last look in his eyes that said *Trust me*, he turned around and walked back to the others. Eldor frowned and returned his gaze to the auditorium.

THE FOG OF LE'MAR
CHAPTER SEVEN

Chenesia lay still under the satin sheets, the morning sun not yet streaking against the curtains. Her mind was lost to sleep that she had not felt for a very long time. The sheet over her nude body was a comfort to her skin, as was the gentle pillow beneath her head.

As the last remnants of sleep ebbed away, her eyes slowly opened to the dimly-lit room. She could tell that the sun would be out soon. She stretched her legs out, her soft flat stomach resting against the mattress and her fingers stretching out to the top of the bed. She opened her legs and relaxed her body again, letting the calm of the morning suffuse over her.

She twitched suddenly when her breasts grew warm. She ran her hand between them, rubbing the muscles that covered her heart softly. As Chenesia caressed her breast, she remembered how her father had always had heart problems. She was tempted to believe that she had inherited the same condition, but then she remembered the Heart of Tigers that lie within her heart.

When the war was over, she would have to ask Lesan how she could remove it. It was a great blessing that the Heart could protect her from death, but if it was going to give her the same condition as her father then she would rather have it removed.

She turned on her back and pulled the sheet down with her feet until her upper body was exposed. The tips of her fingers still massaged the muscle which was starting to relax its throb now. She could feel goosebumps across her chest and arms as a light breeze blew into the room, but she allowed it to cool her if only to relieve the slight pain in her heart.

And then her thoughts travelled to the prince. Lesan had offered her the room before leaving to find the Elders and his father. There were rumours that Shadowolf had approached the Elders already, and she prayed whole-heartedly that they would listen to him.

Yet the thoughts of Lesan were neither about Shadowolf nor Lesan's absence. She imagined a future together with him, and her hand travelled down to her navel as she started tickling the skin with her fingertips. A smile crossed her lips as thoughts of being a mother one day crossed her mind once again.

Chenesia wondered whether their children would be accepted as elves or humans; or possibly both. She thought of Le'Mar, who had elven blood in him through T'Mar, and how the elves rejected him. She knew in her heart that it was through his own actions that he had been rejected, but what would the fate of her children with Lesan be?

She let her feet move over the soft sheet of the bed, enjoying the warm sensuality that was flowing through her veins. Her heart began to throb for a different reason now and she wished that she could taste Lesan's sweet lips once more. His voice passed in her mind and she could almost feel him beside her in the bed. The wind seemed to whisper sweet promises to her of long passionate nights with her prince.

There was a knock on the door and her upper body shot up in fright. Her head pulsed wildly as she tried to find her voice. She clutched the sheet over her breasts, not quite sure what to say or call to the visitor.

"Are you up, my love?" Lesan asked softly at the door. She closed her eyes and breathed deeply. Her heart was still pounding hard, yet gently subsiding.

"Yes, dearest," she finally answered.

Lesan entered politely with a loving smile. He closed the door behind him and sat down at the edge of the bed near her feet.

"Did you sleep well?" he asked.

"Very, very, exceptionally well," she replied and put her head back down on the pillow. She lifted her arms and rested her hands above her head. "What do the Elders say?"

"Well, Shadowolf has spoken to them," the prince confirmed. "It seems they are very indecisive about the matter. I have informed my father this morning that I will be joining the war with or without the Elders' consent, and I will not stop any elves who wish to follow me."

"Oh my goodness," she said, sitting up on her elbows. "What did he say?"

"He said he will not stop me if that is my decision. He has told me that, should the Elders decide not to join us, that I and the elves that follow me will be banished from the Isles."

"A bit harsh, don't you think?"

"The Elders said the same thing when my father's elves left to live on the continent," Lesan replied. "Give them a few centuries and they'll get over it."

Chenesia laughed. She was overjoyed that Lesan was taking his own steps in the war and would not let politics interfere. She could not wait to tell Shadowolf the good news, and was about to ask Lesan when they could leave when the prince interrupted her.

"There's another matter I want to speak to you about," he said. "I've spoken to your mother, and she would be more than happy having me as your husband."

"What!?" Chenesia bolted upright again, not caring that the sheet fell off her upper body.

"I assumed you would be happy," Lesan said, frowning at her reaction.

"Oh, but I am!" Chenesia said. "I just didn't know you spoke to her."

"Well, she's here on the Isles now and I think you should get out of bed so we can start the wedding preparations."

"Are you being serious?" Chenesia said, her hands starting to shake.

"Quite serious," he smiled.

"Oh my love," she whispered and then crawled out of the sheet and into his arms.

The air suddenly shimmered and Chenesia released the prince. Her hair stood up on her arms as the power intensified and seemed to heat the whole room. Lesan looked into Chenesia's eyes with concern.

"Here we go. Le'Mar's getting ready."

***

The waters were warm upon the surface of the ocean north of Horlorn's Gate, despite the fact that the sun had not risen yet. The tide washed up on the beach in the silence of the morning, but further inward the surface was still except for the occasional fish that disturbed it.

The reflection of Sothos the moon was accompanied by that of Ringos beside it. It was brighter and larger since its initial appearance in the sky. The rings that littered the surface were that much clearer to observe.

Deep beneath those reflections, where the water was much colder, swam the mermen and mermaids of James. He led them with the light of the trident forward, still unsure of exactly where they were supposed to wait for Shadowolf.

They had left no one behind. Everyone from the kingdom was with them, even those with children. James knew the journey would be far, and leaving the weak behind while they went to war was not an option. He had decided to leave their homes empty and build a new place for them once they reached the northern oceans.

His main concern was the sirens, or rather, the lack of any. He had been keeping his senses tuned to that of the trident, and even the magical weapon could find no trace or existence of the sirens. He could feel a strong presence ahead of them though, and he wondered if that was where he would meet Shadowolf.

The land south of them ran parallel to their route. James felt them pass the strong presence and he stopped. His kingdom waited behind him as he scanned the seas around him, but all he could sense was the presence on the land to the south. He was sure Horlorn's Gate was on that land.

James frowned. He wondered if Shadowolf expected them to fight on land and thought that he would not put it past that man. Vexed at the thought, he changed direction and headed south.

As they neared the continent, he could feel the soft crashing of water against cliffs. No longer comfortable just feeling his way around the ocean, James swam up and surfaced from the ocean. True to his feelings, a cliff ran before them from west to east, a cliff that he knew ran south to Horlorn.

Yet, the presence still came from within the cliff. James went down to the other mer-people waiting on him and led them towards the cliff. As they got closer and closer, James became more apprehensive and the trident began to glow as he activated its power.

Someone was swimming towards them from the cliffs. He let his senses drift before him and he could feel that there were several of them approaching. James held his hand out to stop those behind him and waited for the party to reach them.

His senses had warned him, yet he had still doubted until he could see them. Their tails pushed them forward and their naked torsos were visible even in the dim light of the morning. He knew they were mermen, but he did not understand how that could be? The trident had never informed him or any previous mer-King of their presence.

Welcome, lord of all fish and mammals that reside in the oceans. We have long awaited your gracious arrival.

James remained silent, but let the power of the trident subside. He could sense nothing suspicious about them, yet his instincts warned him to be careful.

We've lived here for centuries, sent here a long time ago by the King at that time, Merania. Long have we anticipated that the King would come to our kingdom again.

You mentioned you've awaited my arrival? James asked them mentally. He needed some evidence that this was part of Shadowolf's plan. For all he knew, this was just another devious trick of the dark lord. *Is that as your King, or were you forewarned of my coming?*

We were forewarned. In as little as a year ago, a man approached us and told us of the ocean's peril to the south. We have not seen any sighting of sirens in the north until a few months ago, and were glad for the warnings.

Did this man have a name? James persisted.

He went by the name of Elgoth.

James sighed in relief. He had heard of Elgoth many times and was almost certain he was at the right place. The merman he had addressed seemed to realise that James was still distressed.

He said that if you doubted us, we were to mention Shedaaij and Shadowolf.

His instincts still warned him of caution, but he sensed nothing false in the mermen before him. James nodded to them and they turned to the cliffs. James led the mer-Kingdom after them, keeping his senses open.

The presence within the cliffs grew stronger the closer they swam. Even the trident vibrated in his hands and began to pulse. Yet when they finally reached the cliffs, there was nothing but seaweed and stone to greet them.

The mermen that they followed swam through the seaweed, their hands gently caressing it as they passed. James knew instantly what the plant was and turned to address one of his generals.

Marcia, let the others know its Argo Stir. The children need to be assisted in passing through.

Marcia nodded and left to do as instructed. James watched her pass the information to the other generals before attempting entry into the cliffs.

He approached the Argo Stir and saw the leaves tense. The water surrounding the plants reverberated with sparks and James knew that these had been somehow modified. The trident glowed softly and it seemed to ease the plant somewhat. James let out his hand and softly stroked the plant until its anxiety eased.

He drifted his way through the plant until he reached a rectangular aperture in the cliff wall that was wide enough to let him through. Glancing down the sides of the cliff, he saw that it was lined with other such entrances. He made his way through into the inside of the cliff.

James stopped and opened his eyes wide. The coral along the vast walls were lit enough that he could see the structures and domes that filled the huge city. The mer-King only moved forward to allow those behind him through, but he was so shocked that he could do nothing else.

It was all too much for him to take in. He saw no end to the city. For all he knew, it extended all the way below the earth to Dwarf Mountains. He looked from side to side and realised he could see no walls either, except the foundational structures upon which homes stood.

Unlike the cities James was accustomed to, there was minimal dry land. On the odd locations, domes had been constructed and the space within it was dry. He could see mer-people walking on their legs in those few areas, but the rest was water.

Everywhere he looked, there were mer-people. His own people had just finished entering the city behind him, and their amount was miniscule compared to that before him. He could not even guess how many there could be, for James's people only filled a portion of the entrance.

Concentrated light caught his attention. It was a large distance away, but the structure that the light was centered on was large enough to view. A mer-King held a concrete trident high in the waters as if in victory. James did not recognise the face of the statue, but it was majestic and filled him with awe.

He realised that the mer-people within the city had stopped moving and were all facing the new-comers. The merman that had led them in swam before him once again.

Welcome to Selandil, my lord, he said.

The mer-Kingdom before him suddenly all bent over or knelt where they could. James remained still before them, watching their subservience to a King they had never met but had been apparently serving their whole existence. The trident in his hand burnt a brilliant yellow.

Oh stop showing off, James told it.

A liquid form formed before him and once again James's eyes popped wide. He bowed now before the being, recognising the elementël immediately.

My lady, he addressed *Merlandsi* politely, *it's a great...*

James's words of honour were cut off. The water within *Selandil* shook as tremours passed through it. James gripped the trident tightly, waiting for the outcome of the invisible assault.

Your timing is impeccable, James, Merlandsi said as the waters kept rocking. *You need to get the mer-Kingdom ready. The war is about to begin.*

***

Le'Mar sat on his throne chair staring out of his convex window. He quietly ran his fingers over the wooden arms of the chair, his gaze fixed on the armies gathered below him on the earth.

The creatures above the Alcove of Light stirred restlessly on the ground and the commanders and generals awaited the command to move out. Le'Mar sat still, breathing deeply. He knew the warriors within Eldor's old forest were just as restless, as were the demons waiting to be released. He could feel their anxiety, knew they longed for this battle. A similar blood lust ran through the creatures of the Dark Boundary.

He had his hood drawn over his face, if only to give him a sense of composure. He remained hidden, containing his power and the vexation that ached to be released. His fingers kept running over the wood in tune to its own melody, his hand longing to lash out and splinter the chair.

The door to his throne room opened and footsteps fell on the floor and stopped behind the desk. He remained still, his face hidden and his back to them.

"The summoners are ready, lord," the general said. "The four elemental knights have also arrived."

Le'Mar did not reply. The general waited a few more moments in case the dark lord chose to comment before deciding to leave with his guests. The door closed quietly and Le'Mar continued staring out onto the earth.

Shadowolf had been a mere adolescent when this had all started. Le'Mar's plans were clear; force Masara to emerge from the Far Isles, destroy him and any who got in the way, and conquer the earth for the Gemetrashef.

Yet, Shadowolf quietly interfered with matters since the start, growing in power and knowledge until he was ready to challenge the dark lord. He had taken care of Mercius while Le'Mar was trying to enter Eldor's Forest through *Pernonil*. He had released the power node beneath the school and obtained its energy.

Le'Mar's hand became a fist. He relaxed his hand, quietly tapping the chair's arm again. Sonersaat had been a very good choice for a DragonRider, but his arrogance was his downfall.

Le'Mar had to continuously contain Sonersaat's zeal for battle and victory in order to delay the Dragon War for his own purposes. Sonersaat had been much more powerful than Shadowolf, yet in the end, Shadowolf had defeated him like a mere puppet.

Le'Mar remembered meeting Shadowolf for the first time in

Eldor's Forest just after his dragon victory. He had been powerful, but compared to Masara he was a weakling. It was simple to thrust the man aside with nothing more than a blink.

His recent battle with Shadowolf had proven just how fatal the elemental was now. Le'Mar was still much more powerful than him though, but something told him Shadowolf had a secret up his sleeve. Recent events made him feel there was more to the elemental than what he had shown during that last fight.

How had Shadowolf convinced so many to join him at Horlorn? Le'Mar had returned to a destroyed throne in the forest with Darcwulf gone. Sona had been killed. And Le'Mar's attack at the River of Light seemed like a mere inconvenience to them.

For all Shadowolf's actions, he had not gone out of his way to destroy any of Le'Mar's creatures. His sole purpose so far had been to gather forces, armies that could have crushed any of his small tribes. Shadowolf had left them well alone.

Le'Mar realised his hand was a fist again but this time he let it be. He had to get rid of Shadowolf. He had been a thorn in the dark lord's side for too long. If it was a war with the *Sadgi* that he so longed for, then Le'Mar was going to comply.

Darkness shifted in his aura and Le'Mar bit into his teeth out of anger. He gripped the arm of the chair hard, his temper getting the better of him. It was time to destroy this world, destroy all those that now attempted to be released from the fog. Just like Trimistus's people that had tried to build skyscrapers to escape the Gemetrashef's last demonic prince.

The throne room began to shake. Le'Mar's eyes burned red under the hood until the lights could be seen through it. The whole castle shook and the creatures on the ground below wailed in fear at the power.

The fog began to move on the land. Like a wind blowing away the dust of centuries, the fog swept off the land towards the castle. It drifted over sand and stone, water and tree. It passed over all the creatures of the earth until it climbed the high walls of the castle and entered Le'Mar's soul.

It had been a while since he had felt so complete. His power was growing again to a force that he knew Shadowolf could not contend with. He laughed darkly, his throat groaning through the castle as the fog drew its energy into him.

"YOU THINK YOU CAN FACE ME!!!" Le'Mar shouted as he stood. The glass of the window shattered outwards and the castle walls cracked. Waves of power crashed over the earth from his outburst and the last of the fog passed into him.

Le'Mar calmed down and stood looking over the land.

"Prepare to die."

THE GUARDIAN OF THE BOW
CHAPTER EIGHT

Shadowolf cringed and dropped down on one knee. He felt the fog withdraw and the power travel across the continent. He bit teeth, his nerves stinging his muscles and his veins boiling in his blood. His hand gripped his shirt by his abdomen as the power subsided and finally died away.

"Are you ok?" Shedaaij asked. Shadowolf's senses had heightened in that release of power and her voice echoed in his ears. He opened his eyes wide as his sight heightened. He could see each grass blade beside his foot and he could smell every essence of nature around him. He could even hear the soft footsteps of Eldor as he paced the land in thought.

"I'll be fine," Shadowolf said as he stood. Shedaaij and Crystal's auras glared to his supernatural sight as he tried to calm his power. He called the energy back into his soul and took deep breaths. "Le'Mar's pulled the fog back. I think we'd better head back without the elves. We've run out of time."

"The Masaran Phenomenon is within the week," Darcwulf added as he joined them. "I'm not surprised that he's feeling edgy. I agree with Shado; it's best if we head back now. Le'Mar's not going to wait."

"We need to meet up with Eldor, Elgoth and Ursula," Shadowolf said, looking around for Fransiska and finding her walking up behind Darcwulf.

"Where are we going to find them now?" Darcwulf asked, looking back over the hills that led to the elves. "I can't remember seeing Ursula much lately."

"Give me a moment," Shadowolf replied. He turned his back on the small group and closed his eyes. The others held their breaths tentatively, awaiting the outcome of his mysterious action.

Shadowolf could sense them somewhere on the island, perhaps not their exact location but at least their approximate whereabouts. He whispered on the wind, their names travelling on the breeze like a fallen leave gliding to the earth.

Eldor stopped in his meditative wandering and turned his head to the call of his name. Ursula gently stayed her hand on the curtain she was drawing as she her name blew through the window. She knew that voice and she guessed its meaning. Elgoth slowed his walk down the passage to Chenesia's room as the voice called to him upon the bricks of the building.

Shadowolf faced the others again with a smile on his face. To comfort himself more than for anything else, he summoned the wind to blow upon his warm skin and tense nerves.

"Look, if you wanted to cry we could have left you alone," Darcwulf attempted a joke, and Shadowolf laughed in response. Fransiska slapped his arm.

The sound of hooves broke the nearby hills and, before Darcwulf turned to look, Ursula was there as a unicorn. When she became human again, a portal appeared and Eldor stepped through clutching his aged staff. The elf's portal had hardly closed when the wind shifted in direction and Elgoth materialised in their midst.

"I'm glad you could all make it," Shadowolf greeted them. "I'm sure you all felt Le'Mar's power on the land and understand that we have to leave. Eldor, you will have to let me know the Elder's decision."

"Whatever they decide, my son has already expressed to me that he will be there with the elves that wish to follow," Eldor said.

"Will you be there?" Shadowolf said cautiously.

Eldor did not answer. He looked down at his hands and his eyes seemed to lose emotion. Shadowolf did not have to search his feelings long to know that the elf did not want to be pressured for an answer. Shadowolf also had an instinctive feeling that facing Le'Mar was something that the elf lord hoped he would never have to do again.

"Chenesia's wedding is tomorrow," Ursula interceded. "I'm sure she would be honoured if we joined the celebrations."

Shadowolf stared blankly at her, absorbing the news and containing his anxiety. He knew how much Chenesia loved the prince. With a sigh, he conceded that he should be there for her. Maybe the wedding would give him the strength he needed for what lay ahead. He needed to head back to Horlorn soon though as there were a few things he had to do before…

"I'll go back so long," Darcwulf interrupted his thoughts. "I never really got to know her."

"I'll go with him, my love," Shedaaij said, planting a kiss on his cheek. "I need to make contact with James anyway and Deihlia can look after Cry…"

"No," Shadowolf interrupted her. "Go with Darcwulf, but wait for me before you leave for James. I'll be back after the wedding. Eldor, I need…"

"On my way," the elf said and opened a portal beside him. The portal shimmered as he passed through and remained humming there while they waited for his return.

"Fransiska, I assume you're going with them?" Shadowolf asked and she nodded with a deep frown on her face. Tyler's head leaned on her shoulder as the boy slept.

"Darcwulf, can you spare me a moment?" Shadowolf asked. His brother frowned but gave him a slight nod. They walked away from the women and children until Shadowolf stopped.

"It works on the nerves, doesn't it?" Darcwulf said into the breeze. "I find it difficult to contain the fire inside me with all this stress."

"Don't worry, you'll find release soon enough," Shadowolf promised. "There's something else I need to speak to you about."

"I'm listening," Darcwulf replied. He looked ahead, having never heard Shadowolf sound so serious before.

"Remember two years ago when I returned to the earth in Bentley Strip with Asgorna?"

"Vaguely," Darcwulf frowned. "You had just returned from the dragon world, or something to that effect."

"I discovered something while I was in uPendus," Shadowolf said. "I didn't know when to tell you this with everything that's been happening."

"Look, I know we've known each other since birth," Darcwulf

cracked a smile, "but I'm not really into men."

Shadowolf curled his lip into a smile in reply to his joke, but Darcwulf crossed his arms in anticipation of Shadowolf's news.

"One of the kingdoms we were battling against actually belongs to your biological father," Shadowolf said calmly.

Darcwulf dropped his arms and looked at him astounded. At a loss for words, Darcwulf screwed his face up while waiting for clarification.

"It's a lot to explain, which we don't really have time for now, but Asgorna finally found word of the child that was brought to Celenic Earth 26 years ago. Apparently, you're expected to return one day and herald the coming of the united kingdom for your father."

"You're kidding?" Darcwulf said with a trace of humour. "You're saying I have a prophecy too?"

"Pretty much so," Shadowolf laughed, but saw Darcwulf go quiet again. He held his breath. "I've told Shedaaij that I will be returning with Asgorna to that world after this war."

"What?" his brother asked, turning to him. "Why would you do that?"

"It's a promise I made to Asgorna a long time ago," Shadowolf replied. "To this day, I intended to keep that promise. And I owe Asgorna for losing his kingship over the dragons.

"But your choice is important," Shadowolf continued. "I would have asked you to come with me anyway, but there are two matters to consider. First, is that your father is in an opposing kingdom. Second would be your new-found family."

"Is Shedaaij going with you?"

"No," he replied. "I have every intention of returning to Celenic Earth. I want Crystal to grow up here. You, however, can start a new life there with Fransiska if you wish."

Darcwulf turned his head to look at Fransiska and Tyler. His arms tensed suddenly as he curled his hands into fists. Shadowolf could smell the heat rise on the skin of his arms and Darcwulf tried to contain his unease.

"It's not fair that this decision is put on me now," he said finally.

"I know," Shadowolf replied sympathetically.

"I would have gone with you despite my family, but the knowledge of my father does put a different perspective on things."

"It's up to you, brother," Shadowolf said, placing his hand on Darcwulf's tense shoulder. "I'm sure once we're there, we'll work out what to do."

"But for now, I need to discuss it with Fransiska," Darcwulf said, to which Shadowolf nodded.

They returned to the others and Darcwulf tugged softly on Fransiska's arm to call her aside. They walked away from them and Shedaaij raised her eyebrows. Ursula and Elgoth held their silence between the two couples.

"She should take it well," Shedaaij said, but looking at Fransiska's face they could both see that she was not. Darcwulf had just returned into her life to be told that he might be leaving again. "I know how she feels."

"I'll return as soon as I can," Shadowolf told her again. "There are a few matters I need to clear over there, and then I should be home in no time."

"I'll give you two years," she joked and he laughed.

The wind stirred close to them where the portal was still twisting and Eldor stepped through with the blue, crystal bow gleaming in his hand. Shadowolf smiled in greeting and the portal closed behind the elf. Elgoth and Ursula joined them.

"Here you go," Eldor said, holding the bow out to him. Instinctively, Shadowolf stepped back out of reach. The crystal bow glittered before his eyes and seemed to call out to him, but he calmed his spirit and shook his head. Elgoth seemed to twitch with unspoken fear.

"It's not mine to hold," he said and looked up at the other couple. They were embracing each other with Tyler between the two of them. Shadowolf gave them a moment together and it was not long before the two joined them again.

"Fransiska, Eldor has a gift for you," Shadowolf said, looking at Eldor meaningfully.

"Yes," the elf followed his lead. "It once belonged to the maiden Celene and I would like you to have it. It will assist you in the war and be your guiding hand."

"Wow," she said, but appeared hesitant in taking it. "Are you sure I can use it?"

"Only someone who has mastered the water element can take

it," Elgoth informed her.

"I haven't mastered it," Fransiska chuckled. "I haven't even been tested yet."

"Not everyone that masters an element is tested, only those chosen by the elementëls," Elgoth explained. "I can sense the power of *Merlandsi* in you and have no doubt that you would pass her test without even a thought."

"Your confidence in me is inspiring," she said shyly, "but how sure are you?"

"Darcwulf," Shadowolf said, "try touching the bow."

Darcwulf complied by moving forward and reaching out for the bow. As his skin was about to touch the crystal blue surface, his hand broke out in fire and he retracted his hand in pain. He hissed and held his hand as if it had been scorched. Eldor looked sidelong at Shadowolf in thought.

"Now you try," Elgoth offered.

Fransiska moved forward and carefully reached for the bow, pulling her hand back twice in fear before grabbing it firmly. The crystal of the bow began to flow calmly as if it had become a river that passed into her hand. Her skin changed into water that flowed over her body until she was complete liquid standing amongst them.

From the depths of her watery spirit, a song sang to their minds. It called to the men, calming their minds and seducing them to close in on her. Shadowolf closed his eyes and shut his mind to her sirenic powers. Darcwulf had no inhibitions to the mother of his child and moved in to kiss and hold her. Eldor rubbed the sweat from his palms onto his shirt and Elgoth cleared his throat audibly.

"Oh sorry!" Fransiska said. The song of seduction died and she became human once again. She strapped the liquid bow over her shoulders and the liquid froze into crystal once again. "The bow is very overpowering."

"You'll learn to master that too," Elgoth said, and then stepped back as if to show that his part was done.

"Ok it's time to get done," Shadowolf said and turned his back on them. He closed his eyes and stretched out his hand, picturing the Sky Tier at Horlorn. A portal tore the air before him and when it was stable he looked at the others again. "Fransiska, find Lucian or

Lanel as soon as you can. They will help you with the bow."

"I'll take her," Darcwulf offered.

"Very well," Shadowolf said. "I would suggest you get Tyler acquainted with Deihlia as soon as possible."

"Become the permanent baby-sitter, has she?" Darcwulf jibed.

"She's good with Crystal," Shadowolf conceded. "She'll protect them should the need arise."

"See you on the other side," Darcwulf said, embracing his brother. They all greeted Eldor, Shadowolf, Ursula and Elgoth as they passed through the portal to Horlorn's Gate.

"Shall we?" Shadowolf said as his portal closed. "I believe we have a wedding to attend to."

LIGHT BEFORE THE STORM
CHAPTER NINE

Lucian walked sleepily to the main hall on the Sky Tier. He yawned lazily, almost wishing he had never left his wife's side in the bed that morning.

As he passed the opening to the Tier, he saw a shadow cross the light towards him. He looked up and watched as Trimistus joined him on his journey to find breakfast.

"Have a good night's rest?" the reptilian man asked.

"Surprisingly, yes," Lucian replied pleasantly. He waited for Trimistus to say something further, but silence passed between them until they entered the main hall.

As was becoming the norm now that things had settled to a general calm, the tables were filled with most of the warriors from the Sky Tier, with a few from the lower tiers mingling amongst them. At the distant end of the hall was the counter where beverages and bounteous food from the kitchens lay.

Lucian started to step forward, but stopped when he saw a group together at a centre table. Trimistus continued on without him, walking without hesitation or thought to that very table.

He spotted Darcwulf at the table, an angst expression on his face but his demeanour joyfully active. Fransiska sat beside him, his arm tucked in hers. Shedaaij also sat on their side of the table, but he did not see Shadowolf or Crystal among them.

Further on that side of the table sat Angelia, Skywolf and Lastgorn. Lucian looked on the other side to see who the group was listening to at that moment. Sorceress seemed to be speaking in low tones, but for all the noise in the hall Lucian felt it was somewhat unnecessary.

Behind her stood the Alcove centaur, Heltaur. With him, Glamidon, Mirentaur and Millon listened intently to what Sorceress was saying. Heula sat on her right side while the gargoyle Glasden sat on her left.

Lucian had no doubt that the Shadow Clan had reformed. The remaining members from the previous Clan were nearly all present. His head told him this was not a good idea as the entire army had to fight together as one. Groups would only fight for themselves and not worry about the rest.

Yet, his heart told him it was needed. The Clan had been strong together and perhaps it would be the strength of the Clan that would pull them through. He smiled softly, and decided to let it be without causing a fuss. They would not listen to him anyway.

Lucian began to walk forward when the group's eyes turned towards him. He froze, unsure as to why they were alerted to his presence, when he heard soft steps behind him. He turned around and looked straight up into the maw of Anuxis.

"Welcome back," Lucian managed to say while swallowing hard, trying to contain his fright.

"Thank you," Anuxis replied. "Everything still going according to plan?"

"It would seem so," the Windfarer said while trying to look passed Anuxis's broad shoulders. "Have you managed to gather your warriors?"

"Yes, they are all here," Anuxis said, walking passed Lucian and joining Trimistus at the Clan's table. Lucian's frown increased as he left the hall and made his way to the Tier outside.

When he got to the overlaying edge of the Tier, he looked down on the lower ones. He scanned the creatures and people milling around, but he could see no evidence of the Underworld warriors. He could only guess that the wolves were in human form and he did not recognise them.

Once again his attention was turned to steps behind him. Anuxis was walking towards him with Simnab at his side, the Crethan's head bowed in concerned anticipation.

They stopped a short distance from him at the edge of the Tier, and Lucian let the wind carry their words to his ears.

"I swear I did not betray you," Simnab said, his voice a mixture of fear and honesty.

"I know," Anuxis replied. Simnab's head shot up and looked into the wolf's eyes. "It was forever their goal to rid me of my most faithful servant. I am humbled to regret that I ever banished you from my kingdom."

Simnab looked forward over the land, finding himself at a loss for words. His eyes shone with many strong emotions, but his lips held them sealed in the crux if his heart. The foremost was anger and resentment of his kind and his mind swam with the possibility of denying any request that Anuxis might have.

"This war will take a lot from this land," Anuxis continued. "I am proud to see that you have done well here and made it your home. It's not something I wish to take away from you."

"There's nothing left to take from me but my family," Simnab said, not sparing any moment to look up at Anuxis. "I still live in fear that I will face a *Haniegke* in this war that will transform me against my will."

"That is why I sought you out," Anuxis muttered. "Kneel before me."

Simnab twisted his gaze upon Anuxis's wolf face. The anger he had contained was upon the surface of his face now as his mouth formed the brazened words he was about to utter.

"I said....kneel," Anuxis said with a stronger command, "for the sake of your family and this world that you have come to love."

Simnab obeyed hesitantly, falling lightly on one knee with his hands resting upon the other. He felt power rise from with Anuxis and bowed his head as the wolf-lord lay his left hand over it.

"What are you doing?!" Lanel's voice shouted from within Horlorn. He ran towards them with Harmony at his side, their hands balled into fists.

"Lanel, stop!" Lucian shouted. The two slowed their pace and watch anxiously at the scene before them. Lanel seemed to be waiting for a moment to strike Anuxis.

Soft lights broke from the air surrounding Simnab. He kept his eyes closed as the yellow cloud formed and turned around him. Simnab's skin glowed intensely white, pulsing as the power within him grew. A low moan escaped his lips and his muscles tensed, but Anuxis continued streaming power into him.

"No!" Lanel shouted, misunderstanding the groans that were growing louder. He ran forward again to attack Anuxis, but halted instantly when a shape jumped out from under Anuxis's cloak. An oddly-shaped wolf growled deeply at Lanel, its fangs dripping with saliva and its eyes warning him not to approach.

"Lanel," Lucian said, grabbing his arm and pulling him aside. "Leave them."

Anuxis moved his hand away from Simnab's head onto his staff. The power continued to feed into Simnab as he gripped the staff with both hands and lifted the lower end off the ground.

The cloud lifted the shining man off his knees until he was floating before them in the air. Simnab stretched his arms out on either side of him as the power increased, anxious to release it at the same time. It felt like too much power, more than he could ever contain.

His cry died as Anuxis released him and he fell to the ground. The concrete of the Tier cracked slightly as his knee connected with it, but Simnab felt no pain. He stood up before Anuxis, the light in his eyes fading back to normal. Anuxis whistled and Cerexus walked onto the Tier from behind Lanel with a ruby staff in the central head's mouth.

"What have you done?" Simnab asked, watching as Anuxis took the staff and offered it to him. "I feel... almost equal to you."

"You are," Anuxis replied. "As I am lord of the Underworld, so you too shall be lord here on Celenic Earth."

"But where will I get warriors?" Simnab asked.

"They have already been provided for," Anuxis smiled. "Those within the grounds of Le'Mar's castle will be yours. They came from this world anyway."

"But the *Haniegke* that control them will..."

"...fall under your command," Anuxis completed for him. "Remember the power you now hold."

Simnab went silent in thought as Anuxis offered him the crimson staff again. He took it, and watched as Anuxis turned and walked back inside. The wolf that had fended Lanel off merely crawled under the cloak and vanished into him with a jump.

***

Shadowolf walked in the open field that was filled with the elves making the final arrangements for the wedding. The stage for the ceremony was already set, and the trees that lined all sides were dressed with a large array of décor.

He found himself wandering in the centre isle between the rows of seats. The chairs looked like branches and leaves intricately woven together. Small, blue dusts of cloud drifted at the feet of the chairs like small constellations floating through the galaxy. Above him in the overhanging treetops birds and a few fairies flew around, their sounds echoing in the forest as if in a harmonic dance.

The clothes Eldor had sent to him that morning hung loosely on him. Like most of the décor and clothing around him, it was silver in colour with strange designs on the short sleeves and back. A female elf had arrived to brush the mop of hair on his head. It was the tidiest his hair had been in a very long time.

He heard small feet running towards him to the left and, without turning his head, he looked through the long strands of hair falling down his cheek. It was an elfling that seemed very excited to be carrying a message of some importance. A smile crept on Shadowolf's face.

"Mr Shadowolf sir!" the elfling shouted gleefully and quickly. "Chenesia wants to see you."

Shadowolf looked at the elfling confused. The elf took a step back from his gaze and he offered a polite smile.

"Lead the way, little one," he said.

The elf nodded, a mixture of fear and awe on its face. He turned and ran for one of the trees and went up on the stairs that spiralled up the height of the trunk.

Shadowolf was in no mood to walk up those stairs. He looked up at the apex of the stairs and it only hardened his resolve. He summoned the wind, feeling the air stir from the ground beneath him to lift him up in the air. His hair whipped around his face as he rose up to where the elfling was steadily climbing the stairs.

The elfling ran at a battered pace, his arms flinging from side to side as he looked sidelong at Shadowolf spiralling up on the air beside him.

"Come on," Shadowolf said, stretching out his hand. The elfling smiled broadly and jumped towards his hand. Shadowolf grabbed it and flung the kid onto his back. The elfling giggled and laughed as Shadowolf increased the wind and they flew to the treetops at a high velocity.

"Here!" the elfling shouted into the wind as a platform broke out from the trunk. Shadowolf could see Chenesia in her wedding dress, being preened and fitted by several female elves. "Bye bye now!"

Without warning, the elfling jumped off his back and landed on all fours on the trunk of the tree. He ran down its length like a squirrel, and suddenly Shadowolf's flying feat didn't seem so impressive.

Shadowolf let the wind carry him to the platform. He landed gently, but Chenesia was alerted to his presence by the reflection in the large mirror on the wall. She turned around with a very welcoming smile and left the workings of the elves to rush into his arms.

"I'm getting married," she whispered excitedly in his ear.

"You don't say?" Shadowolf teased her. "You smell very lovely."

"I'd hope so," she replied, leaning back in his arms to look into his eyes. "I'm surprised I don't hear wedding chimes from your corner of the world."

"To be honest, I haven't thought about it yet," he said. "Too preoccupied with this damned war. But Shedaaij and I will be married, that I assure you."

"I can't think of anyone else to complete your life," Chenesia agreed.

She let go and walked towards the mirror thoughtfully. Shadowolf frowned and waited to find out why she had called him. She looked at him again, the freckles on her cheeks highlighting the beauty of her face.

"I wish my father could be here," she said sadly. "I know within my heart those tigroys were sent by him to protect me. But I still wish he was here instead."

"I'm sure he wishes the same thing, Chen," he said soothingly.

"Be that as it may," she said, and he could see she was trying to keep the tears down, "I have a favour to ask of you."

"Anything," Shadowolf replied.

"I would like you to be the one to walk me down the aisle."

He took a step back. His face showed that he was clearly caught off-guard. This was an honour he had not expected.

"Chenesia, I…" he choked on his words.

"Shado, there's no one else here that I can ask," she replied. "My mother will be standing at my side on stage. You are the closest friend I have."

"What about Hargon?" Shadowolf asked. He had seen the dwarf earlier that morning, his face lost in glee as he looked at the magnificent forest of the elves.

"Hargon and I have a bond that is very great," Chenesia said, twisting her hands together. "He will carry the rings. I know he finds that a great honour."

She walked up to him, her eyes pleading that he consider it. She reached for his hands and held them in hers, not once looking anywhere else but his eyes.

"Ok," Shadowolf said, "I'll do it for you."

"Thank you!" she said, jumping into his arms once again. "You don't know how much that means to me."

She planted a kiss on his lips and returned to the elves. They started to usher him out when they requested that the dress be taken off for a readjustment. Shadowolf turned at the platform to look at her one more time and then let the wind carry him back to the earth.

A few hours later, everyone was seated and bustling with excitement. The stage shone brilliantly in the late afternoon sun. Lesan made his appearance at the bottom of the stage with his father Eldor beside him.

Soft music played in the air surrounding them. To Shadowolf, it sounded and felt as if the music drifted from the trees and the birds that sat still in the branches. Even the air was still and the grass beneath his feet exuded a sense of anticipation.

As hard as he tried to avoid it, thoughts of the impending war were determined to plague his mind. Often he caught himself staring at the ground and thinking about the things that still needed to be done and whether Horlorn's preparations were nearly completed. He had wanted to get hold of Hargon and ask the dwarf about it, but he had not seen him since earlier that morning.

It would have been a simple matter to project his spirit across the land to Horlorn and see how far they were, but the sense of anxiety that the ceremony pressed upon everyone made his spirit too thrilled to calmly manage such an act. If anyone suddenly approached him or alarmed him with their presence, he would be pulled back to reality and the consequences of such shock would have been dire.

Chenesia needed his full attention and so he pulled out of his thoughts for the hundredth time and scanned the forest for her entry. Larnesia had mentioned that a horn would sound when it was time for her daughter to arrive, but he could not help but look around for her. Watching Lesan, he could see the prince was having the same problem.

He noticed then that Lesan's demeanour changed pleasantly as the elves turned to look at the skies behind them. The horn that they had all awaited sounded around the forest and Shadowolf stood and turned to watch her descend.

The tigroys led the convoy. Their brilliant fur wings flapped as they headed for Shadowolf, their colours orange with black stripes instead of the usual white marble that everyone had grown used to. They bore their fangs majestically and roared magnificently as they neared the earth.

Behind them, Genewiu carried Chenesia on her back. The bride sat with her legs off to the right of the pegasus's body just in front of the wing. She looked very regal with a placid smile on her face. The train of the dress trailed off Genewiu's back and floated in the air behind them like an extension of the pegasus's tail.

When they landed and Chenesia dismounted, Shadowolf approached her with pride shining in his eyes. She gave him a smile that conveyed little, but the twinkle in her eyes confessed her inner gratitude. He held out his arm, and she tucked her hands over it.

As they walked up with the tigroys before them and Genewiu and Hargon falling in behind them, the music changed to the ceremonial tunes of the elves. Lesan stood tall upon the stage now, his father just behind him, as they waited for her to reach them.

When they had climbed the stairs up onto the stage, Shadowolf handed her over to Lesan and stood behind Eldor. He watched as Larnesia and Hargon took their places behind Chenesia, the dwarf holding the pillow with the rings firmly.

Shadowolf felt them before they appeared. One by one, each of the elementël angels appeared on the stage and stood in silence. Shadowolf could not help but feel that their eyes were on him, especially *Enodhim*'s, but he convinced himself that he was just being paranoid.

The melody of the ceremony mellowed down while Ursula and Elgoth made their way from the far end of the stage until they were visible to all the elves below. They were both dressed in stunning, purple robes with patterns of stars spotting the cloths.

And so, with the heart of the elves fired up and the love of the nature surrounding them, the ceremony began.

LE'MAR'S LAST CHANCE
CHAPTER TEN

The large hall was very quiet and lit with torches at regular intervals on the long walls. The walls were crude, unlike the smooth, dwarven work that Lucian had become accustomed to. He could not put blame on them though; it was quickly constructed with emphasis that the hall would in all probability be used very few times.

He had invited the essential members of the War Council of Horlorn earlier that morning, but he knew that they would bring others with them. He waited patiently on their arrival, the three seats beside him personifying the emptiness of the hall.

The suffocating space of the hall was finally broken with Treville's arrival. The former lord of Horlorn nodded in greeting as he led Lanel, Harmony and Nashela to seats at the huge, elliptical table. They whispered amongst themselves, leaving Lucian to his patience.

After a few minutes more groups entered. The Shadow Clan found seats closer to Lucian. He noticed that Shedaaij and Fransiska were among them, but their children were absent. Darcwulf looked anxiously at Lucian, and he could see the *KariemsaPh* was wondering the same thing as he.

Chenesia entered the hall with Genewiu, Lesan and three of his elf generals. Lesan and the elves found seats, but Chenesia left their side to join Lucian at the head of the table. She greeted him quickly, but waited with him for the others before starting a conversation. Genewiu stood by the far wall opposite them.

Ursula and Elgoth entered and quickly found seats by the Clan. They were followed shortly by lord Gallon, Hargon and a few dwarf generals. Anuxis entered the hall with Simnab at his side, but Simnab found his own seat as Anuxis headed for the main table and took a seat beside Chenesia.

Larnesia entered the hall with a few of the Vale's warriors. The last to enter were the Avalion tribe lords Nighthale, Malkius, Jasnon, Sjedwolf and Salinos with a few generals from each of the tribes. Lucian wondered if his wife would attend, but it became obvious after waiting several moments longer that no one else was going to arrive.

"I'm glad to see you all here," Lucian opened the meeting formerly. There was no need to interrupt anyone to silence. The audience was so wrapped in tension that they waited on his every word. He looked sidelong at the empty chair beside Anuxis, the question burning within him again.

"Everything is prepared in Horlorn," he continued. "I believe our warriors are all in place. We have two days until the Masaran Phenomenon, and I have no doubt that Le'Mar will strike before then."

Members of the council looked at each other thoughtfully, but held their silence.

"We're here to deliberate for a few hours," Lucian said. "To discuss the creatures we know we will encounter and those that Darcwulf knows of. These matters have to be discussed with your highest generals so that they may be passed down to others."

"Bit late in the day to be discussing these things," Malkius commented.

"Unfortunately, with how things have been, we've only had the opportunity now to put things together," Lucian replied, and then added snidely, "No point wasting time on useless meetings when only the most necessary will do."

This comment seemed to set the tone for the rest of the meeting. Lucian had not meant to sound so stern, but he knew that several of the members were used to running meetings their way, and he was in no mood to entertain them.

"Lucian, where is Shadowolf?" Darcwulf finally asked. "He should have returned with Chenesia."

Lucian was about to say that he did not actually know, when Chenesia spoke up.

"He didn't return with us, Darc," she said. "He told me that he had one more thing to do before he could join us. And then he vanished into the air."

"Do any of you know where he went?" Nighthale asked the three at the head of the table. "I believe there is some sort of magical communication between you."

"This was not part of the plan," Lucian said, thrumming his fingers on the table top. "I have no idea what Shado is up to."

***

Le'Mar looked at the army before him. The lines appeared to form darkness around them just by their mere presence. The creatures groaned and waited patiently for him to tell them they could relax, but his glare only gave one command: do not dare move.

As far as he could see, the creatures stood row upon row in their ranks. They almost filled the entirety of what was once Eldor's Forest, and yet they were only a third of what was available to him.

Le'Mar believed in his heart that the masse in Horlorn would not be able to withstand such a force, but he still had concern. The advantage they had at Horlorn was that the fields could not contain all the creatures Le'Mar intended sending their way, but there were ways to get around that. If all went well, Le'Mar would not have to use his entire force.

He rose into the wind and when he blinked he was back in his Alcove castle. The army on the grounds below stood just as ready for the war. He saw no way out for Horlorn, and he knew his power was immensely greater than anyone there. It was not vanity; it was a fact.

He strode from his observations and turned to sit down at the throne chair that faced the large window. He felt the presence approaching the throne room and sat down tentatively. He cleared the frown from his face as he felt the man touch the double doors and push it open.

Shadowolf looked down at him, no expression on his face and no emotions betrayed. He walked forward slowly, the silver ceremonial suit shimmering in the reflection of the light outside.

Le'Mar tried to keep his face as serene as Shadowolf's, but eventually the inevitable frown formed again. Le'Mar felt the anger and confusion rise within him, but held it down. He guessed it was what Shadowolf was hoping for.

"Can I offer you a drink?" Le'Mar said, feigning hospitality and stretching out his hand to offer him a seat. Shadowolf smiled and stood at the edge of the table instead.

"You're armies are impressive," he said tartly.

"I find it hard to believe you came all this way to compliment me on my forces."

"You know by now what awaits us in two days," Shadowolf gave in. "We both know what will happen when the sun rises."

"If you want me to believe that you will become the *Sadgi*, think again," Le'Mar replied, standing up and turning his back on him to look out on the world. "That prophecy holds no worth to me. I've only ever used it to my advantage and the world played to my tune."

Le'Mar waited on Shadowolf to say something, but instead received silence. He looked on the man's face and tried to read his eyes.

"But it seems you already guessed that," Le'Mar continued. "You and I both know my hordes far outnumber yours, and that my power can undo you at any time. Why do you persist? Why is it that you truly came to see me?"

"You are not a *Sadgi*," Shadowolf answered, and waited while a laugh escaped Le'Mar's lips. "We want you to leave the earth and take all your foul creatures with you."

"You are in no position to negotiate or threaten me," Le'Mar said calmly as if explaining things to a child. "If I do not remove them, what could you possibly do?"

"I came to give you a message, one that I should have given you once I returned from uPendus," Shadowolf said, and now Le'Mar saw emotion break on his face. It seemed like he was having a hard time with his task. "But until now I did not see fit to bring this message to you."

"Message?" Le'Mar asked. "From whom?"

"From Bontu," Shadowolf said, turning his glaring eyes upon the dark lord. "As much as it galls me to say this, he is offering you a chance to repent for turning against him the day your father died. Your sins and actions will be forgiven..."

"You must be joking?" Le'Mar said, watching Shadowolf swallow hard. "Did you actually think I would believe Bontu sent you to get me to repent?"

"I am sincerely hoping you don't," Shadowolf said with a smirk, "for selfish reasons of course. I would like nothing more than to see you burn in hell for what you have done."

"That power is beyond you, young boy."

"It is now," Shadowolf said, and finally said what he had waited so long to say. "But the angels have promised me the power of the *Sadgi*, and I will receive it on the rising of the sun two days from now."

Le'Mar stood very, very still. He knew Shadowolf expected him to act in rage, and for a moment that was exactly what he wanted to do. How many times had he not passed the elemental tests and beseeched the elementëls to grant him the power of the *Sadgi*? And now they offered it to this young boy.

"My final test is one that you could never pass," Shadowolf cut the silence.

"And what is that?"

"To destroy the darkness within you," he replied. "It is something you are incapable of due to your bond with it, and something I will do everything in my power to achieve."

Le'Mar banged his hand on the table and his aura seemed to shift with darkness as he glared up at Shadowolf.

"Even now it is angered into action," he continued. "But if you can change your heart and give up the darkness, Bontu will forgive you and you will be rid of it forever."

Le'Mar laughed heartily and stood up tall and with shoulders broad. He completed his laugh and then stared into very serious eyes.

"So, you quake in fear and hope I will stop my armies?" Le'Mar said. Shadowolf realised that reason had left the dark lord. "You underestimated me and now hope I will stop my attack and forgive you and the earth for your treacherous actions."

"You are a fool," Shadowolf said with a sigh. "Your armies will be defeated and I will destroy the darkness within you; that is a promise."

"You insolent idiot!" Le'Mar shouted, unable to contain his rage any longer.

"See you in battle," Shadowolf murmured and vanished from his sight.

"Indeed," Le'Mar said to the air and left to start the war.

PART FIVE

SOUL OF THE *SADGI*

UNITED SOULS
CHAPTER ONE

He strode anxiously across Sky Tier until he was within Horlorn. The morning sun caressed his back, tracing the hair that fell gently against his neck. He relaxed his fingers and let the wind pass through each of them as he made his way to the main hall.

Shadowolf searched the faces within the hall for a sign of the others. Although there were many people milling about, he could not find anyone he knew that he could make contact with.

"Master dwarf!" Shadowolf shouted politely to a dwarf that had just crossed his path. "Do you know where Lucian and the others are?"

"They are in the council meeting," the dwarf replied. "I'll show you the way."

He stood aside to allow the dwarf to pass and then followed in his steps. He didn't bother keeping track of the tunnels that led to the council hall as his mind was too preoccupied with the immediate actions that he needed to take.

He knew though that these thoughts were mere distractions from his conscience. His short words with Le'Mar played in his mind, ridiculing him for not trying hard enough to convince the dark lord to change his heart. Shadowolf knew that he did not want Le'Mar to repent, that he had wanted to push him so hard as to instigate this war to its conclusion.

Resentment for Le'Mar filled him again and he knew it was wrong. His nerves stung him as he walked down the tunnels, his hands flexing at his sides. More than resentment, he was disappointed in himself for letting his emotions override his sense of wrong and right; for letting his passion for justice overrule his pursuit of virtue.

Shadowolf knew the words he could have used to sway Le'Mar. Inside, he knew he had the ability to reach out to the dark lord and make himself heard. Yet his arrogance had gotten the best of him, and he had deliberated avoided those words in the hopes that Le'Mar would stay his course. And the guilt was starting to eat at him. More so did the fear of consequences and the judgement of his actions before Bontu.

He heard voices from the hall they were approaching and cleared his mind of thoughts and his conscience of guilt. He took a deep breath as the dwarf left him and entered the hall.

It was musty inside, but in a way that was pleasantly warm. It went a long way to soothing his nerves. He watched the groups huddled over rough drawings on the table before them, their mutters and determinations dancing in the stale air.

Without alerting anyone to his presence, he drifted on the rough floor towards his companions to his left. He stood behind Darcwulf and peaked over his shoulder at the pages on the table. There were sketches of various creatures within Le'Mar's army, and the discussions around the table among the groups seemed to centre on them too.

"Just leave the Firestroms to Shado," Darcwulf commented. "He's the only one who can face them, Bontu bless his sad soul."

"Hey!" Shadowolf blurted out, and Darcwulf turned with a broad smile that indicated the comment had been intentional.

"You really think you can sneak up behind me without me sensing you?" his brother asked.

"I may surprise you yet," Shadowolf replied. He looked up across the table at everyone present, nodding at the few that greeted him. "I'll be back."

Anuxis moved up a seat to allow Shadowolf to sit between him and Chenesia. He calmly placed his hands on the table where he could find a vacant spot among the papers.

"Care to elaborate on your latest absence?" Lucian said in mild humour beside Chenesia.

"I paid our old friend Le'Mar a visit," he replied candidly. "He is very much insistent on the war still."

"If you're being facetious, I should probably let you know I'm taking you very seriously," Chenesia said.

"I'm being honest."

"How was his reception?" Anuxis asked.

"Surprised to say the least," Shadowolf smiled. "Had a lovely chat to him about the war and if he still wants to go ahead, and he confirmed."

"Well," Lucian said, "as long as his highness gives us the go ahead."

"Any indication of when he plans to make his move?" Chenesia asked.

"Not really," Shadowolf replied. "But I made it clear how important the Masaran Phenomenon is, so the chances are he will attack us before tomorrow night."

"And if he doesn't?" Chenesia asked.

"Then things will really get interesting," Shadowolf smiled broadly. "Then I will definitely be taking the war to him. I want them off this earth."

He looked up at the entrance as Shedaaij walked in. On her sides he spied her twin daggers that she favoured so much. Shadowolf gave her a warm smile and then excused himself from the table. He reached her and led her back towards Horlorn proper.

"How did things go with Le'Mar?" she asked.

He looked at her and explained the discussion between him and the dark lord. When he was done, he hung his head down in thought.

"What's the matter?"

"I just feel I could have done more," Shadowolf replied.

"Oh, Shado," she said comfortingly. You're forever being so hard on yourself. Do you honestly think he would ever change his mind, no matter how much you plead?"

"I guess we'll never know, now will we?" he said, and she looped her arm in his and rested her head on his shoulder.

"You could probably slap him a thousand times in the face, and still he would be obstinate."

"Thank you, love," Shadowolf said and planted a kiss on the top of her head. He turned down one of the corridors to their left and headed down to the large basin that they had bathed in so many years before.

As the oval basin appeared before them, Shadowolf had fond

memories of Nelnar swimming in the water with them. They reached the outer rim of the basin that filled the expanse of the cavern floor, removed their clothes and climbed into the lukewarm water.

"How is our girl?" he asked as they floated together.

"Fast asleep," Shedaaij replied. "I had just paid Deihlia a visit before I came back to the council. She so loves Crystal and Tyler's company, despite how she kicks up a fuss about their naughtiness."

"She'll make a good mother one day," Shadowolf commented.

"I think that will only happen once she knows Lastgorn will be ok," she replied. "She never stops asking about him."

"Is he coping?"

"He is very eager for this war," she replied with a concerned look on his face. "You should have seen his face when drawings of the Ma-Wreths surfaced."

"I'm going to have to watch him," he said. "His anger and lust for vengeance might undo him."

"He gives me the idea that death would be a great respite from his pain, and that worries me."

"Do you think he will just stand by and let them kill him?" Shadowolf asked.

"I doubt that," she replied. "Have you seen what he's wearing on his side?"

"His blue sword?"

"No, that's in the armoury. One of the elementals from Carmel brought Scarlette's old sword that he had salvaged from the last war."

"The sword that had killed Gwyn," he said and she nodded.

"He's wearing it on his side now, and I'm pretty sure he plans on using it."

"Ok that's good to know," he sighed in relief. "You know I'm going to need you to leave soon?"

Shedaaij's face became sad and she turned from him to hide her emotions. Shadowolf swam behind her and crossed his arms over her, her back pressed firm into his torso. She crossed her arms over his, her hands gently teasing the skin of his biceps.

"I'm scared," she admitted.

"I'd be utterly surprised if you weren't," he joked lightly. "I have something planned for both of us, something that might take the edge off being apart."

"What's that?" she asked. He could feel that she had wanted to turn in his arms, but instead she pulled his arms tighter around her.

"I want to unite our souls."

"Excuse me?" This time she did not refrain from turning. She looked into his eyes with confusion written on her brow. "What do you mean?"

"There's a way that I can unite us more than we are now," he said, taking her hands in his. "Our thoughts and feelings will be one, we will share the same abilities; it will be as if I'm always with you."

"Is it safe?"

"Not entirely," he laughed softly. "It can be very dangerous if something goes wrong, but it's a risk I am willing to take."

Shedaaij swam away from him for a while, drifting on her back as she thought about what he had just told her. He could read the fears scrawled on her eyes, could almost feel the concerns seep from her pores into the water that surrounded them.

"Ok, let's do it," she said and drifted back to him. He did not bother asking her if she was sure; he did not want to give her more time to think about it.

He took her outstretched hands firmly and closed his eyes. She did the same, and waited for the familiarity of his powers to warm her skin. His mind thronged with the summons of his powers as his fingers lightly touched hers.

Shedaaij murmured involuntarily as his powers increased. It flowed like a river from him into her. It felt like a cloak had covered her aura first and her body second before it dissolved and then diffused upon her spirit.

Shadowolf opened his eyes instantly and hers sprang open at the same time, their eyes lit magnificently from within. The water slowly formed into a whirlpool around them, circling them furiously until their feet touched the bed of the basin and they stood in a pocket of air within the water.

An all-pervading white light broke out that was so bright that they could barely see the silhouettes of each other's bodies.

Without moving, their bodies floated into one another until there was only one of them, neither in form of Shadowolf or Shedaaij. Their face looked like each other and neither of them at the same time.

"I am now one," they said in one voice, both theirs and not theirs. "My duality exists for only as long as necessary and then I may return to myself."

They nodded their head and drifted down from the dimming light. When their feet touch the soft sand, their shared body separated into two separate beings, and the land surrounding them became real.

The waves broke on the beach behind Shedaaij. She looked around her in fright, for a moment only seeing the clothes and daggers she had left on the floor beside the basin. At first, she thought that she was utterly alone, but when she heard footsteps, she raised her head and looked up into her lover's eyes.

"I don't feel any different," she said.

"Our bond will be a conscious act," Shadowolf informed her. "It's a safeguard against a rush of emotions or involuntary acts. If I purposefully wanted to…"

He raised his right arm horizontal so that his palm lay open to the sky. Shedaaij exclaimed in shock as her right hand broke out in flames, a torch at the end of her arm. She looked at it, amazed that it was there without harming her hand in any way.

"Will I be able to learn this new ability in time for the war?" she asked gingerly as the fire died out.

"You don't have to," he replied. "It's more for your safety that I have done this than for mine. I want you to focus on your battles, and I will do the rest."

Shedaaij walked up to him, knowing their time together before the war had run out. She embraced him, laying her head firmly on his chest and sighing in relief as his arms crossed over her. He was warm in so many ways; the chill she had felt in the breeze evaporated from her body, and the tension that had frozen her nerves abated.

The moment was over too soon for her. He pulled back and looked lovingly at her, wearing the most comforting smile on his face and a content, protective look in the vast chasms of his eyes.

"I love you with all my heart Shedaaij," he told her, and her heart almost burst from poignant joy. Her eyes welled up with rivers of love as she barely whispered the reply.

"I love you too, babes."

They held each other a moment longer before she took a deep breath and left the comfort of his arms. She knelt down and claimed the coral armour hidden under the sheets of clothes. Once she had strapped the two parts over her breasts and waist, she took the dagger belt and clipped it around her hips.

She turned and strode bravely towards the ocean. Shedaaij didn't look back as she entered the waters and dived into its depths. The last greeting Shadowolf received as he watched her leave was her mermaid tail that slapped the surface of the water.

THE CHOSEN
CHAPTER TWO

The wind picked up around Horlorn, its concentration focused on Sky Tier. It became denser at the end of the tier, a hard volume of air that formed into a shape of a man until he was solid and his feet stepped on the concrete.

Shadowolf walked towards the entrance, but stopped almost immediately. His clothes whipped on his body in reminiscence of the wind that had brought him there, but it wasn't the wind that bothered him. He could feel the summons from the peaks of Dwarf Mountains.

A familiar presence made him turn. Trimistus was almost by him already, sensing the call of the dragons just as easily as him. The black sockets of the reptilian man's eyes flared orange to the call, although Shadowolf was sure it was dim in contrast to its initial intensity.

"Shall we exercise our wings?" Trimistus jibed.

"We might as well," Shadowolf replied. "You know we're going to need them in the war."

"That I do," the DragonWourd replied grimly.

They stood beside one another, both facing the southern range of Dwarf Mountains. Power surged from within them, light flames racing upon their arms to their shoulders and down to their shoulder blades. The skin of their backs ached and squirmed, forming and deforming behind them.

Ethereal wings stretched out from their spirits, but they did not dim their powers. The wings solidified, hardening to their true form until real dragon wings suddenly broke the skin of their backs and complimented the flames of the ethereal wings.

They dimmed their energies and flexed the scales of their

wings. Shadowolf beat the air a few times to send the blood flowing up the lengths, enjoying the sensation of having them on his back once more. His heart beat harder, pumping the blood further into the new veins.

Trimistus ran and jumped off the cliff. Shadowolf felt his competitive nature rise and he grinned as he followed in pursuit. The wind took to him easily as he flew after Trimistus, the DragonWourd itching to keep ahead. Shadowolf came up close to him and when Trimistus swayed to the side to knock him off course, he circled underneath him and glided to his other side.

The two DragonRiders frolicked and chased each other to the mountains, enjoying the freedom of the skies and becoming acquainted again with flight. Coupled with that was the heightened senses of the dragons and the increased heart-rate and adrenaline that always accompanied the draconic transformation.

Yet, despite their short-lived respite from the tension of war, they ceased their fooling around and straightened their flight as Mynisna and Asgorna came into view upon crags at the very top of the mountain. Shadowolf and Trimistus landed gently before them, the dragons not turning their heads at their arrival.

"Le'Mar is heading out," Mynisna announced.

"Now already?" Trimistus asked.

"Indeed," Asgorna replied. "Look for yourself."

Hardly had the instruction been uttered when Trimistus's sockets filled with an opaque mist. Shadowolf's eyes became translucent in turn, his draconic sight penetrating the distance to the forest that had once belonged to Eldor.

He sensed massive shifts upon the land within the forest. Armies forming ranks and groups near the arid area that had once been the Pool of Radiance. The armies covered the land far south like a dark sheet over a bed.

Shadowolf narrowed his search to the place he assumed was the head of the forces. Four heavily cloaked men, or beings, were carrying staves in their hands. He recognised the ritual easily, for he and Darcwulf had assisted Masara with it once before.

"He's preparing a hyperportal," he voiced what he knew the others must have assumed already. "He's going to start the war early."

"Early relative to us," Mynisna reminded. "You can't set a deadline for war, I'm afraid."

"How much does this affect our plans?" Trimistus asked.

Shadowolf looked up at the sky, his eyes returning to normal. The sun was now at its peak, and trailing behind it like a lap dog was the planet Ringos. It's diameter to sight was now one and half that of the sun's. They would experience one last full day before the Masaran Phenomenon took place.

"Looking at the size of his armies," Shadowolf speculated," he might actually be playing into our hands. This could very much work in our favour."

The others remained silent, but he knew they were questioning his judgement. He turned to look at the west and used his supernatural senses to spy on the Alcove's castle. The same amount of movement and formation was taking place, but there was the absence of the hyperportal preparation. Shadowolf frowned.

"What's wrong?" Trimistus noted his expression.

"He's not making any plans as far as the castle armies are concerned," he replied. The others joined him in his observation. "He plans on using another means for them."

"Or they are the reserve," Asgorna suggested.

"All I know is it makes me more nervous," Trimistus said.

"Shado, you need to get the weapons ready," Asgorna warned. Shadowolf nodded in agreement and took flight back to Horlorn with Trimistus.

"Trimistus, I need you to find Elgoth and tell him we need to meet in the courtyard," Shadowolf said as they neared the Tiers.

"Where are you going?"

"I'm going to see the pegasi," he replied. "Elgoth will know who to search out."

"Are you sure?" Trimistus asked.

"Yes," Shadowolf said and then smiled. "If he asks, just tell him it's time for the kids to open their presents."

"Do you need me there?"

"No, my dear friend," Shadowolf replied. "This is something we need to do alone."

With a confused look on his face, but a nod nonetheless, he

separated from Shadowolf and headed for Sky Tier. Shadowolf diverted his flight and banked down to Mountain Tier.

When he landed, he was fortunate enough to find Cavella standing near the rim looking over the land in thought. He wondered where Hargon was, but put any other questions aside for his main purpose.

"Cavella, do you know where Treya is?" he asked the jaguar.

"I think she's still with Ursula and Elgoth in the main hall," Cavella purred. "Is everything ok?"

"Le'Mar is getting ready to move his troops, so we should start warning the others," he replied. "Would you mind getting the message out to the council lords?"

"Not a problem," Cavella smiled as much as a feline could and headed out. Shadowolf was about to take flight again when he spotted Chenesia and Genewiu further in.

He greeted them when he reached them and informed them about the dark lord's movements.

"I'm going to warn Lesan," Chenesia said and left them.

"It's time to summon the relics," Shadowolf said to Genewiu meaningfully. "Are the pegasi available?"

"I'll find out," Genewiu replied. "I'll see you in the courtyard."

After she left, for some strange reason Shadowolf felt very alone. He was surrounded by a sea of creatures and people, yet he felt like everything and everyone he had ever known had just departed him. His nerves stung with panic and he breathed and flexed his hands to relax.

He closed his eyes and saw the ocean before him. He was swimming towards *Selandil*, the vast mer-Kingdom hidden within the robes of the land. No threats surrounded him; it was almost as if they expected his arrival.

Shadowolf opened his eyes and left Shedaaij to her travels. He clenched his teeth and calmed his powers, for everyone was burning before him. Their bodies were pitch black, but their auras flared brightly before his vision. He glared at everyone around him. Solar flares streaked out from the auras of the strongest of them, while slow rivers pulsed in the veins of the less powerful.

He was losing control of his powers again. He retracted his wings into his body, calling his energy back into the pit of his soul.

Slowly the auras vanished from his sight to be replaced by the people and warriors of Horlorn's Gate.

Disquiet filled him momentarily. Many things felt disjointed, like pieces of a puzzle that were trying to fit into a puzzle it didn't belong to. He felt the urge to make sure all the warriors were ready, but he needed to trust the council lords with that responsibility. He could not enter the war with the anxiety he felt now; he knew it would be the death of him. And knowing that the anxiety pervaded him made him tenser.

Somehow he knew that he would not be able to find that relative calm he desired at that moment, but he composed himself enough for the task at hand. He had to find the will to proceed and, despite how brave he had seemed since his return from uPendus, the courage to carry this war forth.

He was at the pinnacle of his existence on Celenic Earth. Every decision and action he had taken had defined his character. His chest expanded as his determination returned. The muscles on his arms and back flexed as the virtue of his actions and the immorality of Le'Mar's cleansed his mind of indecision.

With the tension building inside, he teleported and opened his eyes. Ursula, Elgoth and Treya staggered back in the courtyard from the wind that exploded from him. He released the grip in his hands, his fingers relaxing at his side. As they opened, a chill breeze flowed down his body and floated like a thin mist above the grass of the courtyard.

Elgoth's eyes flashed warnings to him. He needed to find peace. Once he was done with them, he would send them out and relinquish his powers to Bontu again. It was the only recourse he could take; otherwise everything he had striven for would have been in vain.

Jilian lay on her stomach in the dimly lit room that had quickly become a nursery. To one side of her was Deihlia with Crystal and Tyler sleeping on either side of her in her arms. Deihlia's eye were closed too, her mind lost in webs of dreams.

Jilian's eyes were anything but closed and her body anything but asleep. Her hands scrawled of its own accord, sketching the man who had exploded with power and scattered the others around him. Small lines from his body indicated the wind that had thrown them from him. Her hand quickly went to the side of the ragged paper and she wrote:

Fear runs untamed and consumes his veins

Without stopping, she continued to complete the sketch.

Shadowolf calmed his nerves and the others before him settled. Ursula's human face ushered caution, while Elgoth composed himself again and waited in silent patience for the others to arrive. Treya merely studied him in the aftermath of his release as if estimating his ability to survive the war.

When Shadowolf heard footsteps behind him in the courtyard, he saw that Darcwulf and Fransiska were approaching them. Shadowolf greeted them mutely with a smile and saw in the background that Lucian and Sorceress weren't far behind.

Lucian wore a confident look on his face, for he knew what was about to happen. The other three were almost as confident, but Shadowolf could see glimpses of doubt and wonder in their eyes. Yet for all their suspicions they looked strong and ready for any task about to be given them.

"Well, we're here for the tea party," Darcwulf commented once they were beside Shadowolf.

"We can tell them why they're here so long," Elgoth instructed. "The pegasi should be here soon."

"Ok," Shadowolf replied, looking on either side of him as he addressed the newcomers. "As you all know, I searched you out for certain artefacts that you had on you; special relics that each of you had surrendered to the elements."

"Ah, and here I thought it was because you loved us," Darcwulf smiled, and then laughed when Fransiska nudged him with an elbow.

Shadowolf joined his smile and stepped forward. He raised his palm to the ground and a knoll rose up. He comfortably sat down on it and faced the four.

"Obtaining the relics was only half the task though," he continued. "There was purpose in making sure that you were entrusted with it until now."

"Does it have something to do with you not being able to touch them?" Fransiska asked.

"That's a minor technicality," Shadowolf replied. "If I channeled one of the elements specifically, I would have managed to handle each of them."

"But not all of them," Sorceress said. "Channeling all four elements at the same time in their master forms would have required excessive energy continuously."

"Well said," Elgoth said from the back.

"That's why I needed four masters to carry the relics," Shadowolf said. "But it's more than that; so much more."

"Alright, mister mystery," Darcwulf lowered his crossed arms, his expression stern. "Are you finally going to tell us the importance of the relics?"

"Yes I am," he replied. "Even though I do not believe that Le'Mar is a *Sadgi*, there is only one way to truly remove all power from someone as strong as he is in the elements."

"Before you carry on," Fransiska interjected, "what makes you think he isn't one?"

"Has he mastered all the elements?" Shadowolf asked.

"As far as I know he has," she replied.

"All five of them?" he asked again, curling his lips up slyly.

"Oh," she said and then looked down. "I have no idea about the fifth."

"I don't think his soul has been much concern to him over the years," Darcwulf said. "He uses it as a tool to form the elements. That's about it."

"Don't get me wrong, he is powerful beyond everyone on this world," Shadowolf said, "and so is his soul. But he has not bothered to try and master his spiritual abilities; he does not have the patience for it."

"What abilities do you get from mastering the soul?" Sorceress asked, clearly intrigued.

"Moving things with your mind," Ursula said. "Levitation off the ground without the assistance of the elements. Teleportation. Astral projection. These are but a few things."

"And most of the highly effective ones are only granted by

Bontu," Shadowolf said, "which is exactly why Le'Mar will never become a *Sadgi*."

"Unless he repents," Elgoth corrected. Shadowolf dropped his head momentarily. Shadowolf had a feeling Elgoth was looking at him.

"So why do we need the relics?" Darcwulf asked, returning to the original question.

"Because, like most elementals, you cannot kill him like you would a normal man," Shadowolf replied. "To finish an *Enodhim*, you would have to remove the wind from him first to make his body vulnerable before you can kill him."

"So we need to remove all the elements from him first," Sorceress said.

"My father was not just holding back in Eldor's Forest because Le'Mar is his brother," Elgoth said. "They could combat each other with the elements all day if they wanted to, but neither would win until their elements of power are removed."

"Is that why Masara lost?" Darcwulf enquired.

"No," Ursula countered quickly and a little defensively. "Masara was aged and ill. Le'Mar's victory was nothing more than...."

What the victory amounted to went unsaid. Shadowolf waited for her to finish, but her words failed her. His sympathy for her loss and moment of weakness made him continue what he was trying to say.

"If you tire your opponent out to the point where he cannot summon his powers anymore, then defeat is also possible," Shadowolf said. "The chances that we can wear Le'Mar down though..."

"...is minimal," Lucian finished.

"So our only recourse is to something more powerful than Le'Mar, something that can easily remove his powers from him without struggle," Shadowolf said. "Something so powerful that not even Le'Mar can stop it."

"The relics," Fransiska assumed.

"Time," Shadowolf corrected.

"What?"

"Do you remember the scrolls we read?" Shadowolf asked Darcwulf. "And the tales we heard of the ancestors?"

"Vaguely, yes."

"When Saldheron fought Bentley, he was nowhere near worn down," Shadowolf said. "Do you remember what had happened the instant before the battle turned and Bentley won?"

"Saldheron had summoned the wind and formed it into a dagger," Darcwulf said as he thought about it.

"In a desperate attempt to end it, he had placed all of his elemental powers into that instrument," Elgoth said. "Bentley had used his own powers against him to kill him."

"As did the others in the tales," Shadowolf added. "These relics are not only filled with the elements that the owners had used, but with all the powers the masters could summon and placed within them."

"But what has this to do with time?" Fransiska asked.

"Through time these relics have been left to the earth, either lying still where they had been left for centuries, or being used for other purposes," Ursula answered. "The generations of time have only made them that much stronger, more powerful than even the owners could ever have been."

"It's the main reason Le'Mar was able to become so strong so quickly in the years following his acquisition of the staff," Elgoth said.

"And why I was able to master earth so quickly once I got the butterfly pendant," Sorceress assumed, and received a nod from Ursula.

"Hang on a second," Darcwulf said. Shadowolf could see his mind was working overtime and was curious to see if his brother had caught on. "During the last Masaran Phenomenon, when the sun rose, time stood still while the sun returned to the horizon for the second rising."

"Well done," Shadowolf smiled broadly.

"I don't understand," Sorceress said. "If times stands still, we will all be frozen. What difference does it make?"

"Because Shado will be the *Sadgi*," Darcwulf said proudly. "Only the *Sadgi* will be able to overcome time."

"Are you serious?" Fransiska said with shock on her face. Shadowolf tried not to laugh. "How certain are you that will happen?"

"When I received the power node," Shadowolf replied. "I was the only one that moved when I received that power. I am almost certain that power will waken within me again."

"That's a big gamble to take!" Sorceress said, exasperated.

"It's one that I am willing to take," Shadowolf replied. "Failing that, we have the relics."

Fransiska and Sorceress went silent, their thoughts racing and their minds boggled. Lucian waited patiently for proceedings to continue, as he had been part of this discussion in uPendus. Darcwulf's face exuded complete faith in the matter.

"So…everything that started four years ago is finally coming to a close?" Fransiska asked, her tone soft. "You really are fulfilling your destiny?"

"Not one I chose, I assure you," Shadowolf replied humbly. "This power will awaken like it did every four years since I was born. When it awakens this time, I will be the only one able to what must be done."

"Unbelievable," Sorceress muttered, "but still, it's the only thing that makes sense. But what can we do?"

"I need you to hold the relics for me until the time is right," he replied. "You can't use it; it can't be tainted with blood or death once it's been purified. But you need to keep it for me."

"How will we know when and what to do?" Fransiska asked. He could see she was panicking and confused.

"Don't worry about that," Shadowolf replied. "Leave all that up to me. We just need to bind the weapons to your souls now."

"What?" Darcwulf asked again.

"It's the only way to keep it safe and at hand for when I need it," he said. "You four have been chosen to guard the relics with your souls."

"How are we going to do that?" Fransiska asked.

"With their help," Shadowolf nodded behind them.

They turned to see a group of five pegasi standing behind them, along with Nelnar and Cavella. Genewiu, Nelnar and Cavella moved away to join Ursula, Elgoth and Treya while the remaining four pegasi approached the relic masters.

"'With bow, horn, staff, dagger and sword he will kill the *Sadgi*,'" Darcwulf muttered. "So I guess we have as much part to play in this prophecy as you, Shado."

"Wait, what about the sword?" Fransiska asked suddenly.

"Oh, Shado has the sword, don't worry," Darcwulf replied, turning slightly to look at Shadowolf from the corner of his eyes. "I've been wondering why I haven't seen him use Ruben-Willow since his return."

"You have it all worked out now, do you?" Shadowolf smiled.

"You're a sneaky one, Shado," he replied, facing the pegasi again. "A nanoo nanoo, that's what you are."

"You and your damn nanoo nanoo," Fransiska reprimanded. "One day, I'm going to whack you on the head with a nanoo nanoo."

"As long as it's not a piece of chicken again," he said, and everyone burst out laughing. Even Fransiska could not contain her giggling.

SHADOWOLF'S PRAYER
CHAPTER THREE

Shadowolf watched with numb interest as the ritual was performed. Darcwulf, Fransiska, Sorceress and Lucian stepped within the circle of pegasi at the centre of the courtyard. They listened to instructions and summoned the weapons from the elements surrounding them until they held them in their hands.

In much the same manner as Shadowolf bound his soul with Shedaaij, the pegasi assisted the four chosen elementals in binding the weapons to their souls. Lucian took Bentley's dagger of wind; Darcwulf took Falgar's staff of fire; Sorceress took Masara's horn of earth; Fransiska took Celene's bow of water.

Once the binding of souls was done, Shadowolf decided it was time to check up on his daughter. He regretted the time that they had to spend apart, not to mention the approximate two years he had missed out on her life. It was not the type of father he had seen himself being but, as was the counsel of Shedaaij, he was trying not to be so hard on himself.

His mind lingered on Chenesia's wedding, but only because it made him remember that at some point he wanted to marry Shedaaij and settle down. The topic had not once been broached between them, not even a whisper had been spent on the matter. He humoured himself with the question as to whether or not Shedaaij had even considered marriage as yet.

He found himself sooner at the nursery than he had expected. His mind had been lost in thought so frequently that he hardly recalled how he got from one place to another. He took a long, gentle sigh before making his way in.

The nursery was as rough as most of the new structures within Horlorn. The roof of the entrance was as domed as the rest of the room which stretched quite a length down. The room was perhaps not as wide as the mothers and caregivers would have liked, but it looked comfortable enough.

As Shadowolf walked to where he would find Deihlia sleeping, he noticed that the torches were high up near vertical vents at the roof of the chamber. He frowned at the vents, wondering where they led to and how the dwarves had managed to construct them without interference with the outside walls. He was comforted that the smoke of the torches didn't lend an air of humidity or suffocate the nursery.

"Don't worry, we're replacing those soon," a gruff voice beside him said. Shadowolf jumped slightly in surprise and looked into Hargon's face.

"They don't seem to be a problem," he replied, looking up again.

"It's not good for the children, apparently," Hargon said with a hint of sarcasm. "So the elves say."

"Well, I grew up with torches in the castle," Shadowolf said.

"You know the elves," the dwarf said and joined Shadowolf as he walked to Deihlia again. "There's the right way of doing things and then there's their way."

"Do you know what they plan on using?"

"Those green lanterns of theirs that give off that eerie light," he replied. "You know, like their trees do?"

"Oh yes," Shadowolf smiled. "Strange to find you here though?"

"I was…keeping my thoughts company," Hargon said.

"I know the feeling."

He finally reached Deihlia, sleeping on her side with a pillow beneath her head, a woolen blanket stretched over her and the two kids beside her. Tyler and Crystal were sleeping just as peacefully, their breathing calm and slow.

"If only I could sleep half as well," Hargon whispered. Shadowolf looked at the dwarf and noticed for the first time how red his eyes were. The dwarf did not look as sturdy as he once did.

"Hargon, when last have you eaten?" Shadowolf guessed and only received silence as the answer. "You need to keep strong; the war is nearly upon us. Sleep and food are essential right now."

"I know," Hargon replied, looking down ashamed. "I just can't seem to keep a good appetite."

Shadowolf looked at him a moment longer, but his eyes caught something white on the floor by the children's feet. Parchments with sketches on them lay scattered there.

"But let me try again," the dwarf sighed. With a nod in farewell, he left Shadowolf's side and made for the main hall.

Shadowolf knelt down and looked at the strewn papers. The drawings looked very similar to Jilian's sketch that he had seen on their travel on the river. He sifted through them until one particular one held his attention.

A man and a woman were floating in mid-air, only their heads, hands and feet visible past the shading that seemed to be indicative of light. There were strange objects and signs swirling around the two, meanings which he could not decipher. The two people were too close to one another, their faces rapt in serene joy.

At the bottom were the words 'Their souls and powers are bound as one.'

Shadowolf quickly went through another drawing, his pulse quickening and his breathing increasing in tempo. There was a scene in what he knew must be the courtyard. He could make out the pegasus Treya and a man he assumed was Elgoth. Ursula was there too, albeit in her unicorn form. They were lying on their backs, their hands shielding their eyes from the man floating in the air. The drawing was suggestive of a large power exploding from the man and throwing the others back.

Beneath the sketch was written 'Fear runs untamed and consumes his veins'.

Shadowolf dropped the pages involuntarily. He thought back to the first drawing that he had seen. He had thrown his staff forward and Nelnar had emerged from it. He remembered the words she had written: 'Setting free what he had loved and lost'.

Something was tickling his memory. There was something about this scenario that was bothering him. He went through the drawings again. It took him a moment, but the reality sank in. Words from the prophecy were coming back to him and, as it did, he voiced it.

"'For he has bound his soul with another; their powers are one'; 'Fear will drive his veins, until it is fear he tames'; 'He will lose those he loves, only to set them free'."

"Going through the prophecy again?" someone whispered behind him. Shadowolf turned in fright and saw Elgoth.

"Look at these," Shadowolf handed him the drawings. "It seems there is more to Jilian's gift than we had thought. She's been giving a lot of meaning to what has been happening."

Elgoth went through them and raised an eyebrow.

"I need to find her," Shadowolf declared and walked off to the entrance.

"Hold on," Elgoth stopped him. "I don't recall this one."

He rushed back as quietly as his eagerness would allow him. Taking the proffered page, he studied it intently like an eagle eyeing his next prey.

On the sketch, two men stood with their backs to the viewer. He could see the horizon of a vast land and on the tip of the horizon stood minute, shaded figures. They were sketched in a menacing way, indicating their evil intent.

Between the two men and the horizon, almost directly before and around the men, were shaded warriors. Their faces and expressions were general and sketched in such a contrast as to give the two men more emphasis. Once again, words were sketched on the page, but this time on the top above the horizon and its dark figures:

With power undenied will he join all armies under his command

"I don't remember this either," Shadowolf said and handed the page back. "Do you think there is some connection between her grandfather and her?"

"This is very mysterious," Elgoth replied. "I don't think we will find the answers right now. Just be careful not to read too much into this. Focus on the war, not the prophecy."

"I have to find her," he repeated and headed out of the nursery. Elgoth shimmered in appearance and vanished with the papers in hand.

Shadowolf rushed out into the corridors and made his way to Sky Tier, careful to keep an eye out for Jilian's presence. He spotted Darcwulf leaving the main hall and hurried to intercept him.

"Have you seen Jilian?" he asked quickly.

"No," Darcwulf replied. "What's happened? What's wrong?"

"Do me a favour and see if you can find her," he instructed. "There's more going on than I knew about."

"Wait! Hold on!" Darcwulf called as Shadowolf hastened to reach the tier. When he realised he wasn't listening, he lowered his voice. "There's a lot you don't know about."

Shadowolf stormed onto the tier, and then came to a stop. Most of the warriors of Sky Tier were standing before him gazing into the distance. He couldn't see what was happening, so he summoned the wind to carry him up over the crowd.

As he drifted to where he wanted to stand, he saw what the commotion was about. His face took on a very grave expression and he hardened his resolve. He landed on the forward ledge on the apex of the tier, looking down at all the warriors below him on the lower tiers.

The wind shifted around him and he waited as Lucian materialised beside him. They both stood in silence as they looked at the fog gathering on the horizon, menacing figures forming and shaping from within.

"It's Shado!" someone shouted from behind him, and suddenly the crowds started shouting and cheering his name. The warriors from below looked up and began the same chant.

The pride that was rising within him stung his humility. His face remained grim and he did not like them cheering him. He wanted to shout, to tell them all to stop. This was not about him; this was about them.

"Well, you've brought everyone together for this," Lucian said with pride in his voice. He rested a hand on Shadowolf's shoulder. "Let him try and deny your power now."

Shadowolf looked up sharply, giving Lucian a fright. Shadowolf felt like he was losing control. Jilian's sketch was now etched in his mind, and he had no doubt that this moment was what it had been about. He looked down and closed his eyes.

Sometimes you need to know when you're in control, and when you need to relinquish control to Bontu, Elgoth had once told him in uPendus. There are things you will not be able to do that only He can. Remember, all power and things in this world were created by

His hand. All you need to do is submit to His will.

Shadowolf became one with the wind and vanished from the tier.

Once he was within the courtyard again, he fell down to his knees. His hands clutched the grass blades and the soil as he strove to drive the incessant pounding in his veins to a slower pace.

The courtyard seemed to become more serene around him, despite no change in its actual structure or appearance. He closed his panting mouth and breathed calmly through his nose instead. His powers subsided within him.

"Lord," he said, "I need you more than ever now. I've done everything I possibly could to get to this point."

Shadowolf went silent and opened his eyes. He knew this was not entirely true. His conscience warned him that he was not being honest with himself. So he tried again.

"I feel I have failed you in trying to get Le'Mar to repent. I know I could have tried harder."

The wind shifted in the courtyard. He could sense the trees' branches swaying.

"If it is in your will, then please give me the opportunity to try again. I know I can convince him...."

...you need to relinquish control...

"...by your grace, I know I can convince him if you give me another chance."

Suddenly the courtyard became darker. There was an ominous presence in the area, but Shadowolf closed his eyes instead of looking up at it. His fears began to arise in him, his natural concerns for his family and friends were brought to the fore.

All those people outside were prepared to die to save the earth from the dark lord's clutches. Was he prepared to let them?

"Give me strength, Lord," he continued in spite of the darkness. A knot formed in his abdomen and his muscles tightened. "Free me from the oppression of the darkness. I know who my enemy truly is. And I will not allow Le'Mar to be taken."

There was a silent screech, not audible to human senses, but the dark presence that was thrust away from the courtyard. Shadowolf felt warmth and love enter the chamber and looked up into a bright light. He shielded his eyes from the burning figures, barely making out the silhouettes of seven beings.

He heard their wings shimmer behind their ethereal bodies and felt their warm human-like hands close on his shoulders. He stood up, poised like a bulwark against the former darkness, reaching for a pouch within one of his pockets.

He withdrew the pouch containing the five water eggs that Eldor had handed him. With consternate care, he opened the pouch and collected the eggs in his hands. Taking a deep breath, Shadowolf threw the eggs hard enough against the ground that they cracked open violently.

A blue mist rolled out from the shells of the eggs. Shadowolf went slack throughout his body, yet he felt like he was regaining strength he never had. He could not control what was happening, nor move a limb of his body, yet he felt like he could explode with enough power to destroy the earth.

He fell to the ground as the mist passed into him, his face landing on a pillow of sand and grass. He closed his eyes and felt like he had given his last breath. The air left him, together with warmth, moisture and substance. In the end, there was nothing visible of him in the courtyard, yet he was everywhere.

THE HYPERPORTAL
CHAPTER FOUR

Lucian stood with his arms crossed over his chest, his gaze focused on the fog across the distance but his mind elsewhere. The sun was behind Horlorn's hill already, the shadow playing across the fields before them like an ill omen.

The Windfarer had no doubt that Le'Mar would attack in the night. With the Masaran Phenomenon one day away, Lucian knew the dark lord would be quite anxious to get the battle started. And knowing Le'Mar's penchant for the cover of darkness, all Lucian's logical conclusions led him to believe that the dark lord would wait for the dead of the night before he sent his armies forward.

A soft touch to his right made his jump. Kailan stood beside him, smiling apologetically. A hint of sympathy traced the stressed cheeks beneath her tired eyes. He offered her a smile in return, his eyes returning to the horizon.

"Philanus is resting again," she informed him. "He keeps asking for you."

"I'll visit him a little later," he responded.

Kailan joined him in silence as she stared off into the distance. Her fears were almost as palpable as the stone beneath his feet. He drew a deep breath and exhaled it, hoping that his own fears escaped into the coming night.

"Where's Shado?" she said after a few minutes of cursory study through the crowds milling around them.

"I don't know," Lucian replied. "I haven't seen him since the fog arrived."

"That's a bit odd of him, don't you think?"

"Not if you know Shado as well as I," Lucian said, keeping his laugh at bay. Despite the intended humour, he could not find the strength nor contrive the mood to carry his facetiousness through. "I'd better go check on everything."

Kailan was about to remark that someone else could do it, but she knew it would help settle his nerves. He began to move onto the edge of the tier, when she gripped his arm and raised her hand onto his cheek.

With her eyes, she told him how much she loved him. Her heart had always known how fond he was of Telgar, but the fact that he remained and cared for her and Philanus showed her how much he truly loved her. She would never chide him for caring for the woman his late brother had left behind; she only felt a distant sadness.

The kiss that she delivered to him now betrayed no such emotions or knowledge. She closed her eyes as his lips locked on her, and he surprised her by opening her mouth with his to embrace her kiss more passionately. Her body grew warm for him in a way that she had not felt in very long time, but she pulled away and looked deep into his eyes.

Just like the forgotten passion, his eyes held a love it had not shown for years. Whatever loss the war had wrought upon his heart was now overlooked and he gave a warm smile that her countenance had given up on so long ago.

"I'm fighting this war for us," he said, although to Kailan the words were unnecessary. She could already tell he had set his heart right.

The air ripped as he became wind and drifted away from her. Lucian floated higher up than the apex of Horlorn until the setting sun's rays poured through him. He gave a last glance to the fog before looking down at Horlorn.

Gone was the old Horlorn that had been simple compared to the newly-fashioned fortress. Lucian indulged in reminiscing on how it had looked before; the three tiers jutting out from Horlorn's hill, the rough and damaged interior halls that had been empty expect for the whispers of famous tales and heroes.

Within the structure of the new Horlorn's Fortress lay echoes of the former Horlorn's Gate. The Sky, Mountain and Ground Tiers remained, albeit strengthened and renewed by the fine hands of the dwarves. It was the two additional tiers that marked the most significant difference.

On either side of the Mountain Tier were the new Star and Port Tiers. In a similar fashion to the original tiers, they protruded from the hill in a semi-circle. The angles of the hill's sides were such that the three mid-tiers seemed bunched together.

In the way of a casual observer or a foreign traveler, Lucian floated down to look upon Sky Tier. Of Shadowolf's closest friends, the renewed members of the Shadow Clan, only Skywolf and Heula were present. The rest of the people striding around on the tier and looking furtively towards the dark horizon were elementals, none of which Lucian easily recognised.

Although he could not see them, he knew that Glasden and his fellow gargoyles waited within the halls of Sky Tier too. Lucian hoped for them that Le'Mar would opt to attack the evening or within the fog, as it would at least give the gargoyles a chance to join the war.

Drifting down on the air, his eyes spied the three Mountain Tiers. Lesan's archer-elves occupied most of Port Tier and half of Star Tier. Among them, in ranks of their own, were human archers and more elementals. On the central tier he could see the huge bulks of the centaurs and the pristine beauty of the pegasi, the remaining human archers and elementals filling the gaps.

Reaching the stone of the Ground Tier, he was surrounded by dwarves. He materialised in their midst and looked into the entrance of the tier, spying human and elvin swordsmen. Among the heads bobbing about, he was sure he could see Lastgorn.

Lucian turned around to walk to the main gates. His feet left the concrete of the tier and padded onto soft grass that had been trampled down by the many paws of the Nelmurian wolves and the uPendian tigers. Hargon and Cavella passed him, but did not seem to notice his presence.

Before he was even close to the main gates, he had to pass beneath a long bridge between two towers. In a long line that stretched from the north side of the hill to the southern Dwarf Mountains, five towers rose up as high as the Mountain Tiers.

Similar bridges to the one he now passed beneath spanned between each of the towers. The central tower which he walked passed to reach the main gates belonged to Nighthale and a select group of archers, elementals and council members, nominated the

Degron Elite. This included Franklin and Nowles.

In the musty, stone towers to the left of the Degron Tower were Sjedwolf and Jasnon with their Watre and Lowle Elite. To the right stood the towers of Malkius and Orion's Salinos.

The towers all looked the same. They were cube prisms rising from the earth, their four corners facing the main gate, Horlorn and each other. Where the bridges met the towers, semi-circles like those of the tiers circled the front of the tower so that the elementals had clear view of the battlefield.

Lucian rose into the air once again, shaking his head to the guards who were preparing to open the main gates for him. He remained stationary above the gates, hovering as he spied Dwarf Mountains to his right.

The mountains were very still and Lucian would not have noticed the minute rustling or known of the dragons' presence in the crags on the side were it not for his foreknowledge that they were there. He admired their ability to hide their huge bulks within the folds of the mountain valley a little longer before drifting back to the ground within the defensive wall.

What are you looking for? a voice suddenly whispered in the air around Lucian. It had been so distinct, so soft, that he wondered whether he truly had heard it.

You're wondering if I'm real? it said and Lucian whirled around, trying to catch the speaker. The dust shifted on the earth, but there was no sign of who was speaking to him.

Am I friend or foe? it continued. Lucian stood still, using only his eyes and ears to detect its presence.

"Stop playing games and reveal yourself," Lucian invited.

"And if I wanted you dead?" the voice said behind him and Lucian twisted around, raising the wind around him. The wind whipped his hair wildly around his face, his clothes flapping hard, but Lucian held his attack at bay.

Before him was a man fully clad in a black, silky suit. Not one part of his body was revealed, not even his eyes. His head was covered so tightly with the soft fabric that it seemed to form part of his face. By the bulge of his nose and indented sockets of his eyes, he could at least tell the stranger seemed human.

Lucian lowered his powers, not quite sure of the stranger's

intentions. If the man had wanted him dead, he would not have given away his position. He eyed the stranger precariously, studying the two black swords strapped to his back and the throwing knives running up the length of his legs.

Something about the man was vaguely familiar though. Lucian was not sure if it was his aura that gave it away or if it was the scrawniness of the individual, but Lucian felt as if he knew him.

The stranger raised his hand to his neck and pulled off the mask. His bedraggled hair fell loosely on his forehead, his pale face shimmering in the last of the sunlight.

"I've heard about you," Lucian said. "I'm pretty sure Shado has made mention of you."

"Yes, Lucian," the stranger confirmed. "I was once part of the infamous Shadow Clan. The name you might have heard is Nolraldun."

***

Shedaaij swam between the domes and homes of the mer-Kingdom in *Selandil*, aware of the fact that she felt like a stranger among her own people. James had spent most of her first hours there bringing her up-to-date with the defences he had set up.

What bothered them both the most was that the trident still showed no indication of any threat within the ocean. If Le'Mar truly was preparing to annihilate the mer-people, it did not seem like he was going to do it any time soon.

"But how come *Selandil* escaped the trident's notice for so long?" Shedaaij had asked.

"I don't know," James had replied. "The mer-King apparently resided in *Selandil* at the time. The trident must have chosen a successor in the southern ocean at some point."

"We must have lost knowledge of our ancestry here," Shedaaij had guessed.

Yet, the more she thought about it, the more she wondered how much had been forgotten and how much had been kept hidden from them. And the more cynical she became about the trident's knowledge, the more the absence of sirens and demon-queens bothered her.

As much as these concerns disturbed her, Shadowolf's presence within her comforted her. She could feel his love and contentedness resonate through her and fill her with undefinable warmth. It caused a mirror effect to the point where her soul and serenity reflected that peace.

A force suddenly reverberated in the water. Every mermaid and merman stopped what they were doing as a second reverberation travelled like an ultrasonic wave through *Selandil*. They waited in fear and anticipation, anxiously wanting to go see what was causing the disturbance, but too afraid to find out.

The reverberations grew denser and more profuse until the walls and caverns within the mer-Kingdom began to quake. Just when they thought the drumming was reaching its peak and *Selandil* was about to collapse, the reverberations ceased.

James stood at the entrance to *Selandil* with the trident lit within his hands. Shedaaij swam towards him, thinking that perhaps James had managed to stop the shocks. Yet as she neared him, she could see by his face and puzzled demeanour that something else had stopped it.

Denia, the merman that had greeted both James and Shedaaij when they had arrived, reached James's side at the same time she did. They stared past the Argo Stir into the depths of the ocean. What should have been the darkest depths was now lit with an eerie, effervescent wall of light that stretched as far on the liquid horizon as they could see.

That's a hyperportal, Shedaaij informed them telepathically. *Le'Mar is bringing the sirens through it.*

From where!? James shouted in frustration. *Where the hell could they be coming from?*

Why don't we ask Denia? Shedaaij offered, and they both looked at the merman as he drifted backwards defensively. *Don't you think it's so strange that neither they nor the sirens can be detected by the trident?*

I think it's time for answers, yes, James said.

Denia's backward swim accelerated as he tried to avoid the questioning. Before the merman could blink, James flicked his tail and swam behind him. Denia turned around and found the trident's prong's lifted against his neck. He floated back into the coral wall, the trident's sting teasing open the skin of his neck.

Why can't my trident detect any of this? James interrogated.

Do you remember the old war? Denia asked with a trembling voice. James nodded pensively. *Do you remember those that were labelled traitors and were never heard of again?*

They met up with the elves, Denia continued unhindered. *The view they offered the elves swayed slightly from the truth, but the elves offered them sanctuary nonetheless. In the sanctity of the elvin forest, the elf lord Saldheron built the mer-people a fortress, with coral walls that could deflect the probing senses of the trident.*

I don't know of such waters, James muttered.

Of course, Shedaaij said. *The Pool of Radiance.*

Precisely, Denia confirmed. *When Eldor lost the forest two years ago, we had to vacate the waters. Eldor did not forget us and granted us passage to the ocean. We asked that the same silicate of rock be used in these caverns to shield us from tridents as before, not only yours, but those of the demon-queens also.*

And that's where the sirens have been, Shedaaij realised. *Sheltered and hidden within the Pool of Radiance.*

But hasn't the power that the elves placed there waned? James asked.

You misunderstand, Denia said. *It's not the power that shields us. It's the silicate within the rock itself.*

James looked at the coral walls within *Selandil*, suddenly realising what he meant.

All powers have limits, Denia said. *This is the trident's.*

Then why did you hail me as king when I arrived? James asked. *Why did I receive such a great welcome?*

Because Elgoth informed us this was the only way the mer-Kingdom would survive the war, Denia said. *You're welcome here because the alliance is necessary.*

James lowered his trident. There was no point in threatening him further; he had heard more than he had wanted to.

Saddened, he swam over to the wall and looked at the shimmering hyperportal in the distance. Dark shapes were emerging from the light… and they were many.

***

"How have you managed to live among Le'Mar's creatures for so long without being caught?" Skywolf asked.

The Shadow Clan sat in the council hall with Nolraldun, each equally excited by his arrival. He was perusing their drawings of the creatures they assumed the dark lord would use during the battle.

"I'm an assassin," Nolraldun replied, frowning at one of the sketches. "Stealth is what I do."

"Any insight you can give us into the oncoming battle?" Lucian asked.

"Well," the assassin said, spreading the images out on the table, "you have it mostly right. The sirens and demon-queens will be attacking the mer-Kingdom; that goes without saying.

"The wyverns you've seen will in all probability be used against the dragons. He still has the fletchlings, but I don't think he anticipated the fairies returning to join the war. Then there are the pegators, which I can tell you've prepared for. Then there are the orcs, Ma-Wreths, Froth Huns, Dra-hu-Mar, FireStroms and Crethans we all have grown used to.

"And I see you've made acquaintance with the Shriekers. If you can manage to break their resolve, it will stand you in good stead."

"Are there any we have missed?" Angelia asked.

"I assure you, there will even be some surprises for me," Nolraldun said looking up at her. "I left this morning when I heard that Le'Mar had recruited five assassins. Knowing they would either recognise me or know that I was not recruited, I had to leave.

"There are also elementëls in his force, beings of such great elemental power that your elementals might struggle to keep them back. Not to mention the demons and Saemnati he has acquired."

"The elementëls mentioned the Saemnati," Darcwulf said. "We'll deal with the demonic prince when he arrives."

"He's already here," Nolraldun said, much to the surprise of the others. "It will be interesting to see when Le'Mar decides to put him into play. It will take a tremendous amount of elementals and force to bring that being down."

The table went silent. They already knew the battle at hand was going to be overbearing, and Nolraldun's news was not helping.

THE WAR BEGINS
CHAPTER FIVE

James and Shedaaij remained at the entrance, watching with the front guards as the hyperportal finally closed. It had been three hours of tense impatience before the light of the portal faded, having long ago been blotted out by the hordes that now drifted in the ocean outside *Selandil*.

There's so many of them, James, Shedaaij said as she turned to look at him, momentarily seeing the fear flicker in Denia's eyes.

Then we better do our best, James replied sternly, not allowing his own fears to surface. *I only wonder how many demon-queens there…*

As if in answer to his incomplete question, twenty tridents of varying colours lit up along the front line of the hordes. James could see that the sirens grouped behind their respective queens, but there were so many of them that he could see no gaps between the groups.

How long do you think before they attack? Shedaaij asked, barely able to stop her voice from shaking.

I think they're already on their way.

She looked out on the ocean and saw that James was right. The darkness was getting closer, as were the lights that lead them. At first she thought that the lights were growing very intense because they were travelling so fast, but soon she realised that the tridents were powering up.

GET AWAY FROM THE WALLS!! James shouted to all around him. Without waiting to see why, Shedaaij obeyed and swam deeper into *Selandil*. Before she was even close to the first dome or abode, the caverns shook from explosions.

Rocks caved in and stalactites fell from the highest reaches of the kingdom. Cries resounded from within as the rocks crashed on many mer-people.

James didn't hesitate any further. He swam for the entrance, using the trident to summon all the warriors of *Selandil*. When he reached the wall of the entrance, he swung his trident out in a wide arc and the wall exploded towards the approaching sirens. The hole he had created was wide enough for the mermen and mermaids that followed him into battle to charge through.

None of them stopped or slowed down when the sirens were upon them. Raising his trident high above his head and shouting his war-cry to the minds of his warriors, James struck down with the prongs upon any dark creature that crossed his path...

***

Darcwulf stood with Fransiska at his side, the other members of the Shadow Clan walking along the edge of Sky Tier nervously. They eyed the burning fires on the eastern horizon suspiciously.

"It's three hours to midnight," Darcwulf said. "You'd think he'd start his approach already."

"What if it's just a siege?" Fransiska said. "His way of waiting for the Phenomenon before making a move?"

"I doubt that," Darcwulf said, but he sounded very unconvinced of his own uncertainty.

"No, he will attack," Nolraldun said as he came up behind them. "My guess is his men are resting and waiting for us to tire before he makes his move. That could be anywhere between midnight and sunrise."

"Great," Darcwulf said, crossing his arms over his chest. "I might as well have a drink and take a seat. Maybe when I sober up we can get this fight started."

"Are all of you that anxious to fight?" Nolraldun said amused.

"If any here aren't, then they shouldn't be here," Darcwulf proclaimed.

They waited a moment longer in silence before a murmur washed over the people behind them. Darcwulf turned to see what the fuss was, waiting for the crowds behind him to make a path for the man that walked towards them now.

Shadowolf seemed to glare in the light of the torches behind him. Even to his brother, who had known him all of his life, he seemed changed. In a way, he reminded Darcwulf of a glass vase that had once been smashed, but was now made whole without any indication of former damage.

The awed crowd watched as he moved among them. Shadowolf paid them little heed as he reached the tier ledge and placed his palms upon it. He stared out on the distance, his companions waiting for an explanation but receiving none. Any trace of the fear he once held within him was gone.

"I've just alerted my father that Le'Mar will wait until morning before the attack," Shadowolf said non-chalantly. "The armies will get some sleep and the moment the battle begins we will rouse them."

"Is that wise?" Darcwulf asked, sensing that the other members of the Shadow Clan now surrounded them.

"It's best that they try to get as much sleep as possible," Shadowolf said, and then looking at the others meaningfully. "We will however stay up and be on high alert."

"How do you know he won't attack tonight?" Skywolf asked.

"I've surveyed their forces with my mind," Shadowolf replied. "They are all at rest and sleeping. Those fires are a false sign of activity.

"Have you been training?" he asked Darcwulf, his eyes now feasting on the horrific glory of the dark armies.

"Yes," his brother replied and offered no further answer to the others.

"We have new guests," Shadowolf said to the others, and looked up at the high hill of Horlorn above the tier.

Shadows crept on the grass of the hill, moving into position all along its length. Darcwulf squinted into the darkness, barely lit by the lower torches, but the figures hid themselves so well in the rolling hill that he could not make them out. He was about to look at Shadowolf when he caught the shape of a bow in the hands of one of them.

"I thought the archers were on the lower tiers?" he asked, looking at his brother.

The crowd between them and the tier's entrance shifted again as six elves made their way to them. Their green-hued skins glowed sickly in the torch light, their eyes burning with a deep, fervent passion that Darcwulf could not place.

Lesan led the group, but it was not he that intrigued the Clan. Darcwulf recognised the Elders from the Isles. Eldor was at the fore, followed closely by Selgar, Pendum, Brigem and Haligon. Of the other Elders there was no sign.

"Welcome to Horlorn," Shadowolf said revealing no warmth or welcome despite his words. "What made you change your mind?"

"I believe it was something you said," Eldor said, his manner just as grim. "Something to the effect of the land remembering how the elves abandoned them."

By the time Shadowolf looked up at the hill again, the darkness on the grass was denser due to the amount of elves littering the fields as opposed to the night shade. He could not begin to imagine how many there were, but he had no doubt that they would still not match Le'Mar's army.

"Well, you might as well tell your elves to rest," Shadowolf instructed. "There are no signs of Le'Mar making a move anytime soon."

"Elves can go without sleep for weeks if necessary," Eldor replied. "They will remain on guard."

Shadowolf held his tongue. Even though they had last been on good terms, the slight animosity inside of him towards the Elders was not quenched. He could not blame them for wanting to remain idle, but there was a tension between them that did not want to subside.

He realised that he was being obstinate. The elves were here and Eldor had willingly gone against the Elder decree to assist them. Shadowolf dropped his head in thought as he fought to overcome his pride and stubborn heart. He swallowed hard as he addressed the Elders.

"Thank you for coming, Eldor," he said, offering an apologetic smile. "It will be a tremendous help to us."

Eldor smiled back and followed the Elders into the crowd to stand by an opening further down the tier. Lesan thanked Shadowolf with his eyes and left to join Chenesia and Genewiu on Mountain Tier.

Two hours after midnight, Shadowolf returned from the main hall to meet the Shadow Clan on the tier again. Conversation and discussions had all died, leaving the morning to be filled with the sounds of crickets and owls. The false serenity of the scene was only disturbed by a few snores along the tier.

Only a few members of the Clan remained awake, the others trusting their waking reflexes should the war begin. Darcwulf, Heula, Glasden, Lastgorn and Trimistus looked up at him as he took his position by the ledge, sitting sidelong on the cold concrete of the low wall.

"Have you heard anything from Shedaaij?" Darcwulf whispered as he joined his side.

"The war is very intense there," Shadowolf replied. "The mer-people are holding up well, but I don't know for how long they can endure. At least Shedaaij's strength feels sufficient for now."

The brothers looked out onto the quiet fields below them together. Sharing that space and time with him, the same sight and ambitions, Shadowolf felt closer to Darcwulf than he ever had.

"Have you decided what you want to do after the war?" Shadowolf asked.

"Mmm?" Darcwulf said vaguely, and then snapped back to reality. "Oh yes. Fransiska is keen on starting a new life in this 'kingdom' you referred to. I don't see myself coming back to Celenic Earth once I've left. I've always felt out-of-place here."

"Like a stranger on your own planet," Shadowolf smiled.

"Precisely," Darcwulf agreed. "Besides, you're going too, so at least we can postpone the farewell for a while."

"Not for too long," Shadowolf laughed. "I have a family too, you know."

"Why don't you all just join us?" Darcwulf asked imploringly. "I'm sure Celenic Earth will do fine on its own."

"No, that's not something I want. I really love this place...my home. And I fear too much for Crystal's safety. I have no idea how receptive your father will be, especially since I spent a lot of time killing half his men."

Darcwulf went quiet, contemplating Shadowolf's words. He huffed and sighed a few times before speaking again.

"So strange to call him my father, when I don't really know the man. Is he as much of a bastard as he sounds?"

"Hey, I only know the dragons' side of the story," Shadowolf said. "They can be biased at the best of times. For all we know your father could be the..."

His words fell into the morning as if a knife has cut it off. Darcwulf raised his eyes at his brother, wondering at the interruption. His concern only worsened when he saw Shadowolf's pupils light up with a soft yellow glow.

"What's happening?" he asked.

"Wake the others," Shadowolf warned. "Tell the earth elementals to get ready. Le'Mar's up to something. I can feel the earth shaking against his summons."

Darcwulf did not feel it immediately, but something in the air was wrong. He rushed to instruct the conscious members of the Clan to wake the others, and then ran off to warn the other elementals.

Before he could get far, the land around Horlorn started quaking. Shadowolf pressed his palms on the ledge, closing his eyes as he raised his earthen powers. By the cracks and the noises behind him he realised that the hill was toppling down.

With his senses extended he could feel cracks develop in the foundations of Horlorn. Shadowolf strained his powers to match those of Le'Mar, but he knew it would not be long before he needed more *Goudlem*s to join him. He gritted his teeth and jumped to the side as a rock from the hill crashed on the spot where he had been standing.

CLOSING THE CANYONS
CHAPTER SIX

Shadowolf felt power rise all around him in Horlorn as the earth elementals fought to sustain the stability of the land beneath them. He closed his eyes as he added his own powers to theirs, waiting several minutes before the shaking subsided.

It was not over though. From behind Horlorn he could feel the land was still shifting, as if Le'Mar was reforming the earth. A frown crested his forehead as he drove all contemplations from his mind and continued to keep Horlorn stable.

They did not know how long the earth still shook the land to the west, but it finally came to an end. Once again silence reigned and Shadowolf felt comfortable enough to lower his powers.

"What was that all about?" Sorceress asked as her power waned too.

"I don't know," Shadowolf confided. "But I hope Simnab is ready."

The wolf –lord stood motionless as the earth's trembling came to an end. His crimson staff glowed in the soft light of Ringos in the night sky. The planet that would retard the sunrise the next day was larger in the sky now than Sothos the moon. Simnab stood alone under its reign of the morning sky, watching the dust that settled on the land to the west.

Horlorn remained intact behind him. When most of the dust had cleared, he walked towards the canyon that had only been there moments before. It would take him a good measure of time to reach the canyon, but he strode on at a casual pace, his eyes watching the horizon carefully.

Before he was anywhere near the canyon, he knew that it had

collapsed upon itself. The land sloped down to where the canyon should have been, and the soft rumbling of the water that had once run so strongly at its base towards T'Mar's Scourge was now utterly mute. Even the faint moisture that had been in the air was replaced by the taint of fallen rocks and settling dirt.

In the silence immediately following the aftermath of the quake he could feel the trembling of the earth as creatures stampeded from the western reaches of the land towards the canyon. Dark forms that he could make out with his lupine eyes launched into the crumbled platform within the canyon, making their way hungrily towards Simnab and Horlorn.

Besides the Crethans he knew would be in the horde, there were Ma-Wreths and Froth Huns in abundance too. He could detect no elemental presence, but he held no hopes for their absence. The many Creth-Demons that commanded the canines brought up the rear of the army, their staves blinking from power.

Simnab stopped walking. His muscular body held the black armour he wore easily, emerald trimmings complimenting the green sheath on his side. A maroon cape attached to the metal pads on his shoulders brought out the crimson in his staff. The glint of the blades that protruded from the armour on his elbows reflected the bloodlust in his eyes.

His face changed and extended, his human nose growing out to a snout and hair covering his naked skin. He growled and opened his jaws as his lupine teeth extended into fangs. The remainder of his body stayed human as he watched the first of the Crethans cross the canyon and rise onto the eastern side.

Soft footsteps padded to a halt beside him. Simnab looked appraisingly at the two-headed hound beside him. Like Cerexus it looked fierce, its fangs seemingly capable of shredding metal with one bite. Its bulk was also huge enough to carry any weight on its back, including Simnab with all his armour.

"I want you to hunt the Wreths down, Orxus," Simnab commanded. Both heads looked up at him, their tongues panting playfully down the side of their mouths. "I want their corpses ready for breakfast by the time I reach the Froth Huns."

Orxus looked forward and sniffed the air. The Ma-Wreths were still in the bowels of the collapsed canyon, but the hound appeared to have picked up their scent. It gave a belligerent growl and then charged forward.

Simnab watched the progression of the Crethans. The deformed wolves raced to meet Orxus, their gazes fixed on the hound. Simnab closed his eyes and let his senses flow out from his mind, tracing those Crethans with a distinct difference in their auras.

When Orxus was nearly upon the hordes, almost half the distance between Simnab and the canyon, he sent out the silent command. His staff lit up with a faint light, his command reaching the Celenic Crethans alone.

He could have commanded all of them. Anuxis had reassured him that he could have taken them all under his wing. But the lord of the Underworld had made one thing clear: not one of the *Hieragke* or *Haniegke* was to be shown mercy.

A third of the Crethans racing across the plain began to transform. Blue steam rose off their skin as the Creth-Demons lost control of their minds. Their human forms rose up on two legs as they continued to run along the others, only their faces and arms retaining their canine shapes.

Orxus passed Angelicus at the rear of the transformed wolves, the *Hieragke* surrounding her too confused by the change to react to the hound's presence. Angelicus was gleaming white, her body hidden by the light from within her as she twisted around and faced the hordes behind her.

She arced her arm up to the sky, an invisible power throwing hundreds of the beasts off their feet. Yelps and cries broke out into the morning air as their backs and spines cracked or broke upon landing. She growled and joined the other Crethans as they charged into the *Hieragke* ranks with fangs and claws aching for blood.

Simnab watched and waited, sensing the power of the *Haniegke* rise and keeping his sight focused on the canyon. Orxus dropped from sight at the edge of the eastern bank of the canyon, but there were no sign of the Ma-Wreths. The Froth Huns were starting their approach into canyon.

Before they materialised around him, he could feel the *Haniegke* teleporting around him. He watched each of the thirty beings appear in droves, their canine fangs hissing and growling intensely. Their staves gleamed brilliantly, but Simnab breathed slowly, waiting for their attack.

Le'Mar watched with distant eyes, infuriated at this change of events. At first, Simnab's sole appearance behind Horlorn had amused him, but now the humour was lost in the embrace of his anger.

He had planned to summon the wyverns only later that day, but it was clear he needed them now. He would not allow the rear attack to be so dissuaded.

Simnab blocked the first blow with his staff, and ducked as a ray of power coursed towards him. When he rose, a staff knocked him in the jaw and he spun around, drove his elbow back and lifted the blades attached to them up through the *Haniegke*'s abdomen to his chest.

The blood toppled over his cape as he released the blades and used them to block another staff. The rod cut across its abdomen and, before the *Haniegke* recovered, Simnab unsheathed his sword and drove it into the beast.

A blast of power struck him and he twisted in the air before landing on a rising staff. Simnab coughed and hit the floor. Before he could regain his senses, someone kicked him in his ribs and despite his armour he rose into the air and fell on his back.

Simnab looked up, blood trickling down the side of his lips as the *Haniegke* crowded over him. Their fangs grinned broadly, the closest beasts getting ready for the final kill. Simnab felt helpless, unsure of what to do to get out of the situation. Just when he was about to give in to his demise, he saw the shape of a Ma-Wreth fall towards him from the sky.

Simnab's roll surprised a few of the *Haniegke*, but not as much as the bulk that crashed down on them. Simnab heard several necks break from the initial impact and a few groans of pain in the aftermath. He got up on hands and knees and saw the Ma-Wreth lying dead on its back above several corpses.

Trotting into view from the milieu of the battle came Orxus, a very satisfactory smile on the heads. The *Haniegke* turned to view the hound, some of them recognising it.

"I thought I told you to take care of the Wreths?" Simnab said with gratitude in his tone. Orxus grunted and looked at the dead Ma-Wreth, ending the conversation with a bark from the left head.

Simnab rose with renewed vigour, ready to challenge the *Haniegke* now that their attention was divided between him and Orxus.

The Shadow Clan's attention was just as divided; they were not sure whether they should be more worried about the yelps and cries behind the hill or Le'Mar's silence on the horizon. None of the armies marched forward or made any attempt to approach the fortress. For all they knew, the dark creatures were still sleeping fitfully.

Shadowolf heard wings upon the wind and looked up at Dwarf Mountains. The dragons were rising from their hiding places, but instead of heading east to Le'Mar they went west towards the commotion by the canyon.

Shadowolf thought their wings were echoing along the hill, but when he looked north towards the ocean he saw the wyverns heading west too. Suddenly the dragons' intentions became clear and he closed his eyes to summons Asgorna.

The dragon broke off from the group along with Mynisna. Shadowolf opened his eyes when he heard their wings flapping past the ledge. Trimistus was by his side, ready to join him.

"I'm going with," Darcwulf proclaimed.

"We'll stay here," Skywolf said. "I think we should wait for the attack on Horlorn to begin."

"Very well," Shadowolf said. Mynisna looked up at the army of dragons and not long thereafter one of the dragons broke free and joined them.

"This is Soltavia," Mynisna introduced. "He'll be your mount. He's been complaining about the lack of a rider long enough."

Shadowolf, Trimistus and Darcwulf mounted the dragons and rose into the air to join the race to the canyon. As they made their way over the peak of the hill, a single dragon dropped down from the throng and waited by the ledge, looking around at the Clan.

Not finding what it was looking for, it dropped down until he saw the woman waiting by the ledge of Mountain Tier. Beliva turned her back, her wings flapping gently as Harmony jumped on its back.

The group of *Haniegke* now found themselves in the midst of the Crethan battle as they strove to confront Simnab and his hound. Wolves broke over them, blood and flesh tracing the air and sketching the land with their death. Five *Haniegke* managed to make it to Simnab, their fiery staves powering up.

As Simnab called forth his strength, he caught images of Ma-Wreths and Froth Huns finally making the eastern bank of the canyon. All the hordes were out of the canyon now and heading impatiently towards Horlorn, some of the beasts ignoring the mayhem around them.

He focused on the five around him, his ears catching the sound of wings in the air. He dimly hoped the dragons were arriving to assist him, even though he knew they were meant to be waiting until the main battle before Horlorn. He did not allow his curiosity to sway his concentration though.

A *Haniegke* threw a ball of yellow fire at him. He slipped his crimson staff forward and caught the fire within it. Simnab railed his hand along the smooth shaft of his staff, letting his right hand grip the end of the rod and twist it around his body to block the strike from behind. As the rods clashed, he released the fire and sent the *Haniegke* hurtling backwards.

Continuing his momentum, he jumped into the air and brought his leg around to kick a *Haniegke*. The strike to the face missed, but as he landed on his knee he continued to spin and swept the same *Haniegke* off his feet.

As three *Haniegke* ran forward to attack, Simnab tucked his right elbow in, rolled onto the fallen creature and drove his elbow blades into its chest. As he rolled off, he vaulted up with his legs and delivered an uppercut with the same elbow blades up into a *Haniegke*'s neck. The head split vertically in three as Simnab turned to face the other three that were now redirecting their attack to him.

The *Haniegke* that he had struck with the fire led the trio. Simnab heard the wings again and saw the *Haniegke* look up behind him. Simnab ran forward to take the offensive, when jaws closed around his armoured stomach and lifted him off the ground.

He twisted his canine head in the armour to look at wyvern eyes. The skies were littered with them and he watched gravely as they dropped from the skies and started killing Crethans. Their numbers were already low due to the brutality of the *Hieragke* and he knew it was going to be over soon.

Notwithstanding his fears, he turned his body slightly to the left and then spun hard to the right. The metal suit twisted in the wyvern's fangs and screeched as it scraped the teeth. The wyvern cried and, as he slipped from its maw, Simnab unsheathed his sword with his free hand and cut the beast's slim neck clean off.

He tumbled towards the ground beside the headless wyvern. He noticed that a Ma-Wreth was running with incredible speed that belied its bulk towards the spot he was falling to. Simnab crouched against the dead body behind him in the air and waited for its contact with the earth.

As the Ma-Wreth was upon him and the wyvern crashed into the earth, sending grass spraying into the air, Simnab kicked against the corpse and rose above the Ma-Wreth. The giant's speed was delayed in the shock and Simnab's sword flew from his hand straight into the centre of the beast's skull. He landed on one knee as the Ma-Wreth fell on its back with a heavy thud.

Simnab retrieved his sword and looked up at the sky as he heard another cry. Another wyvern was upon him. He had no time to raise his hand in defence and watched as its mouth opened up to rip his head off.

The wyvern was thrust aside as a dragon crashed against it, its largest fangs the size of the wyvern's head. Blood rained onto the ground before Simnab as the dragon bit into its belly and then threw its corpse with its forelegs into a large group of *Hieragke*.

"Are you ok?" Shadowolf said as jumped from Asgorna's back and let the dragon continue the carnage without him.

"Considering the sit... LOOK OUT!"

Simnab jumped to push Shadowolf aside, but it was too late. A Ma-Wreth had grabbed the tail of a dragon and tossed it towards them. That dragon now crashed into Shadowolf, barely missing Simnab but sending the elemental scraping along the ground under the weight of the dragon.

When the dragon's slide came to a halt, the beast rose and limped off Shadowolf. Simnab ran to see if he was ok, sighing in relief when he saw him stand up very slowly.

"You see, that's the only reason I don't like dragons on the battlefield," Shadowolf gave a painful smile. He stretched his back and it sounded like his spine clicked back into place. Simnab watched as Shadowolf removed his torn shirt, his back rippled with grass burns.

"Can you manage?" Simnab asked.

"Yeah, the shirt would have just hindered me," he replied.

Shadowolf tensed his muscles, his hands clenched in fists and his eyes burning with a white light. He cried out in agony as dragon wings tore the top skin of his back and lashed out on both sides. His face transformed until it resembled that of Asgorna's, albeit smaller in scale. The growl that emanated from his reptilian throat was both lupine and draconic in nature.

"Excuse me while I deal with this tosser," Shadowolf said coarsely and flew up to meet the Ma-Wreth that had thrown the dragon.

Simnab had been about to join him when he heard the sound of hooves approach. He saw the black stallions riding towards Horlorn with white steam rolling from their nostrils and wide sockets. On their backs were the large Froth Huns, their skeletal heads burning with blue flames and their huge swords strapped to their backs.

From the sky, a ball of fire soared down onto one of the Froth Huns and knocked him right of the horse's saddle. The fiery man took the Froth's place on its back and gripped the reins in his burning hands.

"I've always wanted one of my own!" Darcwulf shouted with mock exhilaration. He looked down and noticed the reins melting in his hands. In the meantime, the other Froth Huns were turning to face him. "Well now, that won't do. I guess I'll have to make some minor alterations."

The horse reared up on its hind legs as the reins became fire. Brimstone smoked out from the beast's sockets as fire raged from within it. By the time the stallion landed on it forelegs again, its coat was a raging furnace. Blue flames licked the ends of the horse's mane and tail, the ethereal reins still burning in his hands.

"That's better," Darcwulf said. "Let's get them, Flame."

The stallion bolted forward at the same time that the crowd of Froth Huns made for him. Darcwulf lifted his knees up onto the saddle, getting ready to jump off into the attack. The abundant Froths formed in a long line before him, crashing through any Crethans or *Hieragke* that got in their way.

When Darcwulf reached the line, Flame opened its mouth and scorched fire at the black mounts of the closest Froths. Darcwulf smelled burning flesh as he powered up and vaulted off the back of his stallion.

Using fire to propel him forward, he grabbed a Froth Hun in each hand and used his bald head to carry one up into the air with them. He felt the Froths squirm in his grasp and, when he heard one of them unsheathe its giant sword, he exchanged his head and feet and kicked the central Froth up into the air.

Spinning in circles, he released the remaining two Froth Huns and watched dragons catch them and rip them apart. Flying up to meet the falling Froth like a comet from hell, he unsheathed his serpent sword and drove it through its bony skull.

Shadowolf landed on the ground by Angelicus and gripped her arm hard.

"Get out of here," he said over the din of battle. "There aren't much of you left."

"We're not abandoning the cause," Angelicus returned the offer.

"Then get to Horlorn," he replied. "The main battle will be starting any second and I'd rather you fight there than die here."

She looked around and saw that at most there were fifty Crethans left. Hundreds of naked bodies polluted the plains with their corpses among the horrific forms of the dead *Hieragke*.

Angelicus raised her lupine head and let a long, loud howl resound into the morning air. Responding howls collected around them as all the Crethans that lived met her. The hundreds of *Hieragke* corresponded by circling around them pensively.

"Go," was the only word Shadowolf said.

Angelicus closed her eyes. Light rose from her solar plexus again as her power rose. An orb of blue rays broke from her skin and formed a domed shield around the Crethans. Fur sizzled and burned as the *Hieragke* tried to enter the shield, but instead of persuading them to leave it only encouraged them to wait.

The light covered the group within the shield and, as the light contracted into itself, it drifted off the ground in the form of a baby star. Only Shadowolf remained in the centre of the *Hieragke* while the star of Crethans travelled to Horlorn and out of sight.

Trimistus landed behind Shadowolf, his dragon wings stretched out against Shadowolf's. He unsheathed his dragon sword. Shadowolf watched the *Hieragke* around them, unaware that the upper edges of Trimistus's wings were becoming hardened metal.

"Mind if I join you?" Trimistus asked.

"Well, I usually don't share a meal," Shadowolf grinned and looked back over his wing. It was then that he saw the iron edges of the reptilian's wings. "Hey, that's a neat trick."

"Don't you use utensils to eat with?" Trimistus joked.

Shadowolf concentrated and let water seep from his wings to collect on the upper edges. He then cooled it to form compacted ice that became as hard as diamond.

The *Hieragke* barked and howled, ready for the attack. Trimistus and Shadowolf readied their wings and arms, but then had to shield their faces as fire rained down around them.

Darcwulf was hauling balls of fire at the hordes, joining the flames of the dragons that were not occupied with the remaining wyverns. Earth erupted up into the air where the balls struck, together with the *Hieragke* that happened to be standing in those areas.

"NOW!" Shadowolf shouted, and he and Trimistus went to work with the spinning blades of their wings.

.

BLOOD ON THE PLAINS
CHAPTER SEVEN

He wasn't sure how much time had passed by the time they had finished off the last of the creatures that had crossed the canyon, but he knew it had to be more than an hour. The wyverns had left to return to Le'Mar shortly after Angelicus's departure, giving the dragons a chance to assist in destroying the hordes on the ground.

Shadowolf lowered his powers and drew the back of his arm across his forehead to clear the perspiration. Dead bodies and skeletal remains flooded the plains, many being those of his allies. At least ten dragons lay dead in the fields, some of their corpses as high as a large hill.

Deciding to use no powers and walk naturally, he found a path among the dead until he reached Trimistus, Darcwulf and Simnab resting on fallen rocks and disturbed earth. The dragons were returning to their former crags in Dwarf Mountains.

When he reached the small group, he retracted his wings into his back. He noticed that Trimistus had already done so, the reptilian man's face showing signs of weariness. Shadowolf used the few moments of silent approach to listen and sense any sign of battle by Horlorn, but he could detect none.

"At least we have enough meat to last us a lifetime," Darcwulf joked.

"We better head back to Horlorn," Shadowolf announced, not permitting himself any rest yet.

"An hour and a half before sunrise," Trimistus remarked as they made for Horlorn. "I wonder why Le'Mar didn't send the other troops already. He usually loves attacking multiple zones at once."

"He probably thinks we expected it or something," Shadowolf

surmised. "Or maybe this minor defeat surprised him. Perhaps he was hoping we'd divide our forces."

"Whatever the case," Trimistus said, "we still have a large battle on our hands. I…where's Simnab?"

The brother's looked back, but could not see anything past the dead bodies. Shadowolf rose on the wind and surveyed the land, spotting a small figure on top of a two-headed hound bound into the depths of the canyon.

He landed on the earth and nodded to Horlorn.

"Simnab's on his own mission," he informed them. "Let's get back."

Nighthale watched across the land from the Degron tower. He had woken the armies within Horlorn the moment Shadowolf had left to fight to the west, and now he realised he had made a grave mistake.

The troops had been awake during those long hours of battle, anxiously waiting for the horizon troops to make a move. But as time passed, the only significant thing that had transpired was that his men were growing more and more tired.

Even if Le'Mar's failed rear attack did nothing more than keep them awake, it was still catastrophic. He looked to the bridges on either side and watched as several archers' eyes drooped where they stood. They had replenished the torches of Horlorn thrice while waiting on Le'Mar. When the dark lord finally made his move, Nighthale feared his men would be too sleepy to respond or to properly defend themselves.

The sky was starting to become lighter and it was then that Nighthale realised that there was movement on the horizon. None of the fires had moved and so he had assumed nothing was happening, but as the morning became clearer he noticed that Le'Mar was already preparing his armies for the approach on the fortress.

Ranks and lines formed on the distant horizon, marching down the plains in large groups to a point where Le'Mar must have indicated to them. Before studying them, Nighthale sent the word out to his commanders for the archers to prepare.

A thought suddenly occurred to him and he eyed the formations once more. His keen eyes searched the multitude for signs of enemy archers, but he could see none. His eyes flitted to the hill on the horizon, but if the Dra-hu'Mar were there, he could not see them.

As the blue of the sky became clearer, the army on the plains began to disturb him. He could see that the front line consisted mostly of orcs but, where he had expected the dull grey of their skin, he found the silver of armour instead. And the armour was neither crude nor primitive like the orcs; it seemed rather refined.

In the rear of the multiple formations stood the giant forms of the Ma-Wreths and even they appeared changed. Nighthale squinted the distance and noticed that they too had some form of pristine armour but, more importantly, they now held large weapons and shields in their hands. He had no doubt that when those beasts reached the fortress walls, those weapons would be dropped so that the Wreths could attempt to breach the defence.

Whereas a lesser man would cower and drop his weapons in defeat, Nighthale gave a heavy sigh and held his head up high. That simple act bolstered his courage. He clutched the staff in his hand tighter.

"Sound the horns," he said. Men scuttled around him, giving signals to the tiers behind them. Three horns sounded, one from each tier. Nighthale waited, the wind teasing his tense face and his taut neck.

The large gates creaked open and the dwarves, elves and human warriors began to pass through before the movement was complete. Even though the force that entered the plains was not the main army, the numbers were still by far huge. The men and women stepped into the light of the rising sun, no fear visible in their steps and no outward hesitation.

When the initial army had cleared the outer wall and formed up outside, the gates closed. Soft feet landed behind him and Nighthale turned to see his son stepping up beside him.

"What news?" he asked, returning his gaze to the plains, anxiety reminding him that the archers awaited his word.

"We've taken care of the rear army," Shadowolf replied. He gave him a quick rundown of the events of the canyon before echoing his father's gaze onto the plains. "Are they wearing silver armour?"

"I would assume so, although it could be made of anything," Nighthale said. The armour that glinted in the morning sunlight looked very similar to what the dwarves had crafted for the warriors of Horlorn.

The orcs and Wreths began the next approach, a signal sounding along the far hill. Shadowolf could feel soft tremors in the earth from the vast numbers that marched across the plains in an orderly fashion. Shadowolf frowned. It was very unlike the foul creatures to remain organised, no matter who commanded them.

Nighthale raised his hand. Several commanders along the parapets that bridged the towers raised theirs in response, to which the archers, elvin and human, raised their bows. For a moment, Nighthale silently questioned whether or not the arrows would be of any use.

To answer his question, he dropped his arm. The sound of hundreds of arrows whistled into the air, rising like dark slivers of death to their peaks before falling down on the orcs. The steel shafts of the arrows clanged against steel armour and fell uselessly to the ground.

A few cries rang out where the arrows met flesh, but Nighthale was not satisfied. He knew instantly that the effort would waste more arrows than was necessary.

"Send out the word," Nighthale informed his closest commander. "The archers are to lay down their bows and join the battle on the plain."

Shadowolf could see the concern in his father's face, but he was more worried about the increasing pace of the orcs. Horlorn's warriors on the plains began to race to meet them, their steel swords, axes and studded staves shimmering in the sunlight.

Without a word to his father, Shadowolf walked out of Degron Tower and stood on the left bridge. He looked up at Sky Tier until he caught Darcwulf's attention. His brother nodded and moved from sight.

He vanished from the bridge, becoming one with the air and stirring it into wind as he passed to the lower land. He lost sight of the rushing armies behind the gates, making his way to small outcrops on one of Horlorn's rocky surfaces.

He gently laid his hand on the largest group of outcrops. The stone was cold and rough under his palm. Shadowolf closed his eyes and felt deeper within the hill's surface. He could sense various minerals deep within and, choosing one he felt would assist the most, began calling the precious metal to him.

His hand shimmered with a green haze, his fingers trembling as he exerted his powers through his left arm. Several of the guards near the gates looked his way as the area near his hand began to quake, shifting the rocks to roll on the ground.

Shadowolf turned his palm up as a deep red substance bled from the outcrop into his hand. Despite its fluid motion, it appeared to be as hard as the stone it was pouring from, and the more it collected in his hand, the deeper the colour became.

It twined like rope until Shadowolf was holding a length as long as a staff in his hand. It hardened every second that he held and soon the staff was pitch black with a soft silvery sheen glinting on its surface.

Grasping the haematite staff firmly, he turned to face the riders that approached him now. The weight of the staff was reassuring and its cold strength comforted the anxiety in his nerves. He just hoped that, whatever metal the orcs' armour consisted of, it would be of little help against the staff.

As the Shadow Clan met him at the gate, he passed some power through the staff to make sure it conducted properly and was happy with the result. The power did not clog or knot at any point in the stone; in fact, he found it passed through easier than expected.

Darcwulf rode up on Flame, holding Mandy's reins in his hand. The grey mottled staff hung in the left saddle strap, so Shadowolf placed the additional staff in the right one. He mounted the saddle and waited for the large gates to open.

When they opened, the Shadow Clan were greeted by the sound of battle. Steel clashed on the plains in the centre of the mountain and hills' bowl. The din of steel against armour and shield echoed wildly to their ears, the acoustics accompanied by cries of death. If the ring of the battle could have been compared to music, it was a song that Shadowolf hoped he would never hear or sing to again.

They rode out a short distance, just enough to clear the gates, before Shadowolf turned Mandy around to face the Clan. The only members who could not be there to look back at him were the gargoyles, but as yet that could not be helped. The sun was still rising to its peak, and Shadowolf did not want to expend anyone's power to create cloud cover. He had no doubt that Le'Mar would simply remove it.

As much as he wanted Millon to be with them, the centaur had to lead his own army. Shadowolf would never remove him from that duty, although having Millon with them would have been an immense boon. Ursula also remained behind with Eldor and Lesan, choosing to fight with the elves as a defence for Horlorn.

Those that chose to ride out with him now were no less great, either in valour or in might. They sat proudly upon their mounts, staring at him with substantial inner strength.

Darcwulf was the closest to him, his serpent blade on his waist. In a line beside him were Skywolf, Angelia and Heula. Skywolf had her staff and bow in her saddle strap, and a beautiful cyan shield hung on her back, the head of a wolf adorning the front. Shadowolf recognised Malkius's crest, and was awed that her father had given her his shield.

Behind the four were Lastgorn, Sorceress and Fransiska. Shadowolf noted that the red crusted blade of Scarlette was still on his waist, but he also saw that his own blue sword was strapped to the saddle. Shadowolf had grown used to seeing Lastgorn with his faithful sword and was glad it was there.

At the rear was Trimistus on his large Saurex. The reptilian creature stood high up above them, his jaws open in anticipation for the battle ahead. Drool was running down the side of its fangs and, just when Shadowolf was about to shout a warning to Heula below it, it slurped it back in and continued to pant.

Beside Trimistus was Angelicus on a fresh mount. No weapons or armour complimented her body, as she was prepared to face the enemies with fang and claw. She smiled softly at him as he surveyed her at the back.

And the last three beside her were Nolraldun, Elgoth on his stallion and Lucian on Lancenat. Lucian only had a staff whereas Elgoth had a staff and sword. The aged saint held magnificent knowledge in his voluminous eyes, and Lucian held the power of the wind within his.

"I just want to thank all of you for being there for me all these years," Shadowolf said, lowering his head in thought. "Heaven knows I would not have made it this far without you."

"It's because we love you so much that we do it, Shado," Skywolf replied, riding forward from the group. "We believe in you and each other."

"I don't know what I did to deserve love like this or even just your friendship," he said, looking into her eyes. "I've been on my own mission most of the time. But thank you."

He looked up at Darcwulf, emphasising that he thanked him the most. All the things they had been through since childhood suddenly welled up inside him and, before he became emotional, he closed his heart and turned to face the battle.

He didn't ask them if they were ready; he didn't ask them if they were sure. He already knew the answers to those questions. He simply urged Mandy into a sprint... and they followed.

Le'Mar stared down the hill at the dust rising before Horlorn's Gate and, despite every effort not to, smiled. He had been waiting for this. He turned in his saddle to face the six Saneths, Ru-maak being the only one from the original four still remaining in his army.

"Hunt them down and kill them," Le'Mar instructed. "Leave Shado to me. I want him to earn his way to me, even if that means sacrificing his friends in the process. I want him to WATCH THEM DIE."

The six grunted and nodded and pushed their mounts passed the dark creatures and down the hill.

Le'Mar watched with the deepest interest. The Saneths were halfway down the hill, but Shadowolf would reach the battle before them. A dark cloud formed on Le'Mar's hands as he gathered the fog within him. He thrust his hands out in the direction of the Saneths.

The Saneths became two black clouds that floated on either side of the mass fighting in the centre. When they reached the other side, Le'Mar released them and watched them ride to confront Shadowolf's group.

Le'Mar's jaw dropped and his smile faded as the group

vanished from sight. His vision blurred momentarily from shock, and he breathed slowly to refocus, trying with renewed vigour to find them.

The dark lord's hands closed into fists, knowing this would only be the first of Shadowolf's tricks.

The wind stirred on the hill below Le'Mar's main force and behind the battle in the bowl of the plains. It twisted and changed direction, heading for the back of the battle. Unaware to the orcs and Ma-Wreths that were attempting to reach the main part of the battle, the group materialised behind them and raced down to meet them.

The others behind him all picked up speed to ride in a line on either side of him. The Ma-Wreths turned, clearly hearing the thunder of their horses' hooves. Before its lightning reflexes could counter, Mandy shoved her weight into one of them and pushed it to the ground.

Shadowolf could sense it had taken her a lot of effort. The armour looked very durable from that close, but he noticed she had left a dent in its back. Another Wreth was clambering its way quickly to them and, as its fists fell on them, Mandy became wind and passed through the beast. Shadowolf was on the ground, the fire sword in his hand thrust through the first Wreth's neck.

It was Shadowolf's turn to react too slowly as a Wreth hit him across his back. He tripped over the dead body, twisted his body to face the beast that had attacked him, and hurled a ball of fire at it. The fire hissed at it hit the armour on its chest.

Black ash was all that remained of the ball. Shadowolf frowned, sparing as little a moment as he could to put power to his eyes. Besides the beast's natural dark aura, there seemed to be a layer of purple sparks surrounding the plates of silver. Le'Mar had not only protected them from material weapons, but ethereal ones too.

Shadowolf felt a Wreth approach him from behind, but the last second he used to investigate the armour revealed that it was only the armour that held the protection, not the beast itself. The knowledge gave him a small degree of relief.

He vanished from under the Wreth's strike, grabbed Mandy's reins and landed on her saddle. Under normal circumstances,

Shadowolf would have waited a little longer, but he had no time for exaggerated patience now. He grabbed the grey mottled staff, throwing it forward. The staff twirled in a haze of power and Nelnar landed on a Wreth's back, biting immediately into the first piece of flesh it could find.

Flame was burning, its mane a wave of fire as Darcwulf brought the fiery serpent sword down on another orc. He heard a Wreth approach and lifted his feet onto the saddle.

The movement was fluid as he somersaulted back over the enormous hand that swept over Flame's saddle. The hand hit the back of the stallion's head and Flame gave a sick shrill. Before Darcwulf landed, he summoned a bow of fire to his hands, notched a fiery arrow from the hot air and released it. The arrow struck between the plates on the beast's back and helmet, causing the Wreth to slowly collapse.

Darcwulf felt an impulse to check on Flame, but a Saneth rode before him before he could act on it. It seemed feminine, red plates covering most of her skin like a crocodile with the odd yellow patches in-between.

She hissed and glared at him, her mouth opening up to reveal razor-like teeth that were all cropped over each other. Darcwulf let fire pass through his sword as she leapt off her mount and landed on the ground, drawing her blade.

The sword was transparent, with only the outline of the blade and the hilt visible in her hand. She bent her knees slightly and held the blade before her in a stance, eagerly examining him with her eyes. Darcwulf waited, choosing to let her strike first.

The Saneth twisted her blade with her wrist and struck. Darcwulf knew it was a feigned blow and that she was preparing for the secondary strike, so made a light-hearted attempt at blocking the blade with his. His shoulder jerked as his sword passed through hers and followed through. His quick reflexes made him spin around to meet the second blow.

As it landed, the blade became solid and he lifted the serpent sword just in time. The two swords clashed loudly together. He tried to move the sword away, but it became invisible again and passed through his. He ducked and kicked at her knees, making her cry out.

He jumped back, narrowly avoiding the hardened blade that soared towards his chest. Fire rose to his fist and he hurled it at her. It hit her breasts hard, but instead of sending her back, the fire coursed into her and flew back out at him. The speed of the fire was faster as it hit him, and he let it pass into his spirit.

They circled each other, looking for any weakness. Darcwulf spared a glance around him, suddenly noticing that none of the orcs were bothering them. Instead, their battles were a wide berth around them and he could only guess that Le'Mar had instructed them to stay out of the Saneths' paths. As she attacked again, his mind started working hard at how he could use that to his advantage.

Shadowolf blocked the orc's strike with the haematite staff and then knocked the bottom of its shield up and then into its face. While the orc stumbled back, he moved the end of the staff back to block another sword, kicked the orc's legs from under him and drove the sharpened bottom edge of the staff through its throat.

Three orcs rushed to jump on him and he unleashed a circle of fire that raged about him. Two of the orcs fell back in fear, but the third continued rushing through. The flame hardly harmed him thanks to its armour. The shield crashed into Shadowolf and they both fell to the ground rolling. As they came to a stop, with the orc above Shadowolf and the sword ready to fall, Nelnar crashed into it.

The Nelmurian wolf and the orc battled as Shadowolf rose to his feet again. That knock had hit the wind from him and he breathed a moment to recover. He looked around and saw Darcwulf battling a strange feminine creature near the foot of Dwarf Mountains.

Another cursory glance revealed that Skywolf, Lucian, Lastgorn, Sorceress and Angelia were facing similar foes. One of them he recognised as Ru-maak, the serpentine servant of Le'Mar that had been titled a Saneth during Mercius's time already.

He knew it was too soon, but he felt any further delay would have been suicidal. He raised his staff to the sky and a yellow arrow of light flared out into the sky and exploded into many sparks. He was glad that his father did not hesitate and saw the far gates open quickly. Wolves and tigers broke into the plains, followed shortly by the centaurs.

As planned, Horlorn's warriors on the plains moved to the sides of the bowl while fighting, allowing an entrance for the new fighters to break into. Shadowolf continued fighting the orcs surrounding him, grimly aware that Le'Mar would now make his next move.

True to his fears, hundreds of dark horses lined up on the hill. Accompanying the Froth Huns were the blond-haired Dra-hu'Mar, all of them with swords at hand. They waited for the command and then moved down the hill to join the battle.

Chenesia and Lesan rode into battle with hundreds of the elvin archers behind them. Their bows were now strapped to their backs and their swords glistened in their hands. Genewiu rode strong and fast under Chenesia, her wings tucked away at her sides.

Shadowolf continued to strike against as many orcs as he could, delivering death in a dense dance. His staff hit hard against their armour and, where it could, the sharp point pierced skin. His taut nerves reminded him that Froth Huns were nearly upon them and he prepared himself to leave the crowd of orcs.

He looked up and saw the first group of Froths riding towards his general direction. Mandy was galloping to him from behind and he ran forward to time his next strike. As a Froth drew his sword out and brought it horizontal to his neck, Shadowolf rose on the wind and pushed fire into his feet.

He twisted in the air and brought a hard blow with the back of his leg to the skull of the Froth. The beast lurched back in his saddle but still held his head as Shadowolf landed on Mandy's back. He barely had time to duck as a second Froth's sword passed over his head. Warning bells went off inside his head, but a Wreth cut it off as it slammed into Mandy and sent them falling to the ground with a hard thud.

Mandy got up, but Shadowolf could see she was injured. He stood up with some difficulty himself, seeing the Wreth approach him, the beast hungry for the kill. He looked around for the haematite staff, seeing it beneath many orc feet in the battle rolling over the earth.

He clenched his fists watching the Wreth get ready to strike. He breathed calmly, slowly, knowing that he would need the utmost precision to avoid the strikes and, if he was lucky, deal the death blow.

The Wreth drove his fists fast, and within seconds delivered eight blows. The lightning fast fists moved through the air swiftly, the hands narrowly missing Shadowolf's head and chest by mere margins, but the man moved a little faster. His head was a wisp in the wind and at the end his head and chest became as transparent as the air while Shadowolf began the backward flip.

As his head passed back and his legs up into the air, his lower legs became the hardest rock he could manage. His feet connected with the chin of the Wreth, sending him up into the air with a deep groan. Shadowolf was about to launch his secondary attack, but was spared the chance.

A flaming torch soared into the air and struck the falling Wreth from below with its body. The Wreth flew up with the fiery body until it let the beast go and flew away back into battle. Shadowolf didn't wait to see who it was but rose into the air to meet the Wreth. When they collided, he became one with the ethereal armour, hardened it as he passed through the beast and passed through its back.

The Wreth was dead before it reached the ground. The front part of the armour protruded out the beast's back and formed a sickly gap through its chest from which the blood dripped like rain from venous clouds.

Shadowolf landed on the earth, looking for the fiery assistant. Darcwulf was still fighting the Saneth to the side and the more he looked, the less he was able to spot it. His search was cut short when a Froth Hun stepped before him, its skeletal head burning brightly on its shoulders.

He fired up his body in response, the flames licking his skin. The Froth Hun grunted and its skull's fire turned from blue to red. It roared and grabbed the large sword's handle with both hands. Shadowolf in turn summoned a large fire sword to his hands. They stared at each other for a moment, measuring each other up, before the Froth lurched forward.

Shadowolf jumped up from the orc that tried to attack his rear in surprise and landed on its shoulder, avoiding the shield that the orc had hit to his back. He somersaulted over the Froth's sword that entered the orc's head and drove the fire sword into the skull of the

Froth. It exploded, sending the body scattering over the plains and into a few elves that had been fighting nearby.

Before he could land, blond hair whirled into his vision. A blade bit into his right shoulder and Shadowolf fell to the ground. He winced in pain as the blood dripped down his arm. He wanted to focus on the pain, use the earth to close the skin and repair the ruptured veins and muscles, but the Dra-hu'Mar was upon him again.

Darcwulf cried out as the Saneth drove her fist into his face and the sword cut across the surface of his abdomen. She sneered at him as his palm closed over his stomach, the blood like a broken river through his fingers. He ran forward, his vision swimming slightly as he threw fire at her, ball after ball. The first one she slapped away with the back of her hand, but the second hit her on the left shoulder.

She jumped over them, dodging them as she made her way forward. Darcwulf stopped hurling flames and ignored the bleeding as he brought his sword up. Orcs tried to get at him, but he deftly parried and cut them down to get to her.

When he looked up, she was gone. Before he could make a move to look for her, she placed her hands around his neck from the back and pulled. He fell backwards as she rolled on the earth, her legs on his lower back as she vaulted him over her into the air. Darcwulf raised the fire surrounding him as much as he could, getting ready to volley her with it when he landed on the ground again.

His feet landed and he slid back on the ground, his feet scorching the grass and sand and his hand gripping onto the rocks as he tried to stop the momentum. He looked up, growling deep in the flames and his wolf senses smelling for her presence.

He turned around just as his slide was coming to an end and blocked her sword. Flame screeched against metal as they parried and fought, each trying to out-manoeuvre the other. He could see sweat pour down her face as his heat became a raging inferno. He blocked, avoided her blade when it passed through his, and struck where he could, but he knew she would defeat him soon if he could not kill her now.

Shadowolf became wind and blew past the Dra-hu'Mar's side.

When he materialised, his fire sword was whole as he drove it into the beast's lower back beneath its armour. He ducked under another sword, his shoulder aching as he slowly healed it from within. He moved his head to the side, avoiding a liquid ball from a Horlorn elemental and blocked a blow from another Dra-hu'Mar.

The blow was so hard and untimely that his sword fell from his hand, the fire evaporating into the air. Shadowolf stepped back, finally making it to where he wanted to be. The creature turned his sword into a bow, but before he could notch an arrow, Shadowolf leaned down and gripped his haematite staff. He plunged the rod forward, the sharpened tip passing through its throat.

He was then caught off-guard. As if through a silent command, all orcs, Wreths, Froth Huns and Dra-hu'Mar in his vicinity turned and rushed at him. Shadowolf started spinning the staff around him, gaining momentum for the defence. He gritted his teeth, growling deeply. As he brought the rod forward to block the many blows around him, wolves and tigers crashed into the hordes, sending them falling in all directions.

A cry rang through his nerves and time seemed to stand still as he recognised that voice. He tried to look through the new line of beasts rushing at him, but there were so many that not even the light behind them was visible. Not caring who he might injure, Shadowolf gathered water into his rod. It rose from the ground, up the sharp metal tip into its core. His skin gleamed a deep, oceanic blue as his power collected within it.

He swirled the rod and slapped the blunt end on the ground at the feet of the beasts before him. Despite their speed and anticipation, the flood washed them back and any Horlorn warriors that were behind them. His rage knew no bounds as he unleashed the water. His only concern now was to check on Darcwulf.

He flew up into the air and soared over to his brother. Darcwulf lay in a puddle of his own blood, his dormant sword by his side and the fire on his skin slowly dying. Shadowolf fell to his knees and lifted Darcwulf's head onto his lap.

"No, you can't go," Shadowolf cried, his tears falling onto Darcwulf's bald head. He tried to breathe but all life seemed to leave him as well.

"I'm sorry I failed you," his brother replied. "You better take

Falgar's staff before I die."

"No," Shadowolf said, hardly getting the words out as he sobbed. "I don't care about the damned staff! I need you!"

"I'm sorry, Shado," he repeated, coughing in his blood, the fire now mere embers. He smiled softly as the light left his eyes. "Nanoo, na...."

His words died as his head dropped to the side. His mouth lay open and his eyes were empty pools of darkness. Shadowolf sat still, not comprehending what had just happened.

He knew the Saneth was behind him, but for some reason unknown to him she did not attack. She only watched as he cried silently with his brother in his arms. He felt so empty inside that, had she decided to strike, he would not have been able to move to stop her.

Shadowolf watched in horror as Darcwulf's body became ashes in his arms. The dust passed through his fingers and stained his forearms as his brother became a whisper on the earth. He was dumbstruck, sitting there looking at everything transpire.

Something inside him stirred. Compassion and warmth went through his body like the call of love and he knew it was Shedaaij. She had felt his turmoil and was responding to his loss. He looked up and saw Nelnar before him, the wolf staring into his eyes and also passing on his strength and condolences.

The Saneth had turned to face another Horlorn opponent. Shadowolf closed his eyes and wished Darcwulf a silent farewell. In honour of his brother, Shadowolf teleported before the Saneth and drove the end of his staff through her gaping mouth and out the back of her head.

It was a calm fury. It rose from nothing into his veins and powered his arms into action. Like a serene solicitude unnamed and a turbulent transformation uncalled, he broke into the orcs closest to him and handed out death faster than any other on the field.

He went from orc to orc so fast that he was almost invisible, a whir of action as he drove his staff from one orc to another, many times stopping the orcs from killing others. He remained calm, his heart beating steadily and his breathing soft. Orcs fell before him and others raced to stop him only to die on his staff. His movement was so quick that at times it appeared that he killed three orcs at once at varying distances.

The wind stirred and the ashes moved among the grass blades. It became a collective mass that moved among the feet of Le'Mar's army and Horlorn's warriors. It rose and dipped, mingling with the blood of fallen heroes.

Skywolf hit the ground hard before the Saneth that she faced. The beast gave a speech in a tongue she did not understand, but she got on her knees and notched an arrow with the last strength she could manage. The Saneth laughed strangely and slapped the bow away.

The ashes burned softly like soft coals and died again as it floated upon the gentle wind blowing above the sand of the earth. If anyone could have heard it over the noise of battle, it hummed beautifully as the power rose.

Skywolf sat on her knees proudly and stripped the armour off her chest. The blue top reflected the clear skies overhead and her eyes shone brilliantly in the light of the sun as it moved to the west. She spread her arms to either side and waited for her name to pass on to legend.

The ashes landed on the Saneth's feet and it looked down. Skywolf closed her eyes, not realising that the ashes were climbing up the beast's legs. A frown appeared on the beast's alien face and then it howled as fire broke out on it. Skywolf looked up, clearly confused, and rolled away just as the Saneth fell to the ground to douse the fire.

The fire was all-consuming and did not relent. Even though the Saneth's howls died, the fire only appeared to burn brighter and become warmer in the air until there was absolutely nothing left.

Skywolf stood up to see where the other Saneths were. Lucian, Lastgorn, Sorceress and Angelia were standing around equally bemused at the flames by their feet. Simultaneously, the fire winked out around them and flew to the centre of the battlefield. Orcs and Wreths cried out as the fire burned into each of them, their hoarse groans joining those of the Froth Huns's mounts as it scorched their legs.

When the separate lines of fire met at the centre, it formed into the shape of a naked baby. The baby crept up from the sand and slowly grew in size. It became a child, standing up in the flames it was surrounded by. The child shot up into the sky, changing into an adolescent before he became the man he once was.

Light radiated from him, and the flames around his body were more like an aura of fire than anything real. Sharp orange lights burned where his eyes were meant to be. Darcwulf watched the hill, tempted to take his new powers straight to Le'Mar.

Shadowolf turned his awe away when he felt a new heat approach from the hill. Firestroms were moving to them, their fires gracing the grass below with destruction. There were twenty of them, filling the land above for as far as he could see.

As if that was not bad enough, Le'Mar's main force moved from within the Firestroms' bases. Their armour now shimmered with the purple aura. The shimmer was even visible to those without elemental abilities as the armour struggled against the immensity of the creatures' powers.

Shadow Clan members reached him and stood abreast of him. They all stared up at the shark, lion, gorilla and horse heads, hints of despair rising in their spirits when they saw something else.

Deep within the core of each fiery beast was the node that kept the Firestroms in existence. They knew that they would need to separate the heads to get to that core. The problem was that there were elementëls in the form of humans guarding the nodes. The spheres wiggled within the elementëls' abdomens, jostling from side to side in sync with the Firestroms movements.

The gates of Horlorn opened again. Everyone streamed out from within. The pegasi took to the skies with the dragons. The fairies left the comfort of Horlorn's hills. The remaining main force of elves, humans, dwarves and elementals entered the plains. Centaurs thudded with their heavy hooves.

Wings overhead made the Clan look back towards Le'Mar's army. Thousands of troops in the form of orcs, Dra-hu'Mar, Ma-Wreths and Froth Huns marched under the Firestroms to the bowl of the plains. Joining them were the blue fletchlings that rushed to meet the fairies, the remaining wyverns that were eager to battle the dragons, and the black pegators. At the rear were the mighty Shriekers with large, spiked clubs.

Shadowolf dropped his head and sighed.

"We're with you," Nolraldun said by his side. Shadowolf had not even noticed the assassin reach his side, but looked up at his masked face. "I'll take care of the assassins."

Shadowolf looked up. Although he could not see the dreaded stealth killers, he believed that they were around. It did not make him feel any better knowing that he would have to have even more wits about him, but he hoped Nolraldun would deal with them before they could kill anyone.

Shadowolf gripped his staff and looked up with determination, the steel of the haematite gleaming in his eyes.

"Time to give them all I have," he said to no one in particular. "Hopefully I'll have some left for Le'Mar."

CRIES IN THE OCEAN
CHAPTER EIGHT

They crept quietly though the land that was smothered by camps and buildings. Le'Mar's castle stole the view of the skies before them and the beauty of the land was polluted with the armies that lay in wait.

The collective size of the armies was three quarters of the main force now fighting on the plains. The two silent warriors stared with their lupine eyes at the gathered masses, the dark creatures' armour and weapons glinting in the high sun.

Anuxis looked at Simnab briefly and indicated with his eyes that they split up. Simnab nodded and headed left with Orxus, while Cerexus followed Anuxis on padded paws to the right.

Behind them, over the rocks and crannies that formed the hill leading up to the foreland of the castle, clambered the hundreds of Crethans that had survived the canyon battle. Among them were the *Haniegke* that had surrendered and returned their loyalty to Anuxis.

They growled deeply as they approached the crest of the hill and awaited word from beneath the two wolf lords that separated on their own paths. Anxious to kill, the Crethans moved off to the left, not proceeding further than the topmost rocks of the hill, while the *Haniegke* moved to the right.

Quietly, Simnab and Anuxis made their way as close to the castle as they dared. Their human feet barely made a sound on the sand and stone. Their staves glimmered in their hands, aptly being kept away from any obstructions without even a thought. They used all their senses to get to the stairs leading up to the entrance of the castle, and then stepped out in plain view.

The closest orc leaders looked up at the movement and cried

out in alarm. The Ma-Wreths, orcs and Froth Huns in the foreland turned and grunted at the trespassers, moving forward to confront them.

A disturbance in the centre of the armies made them turn around. Cerexus and Orxus had broken into the formations and were tearing into the armour of the beasts with their brimstone teeth. Their eyes flared with the fires of the Underworld.

The dark creatures had just begun to change the direction of attack when a commotion at the rear of the land caught their attention. The wolves rose above rocks and homes rushing to kill as many beasts as they could encounter, the first finding the supple, yet hardy, flesh of the Wreths.

Simnab and Anuxis rose onto the concrete walls on either side of the stairs. When they reached the end overlooking the forces, they jumped with their staves raised above their heads, and brought it down in a fury upon the orcs.

***

The land shivered as the armies battled upon it. The armies of Horlorn drove their weapons and powers upon the hordes of Le'Mar, battling against armour and ethereal shields to bring death to the dark creatures.

Archers ran among the troops, releasing arrows into the necks of their enemies when they found chance to lower their swords. Elves struck true with their swords, weaving a path through the madness. Dwarves found marks for their axes, the infused elements burning into the flesh of their victims where the armour did not prevent it.

Yet, as well as they fought, the armies of Le'Mar were pushing them back to the fortress. The Firestroms' heat were unbearable to all except the *KariemsaPh*'s, and many strove to avoid the incinerating death as they passed over the land. Elementals fought in the air against the Firestroms, struggling to get to the core of the beasts to separate them.

Confounding the terrestrial battle were the deaths from above. Where dragons, wyverns, pegasi and pegators died, warriors tried desperately to run from the fallings shadows. And whoever was trapped beneath the large corpses were instantly slaughtered by the opposing side.

Amidst all the blood and death, the fairies coloured the skies with their beauty, contrasting the power they raised to battle the fletchlings. They flittered and flew in gorgeous swarms, using the other flying entities as shields or bulwarks for surprise attacks.

Angelicus ran on all fours, growling as she raced to assist a Horlorn warrior. Her fur covered her wolf head all the way down over her breasts. Her belly was human, but from her waist down to her knees the fur covered the nude skin she was born with.

Her claws dug into the ground and she jumped and shoved her shoulder into a Froth Hun. The beast dropped its large sword in surprise, leaving the warrior to roll away just as the tip entered the earth.

The Froth Hun recovered and grinned at her maliciously. Unlike the other warriors, his armour was black, but she could detect that the same ethereal shield protected it. It looked taller than the other Froth Huns and spikes rose from its steel shoulder pads.

She realised that her expression was betraying her fear. She closed her maw and growled intensely, her long slender fingers forming fists. The Froth Hun gave a malicious laugh and moved forward.

Angelicus moved faster and jumped the beast on its chest. Digging her lower claws into its legs, she grasped the top of its pectoral armour and pulled before the Froth could react. With a jerk it broke loose, sending the beast and Angelicus falling back to either side.

She rose to see that his chest was open. She could see his skeleton under the long coat that he wore, blue flames circling and burning from within. It floated up from the solar plexus region, along the spine and to the skull where it burned like a torch.

Angelicus moved to finish him off, but stopped when a Shrieker crossed her path. It held a spiked club in its three-fingered hand, the digits fat and long enough to encompass her neck if it wanted to. The Shrieker opened it mouth and screamed.

An invisible barrier jumped up around her body as she cowered back. The ultrasonic waves of the beast's cry battered the shield, tiny ripples reverberating along the surface. She held the psi shield, her mind battling the onslaught in hopes that it would eventually cease.

She cried out as a club hit her shoulder. The shield exploded, sending the Shrieker soaring into the air, but the blood dripped down her arm as she lay in pain. As she stood, an arrow entered her right shoulder and she collapsed to one knee, looking up at a Dra-hu'Mar changing its bow back into a sword.

Lucian removed his sword from an orc's body and blocked another blow. He retreated, realising once again that the Firestroms was nearly upon him. Warriors screamed as the fires consumed them and his face was wet with perspiration.

He circled his wrist and twirled the sword to ward of an orc's blade before striking it into the beast's open belly. Becoming wind, he flew away from the Firestrom and hit the head of a Wreth with a hard gale. The Wreth's head lurched forward, allowing a Horlorn swordsman that moment to severe the giant's knee with his blade.

A Shrieker noticed his passing and screamed at the moving air. Lucian materialised and fell to the ground, the internal sound making his ears ache as he placed both hands over them. Another Shrieker nearby moved to place his kill when Trimistus's Saurex bent down and ripped its head off from behind.

The screaming Shrieker turned and focussed its abnormal vocals on the reptile. The Saurex whined and bent its head in irritation, tried progressing forward but halted when the pitch increased. A Dra-hu'Mar saw the situation and loosed an arrow into the reptile's chest. The beast wailed in pain, but was paralysed by the Shrieker's attack.

The Shrieker heard wings behind it but could not react fast enough. Trimistus landed on the ground and his dragon sword entered the creature from the back, metal screeching through the armour. He grabbed the club from its falling hands and threw it through the air. The Dra-hu'Mar fell to the ground in shock as the spikes entered it forehead.

Trimistus jumped and twisted, trying to avoid the wyvern he heard flying towards him, but the flying beast was quicker. It bit into his wing and tossed him up, tearing at the leathery appendage. He was still able to fly, but it took extra effort to correct himself in the air.

Millon killed another Wreth and looked up at the sky. Wyverns were striking continuously at Trimistus, the reptilian man barely keeping them off him and the dragons too occupied in the skies to assist. Just outside the perimeter of the attack on Trimistus, Millon saw the largest of the group sweep like a serpent in the sky towards them.

Its neck twisted slowly, almost like a snake sliding through a field in preparation for a silent attack. Its fangs were lethal and the look in its eyes deadly. The centaur launched forward, making for one of the Wreths below Trimistus.

The wyvern's neck was ready to lash forward as it broke through the other wyvern's attacking Trimistus. Millon slapped a Froth Hun off its stallion and vaulted onto the horse's back, nearly crushing it with his weight. Using the momentum of the horse's fall, he jumped onto the Wreth's back and pushed hard with his equine legs.

He stretched his arm as high as he could manage and drove his sword through the wyvern's lower jaw just as its fangs flew at Trimistus's face. Trimistus reached out and tried to catch the centaur's hands, forgetting how sturdy his species was. Millon left the proffered hand alone, returning to the earth and landing hard on his legs.

"Trimistus!" Millon shouted as he looked up at shadows stretching in the sky. Arrows entered Trimistus's wings and he yelled in pain. His right wing gave out and he fell to the ground. Millon moved under him and caught him in his arms.

"Don't make this a habit," Millon said.

"Put me down, I'm fine," Trimistus replied, returning his broken wings into his back.

Shadowolf flew beside Darcwulf, both of them making their way to the Firestroms. Their eyes burned with the fervent anxiety to rid the land of the monstrosities before they killed any more warriors. Darcwulf was still a pyric torch while Shadowolf was a gale of enraged wind.

Shadowolf briefly looked down to where Le'Mar stood watching. Their eyes locked, the dark lord tempting him to leave the battle and finally confront him. Shadowolf knew he did not have the power to confront Le'Mar. The dark lord had attacked too early, and he worried that the land's heroes would die before they saw the rising of the sun again.

The brothers entered a Firestrom together, their powers swirling throughout their bodies. Other elementals entered with them and into the other Firestroms too, making for the centre while trying to withstand the heat. The node guards watched them eagerly, but did not flinch even when Shadowolf was upon their one.

The guard evaporated and Shadowolf passed though, but Darcwulf waited until it materialised. He plunged into it with the full force of his powers, fire raging within fire as the guard tumbled away from the node.

Shadowolf gathered the fire from around him to create a sword in his hand and made to attack the shifting node when another guard formed before him. Before the surprise lit his face, the Firestrom formed more elementël guards that attacked every elemental within it.

Just like the morbid litany performed by the orchestra on the land, the Firestrom was a fiery form filled with a torrent of attacks. Shadowolf spent most of time dodging wind, fire, water and earth balls instead of fighting the guards.

He searched for the node. It was bobbing as the Firestrom moved, hardly distinguishable within the fire and among the guards that surrounded it. Shadowolf vanished within the flames, becoming one with the air that fuelled it. Darcwulf slashed with his serpent sword and kicked a guard back, trying tensely to find his brother.

The Firestrom cried out softly like a baby lamb. The sound was so sad and heart-breaking that many on the land, including Le'Mar's forces, looked up at it. The sound amplified till it sounded like a whale calf. Soon, the outer edges of the Firestrom dimmed, the light ebbing towards the centre.

Darcwulf watched pensively at the node, which was all that remained of the Firestrom. It flickered with orange and yellow lights and he could sense Shadowolf's presence within it. The power was remarkable, but he knew it was the Firestrom's power contained within it, and not only Shadowolf's.

Get away!

Darcwulf's eyes went wide at the voice in his head. He started shouting, alerting the other elementals to the danger. They left the guards that circles the node and flew back towards the land, but it was too late. He could not hold it any longer.

The node exploded with magnificent power. The guards and elementals were thrown with such force that they had never encountered before. Even the warriors closest to Horlorn's Gate fell to their knees and turned to watch the walls of the fortress quake as the aftermath washed over it.

The Firestrom was gone. Of the node there was no sign, but the guards still burned brightly on the ground where they hand landed. The other Firestroms still raged with the battles within them.

Shadowolf got up on his hands and knees, shaking his aching head. Feet scurried all around them, but he sensed no danger from them. He looked up through narrow and tired eyes to see the backs of the Clan around him, creating a perimeter of weapons that clashed against the foes trying to break through.

Nelnar nudged its head against his, offering support. Shadowolf obliged by reaching up and grabbing the wolf's bony shoulder until he could stand on his own. There was no sign of his haematite staff.

His loyal wolf realised what he was looking for. Shadowolf had begun to turn around when the transformation happened. He looked down and saw the grey mottled staff lying on the disheveled grass.

"Thank you, my old friend," Shadowolf said, taking the staff and leaning on it for support. He knew the look Nelnar would have given him for the reference to being old and smiled despite his pain.

"Are you ok?" Lastgorn said as he arrived to help him.

"I'll be ok," Shadowolf replied. He looked at the blue falchion in Lastogorn's hand and frowned. "What happened to Scarlette's sword?"

"I got overzealous and broke it in a Wreth's head," Lastgorn smiled sheepishly. "Listen, I think we need to retreat. We're not going to last much longer."

Shadowolf looked over the battlefield, but knew it was unnecessary. Even without Lastgorn's warning it was painfully obvious that they needed the fortress's defence.

"Heula," he called. She finished off her orc and ran to him. "Will you do me the honour of signaling the retreat please?"

"Won't they hunt us down and kill us from the rear?" she asked.

"We will defend the others," he said, a meaningful look in his eye. If this truly was their last stand, he would make sure the others made it to the fortress.

He thought Heula would flinch, but she didn't. With a grim smile, she nodded and raised her hand to the sky. A purple light surged through her aura to her hand and shot a purple ball into the air which exploded among the fighting dragons.

Shadowolf got ready to defend the warriors for the retreat, but stopped when he saw that no one was moving to Horlorn. He was not sure if they were too preoccupied or if they wanted to continue fighting, but not one made any attempt to retreat.

"I guess they're as stubborn as we are," Darcwulf commented.

"Well, we..."

Shadowolf went silent as he felt pain course through him. It was not from the Firestrom attack, but was almost as real. Just as he realised where it was coming from, the orcs managed to break through the Clan's defence and he raised his staff to block the first round of swords....

...and drove the twin daggers into a demon-queen's heart. The trident was stuck in Shedaaij's abdomen and protruded out the back. He took the shaft of the trident and tried pulling it out, but the barbs on the prongs bit into her back.

Are you ok, Shedaaij? James said as he reached her. *I don't think you should rem...*

He looked into her eyes, but it was not her that he saw. He sensed Shadowolf within her and could see the man's power emanating though her eyes.

She'll be ok, Shadowolf said with her voice, trying to be as reassuring as he could. Despite his words, James remained.

He tried using the wind, but her body would not change. It continued to bleed and he could feel the life within her ebbing away. He attempted once again to use the elements, even her own power of earth, but the trident held onto her like a hook.

It's the trident, James said. *Here, hold still. I'll show you.*

James grasped the shaft and waited for Shadowolf to signal him. They drifted to a nearby ledge where it was quiet and not near battle. Shadowolf leaned her body back and grasped the end of the ledge, nodding for him to proceed.

Bubbles sprang from her mouth as James jerked the trident. She cried out again and again as James pulled and by the fourth attempt the trident broke free.

Shadowolf swam to the bed of the cavern they were in. Her organs were injured, but he quickly summoned his powers. This time they responded instantaneously and her body began to heal. Her head slumped forward from exhaustion, but the muscles and organs became whole again. She would live.

Take her away from here, James said with supplication in his eyes. It was the most emotion he had ever seen from the merman.

What about the rest of you? Shadowolf asked

Our time has come, my friend, James said, offering a smile. *I guess legends weren't made to live forever.*

He nodded and wasted no further time. He swam up with her tail and placed her hand on the mer-King's shoulder.

The tale of the mer-Kingdom will live with us for all time.

It won't if you don't get back and defeat Le'Mar, James said sarcastically for old time's sake.

Shedaaij's body shimmered as James turned around to face his enemies one last time…

…and he laid her body gently in the courtyard. She was breathing erratically and he feared for her life. Although he had healed her as best as he could manage, she struggled to hold on. Her will to live was indubitable, but the strength of her body was giving out.

He put the grey staff beside her and waited for Nelnar to arise.

"Stay with her," he instructed with wet eyes. "Make sure you never leave her side, no matter what happens to me."

Nelnar stared into his eyes, clearly wanting to defy his instructions immediately, but its loyalty forbade it to disobey. As Shadowolf vanished, Nelnar lay down and placed its head on its forepaws, watching Shedaaij with the gravest concern.

HEAVEN AND HELL
CHAPTER NINE

Lucian rose up on the wind and entered the Firestrom. He engaged with guards within the fire, matching his strength with theirs and trying to gain the core as quickly as he could. He knew what would happen to him, but they needed to extinguish as many of them as possible.

He defeated three guards and entered the core. Like he had seen Shadowolf do, he drew the energy of the Firestrom from outside the core inward. The Firestrom cried out as he did so until it was fully submerged in the core, and then he released it.

Once again, the land rattled with the release of power, and the guards and elementals were thrown to the ground. Lucian stood up as quickly as his spinning head would allow and raised his staff at the sound of hooves.

"Are you ok?" a female voice asked. He narrowed his eyes, his vision slowly returning. Chenesia looked down from Genewiu's back. She raised her bow and loosed an arrow into an orc behind him before repeating the question.

"Yes, yes, I'm ok," he said. He moved forward and leaned on his staff. Something small moved behind Genewiu into the crowds. He was almost certain it was a little girl, but he knew it could not be.

"What's wrong?" Chenesia said, looking behind her.

"Nothing," he replied. "We need to get back to Horlorn."

She was about to reply when Lucian disappeared into the wind. Her hair blew across her face as he passed her and slammed into a Wreth that had been on its way to them. The jolt of the gale sent it staggering back, but did not push it over. He materialised and made to strike with a blade of wind, but the Ma-Wreth twisted very quickly and hit him across the face with the back of its large fist.

Lucian crashed on the ground, his back making a loud impact. He groaned and swallowed, almost choking as a paper struck his face. He removed the paper and watched as Angelicus bit into the Wreth from the back and taunted it away from the *Enodhim*.

Lucian was about to cast the page aside, when he noticed scribbles on it. A drawing was sketched on the dirty page. On one side there was a large dark figure filling most of the sky and on the other was a similar figure, but burning with flames. Three comet-like figures were stretching towards the fiery figure. Beneath it were written two words:

The Phoenix

"Now's not the time for reading!" Chenesia shouted, offering her hand.

Angelicus flew back as the Wreth smacked her across her cheek. She had barely left the ground when another Wreth rammed into her with its body and sent her groaning to the earth. Shriekers ran to join the group, eager to challenge the powerful Crethan.

She got up and turned in circles, watching the large monsters surround her. She growled deeply, her body weakening but her power still strong. She built it up within her, gathering them in her abdomen.

They must have sensed the large amount of energy emanating from her, for they backed away with great concern etched on their faces. They groaned in fear and started to flee when their armour shimmered in purple sparks.

Angelicus closed her eyes and stretched her arms out as she released the power. The Wreths and Shriekers screamed as they fell, the sparks exploding on their armour. She looked at them in surprise and then her hands, her mind pondering the effect.

The ethereal shields of the four beasts were gone. She searched with her senses, but she was quite certain that it had been eradicated from the armour. To test her theory, she lowered her right palm to a Wreth and sent out branches of lightning from her claws.

The Wreth shook with convulsions as the lightning hit the armour. Foam formed on the corners of its lips and its eyes went completely white. The body became still as the Wreth died, only shaking slightly from the lightning. Angelicus grinned and left to find more victims.

Shadowolf stepped onto Sky Tier's platform, watching the war on the plains before him. The sounds that reached him were in discord with the view because of the distance, but it did not make the horror any less real. The sun had dipped low enough to cover most of the land in the bowl in shadow. There were none on the field to provide light, save for the fury of the dragons and the might of the elementals.

A rush of air blew the hair across his vision as Glasden and the gargoyles ran for the edge of the tier and jumped over it. They landed hard onto Mountain Tier, not wasting the breath humans would take to recuperate and plummeted over that edge too.

When they reached the gates of the outer wall, Glasden stopped. Shadowolf looked up too, feeling the surgence of power from the opposite hill. He moved just in time as Le'Mar's fist flew to his face, ducking under another swipe and jumping away from a ball of water. He became wind, hoping the next orb of fire would pass through him like so many other times, but somehow the orb struck him and sent him hurtling into the hill.

Glasden looked up, his comrades already having left him behind for the battle on the plains. He saw the rock and soil topple over Shadowolf and ran back towards the Tiers. When he reached the side of the hill he dug his stony fingers into it, clambering his way up to them.

Shadowolf exploded from the hill, sending debris towards where Le'Mar had been a moment ago, and flew up to avoid the huge hand made of rock from the hill. It slammed into the concrete of the tier, cracking the fine handiwork of the dwarves and sending rocks falling down over Glasden.

Le'Mar soared out of the sand of the hill, silver sword glistening in his hand. Balls of fire were flying from his other hand, Shadowolf running along the hillside horizontally as they landed in the wake of his footsteps. He twisted just in time, wings breaking from his back, and blocked a strike with a summoned fire sword of his own.

Glasden removed his arm from above him, the debris having stopped. He started climbing again, but a crash resounded close behind him. He saw a dying dragon in the remains of what had been the outer gate and surrounding wall. Four wyverns had taken it down and were now making their way up to the two combatants.

The gargoyle gripped the hill in anger. He had lusted for battle the whole day and had finally joined it when the costs were too high. He closed his eyes, fury burning in his veins. His skin took on a stony exterior, his muscles bulging as his anger rose. He kicked off from the hillside, reaching with his grey arms to the closest wyvern and grabbed onto its neck.

The creature wailed in annoyance, making the other three turn their long slender heads in its direction. They changed their flight and flew at Glasden. The gargoyle jumped over a snapping head and drove his fist down into its back. The hand extended into a long, concrete spear that cracked the wyvern's massive spine and sent the beast falling to the ground.

He kicked off its back, pulling his head back just as a claw raked at his face. He grabbed the leg with his arms, athletically flipping himself higher into the air. Another wyvern opened its jaws to bite into him, but he extended the spear into its throat. It died on his arm and he retracted it, the corpse falling to the floor.

Le'Mar was faster than Shadowolf, his sword singing a legacy as its metal swept the fire blade away time and time again until the sword struck true into Shadowolf's shoulder. He turned the flesh into sand just before the metal bit in, but a sharp pain forced him to scream in pain and sink to one knee on the Port Tier.

Le'Mar let go of the sword, laughing softly. Shadowolf couldn't transform the sand of his shoulder. The blood ran from it like rivulets, coating the metal with its life. The pain still ran through his nerves as if they were there. He looked up at the dark lord through tears that welled up in his eyes because of the agony.

"You've amused me," Le'Mar said, but it was a tone that Shadowolf didn't recognise. His visage appeared darker, and he was not sure if it was because the pain blurred his vision. He shifted what power he could to his eyes. Le'Mar's aura was so dark that it sucked what light there was into it.

"I thought there would be more to the war than this. Perhaps if I had waited until morning you would have been more of a challenge."

Le'Mar looked at him in contempt and before returning his gaze to the plains again.

"My rule would have been so peaceful if these people just learned to obey. Is it so bad having me as your god? You worship a non-entity that cannot even defend you at your greatest peril. Yet here I am. Triumphant. Omnipotent.

"Where is your Bontu now?" he continued to taunt him. He walked over to Shadowolf, taking a lock of hair in his hands and jerking it up until their eyes met. "You have raised them to defy me. It is because of you that they die now. Are you satisfied? Do you not feel joy at having accomplished your purpose?"

Shadowolf did not reply. His breathing became shallow as he drew his power into the core of his spirit. He closed his eyes and his life waned, removing any energy from his aura and body into his central life-force in his solar plexus.

"You are done, boy," Le'Mar said, dropping his head and walking to the edge of the tier. "I've taking everything from you. Do you think the lives of my warriors worry me? I have lost nothing but troublesome beasts. Nothing valuable has been taking from me. But you....."

He laughed again and raised his hands to the dark sky.

"It's still twelve hours before you will see the rising of the sun. I'm afraid I don't have that much patience. This façade must now come to an end. Tell me if you still doubt that I am the *Sadgi* after this."

Shadowolf watched, his eyes void of life. His breathing had all but come to a stop as Le'Mar began summoning the elements. He closed his tired eyes, using the spirit to watch through the proceedings.

The world looked so different through the eyes of his spirit. Blue and white shades covered the land with life as the warriors of the earth stood still. The darker red auras halted their attacks too as the earth began to quake. Shadowolf could feel the fear rising throughout the land, even those that belonged to Le'Mar.

While the dark lord prepared his demonstration, Shadowolf reached out with his hand behind him and touched the hill's sand and rock. He released his remaining power and let it seep into the earth. When he was depleted, he started drawing forth nature's essence, storing it as deep in his core as he could in the hopes that Le'Mar would not detect it.

The earth reacted to his summons, although Shadowolf could feel that it ached in doing so. Le'Mar had power over it, and Shadowolf knew that that was where the dark lord was making his mistake. Rocks rose into the air and vines broke free from it. The plates of the earth started moving apart, causing chasms on the plains to form. And still, the earth fed Shadowolf its essence.

Fire boiled up from the chasms and the sky turned red. Large comets of fire fell down to the earth, scorching the land and killing any that couldn't get out of its path. The flames screeched and seared the earth in agony, the elements raging against each other in Le'Mar's command. Lava broke out around Shadowolf from the hill, and fed its essence to him.

As the warriors of Horlorn's Gate ran in fear towards the hill, the beasts of the darkness running behind them in equal trepidation, the air twisted fiercely into a small tornado, gathering force until it reached up into the sky and tore at the earth and fire that raged around it. Rock and flame joined the twirling horror. The air threw the racing hordes off their feet, whistling in agony. Shadowolf breathed calmly, deeply, as the air offered its essence.

Clouds formed among the chaos, adding its rain to the floods that broke onto the surface off the earth. The hill around the fortress burst open with waterfalls, rushing towards the surviving warriors that were now surrounded by the chaos of elements. They could do nothing as the fire attempt to eat them, the wind attempting to throw them in disarray, the earth wanting to destroy them with its power and the water crying to drown them. The rain fell on Shadowolf's face, cleansing him with its essence.

Le'Mar dropped his arms. The tornado fell away. The earth stopped quaking, huge cracks remaining where the plates had split. The water ran into those charms, the land drying where warriors that had not died either lied on their backs breathing hoarsely or sat on their hands and knees.

He turned to face Shadowolf. He felt no power from the younger man and smiled maliciously before facing the plains for the last instruction.

"Kill them," he said softly. "Kill them all."

No one moved. The orcs and Wreths clutched what weapons they could find, but just stared at the warriors of the earth. Even the Froth Huns that now got to their feet shifted their gaze between the humans and Le'Mar.

"I SAID KILL THEM!!!" he shouted, his voice carrying over the plains.

Yet again, his army did not move to obey the instruction. Instead, they dropped their weapons in defiance, joined shortly by Horlorn's army. The two groups melded into one and turned to face the dark lord high up on the tier.

Back to the east, where Anuxis and Simnab stood among the armies of the castle, the beast's raised their hands and dropped their weapons too. The two warriors stared at them in confusion, but halted their attacks.

"Very well," Le'Mar said, constraining his anger. "Let this world die and be consumed."

Once again he raised his arms. A dark fog started to form on the surface of the plains. It coiled and turned upon itself as it gained substance, moving swiftly over the land and eventually Dwarf Mountains. Shadowolf could feel that it was going further south, reaching over the entire continent until not one part of it was left untouched.

Deep growls resonated over the land. As the fog dissipated, dark spirits with red, burning eyes were revealed. They covered all of the plains and the lands south of Dwarf Mountains, ready to destroy nature and anything that came across their paths.

The dark lord turned quickly as he heard a movement behind him. Shadowolf had risen to his feet, but for all Le'Mar could tell he was still weak and powerless. Shadowolf looked up at the sky, his hand pulling out the sword in his shoulder and dropping it on the platform.

"Your turn," he said to the sky, causing Le'Mar to look up too.

The sky cracked with thunder and broke out with lightning. The seams of the clouds seemed to tear open as light shone forth onto the land. Le'Mar narrowed his eyes at the blinding light. He could hear wings and wheels, a thunderous roar towards the plain, but it wasn't until the window in the heavens closed until he realised what was happening.

Armies of angels stormed down upon the demons. He had barely taken cognisance of their presence when they drove their swords and chains onto the evil beasts and battled them on the earth. Le'Mar panicked, his hands clenching the rim of the ledge before him.

Leading the divine armies was a large carriage pulled by nine horses in rows of threes. The fury of heaven shone from the carriage as the horses rode upon the clouds of the sky onto the earth, and holding the reins of the horses was Masara.

He turned in anger to finish Shadowolf off when the sight caught him off-guard. Shadowolf was burning with an intense blue light. Le'Mar almost thought there was two of him in one being, but the other form seemed to be feminine in nature. He tried to utter words in defiance, but only croaked.

Something made him look up. As dark as the night was, something shifted in the sky. He heard the supersonic sounds of hundreds of bats. They flowed over the top of Horlorn's hill and flew with such speed to the battle field that even he had a hard time tracking them with his sight.

"AAAHHH!!!!" he screamed as Shedaaij's twin daggers bit into his chest. Long chains that flowed like lava joined the daggers to Shadowolf's hands. Le'Mar's tried to pry the daggers from his chest, groaning in agony as he failed.

Shadowolf ran to the edge of the tier and jumped, spinning in the air like a cyclone and yanked Le'Mar up with him. When they had done three full circles, Le'Mar's cries flooding the plains, Shadowolf pulled the daggers free. Le'Mar soared into the sky towards the bats just as one of them transformed.

Nellice flew hard into Le'Mar's body, both of them tumbling towards the earth at a speed greater than the earth's escape velocity. The angels in the area where they headed vanished, the ground shuddering where they made contact. The demons were less fortunate. They scattered and exploded, the remaining demons left to face the reappearing angels.

Glasden rose higher in the air upon the back of a dragon, having scaled more wyverns in the battle of the skies. He jumped off the dragon's back, thumping his fist into another wyvern. His skin started to glow, his fury shining from within. He soared over the dead wyvern, the wind striking his face.

He clenched the muscles of his back and gnawed his teeth. Three wyverns rose up to him, all eager to kill him. He waited for the moment when they struck and kicked his feet onto the top of its head, forcing his body into a somersault. At the apex of his turn, wings broke from the cracks on his shoulder blades. It spread out in glory and light as he propelled his speared hands along its back and jumped off again.

Nellice and Le'Mar were now just flickers in the night, their power and speed surpassing anyone's senses. Arcs and flashes of light erupted spasmodically where their powers clashed. Many times the aVampeyer had almost sunk his teeth in Le'Mar's flesh, nearly drove the sword into his chest, but the dark lord was always one step faster.

The other aVampyere had more success with the angels against the demons as the warriors returned to the fortress, out of the struggle with which they could not contend. They watched in awe and horror at the battle before them, uncertain of what the outcome would be, but knowing it would only end with Le'Mar's victory or defeat.

When they looked around, they saw that the dark lord's minions were among them. Orcs and Dra-hu'Mar looked back at them, baffled by their circumstances. The only creatures that were absent were the Firestroms, who seemed to have mysteriously left the plains with no evidence of where they had gone.

A streak of light lit the sky above them, and the two opposing forces looked up to see Shadowolf leave to face Le'Mar once last time…

THE SOUL OF THE *SADGI*
CHAPTER TEN

Le'Mar managed to shove Nellice away from him and was preparing a counterattack when Shadowolf plunged into him. Le'Mar broke free, summoning a sword quick enough to block Shadowolf's blade of fire. He kicked Shadowolf away against the chest, twisting to cut into the aVampeyer who had attempted to attack from below.

To those on the land, the battle was mere flashes of light, quick successions of combat that they could not follow. To the three combatants, to whom speed was nothing but flecks of dust, their fighting and movements seemed so natural. The elements surged from hands, fire and wind competing to kill their targets, the skies roaring in power and rage.

Le'Mar attempted to teleport back to his hill, his feet landing on the ground just as Shadowolf teleported behind him and Nellice materialised before him. Le'Mar exploded with a barrier of power, sending the two assailants flying in opposite directions despite their vigilance.

Shadowolf jumped up, ready to face him again, but the same power that caused Nellice to hold back made him stop. Arcane energy flowed through the dark lord's body, but it was not aimed at them. It lashed out of Le'Mar's skin, staining the air with tinges of red like solar flares.

Shadowolf turned as the power coalesced on the hill below him. The air shimmered as the soil gathered up from the earth. The monster grew higher until its head was near the clouds, fire and brimstone belching from its mouth and crude horns as high as Dwarf Mountains on its head.

The Saemnati, one of the prince lords of the demonic realms, rolled its giant rocky hands into fists, fires burning from the depths of its core. Its cavernous sockets for eyes looked down at the two men who stood alone on the hill before it.

Shadowolf flew out of the hand's way as it fell down on them. He rose up higher, dodging the beast's rampage. He was by its chest, hoping to make its face, when a shot of flame broke out from the rock and wrapped itself around his body. Shadowolf tried to become wind, but his body only shimmered as the flame pulled him in.

He cried out in agony as the demon's power ripped through him. It was not only through his body that the assault occurred, but he could feel the loss and damnation through his spirit too. He tried to contain his power, as it felt wild and uncontrollable inside of him.

He gasped as something hit his body hard. He escaped the demon's innards, Darcwulf clutching him in his grasp and flying down to the ground with him. They landed on the earth and saw the elementals of Horlorn and the aVampyere attacking the beast from every possible avenue. Balls of lightning, fire, water, wind and earth crashed into it, but the Saemnati grunted and spread his arms out wide.

Similar to Le'Mar's earlier action, a barrier of fire arced out from it and sent the combatants soaring back to the ground. Shadowolf could see that the strike had been fatal in some cases, the corpses falling helplessly through the air.

The Saemnati proceeded towards the ruins of Horlorn's Gate. When it descended the hill and entered the bowl, the warriors still within the ruins, together with Le'Mar's former army, rushed to meet the demon in battle. The demons that were battling the angels retreated to the prince, climbing up its legs and entering the fires within it. The beast's power increased with every consumption, and yet the land's warriors charged to defeat it.

Darcwulf soared back as Le'Mar swept his palm before him. Nellice made to move, but Le'Mar's eyes gazed at him and the aVampeyer fell to his knees on the ground, clutching his ears in pain. Shadowolf stepped back, but his legs gave in and he fell on his back, watching as Le'Mar stood over him.

"Anymore tricks, *Sadgi*?" he asked in contempt. He stretched his palm out to Shadowolf. There was no exterior evidence of

Le'Mar's act, but Shadowolf convulsed as the power tormented him from within, wrecking his own power he held within his soul. Shedaaij's voice cried out and Le'Mar tortured her too, the united souls writhing on the ground like an enraged snake.

Le'Mar pulled his hand back, seeing a sword lying in the red-stained grass nearby. He aimed his hand at hit and it flew into his grasp. Shadowolf couldn't open his eyes, his lips quivering from weakness. Le'Mar raised his sword up high.

"Goodbye, saviour of the world," Le'Mar smirked. He dropped the sword down and, in mid-descent, the tip tilted and entered the dark lord's abdomen.

Le'Mar spluttered and fell back, looking down at the blood forming on his hands. He yanked the sword out so that he could heal, throwing it away. Where it landed, the metal stood up on four legs as it transformed. Nelnar growled deeply at the dark lord, whose wound would not seal.

The dark lord cursed and turned to see the spirit of Masara behind him. The old saint merely stared with an abyss of glorious light at him, penetrating his eyes with such purity that it stung him. Le'Mar raised his palm to banish his spirit, his power rising to conquer Masara forever.

"I offer the last of my power to thee," Masara said, throwing Le'Mar off-guard. He momentarily forgot the power that he had collected in his hand and it suddenly exploded before him, throwing him over Shadowolf's body to the other side of the field.

Masara knelt and placed his palm on Shadowolf's forehead. The power leaked into him, and as it reached its end, Masara began to fade.

"There's too much time, Masara," Shadowolf coughed. "How must I hold out until the sun rises?"

"Why are you waiting for the sunrise," the old man smiled, "when it's waiting for you?"

"Isn't that when I obtain the power of the *Sadgi*?" Shadowolf asked, dazed and confused.

"You will become *Sadgi* when you are ready to obtain it, my boy," Masara said, "when you are ready to accept that destiny. There are no confines or limits."

Shadowolf wanted to question him further, to interrogate his annoyingly mysterious words. Masara's smile kept him placated though and he nodded. The light that kept Masara's spirit visible faded as the last of his energy entered Shadowolf. And then he was gone.

"You better get up," Darcwulf said nearby.

He rose from the ground. Nellice stood beside him too with Nelnar before them. As he watched Le'Mar, footsteps announced the arrival of the other members of the Clan. They stood alongside the group, their eyes fixed on the dark lord.

He stood with his hood on, his head lowered. His hands were clasped before him, fingers entwined. The fog that he had kept over the land for so many years was seeping from him, creeping over the land and around his immediate proximity.

He became the fog. His form grew, shaping into a dark wraith that extended up into the sky. Shadowolf could feel that all Le'Mar's power was being released into the demonic shape. This was the dark lord's last attempt at victory. It was also Shadowolf's last chance to defeat him.

Shadowolf flew up into the air and burst into flames. He joined Le'Mar in the release of energy, filling the sky above him with the glory of his spirit. Le'Mar's transformation was nearing at an end, but Shadowolf was only half-way done with releasing his power.

Darcwulf jumped into the air and flew like a comet into Shadowolf's flames. Lucian saw the shape and remembered the sketch he had seen on the battlefield, suddenly realising what he had to do. He signaled to Sorceress and Fransiska, and together the three of them flew up. Water, wind and earth joined the large phoenix that faced the wraith, their powers facilitating the formation.

The Clan scattered as the wraith engaged the phoenix. The two clouds of power engulfed each other in battle, causing the earth to quake once more. The tremors seemed to even rock the sky, light causing havoc on the air. Everyone fell down within the bowl, either suffocating from the lack of air or from the immense release of power. The angels merely watched and prepared their chains as the demons wailed and rolled on the ground in agony. The Saemnati glanced at the battle and started to make its way back towards them.

Le'Mar erupted with almighty power and the phoenix fell back from the dark cloud. The fog dispersed from the wraith without taking any power from it, covering and corrupting the land as it passed over it. Somehow, Le'Mar increased his power again, choking those on the earth until they were breaths away from death.

Suddenly the balance shifted, and the fog was no more. Blue mists flowed over the land as Shadowolf imploded with power. Le'Mar, Darcwulf, Lucian, Sorceress and Fransiska hurtled to the ground and landed with hard thuds that nearly killed them. The essence of the mist covered the continent as they tried to regain their senses.

The demons cried out as the sanctity touched them. They strove to enter the Saemnati but most didn't make it before the mist caused them to writhe in pain. The prince of demons howled as the mist entered it, its hands moving momentarily to its head.

There was no explosion or convulsion as most on the land expected. The Saemnati just vanished. Where it had stood, sprays of vapour poured down lightly in the mist as if the prince had merely been an inconvenience.

Le'Mar looked up fearfully. He was not on the hill anymore, that much was obvious to him. An ancient forest of power surrounded him from which the mist seemed to flow. He thought long and hard about where he could be, his senses warning him that he was in the deepest part of what he had named the Dark Boundary.

"This was where it all started," a voice said from the mist. It sounded almost like the words had formed from the mist itself, but Le'Mar wondered if that was possible. "The Nether Region, where Bentley had started life for man and the elves. For it was from him that both were formed."

Four figures emerged within the mist, although Le'Mar could only make out their silhouettes. He was still trying to work out which of the four had spoken, when the one on the furthest right moved suddenly and drove something deep into his right leg.

Le'Mar screamed, but no sound disturbed the trees or the mist. The object pinned him against the trunk of a large tree. He looked down and saw a dagger in his leg protruding out the back into the tree itself. Lucian's mystical eyes pierced the dark lord's, his hands clutching the wind of the Dagger of Bentley.

He struggled to breath. The air escaped his lungs and, as much as he tried to force air in or create it within him, the element did not respond. His eyes became foggy, but there was enough breath in him to cry out in silence again as another object pierced his left leg into the tree. This time it was the Staff of Falgar, Darcwulf's hand clutching the wood.

He became cold, very cold. His body began to shiver as the flame of life left him. He tried to control it, tried to force the element to remain within him, but it would not obey. Like the people of Celenic Earth, it would not obey. He tried to raise his hand, just a simple effort to grab Darcwulf, but the Horn of Masara entered his right shoulder, pinning his back firmly against the tree.

His skin aged, his body starting to decompose. Sorceress stepped back and let Fransiska shoot an arrow into his left shoulder. He had no strength to even attempt a shout. He sagged against the tree, his head resting on it as if it were a pillow. Le'Mar's body died, his head went limp and drooped onto his chest, but his spirit continued to linger.

Le'Mar tried to move his spirit, but the weapons kept him on the tree. He tried screaming again, his mouth open wide as the four retreated to allow a fifth shadow to emerge from the mist. No sound collected around him or came from his throat. He wondered if he was deaf, but the approach of the fifth person silenced any further considerations.

"So you're the *Sadgi*?" Shadowolf's mouth moved, but it was not his voice. Le'Mar stared into his eyes that shone like those of a deity, awed by its brilliance and beauty. He could not help but listen, as if the exquisite wonder of it commanded obeisance.

"This can't be," Le'Mar uttered, his own voice fragile. "The prophecy..."

"...never said I had to be the *Sadgi* to defeat you," Shadowolf interrupted. This time, Le'Mar recognised his voice as Shadowolf's. "It merely stated that I would accomplish both. I received the power four years ago at the power node, which was rightfully mine at birth. All I needed was to understand it and learn to use it to its full potential."

"But how?"

"You never quite grasped the significance of the *Sadgi*," the other voice said. "The elements were never meant to be commanded and controlled the way you did. I never gave you powers for you to abuse them."

"Then why was I permitted these powers if I could not use them as I wished?"

"Your powers are your gift from me," the voice continued. "I cannot force you to use them as I wished you would. Your destiny and your choices are your own. Even with him inside of you, you always had a choice to let it go. To return to me."

"Why would I want to return to you?" Le'Mar asked, the pitch of his voice rising in anger. "You took my father from me. You destroyed everything I loved!"

"Did I?" the voiced asked. "Was it I that told T'Mar to sell his soul to him?"

"Was it Bontu that wanted T'Mar to kill Masara, when Bontu willed that Masara stop T'Mar before the darkness consumed him?" Shadowolf asked.

"Have I ever forced you to make any of the decisions you made?" the voice continued from Shadowolf's mouth. "When your father died, you could have turned to me to heal your pain. Even after you learnt the truth of the darkness, you still refused to return to me."

"Well it's over now," Le'Mar said. "Have your way with me and be done with it."

Shadowolf stepped closer, a comforting smile on his face. His eyes held sorrow that a million stars could not portray, his face a grief that a thousand suns could not signify.

"Shadowolf offered you a chance to be redeemed before," the voice said, raising Shadowolf's hand to gently touch Le'Mar's cheek, "but I am now offering you that chance myself. The same offer I granted your father when he died."

Le'Mar looked up quickly. His heart softened as he looked into Shadowolf's eyes.

"I don't understand. You've never interfered before."

"And I haven't interfered thus far," the voice said slyly. "Shadowolf defeated you on his own, with the choices that he made. But he chose to ask for help. That is the only thing keeping you from me now. Your pride."

Le'Mar wasn't sure if he could forgive himself, let alone ask anyone else for forgiveness. He lowered his ethereal head, noticing that there was nothing left of his physical body.

"What of the chaos I've created?" he pursued. "I've destroyed the earth. I've nearly killed everyone."

"Don't you have faith in me?"

Le'Mar knew He was right. He could have recreated everything with a blink of an eye or just a thought. He could have gone back in time and stopped the first sin, preventing ages of chaos that followed. It was not something Le'Mar understood fully, but he knew with a certainty that Bontu could correct everything he had done, for he was a mere man after all.

"Is my father with you?" he asked.

"Why don't you come find out yourself?" the voice asked, love trailing in the words' wake.

"I think I'll do just that," Le'Mar said and started to move when he screwed his face in pain. His head dislodged from another being inside him, but black tendrils gripped his hair, forcing him to move back "I want to be with you again, lord. Give me the grace to overcome my demons."

Shadowolf smiled and diverted his gaze to the demon. The darkness cried out only for a moment before subsiding and releasing Le'Mar's head. Le'Mar passed through the weapons that held him to the tree and joined Shadowolf's side.

"What of the beast?" he asked.

"It will be Shadowolf's glory," the voice replied, "but of that you will bear witness later. Would you like to see the *Sadgi*?"

"Isn't that only in a few hours?"

"I am time, and time holds no limits over me. As you can see, the sun is already rising."

Le'Mar looked and saw the world come to a standstill. Everyone stopped breathing and their lives came to a halt as the sun rose for the first time that day. Shadowolf stepped forward, leaving behind the deity that had spoken through him. Le'Mar saw the light of Bontu, free of Shadowolf's form, and it made him joyful.

Shadowolf rose into the air, but not of his own volition. His body became pure earth, filled with the essence of nature. Le'Mar could feel that Shadowolf was not forcing or summoning the earth to his command; the element seemed to pass into him freely as if it longed to do so.

The other elements soon followed. Fire entered his soul from within, the flames lighting up the earth from below the soil and grass without destroying the flowers on the surface. Wind passed through the cores of the earth and fire, urging the elements to a greater level of power. Water passed through all three off them, seemingly unaffected by the presence of the serene fire.

Shadowolf descended to the forest floor. The light of his soul joined the four elements, bringing them under its power. They submitted to his will in love and without any inhibition, changing his elemental form to one of the purest, brightest light.

He approached the demon against the tree and, without any show or announcement, summoned Ruben-Willow from his soul and drove the sword into the heart of the beast. The demon cried out one last agonising scream, and then went limp. Its form turned to ethereal dust, little flakes of stars, along with the five weapons that were submerged in it. In the end, there was no trace of its existence upon the bark of the tree.

"Why did you never approach that sweet girl in Carmel you were so fond of as a teenager?" Bontu asked as He and Le'Mar started walking away.

"Who, Wental?" Le'Mar laughed, their forms fading as they passed into a different realm. "I guess I was too shy. Besides, I …"

They disappeared from sight. The mist flowed away from them and soon Shadowolf and his companions found themselves standing on Le'Mar's hill overlooking the bowl. The sun set again in the east, and they waited in silence for it to rise again. When it did, the land came to life again without any of them realising that time had stopped.

The Clan gathered around the five, looking for signs of Le'Mar or the demons. The other creatures of the dark lord's army still stood among Horlorn's warriors, but no one made a move to fight them. They couldn't, because they were surrounded and entrenched in snow.

Darcwulf waded through the snow, feeling the knee deep substance with his fingers. He expected it to be cold, to sting him specifically because of his affinity to fire. Yet it was comforting to touch and put him at ease.

"It will take time for the land to heal," Shadowolf said, and then looked at his body, "and our wounds. Physical and emotional."

"Such is the way of things," Elgoth said as he topped the hill with Ursula by his side. "This snow will help the earth to heal."

"Why isn't it cold?" Fransiska asked.

"Because it contains all of the elements necessary for life," Shadowolf replied. "It will be a while before the animals return and this land starts producing food again, but with all the elementals' assistance, that shouldn't be a problem."

Mynisna, Asgorna and Trimistus landed by them. Shadowolf was amazed that the dragons did not look tired at all. Even after the awakening of his powers at the rising of the sun, he still felt like he needed a month's sleep.

"We're heading back," Trimistus announced. Shadowolf looked up at Asgorna, still very conscious of the debt he owed the former Dragon King. He was about to announce his decision to help them, when Asgorna cut him short.

"I'll be staying behind," he said, which made Shadowolf raise his eyebrows in surprise. "I think the kingdoms can do without me for a while. Besides, there's a nice cave at the bottom of the Strip which has recently been vacated."

"You might have to clean it up a bit," Lucian laughed.

Chenesia and Genewiu walked up onto the hill. They both looked exhausted, but each of them offered a smile in greeting.

"I assume it's over?" Chenesia asked.

"It's over," Shadowolf confirmed, embracing her in greeting.

"Not quite," Darcwulf said.

"Oh yes," Shadowolf added. "I was hoping you had forgotten."

"No, I still need to go," he said.

"Well, we're ready to leave when you are."

They stayed the night within Horlorn's Gate, deciding to only leave the following day. The people of Celenic Earth had unanimously decided to accept the orcs, Wreths and other beasts into their cities without dispute. Leaders were selected from each race and a Celenic Council was formed.

Shedaaij informed the Clan that James had survived the war on the mer-Kingdom. The remaining sirens left the oceans surrounding the continent, but the mer-King had no hope that they would not return one day.

Anuxis greeted them as the Clan gathered on Sky Tier. Simnab thanked him for entrusting the Crethans to his care and the lord of the Underworld left on Cerexus's back. Angelicus stood proudly among the Crethans bidding the wolf-lord farewell.

"I guess this is it," Shadowolf said as Darcwulf, Fransiska and Tyler prepared to leave. The dark horse Darcwulf had acquired skittered anxiously beside Mandy, but unfortunately the stallion had to be left behind.

"I'll message you some time," Darcwulf laughed as he embraced his brother. "I hear the elves will be moving into Eldor's Forest with the Elders?"

"I believe that's the case," Shadowolf confirmed. "Will be nice to have them with us for a change."

"Depends on how you look at it," he jibed. The family took turns embracing each member of the Clan and then made their way over to the dragons.

"Nanoo," Darcwulf said.

"Nanoo," Shadowolf greeted and watched as they lifted off. The dragons and wyverns made for the skies. They watched as the flying monsters flew over the hill towards Bentley Strip.

The Clan went back inside, leaving Shadowolf alone with Shedaaij, Crystal and Nelnar. He smiled at her fondly as he put his arms around them.

"Shall we get married?" he asked, trying not to laugh.

"Oh, but you are romantic," she replied sarcastically, slapping his arm.

"Well, we're practically married already!" he said, smiling broadly.

"Still!" she said, pulling out of his arms. "Ask me again next week, and you better make it special."

He put his arms around her again as she put her head on his chest. They walked into Horlorn, ready to start a peaceful life together.

XXX...XXX...XXX...XXX...XXX

ANNEXURE A
HOW THE APOSTROPHETIC
PRONOUNS DEVELOPED

Through many centuries the elegance of our language has advanced, based on the standard of the humans. The language during the original Falgoth Age was mostly based on the elvin lore. Bentley, when he was awakened on the shores of the River of Light and was led to the elvin forest located west of the river, was nurtured in their ways.

Many centuries later, after the fall and separation from the elves, Masara developed runes. Runes were an adaptation of the elvin scripture, but simplified to assist those that forgotten the ancient ways. The Masaran Age brought many changes to the accepted norm of living. Some of them were welcomed, yet he still applied strict rules to the use of the elements, and condemned anything that aspired against Bontu.

This was one of the reasons for the fatal battle that ensued between Masara and T'Mar.

At the Age of Celene, a new system developed to adapt to the ever-changing civilisation. Insignia's assigned to the 'shai' syllable were reduced, as the 'shai' pronouns started becoming popular amongst the people. In the end, it was widely accepted that the apostrophe would serve as the 'shai' syllable.

Therefore, names such as Marsshainar and Teshaimar were reduced to Mars'Nar and T'Mar. The rules for the use of the apostrophe, the reduction of vowels and the capitalisation of consonants are the key focuses of this chapter...

- The Asbec Study of Celenas: Its influence on modernism
             Part B: The Evolved Language
Chapter 6: The Integrated Pronoun
By Farnerd Malerus

ANNEXURE B
NOTE ON THE MASARAN PHENOMENON

Ringos is a small planet, although how small no one is sure. Its natural orbit in the solar system is around the central sun known as Creotos, as is the earth's. The only problem with the orbit of Ringos is that it differs from year to year, called the four cycles.

No one knows how far into the universe the planet orbits till it returns, but the known factor is that the sun is its central core of gravity. I have read a scholar make note in his thesis that perhaps the planet only has once cycle, and that the cycle takes four earth years to reach us. If that were so, several conclusions could be reached:

1.   That the orbit of Ringos takes the planet out to the far reaches of not only the solar system, but also the galaxy. A period of four years to return to earth is rather astronomical, but not impossible if the distance were attainable.

2.   That the sun's gravity is extremely powerful to allow the planet to travel so far and not release it into the unknown universe. If this were so, how could man possibly survive such a force on a planet so close to the source of power?

3.   That, because the planet circles earth and is thrown back into the system before it reaches the sun, it could be concluded that either:

a)   The earth interferes with the orbit of Ringos, in which case it cancels out point 2, the power of the sun's gravity;

b)   The earth itself is the planet's central core. In this case, it does seem strange that the planet only return to its core in fours years, and veers off into the universe. It would then have to be concluded further that the earth itself has an astronomical gravitational force and should in essence itself be a sun or dwarf star. This last point is however considered the most preposterous, as it creates a loophole, justifying once again the sun's immense power to orbit another sun in its presence. The solar system, in theory, should collapse upon itself.

Through the centuries, one possibility has survived the raptures of time, and this theory has been aptly supported by the sages of our world, including Masara. And that is the theory of Penoplus, better known in the last century as the Masaran Phenomenon.

The theory goes as follows, in the words of Masara:

Ringos orbits around the sun in four cycles. Its first orbit carries the planet far away from earth in a wide arc. On the second and third cycles, however, the planet closes in on ours and by the fourth its trajectory carries it towards earth. It does not collide with the earth, but its path is close enough for the earth's gravity to slow down its journey around the sun.

It takes forty-five days before it breaks our tardy gravity. During this period, the following takes place:

-        *The earth's rotation on its axis decreases. This causes the sun to travel from the eastern horizon to the western horizon for a prolonged period. It takes seventy-two hours, or three days, before it finally sets.*

-        *Sothos, earth's only moon, increases its orbital time. After the sun's setting on the third day, it takes the moon forty-two days to journey from east to west. The sun does not appear on the horizon during that time.*

-        *Due to Ringos's position relative to the earth, the planet is the only source of light and minimal heat during the moon's reign. After Sothos rises, it takes an hour before the first sign of Ringos. It travels for three hours in the sky, from the north travelling south to its peak in the sky, and then to the west where it sets. This erratic occurence has a time-lapse of three hours again between the setting in the west to the rising again in the north. The tug of gravity between the sun and Ringos is clear here. This pattern of rising and setting continues for the entire period that Sothos rules the sky.*

-        *Half-way across the sky, on day twenty-two of moon's reign in the sky, Ringos and Sothos align, and an eclipse occurs. But for the remaining days, Ringos slowly reclines into its familiar path, and on the forty-fifth night, the moon sets and earth's system returns to normal for the next four years.*

This is indeed a phenomenon.

- Presentation to the Orion Counsel
By Philgarn Asmuth.

GLOSARRY 1
LIST OF CHARACTERS

The Shadow Clan

Shadowolf Degron (Elemental): son of Nighthale and Karla; he was taken to uPendus after the Battle for Eldor's Forest and returned to challenge Le'Mar in order to save the earth. Has a faithful wolf named Nelnar, who was thought killed by Sonersaat during the Battle for Eldor's Forest

Shedaaij (Earth Elemental): a Merlani; a warrior sent to assist Shadowolf on land with the war, becoming his partner. She gave birth to their daughter, Crystal, during his stay in uPendus

Darcwulf (Fire Elemental): left on the doorstep of Nighthale's room as a baby and soul-brother to Shadowolf. He was changed by Le'Mar to fight against Shadowolf during the Battle for Eldor's Forest and to rule Le'Mar's Forest thereafter.

Fransiska (Water Elemental): one of the trio of girls with Skywolf and Angelia that resided in Costen; became Darcwulf's partner and gave birth to Tyler without his knowledge during his reign in Le'Mar's forest

Sorceress (Earth Elemental): Sole survivor of the 'Hand of Orion' that originally joined the Clan before the death of Mercius. Obtained the Butterfly Pendant from Ursula when the unicorn reclaimed her original horn

Angelia (Water Elemental): Asbec College student; met Shadowolf through Harmony; moved home to Costen at start of war and then joined Shadow Clan

Deihlia: Lastgorn's sister who journeys with the Clan if only to ensure his brother's safety. Looks after the children when the parents are unable to

Heula: One of three witches that attacked Shadowolf in Plastinon, but then assisted him; she joined the Clan and assisted in the Battle for Eldor's Forest

Lastgorn: a sword master who joined the Shadow Clan originally with Gwyn and Sny-Ten. His comrades were killed during the Battle for Eldor's Forest

Nolraldun (Novice Assassin): Sent by the Semhum Kateth to find Trimistus and kill him as per Le'Mar's orders

Skywolf Saphin (Water Elemental): daughter of Malkius Saphin. Met Shadowolf through Darcwulf, and married Dredwolf after the Battle for Eldor's Forest, having a son named Tailan

Trimistus / Lord Danaka: He once served Mercius, but seeing Shadowolf's bravery he had a change of heart. Le'Mar had him exiled to death, but he plunged off a waterfall and escaped. During the Battle for Eldor's Forest, he realised his full power and became the DragonWourd, ruler of the dragons from the Kingdoms

Glasden (gargoyle): Dren's brother that seeks vengeance for his death in the Battle for Eldor's Forest. Leads a group of 'inferior' gargoyles with no wings, found in Le'Mar's Forest

Southern Wolf Tribes

Nighthale Degron (Wind Elemental): Lord of Avalion, Degron Core, and father of Shadowolf; adopted father of Darcwulf.

Franklin and **Nowles**: Personal friends and advisors to Nighthale

Malkius Saphin: Lord of Costen, Saphin Vale, and father of Skywolf, Darna and Claire.

Sjedwolf Watre (Earth Elemental): Lord of Hasner, Watre Hills.

Jasnon Lowle: Lord of Iceland, Lowle Village, after the downfall and murder of Abutja Blue.

Kailan Par'Mar: Lucian's wife, and chosen leader of the Orion tribe after Lucian's refusal.

Lucian Par'Mar (Wind Elemental): former member of the Sandrihelin of Mercius; former Wind Professor of Asbec College; was once advisor to the Avalion War Council. Before the Battle for Eldor's Forest, he left to find uPendus in order to gain the alliance of the pegasi.

Salinos: Represents Kailan as leader of Orion when she is unable to do so

Mannius Saphin (Elemental Weapons Engineer): Skywolf's cousin that imbued Ruben-Willow with the ability to adapt to the sword-bearer's powers.

Jilian Asmuth: Descendant of Philgarn Asmuth the prophet, with the ability to draw visions relating to the prophecy

James: mer-King of the mer-Kingdom that once resided in *Avalendil* beneath New Avalion. During the Battle for Eldor's Forest, Lellian was killed by Blosom, which caused James to kill her with the trident, making him king. He moved the Kingdom to live in the oceans again and has an intense hatred for humans

The Vale of Tigers and Dwarf Mountains

Chenesia: Princess of the Vale and daughter of Maren-Ti and Larnesia; captured by Le'Mar when she sought elfin protection from Eldor, but escaped to assist in the Battle for Eldor's Forest. Escaped with Shadowolf and Elgoth to uPendus at the end of the battle.

Genewiu (Pegasus): another captive in Chenesia's dungeon, who escaped and assisted in the Battle for Eldor's Forest. Led Shadowolf, Elgoth and Chenesia to uPendus after the battle

Gallon (Master Dwarf): King of the dwarves residing in the Dwarf Mountains, and former advisor and friend of Maren-Ti

Hargon (Master Dwarf): Custodian of the Sanctuary of Jin-Tai and personal guardian of Chenesia; assisted with the dwarf kingdom's defence in the Battle for Eldor's Forest; obtains the jaguar Cavella as a mount and guardian

The Far Isles

Eldor (Elf): High King of the elves and former tutor of Masara; he was defeated in the Battle for Eldor's Forest and left with the eastern elves to reside on the Far Isles, much to the dissatisfaction of the eastern Elder Elves

Elgoth (Saint): the son of Masara and Ursula sent by his father to assist the Council in their meetings and report back to him; assisted in Shadowolf's escape at the end of the Battle for Eldor's Forest and mentored Shadowolf during their stay in uPendus

Lesan (Elf): Former prince of Eldor's Forest and son of Eldor; personal friend of Chenesia

Masara (Saint): Centuries-old man who followed the path of Bontu and learned the lore of the elves. Fought in the Battle of T'Mar's Scourge and was victorious. Taken by the elves to the Far Isles to recover health, but returned to the Forest to assist in the war. He was killed by Le'Mar in the Battle for Eldor's Forest and his soul trapped in Le'Mar's staff

Sinor: Elf that once assisted Chenesia in finding the Elvin Throne in Eldor's Forest when she escaped the dungeons. Became guardian of the Fairiwell beneath the forest, awaiting Shadowolf's return from uPendus

Ursula (Unicorn): She had warned Shadowolf about the power node and had informed him to meet Asgorna and ignore Mercius. She had also warned him not to face Le'Mar during the Battle for Eldor's Forest as he was not ready

Centaurs of Philagis

Glamidon: Son of Seridon; he is the guardian and mentor of Mirentaur

Millon: Originally escorted the Shadow Clan with Kentaur to the Butcher of Philagis, joining the Clan after the Butcher's defeat. After the Battle for Eldor's Forest, he returned to Philagis and refused to rule the dark centaurs.

Mirentaur: Son of Millon and heir to the centaur throne when he is of age

Seridon: Accepted the rule of the centaurs after Millon's refusal

Horlorn's Gate

Treville: Former Lord of Horlorn's Gate before the Battle for Eldor's Forest

Lanel and **Harmony** (wind elementals): former AegleDaele students of Asbec College and Shadowolf's best friends.

Theroy (fire elemental): former Feniseraat student of Asbec College, and acquaintance of Shadowolf.

Nashela (wind elemental): former AegleDaele student that had a crush on Shadowolf; her home and family in Shenama were destroyed by Mercius and McCaniban. After the Battle for Eldor's Forest, she and Lanel became partners

Nellice: aVampeyer once aligned to Le'Mar, but choosing not to be slave to any side. Mirelda became his partner and aVampeyer by choice

Treya: Queen of the pegasi in uPendus

Dragons of the Kingdoms

Asgorna: Former Dragon King, and bound to Shadowolf. Lost his reign after the War of the Dragons when Shadowolf refused to return to the Kingdoms so that he may continue in the Battle for Eldor's Forest

Beliva: Dragon appointed as Harmony's guardian by Mynisna

Fereya: Oldest known dragon residing in Bentley Strip

Mynisna: Dragon in Asgorna's army, bound to Trimistus. He became the
Dragon King when Trimistus became DragonWourd upon Shadowolf's
refusal to return to the Kingdoms

Soltavia: Dragon appointed as Darcwulf's guardian by Mynisna

The Underworld

Anuxis: Lord of the Underworld, with the head of a wolf and the body of a
man; thought he was betrayed by Simnab and therefore removed all
his powers before banishing him from the Underworld. Has a three-
headed hound named Cerexus

Simnab: Crethan servant of Anuxis that was banished from the
Underworld and found a home on Celenic Earth through Le'Mar
originally. He married Telgar after the Battle for Eldor's Forest. Has a
two-headed hound named Orxus

Angelicus (Spirit Elemental): Former fiancé of Darcwulf; found during the
Battle for Eldor's Forest as a Crethan, who then overpowered the
Creth-Demons controlling them and led the Celenic Crethans to assist
in the defence of New Avalion

The Dark Lord's Army

Le'Mar (Elemental): The dark lord; son of T'Mar and brother to Masara.
Vowed enemy of Celenic Earth who defeated the earth's warriors,
including Masara, during the Battle for Eldor's Forest, and claimed
them as his kingdom

McCaniban: A general in Le'Mar's army that destroyed Shenama and
Los'Temenar (Morkom Falls) and set a camp in both.

Sona Nelma (Earth Elemental): a former Sandrihelin of Mercius; former Earth professor of Asbec College; Lanel spotted her meeting with the Sandrihelin in the college, but after the school closed, she was never heard of again. During the Battle for Eldor's Forest, it was discovered that she secretly lived in New Avalion and assisted in its downfall

Reference Characters

Abutja Blue: Predecessor of Jasnon Lowle as Lord of Iceland; was betrayed by an Amethyst pendant of Le'Mar that there was no war and was murdered by purorcs when the spell was lifted and Iceland was destroyed.

Blosom (mer-aVampyeric demon-queen): Was a mermaid of *Marsandil* before her change; Mercius's aVampyeric lover after the change; almost killed Shadowolf at Asbec Lake and still regretted not doing so. Killed Lellian during the Battle for Eldor's Forest in *Avalendil*, who in turn was killed by James

Danto & **Mallice** (aVampyere): Served under Mercius, but joined Nellice in the aVampyeric rebellion. Both were killed during the Battle for Eldor's Forest

Dren (Gargoyle): Captured Shadowolf in Eldor's Dungeon, mistaking him for Mercius. Shadowolf obtained the Lapis Pins for Dren so that he would not be affected by the sunlight. He was killed during the Battle for Eldor's Forest when the demonic Lister removed the Pin in the light of the sun and smashed his marble body to pieces

Fornoren and **Masnen** (Gargoyles): Comrades of Dren in safe-guarding Eldor's Dungeons. Joined Shadowolf in an effort to obtain the Lapis Pins, but became stone when Mercius emitted solar energy and orcs loosed arrows into their statue bodies.

Hurticule (Merman): Ruler of *Marsandil* before it was attacked by aVampyere and Lellian became mer-king. He joined Lellian in defending Sea's Reach from sirens and died on a demon-queen's trident.

Gwyn and **Sny-Ten**: Weapon-master friends of Shadowolf through Darcwulf, who were killed during the Battle for Eldor's Forest

Kelsey Hodgsen and Malferus Ar'Mar (Elementals): two of the former Sandrihelin of Mercius; former Water and Fire professors of Asbec College; were killed by Asgorna after Shadowolf killed Mercius

Kentaur: Centaur that escorted the Clan to the Butcher of Philagis. He was killed during the Battle for Eldor's Forest

Kraakis (Centaur): The Butcher of Philagis. Former lord of the Centaurs, killed by Shadowolf when he and the Clan were led by Millon and Kentaur to their home beneath Philagis

Lellian (Mer-King): The destined ruler of the mer-kingdom, with a powerful trident to fight against the sirens. Resided in *Avalendil* beneath Avalion until Blosom killed him during the Battle for Eldor's Forest

Lister (Saneth): One of the remaining Kings of the Knight, who was killed during the Battle for Eldor's Forest and then possessed by a demon before killing Dren. Ma'Kanak was killed by Nellice and Trimistus left Le'Mar's army. The sole remaining Saneth after the battle was Ru-Maak.

Malanite: Old man found wandering in Meëntis during the time of the DragonRider, claiming his village had been destroyed; later discovered to be Masara's split soul that had joined the Shadow Clan in order to guide them. He reunited his split soul before the Battle for Eldor's Forest

Madison, **Trish**, **Dayna-wolf**, **Teristé**, **Markors**, **Mino'Nelar**, & **Midnite** (Crethans): Saved by Shadowolf when their Creth-Demon was killed and the bondage of servitude removed; it was revealed that Midnite was the former Morkom Lenarsa, turned into a Crethan during the fall of the Northern wolf tribes near Horlorn. They were all killed during the Battle for Eldor's Forest

Maerlesa and **Nestef** (Witches): With Heula, they were ordered to destroy Plastinon and make sure the ghost village remained cursed. They were also responsible for raising the undead and demons in the army. Nestef was killed in Plastinon and Maerlesa during the Battle for Eldor's Forest

Maren-Ti: Lord of the Vale of Tigers and custodian of the Heart of Tigers. After the Battle for Eldor's Forest, when Chenesia escaped to uPendus, he had a fatal heart attack and was buried by his wife and the Vale

Mercius (aVampyeric Windfarer): The servant of Le'Mar that was chosen to lead his armies with McCaniban and fulfil the Windfarer Prophecy; died when Shadowolf kicked him into the *Sadgi* power node.

Morkom Lenarsa: former Lord of Los'Temenar (Morkom Falls); Commissioned by the War Council of Avalion to unite the northern villages into a War Council and stand against McCaniban together. The message arrived too late and Los'Temenar was lost to McCaniban and renamed Morkom Falls.

Mourna: former friend of Shadowolf and partner of Lanel in Asbec College of Elements. She took part in the Battle for Eldor's Forest. Thereafter she got married in Carmel and settled down to a quiet life

Nucial: a strange broken peddlar that claimed he was escaping Le'Mar when Chenesia escaped the dungeons; while in Carmel, he transformed back into Le'Mar's real form without anyone's knowledge

Shadowwe, **Scarlette**, **Rennick**, **Trevor** & **Tinonte** (The Orion): Special group of warriors known as the "Hand of the Orion", who were all killed during the Battle for Eldor's Forest

Sonersaat (DragonRider): Chosen by Le'Mar to fulfil the DragonRider Prophecy and initiate the War of the Dragons. He and his dragon Maneto were killed by Shadowolf and Asgorna during the Battle for Eldor's forest

Historical Characters

Age of Bentley

Bentley: First man on the earth, who defended his son by killing Malherin with the elf's dagger, taking the first murder upon himself

Marhelen: First woman and wife to Bentley

Mikinos: Son of Bentley and Marhelen, who fell in love with the elf Elhorin. He let his lust overcome his love for her and tried to force himself on her, causing the first battle on the earth. He repented after Malherin's defeat and married his sister, Shardenel

Shardenel: Daughter of Bentley and Marhelen, who married Mikinos to continue the human bloodline.

Saldheron: The wisest elf, rumoured to be the first elf and was lord of all elves until his passing; established Saldher's Forest on the land of man when the eastern elves left the Far Isles

Malherin: Father of Elhorin and Temelrin; became enraged when Mikinos forced himself onto Elhorin, but was killed in battle when Bentley protected his son

Elhorin: Daughter of Malherin who fell in love with Mikinos, but turned down their love for the sake of the elvin race. Became partner to Temelrin when they left the land of man for the Far Isles

Age of Falgar

Falgar: Son of Mikinos and Shardenel. Decided to leave the Nether Region and met Mehorin, who he fell in love with. Killed Temelrin in battle with the elf's staff when Temelrin tried to keep them apart. Together Falgar and Mehorin founded Carmel

Mehorin: Daughter of Temelrin and Elhorin. Left the Far Isles to return the elf race to the land of man with her brother Melnirion; this action and her love for Falgar, caused Temelrin to challenge Falgar to battle

Melnirion: Son of Temelrin and Elhorin. Assisted Mehorin in her escape to the land of man and was banished from the Far Isles as a result

Temelrin: Son of Malherin that witnessed his father's death at the hand of Bentley and the dagger; refused to let the elf race mingle with the human race; challenged Falgar when he saw the man with Mehorin, resulting in his own death

Selhorin: Son of Temelrin and Elhorin. Watched his father be killed by Falgar and banished Mehorin, Melnirion and the elves that followed them from the Far Isles. Became lord of the elves on the Far Isles when Saldheron established his kingdom of eastern elves on the land of man

Age of Masara

Namara: Son of Falara and grandson of Falgar and Mehorin

Levon: Wife of Namara, who married T'Mar after Namara's death

Masara: Son of Namara and Levon, who killed T'Mar during the Battle of T'Mar's Scourge, using the captured dark power to shape Ursula's new horn

Ursula: Unicorn sent by Elmerion to continue Masara's mentorship; Masara and Ursula fell inlove and became partners, giving birth to Elgoth

Lucas / Lanesara / Firewolf: A boy found by Masara who eventually became his pupil in the elemental arts. He was known for his love for wolves, being the first to form a bond with them. He twisted Masara's teachings and formed his own school, eventually teaching T'Mar the new elemental arts

Eldorion: Son of Melnirion; known currently as Eldor, lord of eastern elves

Elmerion: Son of Melnirion and Masara's tutor

Seimarion: Son of Selhorin, who passed down history of the elves and humans to him. This caused quiet hatred for humans in him, which was further fuelled by Selhorin's early passing. He decided to take a human woman as his partner in an attempt to taint the human bloodline with his own, causing the Elder Elves to banish him to the Alcove of Light.

T'Mar: Son of Seimarion by his union with a human. He married Levon after Namara's death in order to gain the bloodline of Falgar, which succeeded in the birth of Le'Mar. He killed by Masara with his own power in the Battle of T'Mar's Scourge

Le'Mar: Son of T'Mar and Levon from the mixed bloodlines of Falgar and Selhorin; witnessed the death of his father by Masara

Age of Celene

Morlen: Son of Falgar and Namara's uncle

Cailene: Morlen's granddaughter that established the southern wolf tribes after the Battle of T'Mar's Scourge

Celene: Daughter of Cailene and wife to Nitewolf Degron; ancestor of Shadowolf

Telmirion: T'Mar's son and Le'Mar's half-brother who lived in the Alcove of Light. Desired Celene as his wife, but she refused him for Nitewolf. Killed by Celene with his own power when he tried taking Nitewolf's life

GLOSARRY 2
LIST OF CREATURES

Shadowolf's Army

Ocean

Mer-King: Single ruler of mer-Kingdom, with a three-pronged trident as his weapon that assists in sensing any movement or action in the ocean

Merman / -maid: has the body of a human, but its legs are replaced by a scaly tail and lives in rivers, lakes or oceans.

Merlani: born of human and mermaid conception, the only known one being Shedaaij

Sky

Angel: a divine being from heaven with fiery wings who has the ability to chain and capture demons for their imprisonment

aVampeyer: pale, black-robed creature relatively close to being human, except that it is dead. It sucks on the blood of the living to survive, with razor sharp teeth to pierce the skin of its victims. Has adversity to sunlight. Once part of Le'Mar's army

Dragon – great, reptilian beast with sharp fangs, ferocious talons and enormous wings; has the ability to breathe fire from its lungs and can bond with a single human in extremely unique circumstances, but usually only when a bargain is struck. They reside in Bentley Strip in temples linking to their home planets.

Fairdievell: a species of fairy known for their variety of light and colour and mostly for their power. This species resides in the Fairiwell, a haven provided by the elves in tunnels beneath Eldor's Forest.

Pegasus: mythical horse with large wings and special powers for combat. Located in a mythical land called uPendus.

Land

Archer: human or elvin warrior with an affinity for using a bow in battle

Assassin: a stealthy, efficient mercenary hired to kill a target for a price by any means necessary.

Centaur: has the body of a horse, and the abdomen and upper body of a human. The Philagis centaurs have horns attached to their heads as a sign of their superiority, while the Alcove centaurs have no horns and are regarded as more beautiful in appearance

Creth-Angel: a beast with a wolf head and human body; torso usually uncovered and a loose cloth around waist. It is known for its ability to overcome the power of *Haniegke* or Creth-Demons over Crethans, freeing them from its command

Crethan / -thine: a Celenic human cursed by the bite of a Creth-Demon; whenever a Creth-Demon is nearby, they transform against their will into a deformed wolf that does the bidding of the Creth-Demon. Once part of Le'Mar's army when summoned by the Demon.

Dwarf: a short, stocky human with large beard and usually an axe for a weapon. They are masters of dwarven lore and Architectural Engineering. They reside in Dwarf Mountains and are the guardians of the Vale of Tigers.

Elemental: A human or creature with the ability to summon one or more of the four elements, whether in form or essence. Uses power of the spirit to master the elements.

Elementël: A being composed of one or more of the four elements of nature. Has no allegiance and can be summoned by an Elemental.

Elf: one of the ancient creatures that were on the world when it was created; pointed ears and green-shaded skin, with the elder elves deep green in colour. Adept at any weapon, but specialise in staff and bow. They are masters of the elvin lore and servants of Bontu; they reside in the Far Isles and Eldor's Forest.

Gargoyle: Stony being that resembles a human who usually stands guard against evil forces. Sunlight hardens their bodies and they remain motionless until the source of light is removed. Superior gargoyles have wings

Nelmurian wolves: white wolves that reside in the snowy parts of uPendus from which Nelnar, Shadowolf's wolf, originated

Saint: Servant, sage and fighter of Bontu, the one true God. Uses the powers given to him by Bontu to defend the innocent and defeat evil.

Swordsman: human or elvin warrior with an affinity for using a sword and shield in battle

Unicorn: mythical horse with a power sack embedded beneath a single, pointed horn that protrudes from the horse's forehead. Has the many powers, including the ability to fly.

uPendian tigers: white tigers that reside in the snowy uPendus

Tigroy: a flying tiger gargoyle not affected by the sun and used as guardians of tombs and graves in the Vale of Tigers.

Witch: woman with unique powers and spells, using them to thwart their enemies and known for their ability to summon and vanquish the undead and demons.

Le'Mar's Army

Ocean

Demon-Queen: A mer-queen that rules over a group of sirens, with a dark trident of her own. Has snakes twisting from her hair and four arms attached to her body that ends in a twin mer-tail.

Siren: a ghostly apparition or being that can take many physical forms and can travel on air, land or sea; known for its tendency to seduce men in order to kill them, and lures them by beauty and song. Often mistaken for a mermaid when in the form of a water-siren and can be killed when in physical form. Ruled by a Demon-Queen with a dark trident.

Sky

Firestrom: mountainous fire elementël that hovers off the ground; has four heads upon its fiery body – lion, shark, gorilla and horse. Can separate into four elementëls, with a central core keeping them together.

Fletchling: small, blue creature similar to a fairy but three times the size and with bat-like wings and sharp fangs.

Wyvern: leathery, sleek dragon-like beast, smaller in size to a dragon but much faster

Land

Assassin: a stealthy, efficient mercenary hired to kill a target for a price by any means necessary.

Demon: evil spirit called forth by Le'Mar or a witch to do their bidding, which usually results in chaos and destruction. Has an intense hatred for anything good or divine and can possess any living or dead being

Dra-hu'Mar: looks like a human, and has characteristic blond hair and green eyes. Has the ability to transform his bow into a sword and vice versa.

Elementël: A being composed of one or more of the four elements of nature. Has no allegiance and can be summoned by an Elemental.

Froth Hun: a beast with a skeletal head engulfed in blue flames. Carries a two-handed sword the length of a man and rides a black mare with dark pits for eyes and ghostly torn mane and tail.

Haniegke: a Creth-Demon from the Underworld that rules over *Hieragke*. They have wolf heads and human bodies and can change Crethans from humans to wolves with golden sceptres.

Hieragke: a wolf servant of the *Haniegke* not from Celenic Earth. They are spirits of the Underworld that take the form of deformed wolves

Ma-Wreth: large beast, towering twice a man's height with large, oak-like arms that move faster than its weight should permit. These lightning-fast arms are mostly used to break down walls and defences.

Orc: a foul creature with dark, grey skin and putrid smell. Those whose blood are untainted by any other are referred to as "purorcs". Where a human has been crossed with an orc through the dark lord's cruel experiments they are referred to as "hurorcs"

Pegator: kin to the pegasus, but has a black coat instead of white. Corrupted by Le'Mar to fight for him in the war

Saemnati: demonic prince that guards the thrones of hell and used by the Gemetrashef in conquering worlds.

Saneth: also known as Kings of the Knight. It is a leader from a remote planet used to command the troops of Le'Mar when conquering a new world. The four Saneths brought to Celenic Earth were Lister, Ru-Maak, Ma'Kanak and Trimistus.

Shrieker: huge beast that sends out a shrill cry to deafen its enemies before delivering its fatal blow

Succubus: demonic feminine being that enjoys seducing men before killing or possessing them

Undead: the corpses and skeletons of the dead reanimated, usually through possession by demons but can be reanimated without them.

THE WINDFARER
Book 1 of the epic fantasy series
The Celenic Earth Chronicles

CELENIC EARTH: A WORLD OF MIGHT, MAGIC AND MYSTICAL CREATURES

A shadow lurks over the earth, as foul creatures attack the villages. The leader of hurorcs and purorcs commands them to attack the southern tribes, and is captured. But Mercius, once known as the Windfarer, finally breaks free after years of imprisonment and sets his sight upon the Asbec College of Elements where an ancient power is rumoured to be hidden.

Shadowolf is in his last year of studies at the Asbec College of Elements when word of the escape spreads. Strange things happen and he becomes entwined in a world of mystery and murder, using the power of the elements to survive. And as war erupts, Shadowolf returns home and does everything in his ability to protect the five southern wolf tribes. For his effort he merely frustrates Mercius's plans, but significantly learns that Mercius is subservient to a dark lord; someone more powerful, known as Le'Mar.

Between the protection of his family, the loyalty of the Shadow Clan and the new-found love of his life, can he pull himself away to stop Mercius from reaching the potent power node? For neither the elves nor the dwarves can stop him should he gain the power he seeks. Even the dark lord seems troubled.

The Masaran Phenomenon approaches, and the "Prophecy of the Windfarer" is upon them.

REVIEWS AND PRAISE

"Jooste's imagination has depth of both scale and scope, with parallels between this imaginary world and the real world, characterised by an interesting contrast between the industrialised evil forces and the 'natural' forces of good…"

THE DRAGONRIDER
Book 2 of the epic fantasy series
The Celenic Earth Chronicles

DRAGONS ARE COMING TO CELENIC EARTH TO END A WAR
RAGING ON FOR CENTURIES

Pernonil was lost to the Elves....the southern lands forsaken by the tribes....Chenesia lost to the Vale...Shadowolf lost to the world...

It has been two years since Shadowolf released the power node and destroyed Mercius; since he had been mysteriously taken by a dragon to Bentley Strip. But rumours of the dragons are stirring in New Avalion, and one of them is that the son of Nighthale has returned.

The Shadow Clan reform and set out to him in the Strip, and they meet a man wiser and more powerful than before. They quickly learn that Shadowolf had been in another world with Asgorna the Dragon King in what is called the Dragon War, a war that has leaked into Celenic Earth and that the dark lord Le'Mar plans to use to his advantage. Ursula the unicorn joins their Clan, and urges Shadowolf to find a horn lost in the Battle of T'Mar's Scourge. The horn holds untold power and would assist in defeating the dark lord. But on their way they find many obstacles, including the undead, witches, the Butcher of Philagis and Firestroms.

Quietly, Le'Mar is preparing his new champion for the War, Sonersaat the DragonRider. As his quest grows larger, Shadowolf decides to enter Eldor's Forest, find Eldor and Masara and await Le'Mar. It is a war the earth has been anticipating....and it is a war with the direst consequences.

The "Prophecy of the DragonRider" is upon them...

REVIEWS AND PRAISE

SILENT HILL: BETRAYAL

SILENT HILL HAS MORE THAN ONCE CANVAS, PAINTED BY THE
TAINT OF YOUR SINS.
CONSIDER THIS YOUR PERSONAL HELL

Trevor wakes up from another nightmare of Silent Hill just before getting a
call that the police are after him following the apparent suicide of his wife,
Caroline. He barely escapes with his lover Kathy and best friend Jay
Nixon, the police force hot on their tail on the dark highway. During the
pursuit, a mist covers the road and a strange man with a metallic object on
his head causes them to crash on the outskirts of Silent Hill.

When Trevor awakens, he finds himself alone at the scene of the accident
with no knowledge of where the others are. His search for them not only
reveals that the town is haunted with terrifying creatures, but is also
tainted with clues of Caroline's presence. As his struggle through the misty
town leads him closer to Kathy's whereabouts, Trevor learns the truth of
Caroline's death and the link to her brother's murder. And with this
knowledge, he discovers that everyone that had a part to play in her
misery has been brought together to Silent Hill to account for their sins.

In the midst of the pain and the blood stands Caroline's mysterious
guardian with the metallic stained pyramid on his head... and he is ready
to exact justice for their betrayal...

REVIEWS AND PRAISE

"I love this version of Silent Hill, the twists and build up, I almost expect to
see some terrifying creature around every corner. Two words,
HORRIFICALLY STUPENDOUS"